WILD COUNTRY

In two previous adventure-filled novels, SYSTEMIC SHOCK and SINGLE COMBAT, Dean Ing has created a terrifyingly believable portrait of our nation a few years from now: An America devastated by a nuclear strike that destroyed a hundred million lives and wounded the fabric of society.

In Ted Quantrill, a former assassin who has learned the limitations of violence, Ing has fashioned a true hero, a man strong enough to prevail in desperate times, yet filled with the sense of justice and passion to make a better world.

In WILD COUNTRY, Dean Ing brings this powerful saga to its triumphant conclusion. It is a magnificent, towering vision by a master storyteller.

"In WILD COUNTRY Dean Ing gives his readers a fascinating tour of the Southwest during the reconstruction of America after a semi-devastating war. Ing mixes elements * *** *** survival skills of ran*** *** *** *** dope smuggling, *** *** *** *** esnakes with an am*** *** *** *** most exotic chemic*** *** *** London Blitz, and s*** *** *** (including the boar)."**

—Donald Kingsbury

Tor books by Dean Ing

The Big Lifters
Blood of Eagles
The Nemesis Mission
The Ransom of Black Stealth One
Single Combat
Soft Targets
Systemic Shock
Wild Country

WILD COUNTRY

DEAN ING

A TOM DOHERTY ASSOCIATES BOOK
NEW YORK

WILD COUNTRY

Cover art by David Mann

A Tor Book
Published by Tom Doherty Associates, Inc.
175 Fifth Avenue
New York, N.Y. 10010

Tor ® is a registered trademark of Tom Doherty Associates, Inc.

ISBN: 0-812-51171-9

First edition: November 1985

Printed in the United States of America

0 9 8 7 6 5 4 3 2

"For my grandchildren—Jennifer and Ryan—and for Vicki, who defused the family bomb with love."

CHAPTER ONE • • •

Death minus three minutes and counting: Rawson squinted through yellow sundazzle and displayed his Mex dental work as the stranger neared maximum range. The scope of his wire-stocked assault rifle showed only a single, helmeted rider, straight and tall on the hovercycle, its caliche dust trail writhing behind.

Had Rawson been a praying man, he might have prayed for this break. One well-placed round could mean the difference between Rawson afoot in Wild Country, with deputy marshals closing in, and Rawson sitting pretty in that hovercycle with a straight run to the Rio Grande.

On the other hand, a clean miss might alert the silly bastard, and several hasty shots might render that cycle useless. From his cover among the blistering rocks of South Texas, Rawson judged that his prey would cross within a hundred meters of him. If he waited an extra few moments, he would have a good headshot, and time for more if the first round missed. Rawson flicked his fire selector to semiauto, wishing he had thought to drop his beltpac near the tracks his boots had made. A nice fat beltpac would've provided bait to halt an unwary traveler. Well, tough shit; Rawson concentrated on the world as it was—or rather, as he thought it was. It did not occur to him that the target in his crosshairs might be bait.

Death minus two minutes and counting: For an instant, as the cycle passed below on its cushion of air, Rawson's imagination whacked him under the ribs. What if the rider gripped the throttlebar in his death agony? The hovercycle might just continue on out of sight, its whirr fading with the dust trail, a diesel-hearted horse with the bit in its teeth and a dead man in the saddle. The outlaw adjusted his aim to the base of the neck, let the crosshairs traverse to lead the target, and squeezed gently.

The rifle's muzzle suppressor was a custom job, so that the muzzle scarcely moved and emitted only a flat, whistling pop. The slug flew a trifle high, catching the erect rider behind the ear. Rawson sent two more rounds after it; saw the helmet jerk again, saw shards of plastic spray bright sparkles against the sun.

Death minus ninety seconds and counting: Rawson flung himself down from his prominence, bounding to flat, sun-baked soil, cursing the hovercycle as it continued. The damn thing had slowed a lot, but it was still under way, now wandering in a broad arc above the sparse brush of Uvalde County, Texas. The rider was well-zapped, but at this pace Rawson, carrying the heavy rifle, would never catch up. He made a snap decision, dropped the rifle, and sprinted hard. He willed his legs to pump harder. The goddamn rifle had done its job and in any case he still had his little Chink automatic, courtesy of World War IV, stowed in his break-away hip pocket. In a long, gut-wrenching sprint he knew that he was gaining. And so, in a way, he was definitely losing.

Death minus forty seconds and counting: The rider had not fallen, though his head lolled loosely on his neck. Both hands still gripped the handlebars of the cycle, a scruffy, two-place McCullough with a tarp over the rear saddle cowl. Rawson's thigh muscles told him he'd spent too many summer days in the cantinas of Hondo and Eagle Pass, waiting for word that Sorel needed him for a shipment. Trembling, gasping, he drew on his last reserves of stamina and stumbled, nearly fell. But now the diesel stammered too. Rawson hoped that didn't mean the effin' thing was out of fuel.

He found out what it meant as he staggered forward, exulting. Everything became clear with the sudden emergence of the compact, green-eyed blond fellow from under the tarp. Rawson was only three-quarters surprised; in the smuggling biz, you learned to count on fuck-all.

"Michael Rawson, you're under arrest," the younger man called. He wore the shoulder patch of a federal deputy mar-shal on his thin deerskin shirt, a shirt too nice to perforate, though Rawson fully intended to do that very thing.

"Well—ain't you cute," Rawson puffed, stopping ten paces away, putting hands on hips while he fought for breath. Very cute indeed, wiring a cast-off android from Wild Country Safari into the front saddle and steering from under the tarp. The little deputy might be young but he had used guile, forcing Rawson to run from cover and tire himself with a long, exhausting sprint. Not cute enough to have a weapon in his hands, though. If he knew *who* Rawson was, he ought to know how *fast* Rawson was.

Death minus eight seconds and counting: The broad-shouldered little deputy saw something in Rawson's face. "Don't do it," he said equably. But Rawson thought something in the man's face was pleading, *do it*. Rawson did it while the deputy's right hand was fishing out a card, probably to read him his rights.

Rawson's rights ended with an impossibly liquid left-handed draw by the deputy, who flicked a seven-millimeter Chiller from its hidden armpit holster as he bounded from the cycle. Rawson got his sidearm out, began his trusted sidewinder maneuver, swung his weapon to intersect the spot where the deputy would land . . . and felt two paralyzing impacts in his torso.

Rawson crumpled, the slugs hurling him back. He lay with one leg buckled, both arms flung wide, the little automatic a full pace from his nerveless fingers. He understood a great deal more, now. There were maybe a half dozen bad dudes in Wild Country who could draw with Rawson, but only one whose freakish reflexes were said to be absolutely lethal whether flat-footed or airborne; a regular John Wesley Hardin.

And the blond deputy was a wrong-hander, too. Ex-assassin for Search & Rescue, ex-rebel with Jim Street, now a part-time lawman in Wild Country: "You'd be Ted Quantrill," Rawson grimaced, now feeling thick fluid in his throat.

"And you had to find out the hard way," said the blond, reseating his Chiller.

Rawson's eyes were beginning to defocus, but he never lost his courage. "Well, I said you was cute," he said, dying.

For the record, Quantrill noted that Michael Rawson's long countdown ended at 1:54 P.M., central daylight time, on the seventeenth of September, A.D. 2006.

CHAPTER TWO • • •

Quantrill finished rolling the body into a standard bodybag, spat caliche dust, hauled Rawson's bulk to the cycle, and retrieved his own Aussie hat, flopping it on his head after wiping a film of sweat and dust from his face. The old 'droid in the front seat had been emptied of its innards and was soon stowed in back with Rawson.

After he disconnected the rear steering yoke, Quantrill stepped into the front cowl, then pulled a cold bulb of Pearl beer from the right-hand cargo pannier. With his other hand he toggled his VHF set. A moment later, he had Chief Deputy Stearns on-line.

The complaints began almost immediately. "Nope, I never got a chance to read him his rights," Quantrill replied. "He went for a Chinese sidearm; I'm bringing it as evidence."

He waited, pressing the earpiece with two fingers, meanwhile scanning the innocent horizon. Then, "It was Rawson's choice, not mine." Pause. "Sure. If my belt video was working, you'll see me with the chit in one hand and a handful of air in the other while he was drawing on me. I won't kill a man unless he forces me to." Pause; a flare of nostrils below his broken nose. "Well, I don't anymore, sir. You can tell Marshal Teague our Justice Department is still just. Anyway, you've got two more of Sorel's men for a nice showy trial. You'd never have gotten anything from Mike Rawson. Read his file."

This time Quantrill waited longer. He was shaking his head in disgust when he replied, "It's not my fault if they got sprung so fast. Did anybody plant a tracer bug on either of 'em?" Another pause. "I'm sorrier than you are, mister; Espinel was a friend of mine. Sometimes I think Teague is sorrier to see a fugitive come in horizontal than he is when

10

one of us gets it. No, cancel that. I'm just hot and tired and
pissed off—sir.''

As always, the ''sir'' sounded insincere. Marvin Stearns,
grown sleek with inaction, could list a dozen men he would
prefer over Quantrill. Ted Quantrill could list several friends
who'd become casualties through the inaction of sleek men.

Kent Ethridge, for example. Some men put the entire
blame for that on Ethridge himself. Quantrill's reaction had
been a deepening fury against those who had made Ethridge's
death possible. Now he took a final pause and a gulp of Pearl
before: ''I'm near Dabney, just north of Zavala County. You
want Rawson in SanTone Ringcity, or do I freight him back
to you in Junction? Yeah, he's in a bodybag, he'll keep 'til
tomorrow. Right. See you in Junction bright and early. A-a-
and out,'' he drawled, putting away the tiny headset with
relief.

Ted Quantrill hadn't had a mastoid-implant radio in his
noggin for four years, but he still hated any comm set that
reminded him of a mastoid ''critic,'' however faintly. An
explosive critic had executed his lover, Marbrye Sanger, on
command of the murderous Young administration. The postwar excesses of Young's people had driven Quantrill to rebellion; nearly to madness as well. They drove so many good
people to the rebel ranks that the elections of 2004 had cut
across the lines of Mormonism and federalism. Now it was
President Ora McCarty whose cabinet struggled to reconstruct
America. As long as the ex-rebel boss Jim Street was attorney
general, there would be jobs for men like Quantrill.

Like the American nation itself, old Jim Street had suffered
systemic shock during the SinoInd War. The grizzled, crip-
pled old Texan rode herd on the Justice Department, including both the FBI and the Border Authority. Street had to let
other folks wrangle over the new Capitol site, now abuilding
in the District of Columbia, Missouri. He worried about
foreign entanglements when they crossed American borders—
for example, when the Ellfive colonies of New Israel helped
Turkish drug merchants open conduits through Wild Country.

Street knew in his chalky bones that America could not
survive another reign of unjust rule, of government by terror.
As long as he could climb into a wheelchair, he would prowl
the corridors of law and order. If Wild Country and Oregon

Territory were to be parts of the nation again, they must get fair-handed justice. With deputies like Ted Quantrill, Jim Street's justice reached a long way into lawless regions.

On this day, Quantrill was far into the violent border region claimed by both Mexico and Reconstruction America. Here, whole families sometimes disappeared during a feud or a border raid from Mexican *cimarrones*, wild ones. It was truly no government's land, and it could not be reclaimed without rough justice. When it had to be, Quantrill's was as rough as it came.

Quantrill could have chosen a shorter route back, but his years in the region had given him Wild Country wisdom. Back in the eighties and nineties, before the SinoInd War, Texas ranchers and hoe men had wrestled chunks of this sun-broiled land into submission. In less than ten years after the war, most of those chunks had gone wild again, returned to the kind of new-world savagery that Francisco Vásquez de Coronado had fought in 1541. A few places, chiefly narrow creekbottoms defended by grit and gunfire, were still cultivated. Quantrill did not relish a mechanical breakdown, not with a deader ripening under the tarp behind him, and he also went wide of the cultivated areas. Only fools and desperadoes took chances in the trackless wild regions over soil that, locals claimed, was ''hard as a whore's eye.''

Was Quantrill too cautious? Item: During the first cattle drive east from the Pecos, Coronado's men were forced to build pillars of dung and bones to post the way. Not even their herd of cattle could mark the cactus-dotted hardpan enough to let a man backtrack their path. When those cattle stumbled forward toward water, usually it was deadly alkali water and those cattle had to be whipped away from it. Now it was still possible to find a remnant of a buffalo wallow or a dry hole where a Spanish buckle and bones might gleam, burnished by the dusty winds of five centuries. This was a timeless land, and it would kill you for the slightest miscalculation.

The most pitiless of that land lay far to Quantrill's left. His route was made interesting by deep, brush-choked arroyos and hills. Bit by bit, the stupefying violence of Texas weather had whittled those hills down from mountains to mounds. That weather was thought, by people who had never experienced it, to be just a part of Wild Country myth; but Quantrill kept an eye on his horizons. He knew that in any season, a hellbroth storm might fling hailstones the size of his fist so hard they dented the cowls of hovercycles, with a blazing cadenza of lightning tinted gold and mauve by dust hurled on gale-force winds.

To outlanders, it was all mythology to be taken in good humor. If it were even half-true, they reasoned, Wild Country would be peopled exclusively by the insane. To Ted Quantrill, it was taken for granted—and in good humor. If you lived out here and said you liked it, people figured you'd been too long in the sun without your sombrero. So Quantrill cursed it as necessary and told no one but Sandra Grange that he had learned to love it.

He put in a call to Sandy while sliding up into Edwards County but got no reply; expected none, really. Like as not, she'd be tending her truck garden; and there was no one else to take a call at her soddy. Nine-year-old Childe might hear the VHF beeper, but never answered. If you weren't standing in front of her where she could study your face, Childe saw no point in jawing with you.

Quantrill tried again an hour from the soddy, then shrugged and popped open another cold Pearl. He told himself he wasn't worried about the two sisters; though they lived on the edge of Wild Country, they were rarely more than a whistle away from a mind-boggling mass of four-hoofed help.

Reminded of Sandy's huge guardian, Quantrill slowed the cycle and began to scan overhangs of stone. Generally, Texas rattlers grew larger in regions with more rain. Quantrill knew the legend of Sowell's dragon, the nine-footer killed by mustangs in the old days, and discounted that legend by two feet. He was looking for any handy diamondback or prairie rattler that might serve as a snack.

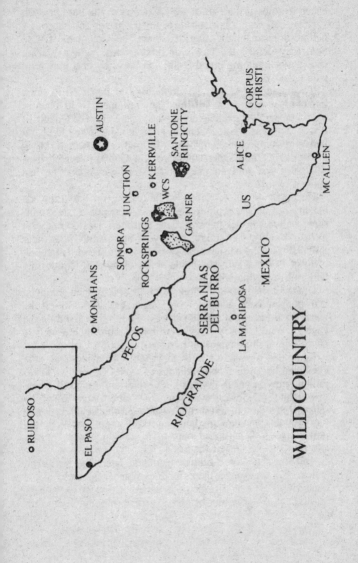

WILD COUNTRY

CHAPTER THREE • • •

The unlucky rattler wasn't even coiled, merely stretched out enjoying a recent meal, when Quantrill spotted him. Moving quickly in the late afternoon heat, the ugly brute coiled a good honest warning to this interloper. Quantrill's ventilated boots and brush trousers were snakeproof, with leg panels that served as chaps; but his primary defense against rattlers was a combination of reflexes and untrembling control. That combination had stunned U.S. Army medics when they'd first tested him for lethal skills.

Once in a human generation, a specimen with Quantrill's natural gifts might occur. Those gifts had been viciously misused until Quantrill turned rebel, pitting himself in single combat against his masters. Now that the rebels had won— and despite the best arguments by Sandy Grange—he still used his gifts in combat. He took them as much for granted as the rattler took its heat-seeking sensors.

For another man, Quantrill's rapid right-handed pass before the snake might have been bravado, but for the deputy it was only a way to coax a snake into straightening out. The rattler lashed his triangular head forward, the S-curve of neck and one coil now the size and rigidity of a baseball bat. And now the yellow-white fangtips lanced for the tempting target, but now too the hand flicked out of range, which was roughly two-thirds the length of the rattler.

And one-tenth of a human heartbeat later, the rattler hit caliche dirt, pinioned there by the treacherous hand while Quantrill's left hand grasped the rattler behind its anal opening to keep that cylinder of muscle from whipping around his arm.

Vaqueros, locally teased by the term "buckaroos," had first learned the trick of whip-cracking a live rattler to remove its head. Once a Mexican cowpoke showed that trick to his Texas neighbors, it became a well-known sport. Some said it separated the men from the boys; some said it separated the smarts from the plain stupids. Quantrill did it because it separated the snake from the sting, and he would not do it while anyone watched. Long ago he'd learned to avoid displays of his quickness. Why put an unknown enemy on guard? Word got around too soon as it was.

A moment later, Quantrill hefted the headless rattler, smiled to himself. Sometimes he brought a toy for Childe, or a spray of wildflowers for Sandy. But this time he curried favor with Ba'al, an enormous Russian boar bred to Texas proportions by Texas A&M researchers before the war. One day when Wild Country was tamed, there would be no room for such a monster, a full five hundred kilos of tusk and gristle, standing tall as a Mex pony and bearing the scars of many encounters with men. It was hard to say if Ba'al accepted Ted Quantrill as a friend. The great animal loved Sandy and, especially, Childe; but Quantrill's odor was the hated mansmell, and the two males had never faced each other without a soothing female presence.

If Ba'al loathed anything more than man, it was a live snake. A recently dead snake was something else again. His forelegs and snout were scarred from rattler punctures, and the boar dined as often from rattler nests as from wild goat, tender shoots, or stray animals from the nearby preserves of Wild Country Safari. Quantrill hoped that this quivering rattler carcass would be the equivalent of a sherbet for Sandy or a praline for Childe. If not—well, whatthehell, he'd tried to pacify the surly bastard. . . .

Less than an hour later, a few kilometers from Rocksprings, Quantrill topped a rise in view of Sandy Grange's soddy. He tried to deny the sense of relief spying the long, semisubmerged dwelling with its grassy sod roof and spiky agarita shrubs planted on the earth berm. Too many times he had seen roofs caved in by concussion grenades, smoke curling from burnt hulks, well-tended gardens ribboned to mulch by *cimarrón* gangs hostile to settlers.

But Sandy's corn stood high and golden, now with a deeper glow from the saffron sun far to the west. Over the years, sunsets were beginning to lose the psychedelic glows brought on by thousands of nuclear blasts during the war years. Atmospheric dust and smoke had brought depressed temperatures and poor crop yields until recently. Quantrill tried once more with his VHF unit, and this time Sandy heard the beeper, complaining that she would not have time to freshen up before he arrived. He thought it better to avoid mentioning his cargo; Sandy tended to get squeamish about such things.

CHAPTER FOUR • • •

Between two and three hundred klicks southwest of Rocksprings, Texas, lay La Mariposa—the butterfly—a sun-splashed village in the state of Coahuila. In the same way that Kerrville and Junction, Texas, marked the northern boundaries of Wild Country, La Mariposa marked its southern reach. North of La Mariposa lay a parched wilderness of jumbled mountains, Serranias del Burro. Beyond that ran El Rio Bravo, which *yanquis* called the Rio Grande. Contraband flowed between Mexico and Reconstruction America by the routes least likely to be discovered; and if you didn't have guaranteed passage through the Serranias, your most likely discovery was death. You would probably not discover the ruined dude ranch from which the contraband flowed.

The man who could guarantee passage, or oblivion, dismounted at almost the same moment when Ted Quantrill stepped from his hovercycle. In well-bred Spanish he said to his wrangler, "Let him cool off slowly," and bestowed a pat on the neck of his lathered polo pony. The little stallion was an unmarked golden brown; a sorrel. His owner took great pleasure in surrounding himself with variations on the sorrel theme, for he, Felix Sorel, enjoyed a golden lifestyle. When Anglos called him Sorrel, he enjoyed that as well.

Born to wealthy Marxists in Guadalajara, Felix Sorel grew from a handsome athletic child into a golden opportunity for Mexico's soccer hopes—an opportunity that country lost when Sorel's father arranged his education in Cuba. Felix' Sorel put Cuba in the World Cup semifinals in 1996, then toured several countries as an honored guest. No one doubted that Sorel would become a millionaire forward on whatever team he chose, until the SinoInd War flared. World War IV embittered young Sorel chiefly because it interfered with his career. Naturally, he blamed the US/RUS allies for the war.

Sorel vanished during the Cuban-based invasion of Florida; was reported dead twice; then reappeared in Cartagena at the war's end as the guest of a Frenchman from Marseilles. Sorel could not have been an honored guest in that context: it is hard to honor a man by entertaining him on the profits from heroin sales.

Yet Mexico, little damaged by the war and enriched by its oil sales to desperate North America, was anxious to honor Sorel. The media reported that he had put on too much weight, and Sorel proved critically sensitive about it when giving interviews. Felix Sorel returned to Mexico and his adoring fans by executive jet, and promised that he would be down to a decent weight in the near future. He shed ten kilos of that weight soon after he breezed through Mexican customs, simply by removing the bags of pure heroin, twenty million pesos' worth of it, from around his waist. His gut pads, and the media hype surrounding them, had provided the perfect cover.

Felix Sorel moved in very fast company. Sorel, in fact, *was* fast company, still in his physical prime at thirty-two. He took good care of his yellow hair, golden tan, blue eyes, and a grin that could scarcely be viewed without sunglasses. Sorel had every reason to grin a lot; his father had taught him that it was eminently proper to grow rich and powerful through flooding the *yanqui* domains with hard drugs—so long as he did not become a user of his own shit.

A dutiful son, Felix Sorel kept his body finely tuned and free of drugs. His addictions could be guessed from his medical records. Urethritis from his gonorrhea; gonococcal pharyngitis; herpes simplex II; and trichomoniasis. The first two of these diseases Sorel got from male friends; the last two from female friends. In the celebration of self, Sorel was willing to share, and as a world-class soccer player he scored as often as he liked in sexual games.

Today, Sorel's exercise on the polo pony was chiefly for show in a Latin culture that valued horsemanship. His private exercises featured loose clothing, mats, and sharp implements; skills he had learned in Cuban commando training and honed with his own lively intelligence. Ambushed once by

Corsican rivals in the drug trade and once by kidnappers, Sorel had yet to be taken.

Cat-sleek, careful in his habits, Sorel ate well, slept well, and split his time prosperously. He spent ten percent of his time among celebrities and ninety percent of it among his own picked staff, who shunned public places.

At the moment he was baring those famous teeth of his, waving to the Brazilian nymph who sunned herself beside the natural-seeming, artificial sweep of his pool. Even from a satellite camera, the old spa appeared far gone in romantic shambles. Sorel's excellent comm set was line-of-sight laser, which defied intercept and was relayed through an automatic translator station near La Mariposa. Sorel's staff was kept small, composed of men who would rather be dead than imprisoned, and who used nothing more mind-sapping than mezcal and an occasional joint. Sorel abandoned his smile as he saw the lounge shutters thrown open. It was a signal that demanded his attention.

"Wait there," he called to the girl in too perfect English. "I shall obtain something to tempt you." He took the ramshackle steps in a springing lope, removed the neckerchief of bronze silk from his throat, dabbed perspiration away as the heels of his polished riding boots echoed down the parquetry of an inner corridor.

He continued past the lounge to a door the girl had always found locked, waited for the voiceprinter to unlock the carved oak door, strode in. In Spanish, he said with deceptive mildness to the two waiting men, "I assume this is worth interrupting me."

One of the men was trained to operate the laser comm set; the other to encode and decode messages. Both had the straight hair and liquid obsidian eyes of Indios, and the look of men in the presence of their demigod.

The tall man with the coder key around his neck ducked his head in respect. "Such is my belief," he said formally, and handed Sorel a folded scrap of paper. The other man, thick and silent, sat waiting for orders. A Yucatecan whose primary language was Maya, he sat as though prepared to wait through a geologic era.

Sorel glanced at the scrap, let his hand drop in disgust, scanned it again, then glanced toward the ceiling as if instructions were printed there. For an instant he stood still, the blue eyes staring at nothing. Then he said to the seated man, "Please go to the kitchen, Kaiyi, and prepare sangarees for me and the woman. Serve them by the pool. Tell her I shall be with her presently."

Kaiyi—a Maya nickname, for the sturdy fellow swam like a fish—arose without comment and left the room.

"Give thanks, Cipriano," Sorel growled then. "You will share no more bad blood with Rawson."

"I never thought you could trust him, señor."

"And I never did; except where his own interests were served. Now it seems the trigger-happy fool has finally caught a fatal case of lead poisoning, if San Antonio Rose is right. He has not misinformed us yet."

"Not that you know of," Cipriano replied impassively.

Sorel studied the mestizo while abrading the scrap of polypaper under his thumb. He peeled its two layers apart; watched them degrade into loose fibers as he spoke: "You have kept something from me?"

"Only my disquiet, señor. Your San Antonio Rose has too much of the gringo in him."

The ghost of a smile: "Not as much as I, you buffoon. If he has arranged bail for Longo and Slaughter, he is still dependable."

"Perhaps so that they can lead the *yanquis* back here?"

"They know better than that. And if they do not, a sniper laser will teach them quickly enough." Now the smile was a grin: "That would please you, I am sure."

A blink and a smile, where a *yanqui* would have nodded.

One elegant finger, backed with sorrel hairs, wagged before the mestizo. "You are a deeply prejudiced man, Cipriano. Were it not for those renegade Texans of mine, it might be you and Kaiyi who would cross Wild Country with our shipments. And you would never pass for TexMex, my friend. You never learned to lower your chin when facing armed Anglos."

"*Gracias a Dios* for that," Cipriano muttered. "Even here in Mexico they cheat at cards. They eye our women too openly. They need humility."

"They need a cold-steel education, you mean," Sorel furnished with a thumb-flick that mimed a switchblade. "Perhaps you are right, but now we need them. For one thing, the two *yanquis* know where the shipment is hidden, and I cannot afford any more losses to the border patrol.''

His Indio eyes slitted, Cipriano asked, ''And how do we know the *yanqui* patrols did not confiscate your demon-powder?''

''Because,'' Sorel said as if to an idiot, ''if they had, they would be holding Clyde Longo and Harley Slaughter without bail. One can learn much merely by understanding how the *yanqui* system works. Now then: since Slaughter is a cautious man, we can expect him to stay in contact with our San Antonio contact. I wish you to encode a reply.''

Cipriano was cautious, too; he handed Sorel a small polypaper pad so that the encoded message would be, letter for letter, Sorel's own. The message was longer than most. Cipriano read it through, understanding most of it.

It was always possible that a transmission could be monitored. That explained why Sorel did not want that shipment's location radioed from Texas. The shrewd Slaughter had no doubt cached the stuff secretly, and well. Cipriano would have bet that Felix Sorel intended to meet Longo and Slaughter personally somewhere near Junction, Texas. But Cipriano would have lost.

The Indio scanned the message again; shrugged. ''Your man, San Antonio Rose: he knows this Cielita Linda?''

''That is not your worry,'' Sorel said curtly. ''Be at ease, Cipriano; I would not entrust such a crucial operation to anyone who has less to lose than I do.''

''But—a woman,'' Cipriano said, fingering his encoder key.

Sorel replied first with silent amusement, striding to the door. Then, ''If San Antonio Rose is a man, why not Cielita Linda? I shall send Kaiyi to operate the comm set,'' he added aloud, stepping through, making certain the door latched. He hurried to change into swim trunks, only half-amused at Cipriano's complaint. The trouble was, Cielita Linda *was* a woman; and while she had much to lose, she also had powerful connections north of Wild Country. It was her infatuation with Felix Sorel, more than anything else, that compelled her to take heavy risks. Sorel would have preferred to rule her through fear for, as he had been taught, in his business fear was by far the most dependable motive.

CHAPTER FIVE • • •

As always after a month's absence from Sandy, Ted Quantrill felt buoyed by a sense of coming home. He always found changes—the corn stood in rosy golden rows, now, ready for picking, and the pumpkins would be turning color soon. Sandy's old windmill generator was gone, too, replaced by new vertical foils with a capstan drive. The new rig made more efficient use of ground winds and did not need to stand on a high tower, so it was not so conspicuous. Also, a secondhand hovercycle had been added since his last visit. Otherwise it was the same familiar little spread, he thought, strolling in the dusk with Sandra Grange.

Time was when Sandy would have crowded near him, even in weather hot as this. Yet her independence had grown with her body. Sandy was no longer a grubby eleven-year-old, staring worshipfully up at him; nor an ardent, full-breasted seventeen, anxious to discover whether love and sexuality could coexist in a world as hard as the one she'd chosen. Now she was within a few inches of Quantrill's height, her arms tan as his, her hands roughened by farm chores. He knew she had changed to the bodiced dress and open sandals for him on short notice, but she walked beside him as an equal, the queen of her small domain.

Pleased at thoughts of her self-sufficiency, Quantrill eased his arm around Sandy's waist, urged her to face him. "I've thought about you every day," he said, kissing her gently, one hand massaging her shoulder.

"Have you thought about changing your line of work every day, too?" Her soft South Texas drawl was like her responding kiss: warm, vibrant, but with a reserve born of long-standing arguments.

"That, too," he said, guiltily because he had done nothing

of the sort. He let the massaging hand shift a bit. "You sure we won't have an hour before Childe gets home? I've missed you, Sandy."

"I know what you've missed," she said, accusing, her full lower lip pursed as though scorning what they both enjoyed. She eased herself away, put fingers to her lips, blew a piercing four-toned blast that echoed from a nearby arroyo. "*Now* I'm sure. She'll be here in five minutes or I'll tan her hide."

His smile was wry, his hands-out gesture full of defeat. "Umm, let's see; those first two notes say, 'Come in, all clear,' right? But I didn't get the others."

"The third said, 'Ba'al, too,' and the last note stands for your name. That's why she'll bust her buns to get home, poor darlin'. She doesn't know what a nasty old man you really are."

"Damn' little chance I get to prove it."

"We've been all over that, and I still say the older Childe gets, the more she understands. If you want to play house with me, Mister Deputy, we do it on neutral territory." Realizing how snappish that sounded, she took his ear gently, circled her forefinger in it. "I'm surprised you're still so randy after the last time, Ted."

"Last time?" It was nearly a yelp. "That was August, you blowsy wench! When do I fit into your bloody schedule again?"

She giggled, raised her face in bogus sweetness, and began to croon: "On the first day of Christmas, my true love gave to me-e-e . . . ."

"Christmas your ass."

She snapped her fingers. "Couldn't phrase it better myself," and then dissolved in laughter at the look on his face. "Ted, I have to get the corn in. Then I'll see about letting Childe stay with friends in Rocksprings, and I'll give you a call. Soon, love."

"That's a promise," he insisted, half in frustration, half-amused.

"No. That's a threat," she replied, raking his stalwart body with her glance, mouth parted. The cool competence in her eyes had the effect she intended. She laughed again as he wheeled away and swore to herself that she would not be so cruel again. Not this trip, anyway.

He was muttering, "Jesus *Christ*, there must be a law against teasers," when Childe rode out of the scrub cedars, waving happily from her mount. Ted Quantrill wondered if he would ever grow accustomed to the sight, one that few others had ever seen and those few scarcely believed.

Childe sat at ease, gangly bare legs astride the great boar, Ba'al, one hand entwined in the grizzled neck ruff while she waved with the other. Quantrill waved back, wondering whether her grip might be painful to the boar. He had never seen the great insolent-eyed Ba'al hesitate from wariness of pain. The significance of Childe's method of sitting her mount was not that it hurt, but that it worked. It seemed that the boar had an Apache's outlook on life. For Ba'al, pain was overrated.

The way Childe communicated with the boar, it was no wonder the kid behaved so much like a white Indian. On the one hand, Childe had been taught the languages of Wild Country by her companion: tracking, weather signs, what you could eat, what might eat you—for bear, puma, and wolf had always lurked in these parts. On the other hand, Childe liked listening to Sandy talk, and Sandy usually had no one else to talk to. In this way, Childe learned a little about the books Sandy read. Dickens and McMurtry, Renault and Buck, Gibbon and Gibbons, Anger and Angier.

The truth is that Childe considered her grown sister slightly dotty about words, 'specially the printed kind. Why, she and Ba'al got along day in, year out without a jotted note or a printed sign, theirs a world of genuine sign and not arbitrary symbols. It was a plain puzzlement the way Sandy filled two composition books a year, writing in a journal that nobody else had ever read.

Childe dismounted with a leap; ran pell-mell toward Quantrill, arms outstretched for one of the few dizzy delights that Ba'al could not provide. Quantrill braced himself, caught her, whirled Childe in a circle once, twice; heard the boar cough his concern. Then he let the girl regain her feet and hugged her briefly without speaking.

"Bring me somethin'?"

"No time, sis—but hold on! I have something for him," Quantrill recalled suddenly. He saw her big eyes ask the question. "Come and see," he chuckled. "For all I know he might not like it."

The leviathan boar had not moved a hoof, only switching his flywhisk tail now and then, the yellow eyes missing nothing. Sandy ambled over to her old protector, watched in silence, and scratched Ba'al under the jaw.

Another girlchild might have squealed in alarm when Quantrill hauled the headless rattler from stowage in the hovercycle. Childe squealed in delight. "Couldn't find a big one?"

"Gimme a break," he joked, holding the massive varmint up for display to show that it was longer than the girl.

She whistled, a quick two-note warble, and Quantrill turned to see Ba'al advance in a bouncing trot, the murderous hooves spurting dust. Then, as he had learned through harrowing experience, Quantrill bent his knees and waited. Ba'al took offense whenever Quantrill stood erect nearby, for then the man's eyes were a handsbreadth higher than the boar's. With bent knees, Quantrill would eye the boar on even terms.

Ba'al planted his forelegs like a cutting horse as he noted the offering; then advanced again, snuffling. Quantrill held the snake out in both hands, nodding, Childe moving to Ba'al's side with odd snortings and head motions. Then—perhaps it was only his imagination—Quantrill could have sworn the great jaws opened in a smile. Ba'al moved his snout across the snake, his enormous tusks long as a man's forearm, curving up and back. Now nearing middle age, Ba'al had to lower his snout even farther to impale an enemy. A product of Texas Aggie geneticists, Ba'al was beyond prediction. It was Sandy's hope that he would live until both tusks formed complete circles, which might take another twenty years.

Quantrill reached out, scratched the boar's bristly jowl, moved back with empty hands. Ba'al shifted the tidbit in his jaws, snuffled in curiosity, then stalked slowly to the hovercycle.

No one interfered as the sensitive snout inquired around the rear cowl and its tarp. The bodybag was, after all, sealed. After a moment the boar backed away, tail erect, and uttered a series of deep grunts before he turned and trotted from sight into the deepening shadows of range scrub.

"Huh; well, I guess it's okay," Childe said, and walked back to the soddy with Quantrill.

As always, he took potluck. Sandy hauled a block of venison chili from her old Peltier freezer and let Childe make the biscuits. Their guest noted, but did not mention, the new microwave cooker. If Sandy wanted to discuss her new gadgetry, she would.

Later, sharing strong coffee and the rich musk of buttermilk pecan pralines, Childe sighed as she heard a rusty old argument grind into motion between her elders. Sandy began it with, "I hear they're paying top dollar for construction work."

"In SanTone Ringcity, yes," Quantrill said. Of the American urban centers that had felt nuclear fury, perhaps half of them had been rebuilt. Some, like San Antonio, had been firestormed to their beltline freeways. San Antonio had been unlucky enough to catch some intercepted nukes, bombs that had been scattered over ground zero without detonating. The center of San Antonio would not be fully safe for human life until that contamination was all scraped away. It was quicker to rebuild this nexus of Texas commerce as SanTone Ringcity, looking outward, away from the inner ruins.

Quantrill knew SanTone well. "No half-built boomtown is a proper place to raise a kid," he said, cutting his eyes toward Childe. "And you'd have to kiss that boar goodbye."

"There's lots of work nearer, at Wild Country Safari," Sandy replied, and whacked her cup down with unnecessary force. "Dammit, Ted, you *have* to work your way into something better than deputy work; you've just *got* to!" She saw the film of stubborn resolve cross his face; tried to attack through it. "Don't kid me about working your way up to Marshal Teague's office; that's a political job, and you can't run with that crowd."

"Don't want to," he grumped. "I prefer the company of ol' Jess Marrow, keeping track of exotic game on Safari lands. It's not as if I were a full-time deputy."

"And someday those freak reflexes of yours will fail you; everybody slows down eventually. And then, instead of having two part-time jobs, you'll be full-time dead. You think I intend to wait around until the day some *cimarrón* buries you?"

Long silence. Then, "Who asked you to wait?"

"You did, a month ago," Childe piped angrily.

Frowning at the girl, a half smile giving the lie to it, Quantrill winked. "You hear too much, sis."

"I hear Sandy cry at night. She wouldn't if you stayed here more."

He nodded slowly. "Sis, these are hard times. I wish the exotic game work would pay a man enough to marry and settle, but it won't. I make more money as a deputy in a week than I do in a month with Jess Marrow. Do you know what a federal deputy marshal does?"

"Manhunter." It was a flat accusation from a nine-year-old, and it hurt. Even if Childe attached very few demerits to the idea.

Grudging it: "Sometimes, yes. Before you were born, this wasn't Wild Country—not *this* wild, anyhow. A lot of Americans suffer today because of smuggled drugs, poorly refined fuel, and diseased animals coming across the border. Somebody has to stop it."

He saw only polite interest in the girl's gaze. To her, these problems seemed very far away. He rarely opened old wounds, but this was a special case. "I had a friend named Kent Ethridge once. One of the finest gymnasts this country ever had." He stopped, turned to Sandy. "Can she handle this?"

"I think so," Sandy replied.

Quantrill faced the memory, gnawing his lip as he proceeded. "Kent Ethridge and I were—manhunters for a bad government. We hated it. Ethridge began to spend his time off with drugs, stuff that made him forget what he was. The stuff is terribly expensive; that's bad enough. But it did terrible things to his mind and his body, too." He saw Childe nod solemnly, considered explaining the terror of knowing that your mastoid implant could be detonated by pitiless masters; decided against it. "Ethridge was a hero in the rebellion, and became an agent for our new government."

"This gov'ment? The good one?"

"Good as we deserve, as usual. We thought Ethridge had cleaned himself up, didn't use drugs anymore; but maybe you never get entirely cured. Anyway, he stopped a shipment of heavy sh—drugs, and he didn't turn it all in." A silence. "I guess he decided then there was no way he could get straight. So he took the best way out that he knew."

"I don't get it."

"He took a massive overdose," Quantrill said softly. "When they found him in his apartment, he'd been dead for a week."

Childe knew about *that*. "Yuck," she said, wrinkling her nose.

"I had to identify him, and yuck is right. I know it was partly his own fault, but Ethridge didn't start the drug smuggling. He just got caught in it. It turns good men into bad ones."

"And you hunt those bad men?"

"Sometimes. Now then: Mexico could help stop it, but too many bad men pay *mordidas*, bribes, to their government."

A moment's confusion. "Is a bribe more like a peso or a dollar?"

"More like a million dollars in good money."

"That's not good money," Childe said, going directly to the heart of the matter.

"Money is just money to most people, hon," Sandy put in. "I know that Ted's job is important. But it is also very, very dangerous, and he has done it long enough. He doesn't think so, and that," she said gently, placing a hand on Quantrill's while she spoke to her sister, "is why we argue."

"Our money's good," said Childe, "and Ba'al won't mind if you come live here." Then, through her shyness: "Me neither."

"I know that, sis," he sighed. "But this little spread of yours won't pay for new dresses or fencewire. Maybe when I've saved some money—"

"We're doing all right," Sandy said, cautious lest she say too much.

"So I noticed. Beats me how you do it," he said.

"What if I won a pile at roulette over in Faro—or something?"

"I'd want to hear all about it," he grinned. Sandy had visited the gambling hells of Faro, the synthetic Old West sin city of Wild Country Safari, exactly once, and she'd gone with a pass.

Now Sandy improvised on dangerous ground. "Maybe I wouldn't tell you. You don't know everything; maybe I do

things you don't know about. Maybe you just have to take me
as I am."

"That was what I had in mind," he said slyly.

Childe reached for another praline, got the lightest of slaps
over her spindly wrist from Sandy. She pulled back then,
bored with her immediate prospects, and innocently changed
the subject. "Can I see the man?"

Too late, Quantrill realized her drift. He and Sandy, simultaneously: "What man?"

"The man in your cycle," Childe said.

"You've kept someone hiding out there?" Sandy wasn't
more than half-horrified. Yet.

"Not hiding," said Childe. "Dead." Quantrill was not
surprised that Ba'al's educated nose could detect the scent of
a dead man. He was astonished that the boar could have
communicated the fact to Childe with only a few passing
grunts.

Quantrill: "Oh, shit."

Childe: "Not s'posed to say 'shit.' "

Sandy: "Ted Quantrill, is that true? Did you actually bring
a—a corpse here?" With a more hopeful suspicion, she continued, "Was it some poor wetback dead of exposure? Snake-
bite?" But her mood darkened as she saw he was not going to
offer some good Samaritan excuse.

He pushed back from the table; took a final sip of coffee
before replying, staring at Sandy. "It was a man named Mike
Rawson, a hired gun protecting a shipment of heroin—for a
man he called Sorrel. You remember Espinel? Friend of your
old hotsy, Lufo; my friend, too. Well, Espinel and some
others were deputized up near Junction to stop Sorrel's people
for a contraband search. Now Espinel is cold in the Junction
morgue, thanks to that brush-poppin' sonofabitch Rawson.
He tried to tomhorn me, bushwhack me, south of here. No, I
wasn't going to tell you about it. I knew you'd get all
spooked."

"I am not spooked. I am repelled, I am disgusted, I am—"

"Mad as hell," Childe supplied with cheer.

"And I"—Quantrill sighed—"am on my way. Thanks a
lot for everything, sis," he said to the girl, and remembered
to flourish his hat to Sandy at the door. "Mighty good chili,"

he said, and then, on his way out, "and by-God first-rate entertainment."

The coffee cup missed him because he was already in darkness, navigating by memory to the hovercycle. Much of Sandy's vitriol also missed him because he was busy muttering to himself. He caught her phrases, "no better'n a goddamn saddle tramp, a hired gunsel" and "might've brought me flowers, but no, he brings me a dead *cimarrón* instead."

The dial at his wrist told him it was half-past nine, and the pounding anger in his head told him he wouldn't be able to sleep anyway. A cold moon showed him the way to the potholed county road and, without lights, he found his way to the Junction highway. He was still vulnerable to anyone with a nightscope, and this was still the raw edge of Wild Country, so he hunkered down and flipped the bullet-resistant polyglass side panels up. He knew he could cadge a free night's lodging at the Junction jail, if he could avoid a drygulching en route.

CHAPTER SIX • • •

First, Sandy Grange located the plastic cup she had hurled into the night. Then she shooed Childe into bed, arranging the woven comforter with its plaited strips of rabbit fur so that it would be close at hand. Next she tidied up, imagined that Childe's snores were genuine, and sat down at the table with her lockbox.

The contents of that box would not have gladdened the heart of a petty thief, unless he knew what he was looking at. A ruled composition tablet of polypaper and ballpoint pens; a curled Polaroid photo, a candid shot of Ted Quantrill in the early days of the war while he still carried a certain innocence in those green eyes; the tarnished engagement ring with its tawdry rutile gem which Lufo Albeniz had once given her (she had never worn it); and finally a stainless-steel amulet of peculiar workmanship. Its central bezel was empty because Sandy had pried the great jewel from it.

Sandy did not know that this unique off-planet jewel, dubbed the Ember of Venus, now adorned the throat of the mistress of a top official of Pemex Oil. She only knew that she had entrusted the thing to her ex-lover, Lufo, hoping that he might sell it for a reasonable fraction of its true value. This, Lufo had done.

Sandy had received sixty thousand pesos, roughly six thousand dollars at the current exchange rate, from Lufo. Lufo had held back a "small" commission. Sandy could not know that commission amounted to four hundred and forty thousand pesos for himself—and for his various wives in Texas and Mexico. So much for trust.

If Sandy entertained doubts about Lufo's honesty, she knew better than to voice them to Ted Quantrill. Once Ted realized that the fortunes of war and Wild Country had delivered the legendary Ember into Sandy's hands, he would know she also owned the steel bezel with its curious black diamond studs, its tiny yield chamber, and the alphanumeric readout on the back. If the jewel was worth half a million pesos, that handmade amulet was worth immensely more. Crafted in desperation by an imprisoned scientist, it was the world's only working miniature of a matter synthesizer.

Rumors of its existence had nearly died through the years. It no longer functioned because the computer terminal to which it had been linked was now fused into slag, a casualty of the rebellion in 2002. Quantrill had once argued that *if* the tiny thing really existed, it could topple governments; would change the face of economies across the globe and on New Israel's orbiting colonies. Sandy had known, even then, that she could set those changes in motion.

For better or worse, she had chosen to hide the thing away. Quantrill, she knew, would have delivered it to the only politician he trusted, Attorney General James Street. Knowing this, she would not share her secret until certain it was the right thing to do. In her youth and optimism, she felt that one day she would be certain, one way or the other. In the meantime, she felt that life was not bad, merely hard. If Ted Quantrill ever learned that she had kept this stunning technical toy a secret, her life might contain a Quantrill-sized void. Therefore, Sandy Grange spent half of her sixty thousand pesos on creature comforts and hoped she could invest the rest wisely.

Of course, once a technical breakthrough is achieved it cannot be hidden away forever. It had never occurred to Sandy that at least two governments were well on the way to rediscovering the secrets of the original Chinese matter synthesizer. Even if Sandy was more cautious than Pandora, others clamored to open the box.

CHAPTER SEVEN · · ·

Sandy's journal, Sun. 17 Sept. '06

And now I have sent Ted away! One day he will tire of my temper, will find some more complacent woman. Perhaps he has already. And that might be best for us all. Let someone else wake on lonely nights to wonder whether Ted Quantrill's luck has finally run out.

I should be more friendly with Jerome Garner, who, with all his father's land hereabouts, is surely the catch in Edwards County. He would not care what I did with this damnable steel toy gleaming in the light before me. Not he! His ethics begin at his fenceline and stop at his beltline. Or so they say in Rocksprings.

I would almost prefer Lufo. At least his dishonesty was transparent and dependable. A pity I did not consider that before I let him sell the jewel. I am certain it brought a higher price than Lufo claimed, perhaps ten thousand dollars American? Twenty, even. Lufo is canny, though. Since I trusted him with the sale, he knows I had my reasons for not having Ted sell it.

And if I made a clean breast of it to Ted, "washed my boobies," as they say on the holo, the least that would happen is the end of their old camaraderie. The most? Mutual murder, for neither of them would ever back down.

The truth is that I can do nothing, cannot even move away without leaving Ba'al friendless, unless Childe should choose his wild ways over mine. And she very well might! Without her caution, he would soon be back among the Safari game animals and the Garner sheep, instead of making do with roots and rattlers. And one day, someone like Jer Garner would hunt him down with a rocket launcher. Ba'al may be the most potent gristle ever created by God and Texas Aggies, but he is not invulnerable.

No more than Ted, who is perfectly correct in claiming that his work is vital. And that no one is better suited to it than he. But sooner or later, if I do not stop him, a bullet must. And I, who cannot even bear to think of poor Espinel's killer lying dead on my property: what will I do when it is Ted who is consigned to the worms? Ah, God, how will it end? For it will end, I know. . . .

CHAPTER EIGHT • • •

The villa of Judge Anthony Placidas shared the breeze off Lake Medina on Monday morning with a dozen other homes, all postwar country residences of neodobe, the envy of those in SanTone whose high-rise windows faced the west. Judge Placidas had done very well for himself while still an attorney; was known in the ringcity as a man sympathetic to the rights of defendants. He was also known as an ardent sportsman; though well into his sixties, he could still shoot an ibex while in the saddle and was not averse to bucking the tiger at the Faro gaming tables—both legal entertainments on the half-million acres of Wild Country Safari. Somewhat less well known were his occasional meetings there with men he would not dream of entertaining anywhere else. The money that changed hands during those meetings had little to do with gambling. It had a lot to do with the rights—and the gravest wrongs—of some defendants.

It was not that Judge Placidas had expensive tastes, but his daughter Marianne was another matter. On this Monday morning, the judge was berobed, earning his money in SanTone. Marianne Placidas had ordered a breakfast for one sent to the villa; chorizo sausage and eggs, fresh orange juice, a double daiquiri, and a slab of butter for the villainous acorn-flour bread that still disgraced the menus of even the rich. (As wheat harvests improved, the acorn content of flour dwindled.)

Marianne slipped off one low-heeled glove-leather sandal by toeing it with the other foot, then shucked the other sandal and stared through the polyglass table. Something would have to be done about those feet, and soon! They were attached to slender ankles, the calves wonderfully long with muscular convexities. The knees seemed too narrow for the demands she made on them, her tanned thighs highly developed. Any

dullard knew by staring at the Placidas legs—and who didn't?
—that the rest of her was equally athletic and well cared for.
Marianne was the perfect image of the synchronized swim-
mer, but she scorned both the strict discipline and the public
titillation involved. Hers were elite sports.

It was only those feet with the heavy veins and prominent
sinews that hinted at approaching middle age. Marianne never
wore heels before dinner, never wore flats afterward; that was
the rule her mother had followed while she was alive. Whether
gifted by genes or by constant attention to her body, Marianne had to admit that the regimen hadn't hurt those gorgeous
limbs any. She pushed the eggs aside, sipped the daiquiri,
and pondered throwing out her dozen pairs of footwear that
showed too much sinew. Perhaps a few pairs of ankle-strap
pumps? The high straps would draw men's eyes upward.
Eyes, and importunate fingers, and perhaps a suitor would not
pause to read the message of those treasonous feet as they
marched Marianne away from her youth.

Her diet would have swollen the waist of a less active
woman, but she was not her father's only daughter for nothing. She eyed the windsurfer sails on the lake, wondering if
she would have time for an impromptu race before her tennis
date. Her wide smile brought faint crinkles to the corners of
her eyes; she could lose at tennis, but rarely did at windsurfing.
Usually she won on superior balance. Now and then she
relied on the tiny hydrazine propulsion system hidden inside
her foam platform. In her lifelong pursuit of admiration, she
had found no advantages in fairness. To Marianne Placidas,
"fair" was strictly defined as a condition halfway between
"pretty good" and "lousy."

She was inside, reaching for her bikini halter, when the
phone chimed. It was probably that militarily correct Englishman, Alec Wardrop, calling to cancel their tennis date. No
doubt he'd heard of her prowess and did not relish losing his
veddy British aplomb. He was hell on horseback, she knew; a
steeplechasing, Indian pigsticking fool from a long line of
English career officers. Well, if she couldn't test him on a
clay court, he would never test her in bed.

"Hello, Alec," she called to the phone. It recognized her
voiceprint, but not her bored resignation.

The caller was not Lieutenant Alec Wardrop. Somewhere,

on the other end of that connection, someone was holding a
cheap commercial language tutor to the speaker. "Marianne
Placidas la linda, *por favor*," the voice said.

She almost forgot the correct response, but: "She is out,
and she is in," Marianne replied in a rush.

"Stand by to record," the voice said after a moment.

She lunged at the nearest speaker terminal. "Recording."

A long series of phone beeps ensued. They meant nothing
specific to her yet, but they came in groups of five, and that
meant a great deal in itself. She coded the doors locked,
opened her jewel case, extracted a small dispenser with its
stack of hormone pills. She swallowed the first pill—it was
candy—and sucked furiously on the second, which was something else.

Before the last beep died away, she had dried her saliva
from the little information lozenge and was inserting it into
her own, very special tutorial voder. Sometimes it taught her
French, sometimes the updated slangs of jazz buffs and soccer jocks. This morning it had already taught her that she, and
not Alec Wardrop, would have to cancel that tennis date.

She remembered to cancel calls from outside, then placed
her voder near the recorder speaker and encoded instructions.
She scribbled the letters out in full caps as the voder, func-
tioning as a very fast version of a one-time cipher code,
began to recite the message, one letter· at a time. There were
faster ways to decode a message, but no way quite so innocent in its hardware, given the possibility that some very hard
dudes might show up one day with a search warrant.

She smiled grimly as the first two words were assembled.
Her father might have heard them in testimony; probably had,
in fact. He could have no earthly idea that they referred to his
darling, his pampered, his celebrated little girl.

The first two words were a greeting. CIELITA LINDA
. . . No, she was not Judge Placidas's daughter for nothing.
She was whatever she was, for all the sorrel-golden gratifica-
tion she received.

CHAPTER NINE • • •

Quantrill handed over his bounty late Sunday night in Junction and slept on a cot in the courthouse annex. It was far from the sleeping arrangements he had intended, and he awoke, Monday morning, with something less than joy. Before drawing his check for hazardous duty he had several things to do.

The most pleasant of those items was breakfast. Then, in descending order, turning in the cycle; filling out forms; and debriefing. In his perverse mood he did them in reverse order—always a mistake.

Marv Stearns eyed the smaller man standing before his desk for debriefing and waved him to a cane-bottomed chair. Stearns had the imposing physique of a defensive end, but these days it was running to meat instead of muscle. His face was more florid than tan. As he spoke, Quantrill listened to the careful diction and wondered, for the umpteenth time, if Stearns had spent his college days as an actor instead of an athlete. "If you're going to slouch, Quantrill, I'd rather you sat." He poured himself a fresh cup of coffee, not offering to share it; lined up the notes on his desk with geometric precision; studied the younger man's face with growing satisfaction. Rumbling it in false good humor: "Hung over?"

"Nope; just lack of sleep."

Stearns glanced at his desk terminal. "Maintenance found several empty beer bulbs in your cycle."

Quantrill knew the rules well enough. And, as a lovely assassin had taught him long before, you don't touch alcohol while under heavy stress. He hadn't so much as risked a cold Pearl until after the Rawson encounter. "Picked 'em up for the deposit," he lied. "They'll buy breakfast, if I ever get out of here. Sir."

39

"I'd have you out of here permanently, if it weren't for
your connections," Stearns said. "Where the hell, and why,
did you steal that old android?"

A sigh. "Call Mr. Marrow at Wild Country Safari; he'll
tell you it was a junker he used for practical jokes. Rawson
used it for target practice thinking it was me. And why is
maintenance going over my cycle when I haven't turned it in
yet?"

"I'll ask the questions," Stearns said, tapping with a forefinger on his desk placard. "Let me make it perfectly clear
that I am chief deputy, and I don't like the way you operate. I
think you drink on duty. I think you probably goaded Michael
Rawson into drawing on you. The first time I catch you in a
slip-up, you may end up on a rock-hockey gang at the county
farm, or worse. And you're never in uniform, Quantrill.
Never!" Stearns fondled the tan silk tie of his own spotless,
sleek uniform. "Ties will be worn, mister. No deerskin shirts."

"Regulations permit a certain latitude in the dress code
during hazardous duty," Quantrill said, quoting exactly from
the book. "That's all you use me for, you know it and I know
it. Sir. I could ask why, but you're asking the questions."

Stearns bit back a furious reply, took a sip of coffee, and
chose to let the harassment lapse for the time being. Most
men, knowing they were under constant scrutiny for the
slightest infraction, began to make more mistakes from sheer
nervousness. Chief Deputy Marvin Stearns liked his world
orderly, neat, and predictable. Wild cards like Quantrill were
burrs in his personal blanket; he would rather remove them
neatly than be surprised by their unconventional ways. Neat-
ness, for Stearns, was a powerful measure of success.

In a trivial bureaucratic way, Stearns was right. But Quantrill
had been harassed by experts. No one could have convinced
Stearns that he was less than an expert judge of men. Pleased
with his strategy, Stearns continued the debriefing. He even
agreed when, at the end, Quantrill asked to study some files
before writing out his final report.

"Go ahead, if it'll make your report sound less like a
goddam telegram and more like a professional job." He
dismissed Quantrill with a wave.

The little deputy walked out without argument, knowing it
was argument that Stearns craved. Obvious insubordination,

or admission of drinking on duty—anything that might give
Stearns an excuse for disciplinary action; perhaps even a suspension. Alone, Quantrill studied holo sequences from official
files, imprinting the faces and mannerisms of Harley Slaughter and Clyde Longo. He was on his own time now, but those
two were free on bail and they might know who had iced Mike
Rawson. For some time now, Quantrill had suspected a leak
in the Justice Department. If Slaughter and Longo had access
to that leak, they might just come calling under false names.

An hour before noon, he cashed his hazardous pay chit and
checked the schedules of freighters heading from Junction
toward SanTone, then hotfooted it to the pickup point near
Interstate 10. With the LOS—line-of-sight—power tower
nearby, the huge-wheeled freight rigs often stopped to soak
up energy through their antennae. Since the war, a lot of the
big rigs were equipped with seats for several paying passengers. It wasn't first-class travel, but if you couldn't afford a
hovercycle and couldn't borrow one from the motor pool, a
freight rig was the best way to travel through the rough
margins of Wild Country.

He found a black double-tandem Peterbilt with a full load
revving its flywheels for pullout onto the freeway and waved
a five-dollar piece. Headshake. A second coin with the first
earned him a wave up, and Quantrill monkey-climbed the
steps into the empty compartment behind the driver's.

She was a surly old specimen who took his money and
heard his destination with only a nod. Pocketing the coins,
she sealed his compartment off, engaged the flywheels, and
hauled her freight with nary a word. She didn't need to speak;
a sign in American and Spanish informed Quantrill that the
passenger compartment was fitted with gas projectors and
bulletproof glass "FOR YOUR OWN PROTECTION." In a
sense it was true. Few rigs were hijacked when, at the first
sign of trouble, a teamster could fill that separated compartment with an assortment of nasty stuff.

Quantrill grinned, seeing the ammo box taped onto the
dash near the old girl's short-barreled shotgun. It was illegal
for civilians to shoot boosted twelve-gauge single slugs, but
not for this leathery old mare to display an empty cartridge box.
If you knew anything at all about those low-recoil, rocket-boosted twelve-bores, you knew they'd go right through most

bulletproof glass. All in all, he decided, this little old lady made her point eloquently without so much as clearing her throat.

For nearly an hour, Quantrill watched the broken countryside and thought about its future. When he'd first landed that deputy job, freighters carried "bulls"—sharpshooters who literally rode shotgun, or with Heckler & Koch assault rifles, in the cab and inside cargo holds protected by armor. In the past four years, the U. S. marshal's men had ambushed, chased, or simply scared off so many bandits that freighters were no longer easy prey. Citizens in SanTone could once again get fresh grapefruit from the southern valley, fresh beef from Abilene, diesel fuel from Odessa.

To some extent, the taming of the freightways had been Quantrill's doing; his and fifty other men's, including Espinel. But Espinel's death proved that life was still cheap in Wild Country. The big landowners often held their spreads with hired guns against squatters. Some of those hired guns worked for little or nothing. Like Rawson and his pals, they needed a base of operations en route between Coahuila and, say, Kansas Ringcity.

How many years before Wild Country could be tamed? With determined law enforcement and honest courts, Quantrill guessed it might be managed in five more years. With things as they were, it might take forever. Especially when too many people moved into the lawless region with high hopes and expensive equipment, but without weapons or ability to defend themselves. Hapless settlers became part of the problem, furnishing easy pickings from Laredo to Yuma. The old issue of gun control was still an issue, despite evidence from towns like Ruidoso and McCook.

Quantrill was fond of Ruidoso, in central New Mexico. It lay in a low mountain range that afforded cover for a robber's route most of the way to the Big Bend region. That being so, a townful of shops and horse race enthusiasts might have seemed a magnet for troublesome brush-poppers. Nearby Cloudcroft had known the nightmare of gun-toting gangs and groups of outlaw hovercyclists. Not Ruidoso!

The township of Ruidoso lived mostly on its horseflesh, one way or another. The town fathers dressed up their horsetown image with frontier celebrations, and they issued fines when they caught a local businessman out of uniform. That uniform ran to Justin boots, rakish Stetsons, jeans with heavy nylon chap panels, and string ties above colorful long-sleeved shirts.

Those jeans didn't really need heavy cartridge belts to hold them up; the belts were for handgun holsters. The postwar city ordinance phrased it as a "compulsory token wearing of sidearms." While urging wearers to peacebond their shootin' irons with ribbon ties to the holsters, nothing was said about ammunition. Roughly once a month, Ruidoso peace officers had to disarm someone. Once a year they had to deal with a shooting. On the one and only occasion when several outlaw cyclists explored Ruidoso together, they soon developed headaches from eyestrain and from frequent darted glances in all directions. They stayed long enough to buy six-packs and aspirin and sought their fun elsewhere. No armed group ever seriously thought about invading Ruidoso. Obviously the town could become noisy, true to its Spanish name, in one hell of a hurry.

McCook, Texas, was a different story; one that Quantrill would never forget. A small town at the southern tip of Texas, McCook leaned on the services of the larger McAllen nearby. McCook's chief of police, wise in the ways of reelection, knew better than to try outlawing personal firearms in his town. With malice toward none, he persuaded most townsfolk to his own version of the Second Amendment to the Constitution. That amendment reads: "A well-regulated militia being necessary to the security of a free state, the right of the people to keep and bear arms shall not be infringed."

The chief, knowing his rhetoric, did not call attention to the final phrase, which, absolutely and positively, *guarantees* citizens their personal rights to keep and bear arms. Instead, he focused on the words "well-regulated militia." He convinced the good folks of McCook that they would display the perfect model of a well-regulated militia by storing their personal weapons in a city armory. Little McCook even had a few dry runs, hoorawed by local media, in which citizens got in line to receive their pistols, plinking rifles and birdguns long enough to handle and inspect them. McCook's brave experiment, and its holovision coverage, was a published invitation for plunder.

A border bandit named Saltillo assembled two dozen

cimarrones and converged on McCook. Some came on horse-back, some on hovercycles, and a half-dozen hardcases arrived hidden in a small van that supposedly carried Mexican diesel fuel for legal sale.

Of course, they overran the police station first. The value of the firearms kept there would have paid for the raid. But Saltillo had seen the old silver icons and the jeweled trappings in the church paid for, over the generations, by McCook's devout TexMex Catholics. He figured to hit the bank as well since the church itself would be such a quick knockover.

Saltillo lost one man at the police station but bagged the chief and over a hundred weapons. *Cimarrones* cleared the streets with rapid volleys and went for the bank next because it happened to be so near the police station. They took forty thousand dollars and three lives there, but they also took their time ransacking the place. Too much time, when the local priest was as thorough and as decisive as Father Quemada.

The good father had heard the worries of his people long before; had agreed to hide the deadly weapons of his parish—or rather, to look the other way when lockers were opened in the church meeting hall. Of McCook's three hundred people, perhaps thirty ran for the church when the shooting started. Most of them intended only to pray for salvation.

Saltillo's men held target practice on the stained-glass windows to terrify the priest and his parishioners, then burst in on what they thought would be a huddled mass of victims. Some, in fact, were screaming and praying near the nave when the *cimarrones* stormed inside.

Saltillo and five of his bravos were shot dead just one pace inside the church by the damnedest concatenation of gunfire imaginable: pellet guns, five handguns, rifles of several calibers, and a sawed-off shotgun firing double-aught buckshot. Father Quemada's combat team was two men, several boys, a half-dozen women, and a pair of teenaged girls. Rumors of a man in black robes firing his own assault rifle were never verified, but it was said later that Father Quemada had the look of a man in need of confession.

Before Saltillo's remaining men fully realized the meaning of this eruption just ahead of them, they were met full face with hot metal blessings from the pure in heart. This was not the kind of greeting the *cimarrones* had counted on and, leaving more of their people flopping in the dust, they lit a shuck for the border.

Three more of Saltillo's men got perforated during the hellish confusion of reversing hovercycles and a van loaded too heavily with stolen guns. By this time McCook's few stubborn Anglos with guns at home got them into play; sniping from cover, shaking with buck fever, steadying down, sniping again.

A few of Saltillo's band got away. McCook got the van and its guns back. Saltillo and the police chief got decent burials. No authority near Wild Country got very far, after that, with schemes for the wholesale removal of personal arms.

Now, Quantrill watched an ancient Volkswagen diesel pickup jounce down a dirt access road near the freeway. He noted and approved of the thick plastic armor bolted to its cab. It obscured part of the windows and it looked like hell, but it said the driver wouldn't be candy in a skirmish. Still, some people came to the region hoping that their claims to government land could be upheld by someone else, without they themselves being ready to operate as a well-regulated family militia. Some of those good people were lucky. Some were driven out by night-riders who may, or may not, have been on payrolls of other ranchers. Some of the newcomers were robbed, raped, tortured, killed by persons unknown.

At least one recent killing bore a clear message. According to a deputy's report, the dead man was found on the spread of a rancher. Perhaps he had been caught rustling a few calves, for he had been treated to an ancient Spanish custom reserved for rustlers: the death of the skins. Apparently while still alive, he was bound inside the fresh "green" hide of a yearling steer and left there without further attention. A pitiless sun, and shrinkage of the hide, had done the rest.

The rancher, old Mulvihill Garner, expressed great surprise when the iron-hard hide was found with its grisly contents. The hide bore the Garner brand. Could the old man have done it? Surely not, for old Mul Garner's arthritis kept him off the range. His strapping, hell-raising son, Jerome? But Jer spurned anything that smacked of Spanish influence and lacked his dad's knowledge of the old punishments. Well, *some*body had done it, and people tempted to lift Garner sheep or cattle understood the message in the death of the skins.

Quantrill knew Jer Garner slightly, as a little dog knows a big dog. Twice, at weekend dances around Rocksprings, Jer had arranged to jostle Sandy Grange's dance partner. The first time Jer demanded an apology, got it, and decided that Quantrill had failed a test. The second time had only been for good measure, to remind Sandy who was the biggest bull on the spread.

Ted Quantrill knew better than to misbehave at a public dance; Sandy had to live with folks thereabouts, even if he didn't. With much of Wild Country's control in the hands of ranchers, and with some of them happy to keep it wild, the region partly justified charges by northern critics. Northerners sneered that when you scratched the veneer of the new Southwest, you found the Old West just beneath, now a mix of high tech and whang leather. Some of the finest families in the Southwest kept that reputation going, claiming you could forge a better new world while keeping a bushel of tradition. Folks in the mold of a Kleberg, a Goodnight, or a Dahlman did what they could to maintain the mixture of old and new. And then, of course, there was Quantrill's destination today: the old Schreiner spread, nucleus of Wild Country Safari.

CHAPTER TEN • • •

Quantrill alerted the old girl with the buzzer as she neared the turnout to the north gate of Wild Country Safari; heard the whine of regenerators as she slowed her big rig expertly. In common courtesy, he climbed down and hit the macadam running so that she would not waste precious energy stopping and accelerating from rest. He turned away from her dusty wake, walked to the untended gatehouse, placed his left thumb against the printmatcher. Then he went inside and selected a surfer. Safari management did not let its help get stranded forty klicks from their work stations.

The enormous spread of Wild Country Safari had begun, a century before, as the "Y O" Ranch, an arid region where the pioneering Schreiner family dug wells to water their stock. By the time Ted Quantrill was born, the Y O brand was famous—not so much for the blooded stock as for the wild game and endangered species that generations of Schreiners brought in. The list ran from addax to zebu; you could find oryx, tiny gemsbok, towering giraffe, shambling bison, and velvet-hided sable for photographs.

After the SinoInd War, Schreiners bowed to necessity and leased the entire spread to LockLever. The giant corporation added nearby lands and now had a spread that covered parts of three counties. A nearby LOS tower sent narrowcast power into the spread, but it took only a little of that power to pump water from deep wells. Much more was needed to run the weird assortment of entertainments LockLever built, and all of it together was world-renowned as Wild Country Safari. LockLever's huge investment was paying off already.

Highrollers floated in a converted delta dirigible from DalWorth to a pad just over the hill from Faro; but they clattered and bounced the last few klicks by stagecoach.

47

Wearing a rented costume, you could easily forget that Faro's plank sidewalks and clapboard saloons were all parts of a careful reconstruction. You could win a pile at faro, monte, poker, craps, or roulette—though more often you lost a small bundle. You bathed, if at all, in a high-backed zinc tub. You slept, if at all, on a cornshuck mattress that rustled louder than coal down a chute, in a room with a pitcher and bowl. If you wore a sidearm, you submitted to a company peacebonder strap that shrilled a microwave alert if broken.

In the past year, more Americans had made enough money to visit the little sin city. This was one good sign of America's slow economic rise from global disaster. Still, many of the moneyed visitors spoke Arabic or French or Spanish, and Faro boasted too many obvious foreigners gawking at each other for Quantrill's comfort. He seldom had business in Faro and rarely went there even for the cheap honest redeye at the Long Branch Saloon. The north road led to Faro, and Quantrill ignored it. The west fork arrowed over rolling lands and out of sight toward the Battle of Britain and Thrillkiller sites. He ignored that road, too, and turned toward the south.

Separated by great distance on the vast spread, connected by macadam ribbon, were other sites of very different entertainment. To the south was the old ranch complex where Quantrill lived. Here, big-game hunters found their cruel sport, and the ranch staff bred cattle: Herefords and Brangalo for beef, Longhorns for show. Quantrill mounted his fatwheeled little surfer, extended its sissy handle and seat, then urged it along the macadam.

For short runs, he sometimes rode a surfer as he had ridden ordinary skateboards before the war. But only a dunce would tire himself by standing up for an hour, creating extra wind resistance, while the energy cells drove him whirring crosscountry. He used the surfer in its scooter mode and wondered if he were getting old.

On downhill stretches he nudged its toe plate, wedging it for maximum speed, hoping to arrive at Marrow's office before midafternoon. Jess Marrow rarely complained about Quantrill's absences, but he could be testy as a bull in flytime when his assistant wasn't on hand to keep tabs on the experimental animals.

Marrow's office was empty but, stowing the surfer on a rack, Quantrill could hear familiar curses floating out from a nearby barn. It sounded like the grizzled veterinarian was not overly pleased. Sure enough, the usually unflappable Marrow was venting his ire at a cranky squeeze chute. Quantrill ran to help.

"About goddam time," Marrow grunted. He paused to reach a hand between metal bars to soothe the panicky Brangalo bull inside the squeeze chute. The Brangalo, a cross between Brahma, Angus, and bison, was in a snorting rage. "The limit switch has come loose on this godless damnable machine's hydraulic ram, an' I can't reach it without lettin' go the chute lever."

Quantrill tried not to grin, noting the bright red sheen that spread back from Marrow's forehead to his receding hairline. While Jess Marrow showed great patience with his animals, he could—as now—lose all patience with rickety old machinery. The squeeze chute allowed a vet to shoo an animal from its corral to the elevated platform where, with adjustable sides and ends on the chute, something as pesky as a Brangalo bull could be lightly squeezed into immobility.

But Marrow's equipment was old, and he knew better than to work a bull in that chute without help. He knew better, and yet . . . Jess Marrow was not a man to let his schedules slip. ithout installing a graze monitor on that bull, he couldn't round out his profile of this new hybrid. So Marrow put himself in a bind where he needed three hands. His plight looked comical to Quantrill, but Quantrill was outvoted two to one. The bull was madder, if possible, than Marrow.

"Sau-u-ugh," Marrow gentled, holding the front-end lever, and, "Soo-o-o, pard," he said, watching Quantrill stretch toward the loose limit switch, and, "There, you stupid sonofa low-balled hellion," he growled as the hydraulic ram began to work. Quantrill busied himself with the rancher's machine shop—pliers and baling wire—to secure the switch while Marrow strapped the graze monitor under the bull's jaw. Quantrill could not help his amusement at the way man and bull stared at each other through the bars as Marrow worked.

Marrow would adjust a strap, eye the bull; pass a strap behind a wicked horn, eye the bull; and continue, talking to the brute as he worked. "Yep, you'd like to catch me—

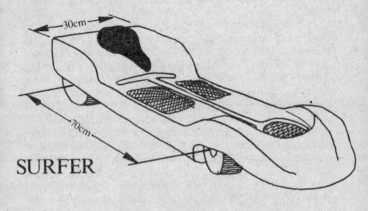

30cm

70cm

SURFER

NOTES: 1. Heel & toe plates crosshatched
2. Seat & sissybar in stowed positions
3. Energy-cell version shown

SUMMARY DATA

DESIGNATION: SURFER
DEPLOYMENT: UNRESTRICTED
SPECIFICATIONS:
1. Speed: 50 kph (elec. versions)
   80 kph (internal comb. versions)
2. Range: 50 km. (elec.)
   150 km. (internal comb.)
3. Power: high-density energy cells;
   competition versions are air-cooled
   rear-mounted internal combustion engines.
4. Structure: Polyskin chassis & shell; primitive suspension
   & high-hysteresis polymer wheels; metal stub
   frames & sissybar.
5. Wt: 12 kg. (typ.)
6. Operational modes: Smooth roads only; some city use;
   competition versions for closed tracks
   only.
7. Mfr: Various; typ. GE, Curran, BMW, Honda, LockLever.
8. Features: Shoulder strap for carrying; plug-in recharge;
   spare wheel in stowed seat; seat & sissybar for
   long trips or hilly travel. Toe plate accelerator,
   heel plates for braking. Aerodynamic shape is
   of little importance except for competition events.
   Helmets required by law in some regions.

nappin', wouldn't you? Run a horn—plumb up my pore spavined ass. And me the only—friend you got." Meanwhile, Quantrill leaned across the machinery only one pace away, a listener whether he liked or not.

Marrow paused, wiped his brow with a thick, hairy forearm, cocked his big round head with its halo of gray hair, and squatted as if listening to the bull. Then, speaking as if to the bull: "Quantrill? Don't shit yoreself, stud. He ain't your friend, he'd make mountain oysters outa your nuts in a minute."

This was an obvious lie, for Quantrill often claimed guilt when using a castrating knife. "Don't believe the old fart, stud," Quantrill said. "He's the one with a taste for your *cojones*."

"Naw, Quantrill don't need your *cojones*, he's got enough of 'em for me and you both," Marrow went on. "Today, at least. If he keeps that deppity job, one of these days he'll show up needin' spares."

So that was the drift of it! "Sorry I'm late," Quantrill said.

Marrow stood up, exhaled heavily; operated the chute lever to release the bull back to the corral, slapped the bull's flank, and waited until the chute was empty. Only then did he turn to his assistant. "Late, schmate," growled the aging vet, whose rough cattleman's lingo masked an excellent education. "That ain't what puts the hole in my boot. Well, yes it is, too; every time you come strollin' in with that gawddam space-pirate sidearm"—Quantrill had completely forgotten to remove his Chiller—"I wonder if it's the last time before your number comes up." He turned, leading the way back, and gestured toward distant oaks and cedars. "There's not a bull on that range that won't one day find another 'un that can thrash his ass, if he keeps bellerin' and searchin' long enough. But they'll all do it, ever' one of the dumb bastards, and it must be catchin' because, Teddy boy, you've caught it!"

"That's what my lady friend says," Quantrill admitted.

"The Grange girl? I remember her; who wouldn't? Why in the world and three Jewish satellites don't you listen to her?"

Quantrill, trudging beside the burly vet, did not want a repeat of his argument with Sandy. He jogged Marrow's elbow and said, "Hey, Jess, tell me about Klamath Steamboat again, and how you owe all this to him."

"Go fuck a duck." Marrow chuckled and dropped the

subject. Jess Marrow's rodeo career—like most Texans he pronounced it "*rode*-ee-oh"—had been ended in 1985 by an Oregon bronc that tucked its nose into its belly button and wound up on top of Jess, who had bone splinters poking through his jeans and blood pouring from his ear. As Jess later explained his switch to veterinary medicine: "I didn't need a house to fall on me to tell me I was past my prime. A horse, yes. A good man needs a good strong sign, an' Klamath Steamboat gave me all the sign I needed."

Marrow still walked with a slight limp. He could tell an outlaw horse or a mean bull just by eyeballing it, and he respected animals enough to treat them right. He respected humans a bit less, on the whole, but he'd known Ted Quantrill's background from the first and tried hard to keep his affection from showing. Now he scraped his boot heels before entering his office and repeated a snippet from his old monologue: "Okay, a good man needs a good strong sign, Ted. I just hope your sign ain't a skull an' crossbones."

The two men shared coffee while Marrow attacked his office computer terminal with stubby forefingers. By running his legs off, Quantrill could do a decent half day's work by quitting time, and knew Marrow would pay him for the half day.

An hour later, Quantrill returned to the offices with an ancient clipboard filled with notations on feed ingestion rates for their hybrid antelope. It would have been quicker to feed the information to the computer from a remote pocket terminal, but Marrow trusted pencil and polypaper more.

The vet nodded, completed his talk on the vidphone, then punched out and faced his helper. "You happen to know where—no, 'course you wouldn't. One of these days I'll put tracer bugs on every animal on the Safari preserve, swear to God I will. Well, Teddy, there's an Englishman in SanTone who's heard we've got those feral Russian boar runnin' loose down near the southeast corner. He's bringin' his own horses out tomorrow—must be filthy rich—to see if pigstickin' is the same here as it is in India."

"Pig*sticking*? You mean with darts, or what?"

"Lances." Marrow traded doubtful glances with Quantrill and admitted that the sport was more than half insane. Using short bamboo lances, English officers had developed the sport over a century before, riding down the wily boar from horseback. Lieutenant Alec Wardrop was one of the few who'd kept the sport alive during postwar occupation of India, and Russian boar were just as hard to bag in Wild Country as in Asia.

"Wardrop's experienced, and willin' to sign waivers. And he has political clout. In the old days, the Schreiners woulda told him to go piss up a lariat. It isn't a quick kill. But LockLever wants some of those big Muckna boars thinned out. I gotta go find where the singleton boars forage; goose 'em out a few miles, if I have to, for tomorrow."

"Want me to fly the chopper while you search?"

"Nope. I'll fly it; you get the Nelson rifle and some orange markers, and I'll tell you what to shoot at."

Quantrill removed his Chiller and, from a lockable cabinet, took the coldgas rifle with a handful of paint pellets. The Nelson rifle fired a harmless plastic ball that splashed bright paint against the target. Big game was often marked this way to identify a "takeable" trophy particularly when the hunter was a newcomer who might otherwise draw a bead on a female, or even the wrong species. Marrow still cursed the time a hunter, hoping for an elk trophy, shot a Brahma heifer despite the letters "C O W" whitewashed on her flanks.

Quantrill stowed his gear in the four-place chopper, watching Jess Marrow's preflight check. "Seems to me," he said, speaking into his helmet comm set as Marrow brought the turbine up to speed, "if this guy Wardrop is so experienced, he won't need us to pick the trophies from the sows."

"*He* won't, but he's bringin' a friend along. I told you he has clout; well, he's bringin' Judge Anthony Placidas along."

"Old Tony Plass? I heard he's got more trophies than Teddy Roosevelt."

Now they were lifting, Marrow going high before swinging away to the southeast. "He's older'n I am, Ted. It ain't enough to be mean and crooked and a good shot when you're after a big hog with only a lance. Nobody over the age of thirty-five has any business at pigstickin'." Waivers or no waivers, he added, Placidas would have been refused if not for his importance and for the endorsement of Wild Country Safari's best guide, Cleve Hutcherson.

"I hope Hutch knows what he's doing," Quantrill murmured.

Marrow: "He's no genius, but he knows pig an' he's dead steady with a Colt. Before you came here, Hutch saved a whole group of easterners from that monster, Ba'al. You wouldn't know about it.''

Quantrill knew, all right. He often shared confidences with Marrow, but Ba'al's home ground and relationships were items he kept to himself.

From a thousand meters up, the rocky, broken terrain seemed almost flat, with great clumps of prickly pear sharing the range with the water-cheated trees and brush. Twice they spotted wild pigs, flushing them with sudden swoops, finding a pair of young boars and a sow with her brood of striped ''squeakers.'' Piglets like these had flourished in South Texas for half a century and were already replacing the small native peccary as they grew to trophy size.

Ranging farther south, Marrow saw the seasonal sinkhole with its cattails and lush weeds. ''Hog sign,'' he said, hovering near, pointing to the swath where some big animal had rooted up a room-sized area to get at the succulent cattail bulbs.

Quantrill saw the boar first. It was actually crawling through the cattails, its great shoulders heaving with the effort as the rushes lashed in the chopper's downdraft.

''Paint him,'' Marrow said. ''He'll go two hundred kilos.'' Marrow had noted the big curling tusks of an adult boar. The animal would have barely come up to Ba'al's shoulder, but by any other standard it was a fine trophy.

Quantrill studied the animal, saw its intelligence in seeking better cover. ''Back off and take a run from head-on, Jess,'' he said. ''If he hunkers down in that mud, we'll never get him marked.''

Marrow did it. The boar disappeared for a moment, then broke from cover, spurting toward distant brush. Marrow surged the chopper ahead and lower, Quantrill leaning the coldgas rifle from an open window and charging the Nelson's plenum. Then, with incredible swiftness, the harried boar spun on the hard ground, charged his pursuers, leaped as high as a man might reach. Both men felt the solid *thunk* as the boar struck their aluminum landing skid. The boar fell heavily, rolled, was up and running back to the cattails before Marrow could react.

Quantrill had used the Nelson before and knew its range with the big pellets. He fired once as soon as Marrow had the chopper turned, splattering orange paint ahead of the fleeing boar. It jinked abruptly and Quantrill fired twice more. The second round caught the boar halfway down its spine and must have stung because the saffron-splashed animal spun again, facing them, flanks heaving as Jess Marrow brought the chopper low again, backing away. The furious boar followed them for as long as Marrow estimated it would take for the paint to dry. Then they sought more altitude in search of other trophies.

"You realize that little devil leaped three meters high?" Quantrill was wondering how high Ba'al could soar.

"Yup. They'll attack *any*thing, even Bengal tiger. You ask me, Ted, I think Tony Plass is out of his Latin mind."

Quantrill laughed then. Into Marrow's inquiring glance he quoted, " 'A good man needs a good strong sign.' "

"I reckon. Now keep an eye peeled, Teddy, we need to mark more trophies 'fore we knock off. Not much other game out here, it's a helluva long way from the central lodge, but it oughta serve Wardrop just fine."

They found only three more takeables in the next half hour, but Marrow was satisfied, radioing the position of the game for Cleve Hutcherson's benefit. Marrow and Hutch were old friends, and the vet basked in a sense of a job well done. Hutch had endorsed the idea of the hunt, in part, because despite all his experience with exotic game he had never seen Russian boar hunted with a short lance. It would be Hutch's job to protect the hunters, and it was the guide's boast that his forty-five-caliber six-gun hadn't failed him yet. Perhaps Hutch, too, needed a good strong sign.

CHAPTER ELEVEN • • •

Sandy's journal, Mon. 18 Sept. '06

Gloves in ribbons. Wish I could afford to autoharvest this corn! Should be finished by Friday.

Called Ted tonight after Childe asleep. My turn to apologize, his to be tender; but Lordy, that man can be vexatious! I hinted at availability & he gallantly suggested a tryst. Wonder if he knew I've been having kinky thoughts all day? Are corn tassles an aphrodisiac? He thought my ideas outrageous, but agreed. There must be a million ways to get a husband—have I grown cynical in thinking this may be the best way to keep one? Stay tuned, journal. . . .

CHAPTER TWELVE • • •

Quantrill spent much of the next day around the breeding pens, too busy to think about the Wardrop party, which had left early. The trained Wardrop ponies had been transported by hovervan to the far southeast reaches of Wild Country Safari. It was really none of Quantrill's affair.

It became his affair in midafternoon. He heard the emergency hooter, came running toward Marrow's office, saw Jess in a limping trot toward the chopper and beckoning him to follow. Not until Marrow dropped the little recorder in his lap did Quantrill ask what the hooting was all about.

Jess Marrow sped the turbine's warmup and jerked them away at low altitude, spooking their penned stock. Quantrill knew then that it must be serious. "Hutch maydayed for a rescue chopper; it's on the way from ranch headquarters. Called me and told me to bring you with a recorder."

Hutch knew Quantrill doubled as a deputy, but: "Do I have to guess why?" The younger man fumed.

"Old Placidas got hisself thrown out there. Boar came up under his pony, Hutch says. Couldn't shoot at first, since the boar charged Tony Plass and was all over him trailin' horseguts. Hutch nailed the boar, but SanTone may be short one judge."

"What am I supposed to do, take Hutch's statement?"

"Placidas's. Hutch claims the old bastard's opened from crotch to navel, but wants to talk. Guilty conscience, I gather."

"Good God," Quantrill muttered, staring at the recorder.

Homing in on Hutch's transceiver, Marrow made the trip in fifteen minutes. The rescue chopper was not yet on the horizon when Quantrill bailed out two paces above the dirt, leaving Marrow to set the chopper down.

Erect as a blond Masai, a tall sunburnt specimen with a clipped mustache leaned on an eight-foot lance, its weighted butt on the ground. The long, barbless point of the lance was bloodstained. The man gnawed his mustache and said nothing as Quantrill raced up.

At the blond man's feet squatted Cleve Hutcherson, talking to the old fellow who lay stretched out with a folded windbreaker under his head. Hutch swatted at a deerfly brought by the smell of blood. "You wanted someone with a recorder," Quantrill said.

The old man's eyes fluttered open, seemed to focus with difficulty. "A lawman," he corrected. There was surprisingly little blood puddling the caliche dirt, considering his gaping abdominal wound. Quantrill had seen that transparent gray pallor on swarthy victims before; he judged that he was looking at a man who would not live much longer without a transfusion. The bloodless lips formed words through waves of evident pain, and Quantrill knelt on both knees to hear. The old man was stern: "ID, please." Even in this extreme, Judge Anthony Placidas was a man who could show caution.

Quantrill fumbled out his wallet. Three five-dollar pieces and a couple of smaller coins, the entire contents of his wallet, fell out as he showed his Department of Justice shield. Placidas blinked slowly; dropped the wallet on his breast. "Only seventeen dollars," he said, his voice almost a whisper. "You must be one of the honest ones." A spasm of agony. "I'll chance it. Recorder, please." Quantrill displayed the little machine, flicked it on.

"I, Anthony Somoza y Placidas de Soto, being—ah!—of sound mind and expiring body"—the faintest of smiles from this brave old curmudgeon—"understand and waive my rights to silence."

From time to time Placidas paused for long, shuddery breaths. The others scanned the skyline for that rescue chopper, but Placidas seemed resigned to dying. "Added to my income with—cash contributions from a loose cartel based—in Coahuila, to the best of my knowledge. Its activities include transport of illegal fuels, foodstuffs, and—ahh—drugs to outlets in—DalWorth, New Denver, and Kansas—Ringcity."

Placidas breathed more shallowly now, and quickly. Quantrill had heard nothing so far beyond what was already known. "Can you give me names?" He urged.

"Felix Sorel was—source of my funds," Placidas said,

panting. "I used influence—to reduce bail for his people.
Sorel knows the bail is to be forfeit. Man named Slaughter
is—his favorite bodyguard. Slaughter has special—weapons,
they say."

Quantrill: "There's got to be a regular thieves' highway for
that stuff. What's their route?"

Placidas had trouble swallowing, and for a moment Quantrill
thought he would hear no more. Then: "Never knew—details.
Sorel—cagey. But conduit always—maintained—through Garner Ranch."

"Mul Garner?" This from Jess Marrow in disbelief. Marrow knew most of the cattle barons in Wild Country.

Softly, so softly that Quantrill almost missed it: "The
young one." It was as if the mention of youth stirred Placidas
toward another train of thought. "My apologies to Marianne," he said, loud enough for the erect Englishman to hear.

"The fault was mine, sir," said Wardrop, stiffening.

"*Mierda*," the old man cursed to himself. "My daughter
would like to remember me as an honorable man. Do what
you can," he whispered, his eyes boring into Quantrill's.
"She is—naive about the likes of—Felix Sorel."

"I'll do what I can," Quantrill hedged. "You must know
names of more of the people in that bunch."

A pause, then the faintest of headshakes. "Tell Jim Street—
his channels are not secure," he said, shutting his eyes
against the pain.

Then the old man relaxed. He was still breathing, but even
that effort ceased before the rescue chopper appeared from the
north. Quantrill sighed, stood up; wondered if there was a
cool breeze in hell for men like Anthony Somoza y Placidas
de Soto.

CHAPTER THIRTEEN • • •

"First client I ever lost on a hunt," Hutch admitted, elbows propped on the table in the lodge at ranch headquarters. In unspoken agreement, the four men who had watched Placidas die waited for the daughter to arrive, drinking the time away. "Them ponies of yours, Lieutenant—the ol' man wasn't used to a hog-trained horse."

"First rule with a mount trained for Muckna pig." The tall Englishman shrugged. "Leave your horse alone. The judge should've let the mare have her head. And I should have mine examined," he added in furious self-accusation. "What shall I tell Marianne? Why, that I lent her father the means to suicide!"

"Aw, shit, once he heard what you was up to, you couldn'ta stopped him with hobbles and a Spanish bit," Hutch gloomed. "Crazy old coot, I never seen him happier on a hunt. I think he'd've ridden against Ba'al hisself after you got that first one. He kept askin' me what you was yellin', but I didn't have no idea."

"Oh. *'Woh-h-h jata!'* Just wogtalk, or was in my grandfather's day. It means 'There he goes,' more or less."

"Well, *woh jata* for Tony Plass, too," said Jess Marrow, now slightly drunk on his favorite vice, Old Sunny Brook. "Every boar in his prime thinks he *is* Ba'al."

Quantrill had done more listening than talking, but now he spoke quickly to divert the topic. "Lieutenant, I don't know what you heard out there, but it might be . . . um, kinder to Placidas's girl if we pretended he didn't have any last words."

"Girl! My lad, Marianne Placidas is only a girl the way Horatio was only an infantryman," Wardrop said, draining his glass in salute. "Waaagh, this whiskey—well, sorry. My arse is tough, but my palate is rather tender. As I was saying,

61

Marianne can be very, very hard cheese. And I did lend a mount for the old gentleman's madness. The fault was mine," he said.

"Hope you won't mind sayin' that to my foreman," Hutch put in.

"My pleasure," Wardrop said, and reached for the bottle with something like mortal resignation.

Hutch heard the high-pitched snarl first, turning his head toward the window. Quantrill was first out of his chair. "Christ," he said, "it sounds like one of the little Spits."

But it was not one of the half-scale Spitfire aircraft from LockLever's Battle of Britain complex. It was a gasoline-powered Ocelot roadster, shrilling its turbocharged challenge to anything else on wheels. Useless as an off-road vehicle, on macadam the Ocelot's racing tires could hurl it faster than many light aircraft.

"That will be Marianne," said Wardrop. He stood up, straightened his shoulders and his hunting jacket, then strode outside to meet his fate.

The others watched from inside. Marianne Placidas was a surprise to them all, older than they had expected and beautiful without much femininity. Her helmeted dark curls and scarlet neckerchief, her graceful motions, all reminded Quantrill cruelly of the long-dead Marbrye Sanger. She exited the little roadster, whirled back to retrieve a stained overnight bag, recognized Wardrop, spoke quickly with him. Then something in his response snapped her erect posture, and she sought Wardrop's shoulder for a time. More talk; Wardrop gestured toward the ranch clinic and followed her sprint into the place. She did not relinquish her heavy bag.

"Handsome pair," said Quantrill.

"Oh shut up, Ted," snapped Marrow, who had been thinking exactly the same thing.

Quantrill strolled out to look over the Ocelot, a limited-production toy favored by the shuttle set. He noted the metallic plum paint job, the suede seats, the spatters of mud around the enclosed wheelwells, the sand in the driver's footwell. Marianne Placidas had finally been contacted somewhere north of Wild Country Safari; and the nearest source of mud or wet sand in that direction was the Llano River, which meandered past Junction. He pondered the unlikely notion of such a shuttle-setter as Marianne Placidas tooling her Ocelot along a riverbed, then turned away from the car and the question. The motives of the spoiled rich were not his province—or so he thought.

Quantrill, Marrow, and Hutch returned to the lodge and watched without shame from a window as a succession of LockLever people converged on the clinic. Hunt-party waivers gave the company protection against lawsuits, but Wild Country Safari did not need the anger of a Placidas heiress.

Two glasses of Old Sunny Brook later, the woman emerged from the clinic with Wardrop in tow, the ranch manager at her left. To the manager she was abrupt. To Wardrop she streamed vitriol, slapping his arm aside as he attempted to carry her heavy bag. Again Quantrill was struck by the small anomaly; the scuffed, mud-stained bag was not the sort of accessory such a woman would carry. Why hadn't she left it in the roadster?

The answer—that the contents of that bag, retrieved from a Llano sandbank, could have bought several new Ocelot roadsters—never crossed Quantrill's mind.

Marianne's mascara was smudged, but now, dry-eyed, she stalked to her car and faced Wardrop. Her harangue was designed for the hearing-impaired. "No, dammit, for the last time! If I had never set eyes on you, my father would be alive now!" She swung into the driver's seat, stowed the bag carefully in the passenger footwell.

Wardrop knelt his long frame to make some plea.

"I don't *know* what you can do! Undertake some inane romantic quest in my name?"

Wardrop still knelt, but as he spoke he seemed to be at attention.

An expression of fierce joy spread across the elegant cheekbones of Marianne Placidas. "All right, you pigsticking moron, bring me the head of Ba'al, and then I'll forgive you! I don't know if my father would; he died without last rites." Now she was nodding, pleased with her idea. She unwound the scarlet kerchief, flung it at Wardrop's feet. "Here, Ivanhoe, I'll give you a real Wild Country quest—and a token of my affection! Bring me the head of Ba'al," she snarled, and the Ocelot's engine snarled with her.

The three voyeurs watched her storm off with Wardrop

half-hidden in her dust. "She wants the man dead," Marrow observed.

"That's one hunt I ain't goin' *any*where near," Hutch replied.

"There won't be any hunt," said Quantrill, thinking fast, "if nobody helps Wardrop. Ba'al hasn't been seen around here for years. Probably dead."

"No, he ain't," said Hutch. "One of Garner's fence-riders seen his sign this spring."

"You tell the Englishman that, if you want to see him buried in a cigar box," Quantrill said evenly. "Besides, Wardrop may be a romantic, but I don't think he's stupid."

"He ain't," Hutch agreed, "but he's got bigger balls than a pawnshop where pig is concerned. The way he'll wait for a boar's charge with not even a sidearm to back up that lance just scares the pure-dee ol' shit outa this child. No, I don't reckon I'll help him."

But by now, Lieutenant Alec Wardrop was certain that the name "Ba'al" referred not to some mythical Hebrew demongod but to something tangible. Something worthy of the Wardrop steel.

By nightfall, the body of Anthony Placidas was on its way to SanTone. And by then some fool had shown Alec Wardrop a glossy print of an old infrared photo. It revealed a boar beyond Wardrop's wildest dreams, and all the warnings in the world could not make Wardrop forget the scarlet pennant that symbolized his quest.

CHAPTER FOURTEEN • • •

The fires of Marianne's fury did not flicker low until after she had found gasoline near Norman, Oklahoma. As long as she stayed on interstate highways, the search for this unusual fuel was fairly easy. It was different on secondary roads, where diesel and electric services were the rule and gasoline a rarity. Marianne knew, in any case, that in a pinch she could fuel the Ocelot at most airports. Gasoline was still a popular fuel for older aircraft and, of course, for special effects used in the entertainment industry.

She rolled into a swank new Holiday Inn near Tulsa; estimated that she could get a night's rest, with the bag as her bedpartner. She could then arrive in Kansas Ringcity by noon, thanks to the ID transceiver in her roadster. Most of the shuttle set avoided fast cars, when police were so pleased to hand out speeding tickets. Police did not hassle other police, however, regardless of the vehicle type. The last special gift old Tony Plass had given his daughter had been the police ID unit for her car. Settling between clean sheets, she wondered what the old man would have said had he known the Ocelot had become a drug-running roadster.

Marianne called the SanTone mortuary before breakfast the next day and said she simply could not face the memorial services. Would they cremate the body and turn away reporters' questions about the service? They would. They understood her bereavement; she could count on their discretion in her hour of need.

Halfway through her outrageously expensive steak and eggs, she had shelved her grief and was planning to buy clothes for the big noon event. Something severe and dark; something suitable and sinister to impress a drug buyer.

CHAPTER FIFTEEN · · ·

Sandy's journal, Wed. 20 Sept. '06

Ted's call has disinterred an old nightmare and grafted it to a bad joke! Somehow I always thought it would be a bunch of local vigilantes—but a Brit officer, alone?

Well, mad dogs and Englishmen! This one has two million acres to cover, aside from WCS land. Ted claims this man Wardrop has foresworn bullets, which means Ba'al will not be enraged by the smell of gun oil. The poor man will grow old searching, if Childe can explain the problem to Ba'al in proper detail. Yes, but will he listen? If a lieutenant will not, why should a pig?

CHAPTER SIXTEEN • • •

Any striking latina woman who shows up alone in the North Kaycee slums with an off-purple Ocelot and a half-million dollars' worth of poppy concentrate is a woman well worth watching, if you can catch her. The syndicate's contact man passed up the noon meeting on Tuesday, warned that the woman's plum-colored racer contained a police ID unit. Later he lost her on Vivion Road, unwilling to match her speed on public highways. But the syndicate boasted a good comm grid, and they located the Ocelot at the new Ringcity Motel before dark. After that, every move and telephone conversation by Marianne Placidas was monitored until she left Kansas Ringcity.

Wednesday she tried again. By then they understood, and envied, her use of that ID unit; their channels were *that* good. This time she placed the overnight bag in full view in the little Italian restaurant. She felt a tidal flush of relief as a little man left the Chianti he was nursing and walked with tiny precise steps to her table. His face was the color of pasta; his suit was expensive, playing down the paunch under his belt; his manner was very courteous. He whisked the bag under the table while sitting down, and something in his face told her not to complain.

He knew the pass phrase and advised her that the lasagna was good. She ordered it even though she was far too nervous to eat much of it. Marianne needed several minutes of cautious small talk to realize that he was nervous, too.

He had good reasons for a case of nerves. She was an amateur, though a courageous one; she could still be a plant from the Department of Justice. He had taken a very special commission from another group to pass an offer to Sorel's "man," who'd turned out to be a woman, and a real hotsy at that. Okay, this was soldiering time. This was what his sources paid him for.

He was wholly unaware of his own fidgets but, watching him, Marianne found her own anxiety dying. Eventually she found herself wolfing lasagna. While he talked he unzipped his beltpouch. He scratched his blue chin. He tapped his forefingers together; cleaned under his nails with his opposite thumb; patted his knees, interlaced the fingers of both hands, scratched his little potbelly, rezipped his beltpouch. Then he did it all again in different order. Marianne was positively at ease by the time he took her bag to the men's room.

When he returned he was smiling, and his was the kind of smile to unsettle a tummyful of lasagna: the smile of a well-fed rat. He suggested that she repeat what he had told her and paid close attention while she did it. He corrected her several times, too scornfully to suit a Placidas. Then he gave her a thin envelope, told her fair exchange was no robbery, and left with the bag.

While scanning the single sheet of polypaper, Marianne realized that there must be some trust among really big thieves, for the man had paid for that heroin with only a code for a numbered account in a São Paulo bank. She knew the advantages of Brazilian banks well enough. Idly, she wondered what Felix Sorel would do if she used that code for her own purposes—and then she shuddered and sought the waiter's eye.

An amateur, yes; but Marianne was not stupid. She did not write down the little man's instructions until she was locked in the ladies' room, and she tucked those instructions where only a lover, or a ravisher, would find them. Then she took a sightseeing tour of Kansas Ringcity and, again without realizing it, ditched the man tailing her.

On the other hand: while not stupid, Marianne *was* an amateur. She returned to her motel room for a nap before placing her call, and of course the Ocelot bore a tracer bug behind its Texas license plate by the time she awoke that evening. A professional would have made that call from a row of booths at a busy bus station. Marianne had the brains to avoid her car phone. She found a quiet booth off North Broadway and paid no attention to the kid—actually he was twenty-seven years old—who skated his old surfer into the alley a half block away and then did odd things with the cardboard box he carried.

Felix Sorel was nothing if not a pro. He could have had her call relayed through La Mariposa, but then two of his own people would have heard him talking in clear uncoded speech with an amateur. Risky business, that. He could have told the woman to call him at Nuevo Laredo, but too many American undercover spooks maintained watch in that known border conduit. Instead, he had given her a number in Monclova; the number of a well-protected place where one could disport with male prostitutes without any hassle from the Mexican police.

Sorel enjoyed his sport on Tuesday evening, having nothing better to do. On Wednesday he was listening to a youth with a twelve-string guitar and a lovely clear castrato voice when the phone buzzed. A young woman calling herself Quiet Mary needed to speak to someone named Caballo, the horse. Sorel took the call.

Thanks to the "kid" in the alley near Marianne's phone booth, an excellent typed transcript was made from the monitor on the cardboard box. The syndicate made no immediate move against Sorel or his latina. But a pasty-faced little man with nervous mannerisms soon got concrete galoshes and a resting place on the bottom of the Missouri River for guiding Sorel to what could be considered as a rival syndicate. They already knew Marianne from her license plates. Voiceprints told them she was talking with Sorel himself.

The transcript read as follows:

: *A su servicio.* . . .

P: *Buenas tardes, señor. Soy Quiet Mary, y quiero hablar con el caballo.*

:*Uno momento, por favor.*

S: This is the horse, Quiet Mary. You have been quiet a day too long.

P: I did as you said, but nobody showed up yesterday. It went okay today, only . . . well, do you want me to give you a set of letters and numbers I got in return?

S: No. There is no hurry. Memorize it and destroy the paper. But you said "only." Only what?

P: Uh . . . this funny nervous little man told me you might be interested in a, um, farming venture in Oregon territory.

S: I cannot imagine what he has in mind.

P: Well . . . I gave him a bag of corn chips; got it?

S: Continue.

P: He told me that a group of scientists have developed a strain of corn that could be grown in poor land. And that it does not look like corn at all. Still following me?

S: Yes. I wonder who else may be following you.

P: I've taken care of that.

S: Are these . . . scientists the same people who took your corn chips?

P: I don't think so. I'm sure of it, unless my man was lying.

S: What do the scientists want from me?

P: They think Oregon is a fine place for crops, Horse. They think you may want to expand as a grower. A very big grower. (LONG PAUSE.) Are you there, Horse?

S: This is completely . . . I do not want to hear more details over the phone, Mary. Did your man tell you how one might contact these geniuses of farm management?

P: Yes, he said I can—

S: Don't tell me! Set up a meeting for me, and inform me through your usual channel.

P: You mean Sa—

S: Yes! I mean that is satisfactory, Mary. You have not been trained for some parts of this work, but you must learn quickly. Can you follow instructions and use good judgment?

P: I found your damned corn chips and delivered them, didn't I?

S: (LAUGHTER). That you did. Now, before you do anything else, draw out enough cash to operate. You can do that on your own?

P: Yes. Did you know my father was—

S: I know your father, Mary. Please attend to business. Do you have a car there?

P: My roadster.

S: *Dios mío!* Why not carry a banner? Garage your car, go to some store with many exits, dress plainly, change everything about yourself that you can, as soon as you can. You must disappear. Change your appearance often. You may think you are alone, but the chance is very great that others are studying you. You must lose yourself. When you change clothes, change *every*thing and leave the ones you wore. I am sure you can imagine ways to move around without using credit cards. And you must. Are you getting all this?

P: Yes. Are you sure?

S: I am sure I do not want to lose you, Mary. When you are *certain* you are not followed, go to another town, smaller but large enough for bus, rail, and air terminals. Change appearance again and go to another large city, making sure you are not followed. Only then, Mary, *only then* are you to contact these scientists. Make an appointment, change appearances yet again, and tell me the arrangements by our usual channel. Can you do all that?

P: I think so. Can you hear my knees knocking?

S: Your knees do not knock; but they beckon, Mary.

P: Now I feel better. Uh . . . Horse?

S: *A sus ordenes*.

P: This is the big time, isn't it?

S: Very. You must be paranoid. If I thought it would not endanger you, I would suggest you carry a weapon.

P: You know about me and weapons, don't you?

S: I do, Mary. I also know this phone may not be as secure as you think. Now, do everything I told you, as fast as you possibly can, and pretend that you are pursued. Do not underestimate others; let them underestimate you. And do not hesitate to act in self-defense.

P: I'll do it.

S: Do it now. This instant, Mary. (TRANSMISSION ENDS.)

CHAPTER SEVENTEEN • • •

Marianne was fleeing up North Broadway before the syndicate had time to react. Within twenty minutes, she reached the sprawling shuttleport outside Kansas Ringcity; in another five minutes she parked her Ocelot in an expensive sealed compartment deep inside the fifth underground level of the shuttleport parking complex. A shuttle-setter herself, Marianne knew that such parking compartments were available for storing an automobile while you spent a month on New Israel/Aleph, if you could afford the tab.

A tracer bug will not transmit through five layers of ferroconcrete, so the syndicate only knew that she had gone to ground north of the Ringcity beltline. Marianne was smart and lucky. Smart to hurry aboard the first monorail to St. Joseph; lucky to find a suburban mall immediately in old Saint Joe.

By the time Marianne had outfitted herself in cotton work clothes, the syndicate had called off their womanhunt. They knew Marianne Placidas lived near SanTone, and they knew what their own man had told her because they had him under narcosis. Very soon after the interrogation began, they knew that they were not going to muscle out the rival outfit.

For one thing, the rival's address was on Sharon Square in the satellite colony of New Israel/Beth. Had it been New Israel/Aleph, they might have entertained a hope that some Earth-based drug baron was taking it easy in the low-gravity spa on that carefully groomed tourist haven. They could get an ID check and, when he shuttled back Earthside, deal with him in customary ways.

But Beth was New Israel's second satellite colony, the one devoted to research. *No* one could visit without a special visa, except for Israelis with expertise in weapons, physics, agronomy, or some other skill vital to the survival of a spacefaring people.

The syndicate knew its limitations. It enjoyed traditions as old and honored as the island of Corsica, and no doubt it could find—or force—some accommodation with any government on Earth, at some level. But New Israel? Every year those hardnosed sabras seemed to care less about the world they had left; a world they felt had exiled them to space colonies. Oh, they still had friendly arrangements; for example, with Turkey, the site of their original spaceport. And of course, Turkey was a prime region for producing poppy heads. Who would know that better than Corsican middlemen?

Now, perhaps, the middlemen were to be thrust outside. The syndicate resolved to peel every eye, prick every ear. It would *not* be wise to insert a tendril into New Israel's business, for that tendril could be reeled in like a string on a bobbin. No bunch without its own seat on the World Council could afford to be pulled in by New Israel's Ha Mossad agents. Anybody without a standing force of military spacecraft was plain *upazzo*, crazy, to take on those guys.

But why had the Mossad converted a good syndicate soldier merely to contact Felix Sorel? Maybe because Sorel's own operations were so cagey, so condensed, so carefully interwoven with the politics of Mexico and Cuba. New Israel did not want trouble; it coveted only success—on terms that few men on Earth could appreciate. When you feel that you have been expelled, literally, from your mother planet, you are not likely to harbor tender thoughts about the people still living there.

The syndicate learned from their wigged-out soldier that New Israel had offered him a reasonable bribe: a sex-rejuvenation operation. Syndicate bosses smiled at this for two reasons. One was admiration: not many mobs could offer bribes like that. The other was savage satisfaction: the soldier would not live to enjoy it. The Placidas woman might be harder to catch.

After drawing a great lump of cash in St. Joseph, Marianne slept the night on a slow local to Des Moines, fretful at every stop. The Corsican soldier slept without further cares on the bottom of the muddy Missouri, undisturbed by the fish that nibbled at his eyes.

CHAPTER EIGHTEEN • • •

On Thursday, Marianne fretted through the contact from her Des Moines uplink to a terminal on Sharon Square, New Israel/Beth. The man's accent was clearly American, and his holo image reminded her charmingly of a witty professor or a successful salesman. He and two others just happened to be slated for shuttledown to Kingsley, the southernmost shuttleport under Canada's control, near Klamath Falls in Oregon Territory.

Could the lady and her friend Felix meet them in the little tourist haven of Ashland? The lady thought it might be arranged; border authorities rarely bothered tourists crossing into soil that had been American only ten years before and seemed likely to revert to statehood again, once the resentment over wartime quarantines had faded.

The man on the holo was nearly bald, with a strong nose and expressive brows. He assured Marianne he would recognize her by sight in Ashland's famed Lithia Hotel. He would be accompanied by an agronomist, Aron Maazel, and an attorney, Zoltan Azeri. His own name, he said, was Roger St. Denis; a trained negotiator.

Negotiators are good at half lies. He was trained all right, but his name had not always been St. Denis. Until the overthrow of the Young administration he had been Boren Mills, chief exec of International Entertainment and Electronics. As Mills, he had fled his collapsing corporate empire four years earlier, on the eve of the rebellion. Now, as St. Denis, he was returning Earthside with New Israeli credentials.

Marianne accepted her Ashland rendezvous and overflew the ruins of Omaha en route to Lincoln, Nebraska. After a change of clothing and a bleach job that infuriated her by tinting her dark hair a floozy red, she caught a bus to the university campus, where she disappeared into the main library. Though changing purses twice, she kept the contents. In the hubbub of young Cornhuskers flailing among their first library assignments of the fall season, Marianne managed to encode a message into her voder.

She refused two invitations to fraternity brawls while waiting for a phone booth in the bowels of the library, and the booth she claimed had no video. No problem; she did not intend to transmit her image anyway.

Marianne punched a SanTone number, unwilling to commit her voiceprint to the system. The voice that responded was obviously that of another voder. San Antonio Rose would return pronto; did the caller want to leave a message?

She thought fast and put the call on hold while she punched a brief message into her own voder. Her little machine then said into the speaker, in its professional baritone: "Cielita Linda is out, and she is in. She wishes to send a message and will call every hour on the hour until San Antonio Rose is ready to record." Then she punched off and sought a less crowded place. She was damned if she'd transmit until she *knew* an honest-to-God human was on the other end.

Like an army, a university advances on its stomach. While thousands of youths filled their bellies, Marianne had her choice of phone booths, and at seven P.M. she reached her contact in SanTone Ringcity. She transmitted the long string of numbers by voder tone, waited through the longest twenty minutes of her life, and finally got a coded response before she abandoned the campus in search of a hostel.

That response, when decoded, was a big relief. The Horse agreed to her Oregon rendezvous. He would be strolling on the monorail platform in Ashland before noon on Saturday. He expected Cielita Linda to do the same.

Because the hoverbus to Ashland would not leave Lincoln until early morning, she relaxed in her spartan room, watching an enhanced holovision remake of *Duel in the Sun*. One good thing about holo enhancement: it let a director choose from the entire array of entertainers who had ever been committed to film or tape. The cast of *Duel* now included Leslie Howard, young Henry Fonda, Evelyn Keyes, Gloria Swanson, and William S. Hart—plus the ungimmicked Jennifer Jones, whose willful, half-mad, half-caste Pearl Chavez could not have been improved by any video gimmick. Marianne also enjoyed Fonda as lewd Lewt McCanless; she'd always had a weakness for men of action who were also men of ideas. Why the hell else, she asked herself, would she look forward to third-class travel halfway across Reconstruction America?

CHAPTER NINETEEN • • •

Feeling slightly raffish in his new finery, the young man found the Al Fresco Cafe in the western outskirts of SanTone Ringcity in time for a late lunch on Saturday. Al Fresco, with its outdoor canopied tables and a view of the new high rises, managed to combine TexMex and Creole trappings without being pricey or pretentious. He admired the available women as he ate a single crepe; noted that one or two of them made the admiration mutual; ordered a Dos Equis and waited for something better.

Something very much better arrived within the hour. He needed a double take, but with his second glance came an instant erection. Her fine straight hair was gathered loosely over her bare right shoulder in a cascade of reddish gold with auburn highlights, her flowered Mexican peasant blouse tucked into a wide belt decorated with flashy conchos. She carried a big cheap shoulder bag. Her skirt, a pleated black lace affair, showed off exquisitely modeled calves, her ankles accentuated by colorful needle heels. He had never seen anything in his life that looked more like instant nookie—and at a modest price.

She sat near the entrance, gripping her bag as though fearing it would wander off. He shouldered his first impulse aside—it would have been a blunt frontal approach—and waited, sampling her with his gaze. He wasn't the only one.

The waiter seemed to regard her as special new talent and leaned over her chair in a frank assay of her cleavage, his grin insolent and knowing. When she had to wave the waiter on his way, the watcher broke into a smile, which she discovered by some kind of personal radar. She looked away quickly, a blush mounting from her bare shoulders, and he found his erection throbbing at this lapse from her commercial appearance.

Presently, while studying a new arrival, he saw that the honey-blonde was staring at him with new interest. When the waiter appeared with her drink, a bulky gentleman wearing expensive rings, who had never let his eyes stray from her since she arrived, tried to pay. She seemed to consider the offer but refused it with a winning smile. The young man across the patio relaxed; this time, his impulse had been to weave himself a potholder using a few of the man's ring fingers.

Now the blonde's appraisal of the young man involved something between a glare and a leer. He let her look, gripping his beer to show the cords in his forearms, the open collar of his yellow shirt revealing sinew at his throat when he smiled. Then he came to an internal decision and stood up slowly, running a hand through his freshly barbered black thatch, shoving his chair back with a careful thrust of a sharkskin boot that matched the color of his hair. In those new western boots he stood tall and knew it.

Neither of them had any doubt about his intentions from the very first. "Waiting for anyone special?" He wondered if she suspected why he was holding his Stetson over the bulge at his crotch.

She must have known, for she studied the hat before meeting his gaze. "I could be. Are you anyone special?"

"I'm Sam Coulter from Monahans, ma'am, and that's special enough for most folks."

"I'll just bet it is," she said, and took his hat. Her smile was wide and innocent, but the hand that brushed his fly was deliciously guilty. "Sit, Sam Coulter from Monahans—if you can, in those tight britches."

He sat down as if poleaxed. "My Gawd, you're really something," he said, laughing.

She nodded, studying his face. "Those big brown eyes of yours affected my judgment," she murmured. "Buy me a drink?"

His turn to nod. He gestured to the waiter, pointed to her drink, made a two-finger V. "What do I call you?"

She drained her glass, licked her lips carefully before answering. "Margarita. Like it?"

"A blond Margarita; why not?" Suddenly, with an intensity he could not mask, he was leaning forward, gripping his elbows with opposite hands: "Let me tell you something for your own good, Margarita. You're lookin' at a man who's been hungry a lo-o-ong time. If you're not careful, I just might make a crepe out of you right here in front of all these people. Consider yourself warned."

She found his knee with hers. As the waiter set down their drinks, she spoke as if they were alone. "What flavor?"

"Hm?"

"I mean, will I be your main course, covered with cream cheese and spice, or more like a light dessert crepe?"

The waiter, wearing a freshly-goosed expression, wheeled away only after a pointed stare from both of them. Then the young man nodded at her, picked up his drink, sipped, nodded again. His aspect was friendly but determined. "You're gonna pay for that, Margarita. Wait and see."

She grinned, a bright, salacious challenge, and said, "It's you who's supposed to pay, cowboy. Didn't they teach you that in Monahans?"

Helplessly amused, he let the drink dilute his excitement. The drinks did not last them long. "We sure don't have anything like you in Monahans," he said finally. "No professionals, anyhow."

"Actually," she said, purring it, "I'm only a gifted amateur."

He leaned back and guffawed, then wiped his eyes and, after a glance around, said, "There's not a man in this cafe who couldn't make a list of those gifts from memory, twenty years from now."

"That was the idea," she said, and emptied her glass. "Now that you've won my heart with sweet talk, I wonder what else you can win. No, don't get up yet," she said, rising, probing in her bag. She swept around the table, bent down, cupped his head between her hands. The kiss she gave him was enough to raise the local humidity. The twenty dollars, clinking from her fingertips to the table, broke a silence maintained by a dozen envious idlers.

She crooked a finger to bring her young man up from his chair, linked arms with him, then glanced at their audience. "This one," she said to them all, "will be on me." She noted with joy that her companion was too flustered to hold his hat down where he really needed it.

She expressed surprise at his Lectrabout, an obvious rental but still expensive for a West Texas saddle-slapper. Was he, perhaps, a foreman? No, he said, not even a cowpoke; he was one of the lucky ones who'd taken a chance with a wildcatter outside Odessa and hit a pocket of natural gas. And by the way, it was almost siesta time. Before doing the town, would Margarita care to see his motel room and catch a few winks?

She agreed with a single wink, the only one that counted, and played the ticklish tease while he drove as she let his free hand wander. In ten minutes and after one near collision he navigated them to the underground parking at his motel.

Like many new motor lodges, this one offered maximum privacy by placing the whole complex into insulating earth, with one glass wall of each room facing a sunken private sundeck. This man who called himself Sam Coulter, she mused, may have carried a heavy need out of Wild Country, but he wasn't too antsy to put careful planning into a private conquest.

Once inside the room, she took her shoulder bag into the dressing alcove and prepared her tawdry magics. When she strode out, he was still standing by the sunlit deck, hat in hand. Her forthrightness had a devastating effect.

He turned and saw that her skirt and blouse were gone, the gold-auburn hair parted so that it flanked her throat, hiding her nipples while permitting a view of the undercup bra, itself an architectural marvel. Under the skirt she had worn—still wore—a black lace apron no larger than a doily, with a similar tiny tapestry over her ample behind. And she still wore the stylish needle heels, hardly more than stiletto-tipped sheaths, cemented lightly to the soles of her feet.

He watched her approach, scanning every centimeter of her, and his Adam's apple bobbed convulsively. Then: "I just discovered there's such a thing as too much," he said with an idiot grin, and put his Stetson on. She saw that he had intended a modest surprise of his own, protruding through his open fly. It was now a limp surprise.

A series of unspoken responses wafted across her face, and the one she kept was with narrowed eyelids, hands on her hips, one seminude foot tapping in pornographic satire of a vexed schoolmarm. "I told you and told you, don't touch it 'til I get there," she said.

"What? No, I—uh, dammit, I didn't! I *said* you'd be sorry," he said, palms out at pocket height.

"No you didn't, lover," she replied, near enough for him to feel the heat of her body. She took the hat from his head, her smile full of warmth and promise and without the faintest hint of smugness. "You said I'd pay for it." Her brows asked for endorsement; he nodded. "And as it happens, I will love paying for it," she said, tossing the hat into a corner. "Get over on that bed, mister; your first payment's going to be a massage."

By the time she got his boots off, he was already functional. When she pulled his synthosuede briefs down, he met her with a salute of sorts. "No you don't, Mister Coulter," she said, even though she was brushing it with her hair as she continued, "it's your shoulders that I massage first. Just stay there on your back, buckaroo."

Of course he had taken a room with mirrors on the closet, and she caught him watching as she kneaded the muscles across his shoulders; and the sight of herself astride him, his erection fully vertical and only a hand's span behind her buttocks as she rubbed the bronzed shoulders, made her gasp with desire.

Now their glances locked in the mirror and held as she moved back, still massaging, pretending to ignore the probe between her thighs, and even when he slid into her she did not abandon her attention to his upper torso.

His arms had been flung wide, but as she began to utter soft moans to pace him, he reached up and separated the bra, titillating her breasts with feather touches. She wanted to look directly at him but remained fascinated by the sight of herself, somehow not herself, ravishing a man in ways both familiar and strange; plunging on him, turning to favor one nipple or the other for his attention, controlling and dominating him through raw sex. And with his wholehearted assent.

When she felt the warm climactic flood spread through her body, she urged him to accompany her; felt him thrust more slowly but more deeply, too, and when they began to cry out, the name each of them called was not the name the other had given. And this was somehow an added ecstasy.

She collapsed on him eventually, and now it was he who gave the massage, progressing to her buttocks, clasping her, rolling her over. She lay with lips parted, her face partially masked by masses of honey hair with those strange auburn highlights he had never seen before, an addition to his joy.

He never withdrew but came to his knees, his blunt nails running gently down her legs until he gripped her feet, now holding her legs up, using those lascivious heels as handles. "A very, very gifted amateur," he teased as she reached down to tickle him.

"I watched a holoporn cassette," she said in bogus innocence. "Can you really come again?"

"I faked it," he said, burying himself in her. "You're not through paying yet, Margarita."

"You bastard," she said, more blessing than curse. Then she reached up and grasped her feet in glorious abandon. "Fake it again, Mister Coulter."

"Never trust an oilman," he began, and ended, "from Mon—a—hans," and this time there was no question of fakery.

They lay together for a long while, exchanging kisses, caressing one another as though afterplay were foreplay. Presently she disengaged, showered, and dressed while he showered. Then, before emerging into the sunset for dinner and dancing, they enjoyed a second engagement featuring broad variations on oral and manual themes.

Sometime before midnight, after touring half the ringcity, they sat through a short double feature "living presence" holoshow, the first feature a broad farce, the second rated X, and Y, and Z, and just as comic in its own way. Later, they found that they could not copy every position they had seen— but it was not for lack of trying.

On Sunday they went to church together. Neither of them found anything odd in that. In parting, they agreed to repeat their liaison "sometime soon," but they were cheerfully vague about details.

CHAPTER TWENTY • • •

Sandy's journal, Sun. 24 Sept. '06

I am going to sleep for a solid week. Poor Ted, those brown contact lenses had him teary-eyed until I convinced him that his hair-dye deception was enough! I could convince myself that all this was entirely a stratagem toward marriage. But no lies in these pages. Liked it so much it scares me—but only because the illusion of sex without love was an illusion, and one that we discarded during the night. Perhaps if he did not give up male domination so easily, I would like the illusion less. And will he still like it, after sober reflection?

We did not talk as we usually do—but why should we? Often, words between lovers are slaves of the poor, a few doing the work of many, doing it tiresomely, over and over. This may be a blessing, since it sometimes bids us hush. It is only then that we can hear the silence filled with the sibilance of unspoken yesses.

Mutual oral sex may be the most profound communion of all, if for no better reason than that our tongues are silently occupied!

God, I miss him already. . . .

CHAPTER TWENTY-ONE • • •

On Saturday, Felix Sorel arrived in Oregon Territory with papers claiming he was one Ernst Matthias. Within the hour, he and a second man were seated in a monorail lozenge as it slid up broad green valleys toward a tumble of mountains on the horizon. Sprawled like an apron across the lap of one of those mountains lay their destination, the southernmost township under Canadian protection: Ashland.

Sorel studied maps and promotional pamphlets, noting that many of the prewar roads shown on the maps were "no longer maintained," to quote the map legends. Now and then Sorel stared at some local landmark, identifying it on the map. Long ago, he had learned to use every means to brief himself on an unfamiliar region—especially one where his pelt had a price on it. By the time they reached Ashland, Sorel had a bare-bones working knowledge of the town and the arterials that fed it.

The second man, Harley Slaughter, carried forged ID as well. The lank, yellow-haired Slaughter talked little and, as he stepped from the lozenge into sunshine, watched the crowds a lot in his heavy-lidded way. From the first, Slaughter was uneasy among the tourist throngs who made Ashland seem a major city in miniature. If he felt any premonition, he kept quiet about it.

Harley Slaughter enjoyed perfect health but had hollow cheeks and gaunt limbs suggestive of a man recovering from serious illness. His expression said he was half-asleep, if you missed the way he scanned his surroundings for trouble. He had the trick of noticing everything without the faintest show of recognition, and he carried another trick up his sleeve—literally. Strapped to the underside of his right wrist was the barrel of a coldgas weapon, its pressure cartridge snugged into his armpit, its trigger mechanism a flesh-colored tongue of plastic hidden by a long shirt-sleeve. By flexing his wrist sharply outward, Slaughter could fire the weapon through his sleeve without the wasted time and effort of a fast draw. Though its range was limited, the weapon was quiet and flashless.

A product of North African genius, the coldgas mechanism was semiautomatic, firing porous metal balls of medium caliber. Each ball was coated with a plastic film that peeled away when penetrating a target, and then the ball tended to disintegrate. The pores of the ball contained formic acid, the same stuff that fire ants used to such effect, except that a hundred ants did not carry as much formic acid as a single ball from Slaughter's weapon. Harley Slaughter did not depend on muzzle velocity or impact effects; anyone who took the slightest flesh wound from him became hors de combat from sheer agony, tearing at his own flesh, sometimes dying from toxic shock. Slaughter's was not a very nice weapon, but Harley Slaughter was not known for nicing.

Marianne Placidas found the men at the monorail platform and did not remark on their roundabout route (Chihuahua to Portland by laserboost, before the long glide through Eugene to Ashland by electric monorail). She was too nervous for small talk and guided them to her rented diesel-electric Chevy without preamble.

"I assume," said Sorel once they were inside the Chevy, "that you are not as unarmed as you seem to be."

In answer, she reached under her skirt to produce a tiny six-millimeter automatic. It was flat enough to fit a thigh holster but, "Strictly for point-blank use," Sorel criticized.

"I didn't need it at all," she said.

"The need may yet arise," he said. "Do not imagine that these Israelis came here for a harmless weekend of costume drama at the local Shakespeare festival. Are you ready to use your weapon if need be?"

"You know I'm damned good with a pistol."

"Against two-legged targets?"

Licking her lips: "If I have to."

From the backseat, Slaughter drawled, "They'll all be packin' some kind of heat behind the smiles. Count on it."

"Ah: Marianne Placidas, meet Leo Cherry. You must introduce me as Ernst Matthias. You may as well start using the name now," he insisted.

"Shouldn't I have an alias, too?"

"No. They will check and discover that you are operating without cover, and so they will consider you harmless. It is your best protection," he lied. "Now, put this thing in motion and take us to the hotel."

She glanced at the man behind her, then at Sorel. "No more preparation than this, Fel—Ernst? We're just going in cold?"

"You and I will seem to. Smile often, and listen as if you were bored. Leo here"—he jerked his head to indicate the man behind them—"will join us when he has seen to exits and—monitors." He had almost said "ambushes," but the woman was already agitated enough. Her silent beauty might be useful in several ways: as distraction, as apparent proof of his own harmlessness, and if necessary as a shield. Women never seemed to expect a man of Sorel's reputation to use them this way. Yet Felix Sorel owed his reputation to planning for the unexpected.

Slaughter left them two blocks from the hotel. Marianne found a parking lot and made a good entrance on Sorel's arm. Her spirits were buoyed by the trappings of the Lithia, an excellent hotel in the old style with a subdued opulence. Glass walls on two sides of the lobby added an informal western touch, bringing passersby on the street very close to the interior. The Lithia's ambience seemed to deny the remotest chance of danger.

Marianne and the balding Mills recognized each other instantly in the crowded lobby, he rising to greet her from one of the booths that lined the great glass-enclosed room. She introduced Mills as "St. Denis" and Sorel as "Matthias." Mills turned and included a confederate. "Mr. Matthias, you may have heard of my colleague, Professor Aron Maazel-the-agronomist."

Sorel nearly laughed to hear this homely phrase. "Your accent seems very American," he said to Mills, then extended his hand to the seated man.

The ex-American's handshake had been firm, his summer suit almost offensively stylish. Maazel, the rumpled fat man in the booth, seemed to lack vitality, and his smile was as welcoming as a slit cut in thin cardboard. Maazel's round, hairless head perched on a body that had been too long inactive in reduced gravity; when he stood up to acknowledge Marianne, flesh quivered at his chins. Sorel guessed that this was not the sort of agronomist who got dirt under his fingernails. Perhaps he was the sort who studied computer graphics in the search for hardier stock, faster sprouting, more deceptive poppies. No telling what his attaché case contained, but Maazel never let go of it and replaced it against his ample belly as they ordered a round of champagne cocktails.

"I understood there would be three of you," Sorel murmured as the waitress swept away with their order.

"One of us was . . . delayed. We expect him any moment," said Mills.

"With *your* third member," Maazel added in a wheezy tenor, drumming his fingers against the black case in his vestigial lap. "How was your trip to Ashland?"

"Very nice," said Sorel and the woman simultaneously, prompting grins all around. From Sorel's grin, no one would guess that he was damning the woman. Obviously, someone had spotted her earlier; had seen and reported the threesome before Slaughter separated. Now Maazel had told him, in so many words, that the Israeli surveillance and comm network were superior. It was supposed to make him feel outclassed. It did, and that was Maazel's mistake.

But the agronomist, if that was what he really was, looked at Sorel expectantly. "I rarely travel for pleasure," Sorel said. "It is only a means to conduct business," he added with a shrug.

"Then you honor me," said Maazel, fiddling again with his case, and Sorel felt a wave of satisfaction flow like damp heat from the fat man.

Mills saw something dangerous in Sorel's expression. "Don't worry," he said, "I'm sure they'll both be along any minute. Excellent service," he added, beaming as their waitress unloaded her tray. "Prosit."

"Ah, they are coming," Maazel said, and reached for his cocktail as he continued. "Surely you realize, sir, that if your voiceprint did not match that of Felix Sorel, I would have little to say to you." Into Sorel's glare the fat man made a half salute with his glass and bestowed a genuine smile. "I have long been a follower of your athletic feats. Would you prefer that I kept my knowledge to myself?''

Marianne had frozen in midsentence while talking with Mills. Sorel glanced at her, then saw Mills shrug. The natty Mills reached for his cocktail and murmured, ''Dr. Maazel deals in science, and I'm afraid that scientists have a horror of hoaxes.''

During a slow count of perhaps four heartbeats, Sorel smiled and nodded as always when he contemplated violence and did not want that contemplation to show. During that time he concluded that Maazel's attaché case contained some kind of comm set with a readout visible or audible to him only; that he, Sorel, had underestimated the speed with which these clever bastards could analyze new information; and that Maazel was a fool for tipping his hand. A fan of Sorel's, perhaps. A cool negotiator backed by high-tech gadgetry and an unforgiving government, yes. But when dealing with a man like Sorel, a fool for all of that.

Encouraged by Maazel's foolishness, Sorel relaxed. ''Forgive my caution, gentlemen,'' Sorel said, and sipped his cocktail, letting his eyes smile at Marianne over the rim of his glass. He was not certain, but he'd had the momentary impression that her hand had been drifting down to the vicinity of her hidden pistol.

Sorel sipped and let his glance stray toward the entrance, feeling less vulnerable. Marianne Placidas might be an amateur, but she hadn't panicked; had evidently made herself ready to follow his course of action—or, in this case, inaction. Then he saw the yellow hair of Harley Slaughter, and when the tall Texan knew he had eye contact, he turned with great deliberation and stared toward a side exit before facing Sorel again. That exit, then, was the quickest way out. Sorel scratched his jaw to show that he understood and only half noticed the swarthy, hawk-nosed little fellow who eased past Slaughter, murmuring some excuse in close quarters.

But hawknose spied his friends and moved gracefully to the booth, nodding to Maazel.

''Miss Placidas; Señor Sorel,'' Maazel said, ''meet our third member, Zoltan Azeri.'' The swarthy man made a tiny clockwork bow to them and then stood to one side.

''You may as well ask our third member to join us,'' Sorel said as if enjoying a joke on himself. He smiled at Azeri.

"I believe you have been challenged, Zoltan." Mills chuckled.

Thickly accented, in scorn: "Challenged?"

"Not a well-chosen word, Saint Denis," Maazel said with his own wheezy laugh. "Zoltan, please ask the gentleman you followed to join us."

Azeri's head swiveled to gaze at Slaughter, then back. "The tall one in the denim jacket; you will vouch for his reaction?"

Sorel raised his free hand and beckoned, nodding as he did so. "Mr. Azeri is wise, Professor," he said as he saw Slaughter picking his way around the piano bar. He felt something of a fool himself. What if the little Israeli had confronted Slaughter without hesitation? Harley Slaughter was no trained seal with wholly predictable moves, but a trailwise gunsel who had jumped bail from a capital offense. He just might have wasted little Azeri on the spot. Or he might have said something so offensive that Azeri would— But those scenarios could be ignored now, for Slaughter approached wearing a rictus almost like a smile.

The booth had room for them all, but: "May I suggest something, señor?" Maazel tapped his attaché case. "I have things to show you, and now that we are all here I wonder if you would care to take a stroll."

Slaughter: "Just you two?"

Maazel: "But of course. With my bulk I shall not stray far," he said, patting his belly.

Sorel considered it. The fat man might not want to broadcast details any more than Sorel did, and he wasn't suggesting a hotel room where Sorel could be ambushed. And Felix Sorel did not fear a man like Maazel in public, so: "Excellent. Enjoy yourselves," Sorel said to them all, sliding from the booth.

Maazel needed the help of little Azeri to exit his cramped seat, but moments later the athlete strode out into autumn sunshine with Maazel and that attaché case.

They ambled downhill, speaking guardedly as they passed shoppers. Maazel trudged with the splay-footed gait of a man with poor balance, taking his time, explaining in general terms how agriculture was monitored from satellites.

Certain produce, said Maazel, was of such compelling interest to many governments that orbiting spy-eyes could identify many crops and trip automatic alarms. "A matter of broad-spectrum photography, local temperatures, rainfall—and of tradition," Maazel said with a fruity chuckle. "The French keep what they believe to be a close tally on one crop, for example. It is grown widely in Kampuchea, and in Turkey." He paused as a well-dressed couple passed, then continued softly, "Also, a bit of it is grown in Oregon Territory. Oh, yes, the American authorities learned long ago that this crop could be grown near a town called Grants Pass and even within the city limits of Seattle.

"But what if a much more common and perfectly harmless crop could be imitated by the, ah, Turkish flower?" Now they walked through the grassy verge of a park where strollers admired a showy little waterfall. Maazel indicated a stone bench near the water, nodded, and steered Sorel to the bench.

A constant splash of water was among the best barriers against a listening device and implied that the fat man did not take his security for granted. Sorel replied, "I suppose authorities would be alerted by the crew that slashes the poppy pods."

Maazel's broad face, now gleaming with sweat, registered delight as he lowered himself to the bench. "Correct! Exactly so," he said as if Sorel were a student in some innocent seminar. He fished a set of livesnaps from a vest pocket, studied the labels on their backs, and offered one to Sorel.

In a way, the livesnaps were a test. The little liquid crystal movie cards were still a high-tech curiosity, the images programmed into memory chips so that each flexible card could provide a moving holographic image in full color. Sorel passed his technology test by pressing the dot in the lower-right-hand corner, deforming a tiny crystal to provide piezo-electric energy for a brief moving sequence of images. The blank flexible card instantly became a moving, three-dimensional snapshot.

Sorel watched the livesnap without understanding. He saw a slender plant with long sparse leaves and an elongated pod, waving in a slight breeze. Clinging to the pod, he saw, was a tiny winged insect that moved from a spot on the pod to an unspotted area. After fifteen seconds, the card went blank. "This is a poppy?" he asked doubtfully.

"Yes, but study this enlargement," Maazel urged, offering a second card. "The *Papaver somniferum*, opium poppy, has been mutated to the appearance of an edible plant called salsify. It was a European plant originally but now grows wild in Oregon Territory. It became a food crop here during the last war when food was in short supply. We recognized that the pod-slashing crew would raise suspicion, because salsify is harvested like other shallow-root crops. That is why we applied genetic engineering to this fruit wasp," he said with pride.

The enlargement sent a shiver down Sorel's spine. The tiny wasp busily chewed a hole through the pod surface, inserted a body extension, then moved to another site perhaps a millimeter away and resumed chewing before the livesnap went blank. Sorel pressed the dot again, watched the sequence again. "It seems to be depositing eggs," he said.

"Sterile eggs," Maazel said with a wink. "But the pod soon begins to ooze raw opium through each hole. The female wasp continues to visit pods until she dies—long after she has exhausted her egg supply."

Now Sorel saw the connection. "Your wasp does the job of a field worker," he said.

Nodding, Maazel took the livesnaps and replaced them in his pocket. "And standard machinery separates the pods while it harvests the plant, in a single pass. A crew of three can harvest a square kilometer of *Papaver* in a weekend, with no one else the wiser. How does it look to you?"

It looked damned efficient. It looked like the end of the French connection, that long trail of illegal processing from Turkey through Marseilles to Mexico and then, thanks to Sorel, into Reconstruction America. It also looked like the end of Sorel's usefulness as a middleman. To give himself time for furious thought, Sorel asked, "Where does one obtain the seeds and the wasps?"

"The seeds are free." Maazel smiled. "The wasps, all guaranteed sterile females, will be shipped to the user as eggs—roughly a million in each batch, guaranteed to hatch and grow into adults with eighty-five percent viability. The wasp soon dies, and in any case it will not migrate from the field of choice. In a region with hidden valleys like this, it will be years before some entomologist discovers a specimen. More years before he learns its, ah, very special use.''

Sorel made appropriate grunts, unable to figure why the Israelis had approached him, of all people. When all else failed, he was willing to ask directions. He said, ''And what would you say is *my* very special use in all this?''

''We know your outlook on Americans, and your means of taking revenge on them,'' said the fat man without implying any value judgment.

''But why would you care about that?''

''We do not. We care very much that our ally, Turkey, is becoming difficult as she becomes less dependent on us—and more dependent on her major illegal crop.''

''That seems a very risky thing to tell me.''

''Not so risky,'' Maazel wheezed, his eyes slitting above puffy cheeks as he grinned. ''The Turks know it, and we know it, and so on. We simply choose this way to, um, manipulate the price of their product.''

Sorel sought the missing piece in the puzzle. ''But if the seeds are free, surely it is because the grower can harvest the seeds himself for the next crop.''

''Correct again.''

''Then you will not merely manipulate the price of the Turkish product; you will utterly destroy their market when its price is undercut by processing here.''

''Your first error,'' Maazel said, erecting a finger like a Vienna sausage. ''We are the *only* source of the wasps, Señor Sorel. It is not difficult to predict a precise yield from the number of wasp eggs we ship. We do not intend to destroy the Turkish market. We merely allow a measured amount of competition by someone dedicated to producing all he can for American addicts—someone like yourself.''

''You would also be controlling my end of the business,'' Sorel reminded him.

''Of course; but on a scale far greater than you have ever known before.'' He saw Sorel nod agreement and added, ''Is it not elegant?''

It was more than elegant; it was regal. While marveling at this scheme, Sorel realized with a shock that these Israelis had made a really incredible mistake. They assumed that Sorel cared more for revenge against Americans than he cared for the lifestyle he led. These orbiting Ellfive nabobs expected him to become a farmer in a region where a price hung over his head, instead of a—very well, he would admit it: a player leading a double life in the world's most exciting game.

Maazel's smile said that he expected Felix Sorel to leap at this chance, regardless of its effect on his lifegames. And no matter how long he pondered the Israeli offer, Sorel knew that he absolutely would not, *could* not, accept it.

Which left Sorel holding a satellite-sized tiger by the tail. If he refused the offer, he might not see Mexico again. Even if he did, he would be a prime target for every hit team New Israel controlled. That meant Sorel could never move in shuttle-set circles again; it was one thing to be on an American shitlist, and quite another to find yourself on a Mossad hit list. Americans made you a celebrity. Israelis made you dead.

If only some shrewd Turk had whacked Maazel and his cronies on their way to this damned meeting! The Israelis would have pulled back, analyzed the problem, delayed their plan—perhaps indefinitely. And Sorel would not have been placed with one foot in the frying pan and the other in the fire.

Suddenly, with the clarity of a digital readout, Felix Sorel saw what he must do to remove the heat. "I assume you can advise me on the land I must purchase in Oregon Territory," he said, and with his handshake Sorel offered a lovely golden smile.

CHAPTER TWENTY-TWO • • •

Marianne sat on the edge of the bed, now and then glancing from her companions to the panoroma outside the window of their suite. "This is truly a beautiful place," she mused. "Felix, do you suppose we could come back sometime?"

She might as well have been talking to herself. "It was that little sonofabitch Azeri," said Slaughter, standing with legs apart, arms out and parallel to the carpet, raging as Sorel ran a pocket debugger over every inch of his clothing. Sorel had already found one tracer bug, no larger than a grain of wheat, stuck to the elbow of Slaughter's jacket, "I can't figure when he did it," Slaughter went on.

"I know exactly when—Marianne, close the curtains, please," said Sorel.

"I wanted to look at the mountains. Weren't you listening?"

"Just do it, please." He waited until she had drawn the heavy drapes, then paused in his work, facing her, using the elaborate courtesy of one whose patience is beginning to fray. "A bare windowpane is like the head of a drum, Marianne. A tiny laser beam could be bounced off the corner of that window in such a way that someone far away could hear, from the vibrations of the window, every word we say. We are paying well for three adjoining rooms in a one-floor luxury inn, so that we are assured privacy here in the middle." He resumed passing the debugger over Slaughter's clothing and eventually found the second tiny audio device.

"Azeri needs offing," Slaughter growled.

"A wonder he didn't pick your pocket," Sorel said, taking his turn while Slaughter held the debugger. When Marianne had been pronounced clean in turn, the three of them sat on the big bed for Sorel's briefing. Slaughter put in a few curt questions and a suggestion here and there. Marianne grew

94

silent, lips pale, and responded only with nods and headshakes. When the men agreed on the signal Sorel would give, she knew that this was no optional plan, but a firm decision.

"I don't think my falling down will divert any of them," she said. "Maybe the old man; I don't know."

"We must chance it. Most men will turn aside to help a woman in distress," Sorel replied. "Draw and shoot the nearest one, and do not hesitate."

"Most likely we'll be on broken ground," Slaughter put in. "Problem is, they've probably checked the area already. They could have somebody staked out there, and I don't want none of that OK Corral shit if I can help it."

"Very unlikely," Sorel snapped. His hard look suggested that they would chance it anyway. "But if they are not all three with us from the start, the stakeout becomes a possibility; and in that case we cancel the plan. Questions?"

Slaughter was impassive. Marianne swallowed hard and shook her head, then moved toward the telephone handset near the bed. "I'd better make our travel arrangements," she said.

Slaughter moved faster than she thought possible; his grip on her wrist bit like pliers, but her glance was a plea to Sorel.

"We have your car," he said, and nodded to Slaughter, who made no apology as he released her arm. "After such work as this, you never rely on public transportation, Marianne." She bit her lip and rubbed her wrist gently, more angry than anything else. One day, she thought, this hardcase brush-popper, Slaughter, would pay for treating her so brutally.

It was midafternoon when Maazel called, a half hour later before their two-car convoy eased out of the parking area, Mills leading in a rented Ford. Maazel, using the Ford's dashboard mapfiche, directed him while Azeri sat in the backseat.

Marianne, driving the Chevy as they ascended the blacktop mountain road, tried to quell her nerves in silence. "Azeri is their prime hitter, all right," said Slaughter over his shoulder. "I kinda thought it could be Saint Denis." No answer from Sorel in the backseat, but Marianne realized for the first time that seating arrangements had their own meanings. She wondered whether Felix Sorel was deadlier than the man beside her. In any case, she would soon find out. She fought an urge to pull over, to argue against violence, to— But she knew it was far too late. It had been too late when she'd rented the Chevy. Perhaps she was fated to gamble with men like Sorel, instead of playing out her life with the likes of Lieutenant Alec Wardrop. At the moment, she wished she could be riding with that fool Wardrop as he sought a four-footed killer in Wild Country. Better than a showdown in these mountains with two-legged carriers of death. . . .

The blacktop was old and broken. For long stretches, there was no gravel shoulder to speak of. One wheel off the edge could mean an endless plunge, down and down, headlong through scrub oak and madrone, and once Marianne saw a rusted hulk, prewar limo by the look of it, lying on its side in a ravine far below. She was careful to avoid that crumbled shoulder verge. Then, twenty klicks into the mountains, the Ford nosed off the blacktop to a rough unsurfaced road and stopped for moments while its occupants argued over the mapfiche. "They dunno where the fuck they are," Slaughter said with satisfaction.

"Or would like us to think so," Sorel said from behind him.

"We're leaving Dead Indian Road," Marianne put in, pleased that she had remembered the road signs.

"And headed for dead Israeli gulch," Slaughter said. It was Marianne's first inkling that the man had any sense of humor. Was it possible that some men actually looked forward to the killing of near strangers?

Then the Ford lurched forward, its wheels very near the lip of a roadbed cut by a bulldozer many years before. To one side was a steep uphill slope covered by dry grasses; to the other, a slope that was almost a precipice. The breeze was cool. Far away, Marianne could see glints of sunlight from solar panels on the outskirts of Ashland; she judged they might be a full kilometer higher than the valley by now. The diesel's subdued clatter, the grit of stone beneath her wheels, were reminders that she was really here; and "here" was the last place she wanted to be. She willed herself to remember what Sorel had told her: kill these men today, or be marked for death herself. That would make it easier to use the automatic that lay against her thigh. Would she hesitate? She told herself that these Israelis, alive, meant death to her, and when

Sorel gave the signal she should save her life by killing as quickly as possible. And, if possible, without pausing to think about it.

Five minutes later the road swung in a downward curve, the Ford passing from sight for a moment. Sorel cursed in Spanish and urged her onward. But no ambush had been intended, and a half kilometer farther the road simply stopped at a ruined farmhouse with a barn. Sorel and Azeri were the first men to exit their cars, glancing at one another in mutual respect.

Maazel brandished a plastic map in one hand, still carrying that attaché case in the other, and announced that this property had been worked for salsify during the war. "Or so the agent claimed," he said. "A few soil samples will tell us more." The fat man wheezed louder than ever now, in the thin mountain air. Following Sorel, he trudged to inspect the wood-framed little house with its broken windows and tumbledown porch.

Slaughter pulled a thin cheroot from his shirt pocket, found his lighter, puffed for a moment, then ambled toward the barn, which seemed sturdier than the house. Marianne realized that any fourth Israeli staked out here would probably choose one of the structures for cover—or would he? In any case her companions seemed to be checking the possibility as they made their casual inspections.

When little Azeri followed Slaughter into the barn, the dapper Mills chose to stay with the woman. "I take it that poking around in musty corners isn't your cup of tea," he said amiably. When she fed him the best smile she had, he smiled back. "Nor mine, Miss Placidas. I'm a negotiator, not a dirt farmer. And you?"

As elitists they had much in common. She warmed to the Mills charm in spite of herself, saying she was a friend and courier, her nerve endings all tuned for any sign that things were going wrong.

Boren Mills displayed nothing but boredom. When the others finished tramping around in the wilds, it would be his turn; and in earlier days, Mills had proved one of the sharpest businessmen in Streamlined America. This would not be the first time he had cut a deal with dangerous men. Since his escape to New Israel, he had often dealt with sensitive business issues, always backed by Israeli clout and his own intuition for the precise limits of an acceptable deal. His weapons were all in his head. Like many an intellectual before him, Mills assumed that he needed no lethal hardware. It was Mills's pride that he was a man of ideas, and not a man of action. Surely, he thought, if he packed no deadly physical threat, his opponents would oppose him on his own terms. With the Placidas woman he admired the view, picking their way around clumps of weed as they neared the farmhouse, where Marianne could hear Sorel and Maazel. Presently, Slaughter and Azeri left the barn to amble toward the others.

Sorel emerged from the house, holding the screen door for Maazel, talking all the while. "I suppose it will do," he was saying cheerily, "but there may be other parcels more secluded." Marianne saw no signal pass between him and Slaughter, but perhaps none was needed.

Mills/St. Denis moved smoothly into the conversation, doing what he did best: "We could help finance the parcel you choose, but you will create less of a local stir if you haggle a bit and offer minimum down payment."

Sorel seemed to consider it, nodding slowly, then patting his pockets. "Marianne, do you have my calculator?"

Her mouth went dry. "Why, ah—oh. I guess I left it in the car," she managed to say, and moved toward the Chevy as Sorel, astonishingly, turned away from her, making some reply to the little negotiator. So it was that Aron Maazel was the nearest man to her when Marianne stumbled and fell.

She scarcely cried out at all but Maazel saw her and hurried up, puffing, attaché case in hand. She reached down to her ankle with her left hand, her right snaking under her skirt, and Maazel's fat face held such genuine concern that she could not, at first, command her finger to pull the trigger. His bulk hid her gun hand from the others, however, and in that frozen moment the fat man was the only one who saw the gun in her hand. Maazel's expression turned ugly as he opened his mouth. That change of expression became deadly for Maazel as he faced the pistol at close range, because it was Marianne's release. She fired twice from a distance of three meters, unaware of what the others were doing, her universe suddenly contracting to the bulk of the man above her.

Her first round caught the fat man just below the ribs and did not even stagger him. The second struck him near the heart while he lifted the attaché case as if for a shield, except that he held it edge on, almost like he would hold a guitar, and before she could fire again the end of the little case erupted in a stuttering burst. Spurts of dust surrounded Marianne, and she felt a searing pain in her right breast, flinching away, firing again as Maazel rocked back with the recoil of his own weapon.

Sorel had turned away for two good reasons: first, he saw that Maazel would be near the woman so that St. Denis was his nearest target, and he raised his elbows as if to stretch himself lazily. It brought his right hand near enough to his chest to reach his shoulder holster with minimum effort. Second, with this move he placed St. Denis between himself and Azeri. The cavalier disinterest of St. Denis had to mean the little man was a confident killer—either that or a man so far out of his element that he did not even know he was lost. Sorel had the soccer pro's sense of where his opponents were. Slaughter could see to his own safety. Sorel kept Marianne at the edge of his peripheral vision and did not draw his own H&K parabellum until he saw St. Denis spin toward the sounds of gunfire.

Sorel's victim reacted very oddly for a gunsel, clapping his hands to the sides of his head in horror instead of going for a weapon. For Sorel the job was ridiculously easy as the smaller man turned his back. Mills took two rounds in the back, point-blank, the mushrooming slugs flinging him forward as Sorel skipped sideways to face Azeri.

Zoltan Azeri was very quick, very silent. At Marianne's first shot, he essayed a long shoulder roll, drawing his sidearm from its waistband holster. He came up on one knee with the pistol in his hand before Slaughter triggered his coldgas weapon, arm extended, flicking his wrist repeatedly in a series of chuffing reports. Azeri went down hard, writhing and kicking, and had time to scream once as he clawed at his neck. Sorel's single round at a range of five paces was really a coup de grace into the little man's forehead.

Maazel was still standing, howling something in a language none of them understood, but now the attaché case slid from his hands as he fell heavily to his knees, then face forward, clutching his chest. ''Finish him,'' Sorel called to Marianne, sprinting toward her.

But Maazel stopped breathing, voiding himself noisily as he died, and Sorel knew those signs well. Marianne Placidas tried to prop herself up with one arm, grasping her breast with the other hand. Then, blinking hard and muttering, she slid down very slowly to lie on her back.

''She froze,'' Slaughter said with no particular emotion as he picked up the attaché case. ''What the hell is this thing?''

Sorel reseated his own sidearm without looking as he studied the deadly case. ''Wipe your prints from where you are touching it, fool. And wipe carefully; God knows how many more surprises that damned thing has inside it.''

Slaughter frowned, but did as he was told. As Sorel knelt beside the woman he had sacrificed, he added, ''Leave Maazel's prints. Her own prints are on her weapon. If the Canadians ever find anything, they will find that they killed each other.''

''She don't look dead to me.''

Sorel found the small wound, checked Marianne's breathing and raised her left eyelid, then stood up. ''Not quite. But she took at least one round from that needle claymore, and they are usually loaded with alkaloids. Her eyes are dilated and her heart will soon race itself to death.''

''Besides which, you can't fuck around in Oregon nursing her in a goddam farmhouse, and *I* damn sure ain't gonna do it.''

''Very perceptive,'' said Felix Sorel, smiling. ''We must wind this up quickly, put the car into the river near Portland, get back home, and maintain the position that I never left Mexico.''

''Damn shame about the Placidas bimbo. How do we handle her?''

''Into the barn with everything, unless we find a well nearby.''

''Didn't see one. What about the Ford?''

''*Mierda*! Of course.'' Sorel thought for a moment, then nodded. ''I shall wipe my prints, plant Maazel's, and leave it with him. You check Saint Denis for weapons; he surely has one.''

Slaughter soon discovered that their third victim carried not so much as a pocketknife; nor, for that matter, had Maazel carried anything in addition to his lethal needle claymore. Watching Sorel cut Azeri's leather holster away and appropriate his unfired pistol, Slaughter said, "Man, that little case is better'n a scattergun."

"It could clear out a cantina for you," Sorel agreed. He molded the dead hand of Maazel around the H&K weapon, fired it once more into the hillside to spread powder residue over Maazel's hand, then let the pistol fall into the fat man's jacket pocket. Then, cursing himself for almost forgetting, he fished the livesnaps from the man's inside pocket. He could destroy them later.

"I think I get it," Slaughter said. "The fat man blew away the little farts, and she nailed him, and then he offed her with that claymore gadget."

"Welcome to police forensics," said Sorel.

"So how do you explain my slugs?"

After a pause: "I suppose they came from a handgun that fell from the car while it tumbled down the ravine."

"Shit-I-reckon! *What* ravine?"

"I leave that to you, friend Slaughter. I believe you have gloves; use them to drive the Ford, with the woman in the seat beside you. It will be thought that she left the men in the barn, got away, and then lost consciousness while driving back. When you exit the Ford, I shall pick you up."

"I'm glad you're takin' care of that little detail," Slaughter said, grasping Maazel's feet as Sorel staggered under the load of the fat man's shoulders. He saw the woman shudder, her breathing now faint and rapid, and headed for the barn. "You got it all worked out," he said, grunting with the effort. "Sorel, you shoulda been a lawyer."

"Smile when you say that," replied Sorel, and held up his end of the burden.

CHAPTER TWENTY-THREE • • •

Slaughter nearly bought himself a piece of Oregon after accelerating the Ford with the woman slumped in the seat beside him. Suspension systems simply could not cope with these ruts at respectable speed, and Slaughter's long legs got tangled as he bounced against the doorframe on his way out the open door. Slaughter hit on his stomach, sliding and rolling almost to the edge of the precipice. He got a vague impression of the car's underside, rising near him as the front wheels pitched over the grassy edge.

He got up cursing his ruined shirt and spitting weed seed, and hobbled to the verge in time to see the Ford rise into view twenty meters below as it began its second roll, now moving faster on the slick dry grasses, finally beginning multiple flips, shedding small parts in midair. Even after he could no longer see it, Slaughter listened to its progress with satisfaction. It took a good fifteen seconds before the sound of the last impact died away.

Moments later, with Sorel in the Chevy, he craned his neck to see his handiwork. "Can't even see it for the brush," he said, and spat again. "Good thing our duds are in the trunk; I purely trashed a good shirt—and damn near my hide in the bargain."

"With the bonus I have in mind, you can buy many shirts," said Sorel, turning the Chevy's mapfiche toward himself. "Now get some sleep. We have a long drive over back roads before we reach the old interstate highway. You can take your turn then." Not once, then or later, did Felix Sorel show the slightest remorse over Marianne Placidas. She had been a tool cheaply bought and cheaply expended.

Despite his bruises, Slaughter exulted in a job well done. Before racking the seat back, he saw the deep ravine once more from a turn near the blacktop road. He could see no sign of the Ford. From their high vantage point, it was impossible to see the slight depression where the car had ended its first roll, where its lone occupant had tumbled from the open door into high grass before the car continued its headlong plunge.

Ten minutes later, Slaughter was enjoying the sleep of the innocent and Sorel was figuring their timetable to Portland. Several kilometers behind them a Toyota Scrambler howled up Dead Indian Road, driven with the happy abandon of a maniac or of a man who knew every pothole in the road between Ashland and the high mountain lakes.

Keith Ames had the Toyota's top down to savor all the glory of a fall day and scanned the mountainside above to avoid being surprised by a car coming his way. Blasting along at this pace, he might have passed Sorel eventually, had he not spotted movements in the tall grass high on a ravine, above and to his left. It was some distance from the main road, but when snow began to dust the flanks of Grizzly Peak nearby, Ames would be hunting blacktail in these parts. He slowed the roadster, expecting to see antlers emerge against the sky. What he saw made him forget venison. Like many ex-racing drivers, Ames kept a remarkable memory for the features of roads he flogged. He knew that a path that was almost an access road fed into the blacktop a couple of turns above. "Why the hell," he asked himself as he flicked the gear lever and surged the Toyota forward, "would a woman be crawling up that ravine?"

He would not have much of the answer for some time. He would, however, spend his next twenty minutes driving as he had not driven since dueling a prototype tree harvester against a similar machine driven by a killer, years before. He saw as he scooped the woman into his arms that she was delirious and near death. He buckled her in, trying not to look at the ruined face, hit the blacktop with a squall of rubber, and ignored his usual caution when driving with a passenger because this one was bleeding all over herself and might not live even if he broke all records down Dead Indian Road.

He broke the records, skirting Ashland en route to the city hospital, hanging his inside front wheel in thin air over the verge at every turn because, with its stiffened suspension, the Toyota had enough chassis lean in one-gee sideloads to keep that wheel aloft. On one long straight, he used his radiophone for the emergency freq and had time, before wailing the Toyota through the next bend, to tell them the bare essentials. Still, Marianne Placidas was more dead than alive as Ames burst into the emergency entrance with his gory burden, shouting for his friend, surgeon Dominic Ewald.

CHAPTER TWENTY-FOUR · · ·

Quantrill knew he was in for either an ass chew or a peace offering when, after being summoned to Stearns, he spent only a few moments waiting in the rec room. Either way, he'd be paid for the trip to Junction. And these days he was actually beginning to think about saving these extra dollops of cash. That worried him, because a conservative man tended to be overcautious, and too much caution could kill you just as surely as foolhardiness.

"Take a load off," Stearns told him as he entered, waving him to a chair. "Coffee?"

At Quantrill's nod, the chief deputy poured it himself and brought it, taking the adjoining leather-backed chair and placing a slender faxbook in his own lap. It was standard issue, with a case ID on its cover.

Stearns occupied himself with his coffee in the old Texas way, dribbling some into a saucer to cool it, blowing into the puddle, pouring it expertly back into the cup. Then, over the rim of his cup, he astonished Quantrill by smiling. It was a warm, easy smile full of informality and welcome; a politician's smile.

"No point beating around the bush, Quantrill; I was wrong about you."

Ted Quantrill smiled back and sipped; waited for the other boot to fall. Against his backside, maybe.

"I read your report on old Placidas's statement. Must've been a nasty time."

"For the judge, especially," Quantrill said, and waited.

"So I gather. Never met the old fella myself," said Stearns, his eyes meeting Quantrill's steadily, "but it's a hell of a shock to find he was on the other side. The point is, you did a fine job and you probably deserve a commendation. I listened

to the tape," he added, tapping the faxbook in his lap.
"There are only a couple of little things I thought we might
go over."

Good news and bad news; carrot and stick, thought Quantrill.
He hadn't really done much more than hold a recorder for
Placidas, then describe everything on polypaper. Well, it
would be just like Marv Stearns to give commendations for
paperwork. "Whatever you say," he replied.

Stearns smiled again and flicked the faxbook's cover open,
dialing medium magnification on its display so that he would
not need reading glasses. "I see you never read him his
rights."

"He waived 'em," said Quantrill. "Hell, he was a judge."

"No big deal; wherever Placidas is, we can't indict him
anyhow. But in the future, do it. Just for me, okay?"

Quantrill nodded.

"Second, it seems the judge had quite an audience for his
true confessions. Try not to let that happen again."

Quantrill thought it over; realized that old Placidas's reve-
lations might mark all those who heard them. "I can do
that," he said.

"Okay. I mean, how many people heard Tony Plass say
that Mul Garner hung one on us?"

"Two or three, I— Mul Garner *what*?"

"You got it on tape, remember? Placidas said the contraband went through Garner Ranch, and somebody says, 'Mul
Garner?' and Placidas says, 'He hung one on us,' and then
apologizes to his daughter."

"Damn if I remember that," said Quantrill, who had only
an average memory for dialogue. "I thought he said it was
the son. Jerome Garner," he added as if that explained much.

Stearns repeated the name contemptuously. "A Saturday
night hero, I hear tell. I can only go on hearsay, but Jerome
Garner doesn't strike me as a gang organizer. Anyhow, Tony
Plass didn't say anything remotely like 'Jerome.' Listen to it
yourself," he urged, and punched an instruction into the
faxbook's keyboard.

The digital recording, as well as photographs and written
reports, lay stored in the faxbook for later study. Quantrill
heard a soft thrum of prairie breeze, remembered squatting
beside the old man while Jess Marrow hovered near; heard

Placidas say, "Conduit always maintained through Garner Ranch." Then Jess, unbelieving: "Mul Garner?"

And then, so soft as to be nearly inaudible, Tony Plass: "The young one onus." Or perhaps, "The young one's on us." It was hard to say for sure. Stearns stopped the tape and let his eyebrows ask the question.

But Quantrill's memory was tripped by the recording. "I'm sorry, Stearns, but the man said, 'The young one.' I don't remember that last couple of words."

Marv Stearns tipped his palm toward the faxbook and shrugged. "It's your tape, Quantrill. "But he doesn't say anything that sounds like 'Jerome.' "

"He said, '*The young one.*' I remember it now."

A tiny cloud of irritation was gathering across Stearn's brow. "But you don't remember the other words," he accused. "You'd have him saying, 'The young one on us.' Shit, Quantrill, that doesn't make sense. And I tried the tape on three other people and all of 'em hear Placidas say that Mul Garner hung one on us. Now I ask you—"

"Can I hear it again?" Quantrill listened repeatedly. The quality of the sound was poor, and it still sounded to him as though old Tony Plass had said, "The young one"; but those two following words, slurred and indistinct as they were, threw him off badly. Perhaps . . . "You could be right," he said at last.

With gruff bonhomie: " 'Course I am. Anyway, just between us two, there are other agencies watching the Garners. So we're to keep hands off, and *we* means *you.* Soon as you adjust your report so you don't look silly, I'll get cracking on a commendation. You've earned it." His smile was now a grin; good ol' Marv Stearns, giving his good buddy Quantrill a chance to un-fuck up.

It took Quantrill only moments to revise his original report. It no longer implied that Jerome Garner was more than a barn-dance bravo. In fact, it no longer said anything whatever about "the young one."

CHAPTER TWENTY-FIVE • • •

To be hoodwinked by a politician is bad enough; to admit later that you half knew it at the time is worse. Quantrill arrived at the ranch at dusk, his dull rage tempered only by a suspicion that going along with Stearns had been the correct move. But for the wrong reason—maybe several wrong reasons. He really *had* let Marv Stearns talk him into changing that report. Flailing his memory hard, he still saw the pale lips of old Tony Plass form three words: *the young one*. That meant Stearns had doctored the tape, and then dangled a goddam lousy commendation like a carrot ahead of a jackass, and Quantrill had brayed agreement and, for him, a pussywillow flexibility in order to bask in the favor of Chief Deputy Marvin Stearns. Slamming into his two-room digs near ranch HQ, Quantrill thought he understood why.

He wanted approval from the system, because he was growing tired of living on its margins. The system meant security—only security was a Shangri-la, a charming fiction. Still, there were varying degrees of *in*security, as Sandy and Jess Marrow kept telling him. Maybe they had convinced him against his will. Maybe, just maybe, he was getting too old for the gunsel life.

Too old, in his twenties? Well, maybe "old" was a state of mind. But if he continued to walk that margin, he was likely to die young. Was there any middle ground? Perhaps there was; something he would call "maturity" for lack of a better word, a mind-set that would urge him to begin tapering off from the extreme chances he had taken, for years, as a matter of course.

Yeah; maturity. It had a nice mellow ring to it, and maybe he would be wise to accept it. Tomorrow, perhaps. He found the scrambler modem, one talisman he kept from his days

108

with the rebels under Jim Street, and used it for a collect call.

He might've reached any of a dozen people, but he recognized the smooth TexMex voice immediately. "It's Ted Quantrill, Lufo. Jeez, don't tell me they got you saddled to a desk now."

"Ey, compadre," boomed Lufo Albeniz with real pleasure. "You know how it is, man, you take what comes and wait for an opening." Only Lufo had always made his own openings and had taught Quantrill the same moves. "*Qué tal*? You callin' on the old scrambler, I see."

It may have been the first tendrils of that maturity which made Quantrill focus on the phrase "old scrambler." No telling how many people might have access to the old reb modems; he could tell Lufo more when they met. For now, "Just got myself a commendation, is all. Wanted to share it with the Gov." Even if James Street became President and Pope combined, his old comrades would always call him "Governor."

Sorry, said Lufo, but the Gov was where an attorney general was supposed to be: in the District of Columbia, Missouri. "He flies home most weekends from Mizzou, D.C., now that he has that motorized walker. Saturday you'd most likely find him in Alice."

"Who?"

"Alice, Texas, you Anglo airhead," Lufo guffawed. "Hell, you've been there. Want the number? I think the Gov won't mind if you keep it short."

Quantrill recorded the number and passed a few more pleasantries with Lufo. Each claimed to be considering different lines of work, but the details were vague. Quantrill rang off laughing dutifully at a sexist joke, waited a few moments, then dialed the Alice number. With a little luck and a friendly appointments secretary, he might manage a face-to-face with the Gov on the following weekend.

CHAPTER TWENTY-SIX • • •

The instant he saw Jess Marrow's face the next morning, Quantrill knew something was brewing. Marrow wore an expression somewhere between worn patience and cynicism as he led the way out to the tack shed, actually a well-kept stone structure larger than many stables. Indeed, several stalls in the tack shed were used to stable "temporaries" and to rig such occasional jokes as the saddled tame bison for special events.

To Quantrill's question, Marrow only said, "Words will not do it justice, Teddy. Not if I was Mark Twain." They turned the corner into a stall and Marrow continued, obviously wanting to be overheard, "I thought you'd want to kiss the dumb sumbitch goodbye. It was you, said we'd have to bury what's left in a cigar box."

"Wardrop," said Quantrill, shaking his head at what he saw.

Alec Wardrop tossed a broad grin over his shoulder as he applied a final stroke with a whetstone. "Mr. Quantrill," he acknowledged cheerily. "You're a bit late."

Quantrill studied the carbon filament lance, as long as two men, and the exaggerated, daggerlike steel tip Wardrop had been honing. Then he shook his head and sighed. "Late for what?"

"Why, the great debate," said Wardrop, and now it was clear that he was keeping his good humor with some effort. "Every man jack of my other messmates"—he must have meant Hutch and a few others he had met—"was up at sparrowfart this morning, warning me off this little peccadillo of mine."

"Your quest, you mean."

"Oh, it's not all that serious, old man," said Wardrop.

"That looks damned serious to me," said Quantrill, indicating the lance and then, following Marrow's head nod, studying the little horse that munched grain near them. "But the horse looks like a bad joke."

"Actually, it isn't," Marrow put in, leaning against the Dutch door with folded arms.

Quantrill saw a mud-ugly little stallion the color of ashes, with huge crescent nostrils and belly to match. Under fourteen hands high, he would not weigh four hundred kilos sopping wet and was short-backed and narrow-chested in the bargain. The truth was that Wardrop's mount was smaller than his quarry. "You have God-awful taste in horseflesh," Quantrill said.

"Pretty good taste for this job," Marrow replied as Wardrop strapped on small spurs to his riding boots. "That's a Spanish Barb, Ted. See those forelegs? Cannon bones round and solid as greasewood stumps. Those mean little slant eyes don't miss a single prairiedog hole. Long-winded as an alderman, too. He'll peel out from under you like a quarterhorse if he's got somethin' to chase, and he'll last as long as his rider. Nope, they don't come any tougher than the Spanish Barb."

"Nor any uglier," Wardrop admitted.

"Well, shit, you ain't ridin' in the Calgary parade," Marrow said.

Wardrop smiled at that, nodded, began to saddle the little barb. "Right you are, Mr. Marrow. And I don't care if he looks like a cur, so long as he performs with pig."

"Not with the one you're after," Quantrill muttered.

"We shall see in good time," said Wardrop. "If you'd care to ride out with me and Mr. Hutcherson this morning—"

"Hutch is going after all?" This from Quantrill, quickly, to Marrow.

"Just practice," Marrow replied guiltily. "I marked a few boars for this crazy Brit to try out his new gear with, while you was in Junction yesterday." He turned to the Englishman. "But we won't use ranch choppers to spot Ba'al for you. You'll just have to hire somebody else when you go lookin' for that widow-makin' hog."

"This is all the help I expect," said Wardrop, his jaw set. "Hutcherson is not exactly keen on it, you know. I fully realize that you're all in this conspiracy, Mr. Marrow, but I am not a cadet. Taking this animal, Ba'al, at half face value, I consider him a world-class trophy.''

Quantrill picked up the lance with its weighted butt, walking with Wardrop as he led the barb outside. Looking steadily into Wardrop's face, he said, ''A good recipe for a messy suicide is to take Ba'al at anything less than two hundred percent face value. His tusks are longer than your lancehead, and as somebody once told me, he can beat you at checkers. Or any other game you have in mind, and if I knew a legal way to stop you, I would.''

''You've seen him, then.''

Marrow was near, listening; suspecting. ''Hutch has, and I've seen the pictures,'' Quantrill said carefully. ''If you brought back a really big hog today, maybe Jess could get its head mounted so it'll look bigger. Marianne Placidas would never know the difference.''

''But *I* would, Quantrill. If you intended no insult, I will not ask you to kindly bugger off.'' Wardrop was behaving like a gentleman beset by street urchins, holding in his temper while showing a flash of steel. Quantrill realized his error; shrugged; shook his head again.

Wardrop mounted, swinging up with the easy grace of a man who knew what he was doing. Quantrill handed over the lance without a word. With the best intentions, he had clearly pushed Alec Wardrop past any possibility of turning back.

CHAPTER TWENTY-SEVEN • • •

Quantrill offered the best possible reason to Jess Marrow for taking Thursday and Friday off: Sandy needed help with her cash crop. He said nothing about personally freighting that crop to the big export market at Corpus Christi. Sandy's special hybrid crop of red-pulp, chili-flavored popcorn would certainly bring top dollar around Corpus—but he would also pass very near the little town of Alice.

The fact was, Marrow took care to keep from showing too much pleasure in granting his assistant leave whenever the Grange girl was involved. If there was one thing that might tame this young hellion, it was a good woman. From what Marrow could see, Quantrill was showing signs of getting domestic. But Jess Marrow could not see *all* of the signs. He could not know that Jerome Garner resented Quantrill's presence on Sandy's land. Sandy shared a long fenceline with the Garner spread, but for some reason Sandy was never bothered by Garner hands paying court to her. It never occurred to her that Jerome Garner might have told his hired men to steer clear of anything he had his eye on.

Late Thursday afternoon, Quantrill ran the stitcher across the last "gunnysack" of Sandy's crimson-hulled popcorn and mopped sweat from his face. The old fiberglass pallets, roofed for the moment under Sandy's grungy chickenhouse, groaned under their loads. He had sacked three metric tons in all, a full load for any hovervan and then some, if the route covered much broken country.

The buzz of the stitcher clattered down into silence as he called toward the soddy: "Hey, sis, how about some of that cold peach wine?"

Then he heard another machine, a big one with the whistling throb of a blown diesel with fans, in the near distance.

He walked out into autumn sunlight, stretching the kinks from his muscles, pulling off gauntlets and rolling up his sleeves, and saw the flaking paint on the door of the hovervan. Sandy hadn't told him she was renting the cargo vehicle from Garner Ranch.

Sandy and Childe greeted the driver, a lanky six-footer even without his scruffy boots, with no hips to speak of and a powerful beak of a nose between deep-set eyes. Quantrill considered withdrawing into the shed, saw the man glance in his direction, then resumed his walk. Nearing the trio, he heard the man's resonant basso: "Old gentleman said tell you there's no hurry. He'd be obliged if your driver would pick up some parts from International Harvester, and he'll call it even." But now he was standing beside them, looking toward Quantrill, and Sandy turned, too.

"That's more than fair, Cam— Oh, Ted, finished already? This is Cam Concannon, Mr. Garner's foreman. My driver, Ted Quantrill." Her welcoming hug around Ted's waist said much more.

"Mr. Concannon," said Quantrill, taking the scarred hand. The thinning sun-bleached hair suggested the foreman might be past forty, but still whipcord tough and lithe.

"Quantrill," replied the man softly, with smile wrinkles at the corners of his eyes as he sized up the smaller man. "We heard Miz Grange had some hired help. God knows she can use it," he added, nodding toward the acreage Sandy had not yet cleared.

"We have some iced peach wine, Cam," Sandy offered, and Childe scampered to the soddy ahead of them. They sat inside, sipping chilled glasses of liquid the color and clarity of a partridge's eye, discussing common topics: the price of special crops, the merits of twelve-volt or "house current" tools, their mutual hopes of a warming trend with less savage winters.

Finally, with a glance at his old-fashioned pocket watch, Concannon declined another refill. "The old gentleman expects me back 'fore dark, and my old cycle ain't what she used to be." He sighed, ducking as he passed the low doorway. "Quantrill, let me get you that parts list and check you out on the van."

The two men walked silently to the hovervan, parked

where its air blast would not throw dust near the soddy. "Ted Quantrill, hm?" Concannon's voice was friendly enough, but his message was something else again as he handed over a parts list from the cab. "Ten years ago, we coulda gone to Rocksprings, you and me; knocked off a few beers with the old gentleman. I think Mr. Garner and you would hit it off. But times change. I wisht we could be friends, I really do. Sorry."

"So am I. Is this a nice way of saying Mr. Garner wants me to keep clear of his fenceline?"

"Mul Garner ain't seen his fenceline in years, Quantrill. Pore old man is too sick to run things much. It's Jerome I'm talkin' about. Another year or so and I'm afraid he'll be the only Mr. Garner around." A pause, looking across the hills with a lopsided and cheerless smile. "Garner Ranch is my business. Mul Garner had his boy pretty late in his life, and never kept hobbles on him. Knowin' Jerome is my business, too." The pale, deep-set eyes found Quantrill's again. "He has his eye on this place and what's on it, if you get my drift. He's met you, and he don't like you one bit, and Jerome is mean as a pet coon."

As though asking something of no consequence, Quantrill asked, "Any suggestions?"

Conconnan spat. "Shit, I never in my life told a neighbor to clear out. I won't start now."

"But if Sandy Grange sticks with me, we'd best move on. Is that it?"

"It'd be healthier than stayin' put. For you, anyhow."

Quantrill released a long breath. "Did Jerome Garner tell you to say any of this?"

"No, goddammit! If he knew you was here, he'd of argued the old gentleman out of lendin' the van. Or worse. Hell, I said too much already. The Garners are like my family, and I don't sell my family out. But I can see trouble a long way off, Quantrill. You're trouble. Anybody in this country can tell you how Jerome deals with trouble, and that's about all I ever intend to say about it. I see you again, I nod. That's it."

"Good enough."

Concannon waved a hand across the dash of the van. "Anything here that looks funny to you?"

"Nope. I figure it'll get me there and back. You think I figure right?"

"I wouldn't lend a man a lame horse, damn your hide!"

Quantrill slid back to the cargo section; began to guide a rickety old hovercycle to the loading ramp. "I never thought you would, Concannon. Sorry it sounded that way. Let me help you with this."

"No, you go on back to the soddy, I don't want your goddamm help." Waving Quantrill from the cargo bay, muttering now as if to himself: "Ain't right to take help from a man you can't be seen with. I just hope the old gent lives another fifty years. Keep most of the shit outa the fan. . . ."

Quantrill partitioned this new knowledge off and wandered into the soddy asking about supper. He wasn't disappointed; Sandy was guiding Childe through the first steps of Sonofabitch Stew. They paused to watch Cam Concannon whirr off on his old cycle, and only then did Quantrill remember the Englishman who was training his borrowed Spanish Barb over the horizon. There would be time to discuss it over a second helping of stew; meanwhile he had plenty of time to winch those pallets into the cargo bay.

By suppertime he had scrubbed down, removing the pesky hull fibers that gave a fair imitation of seven-year-itch. Childe bustled about, officious as a Park Avenue doorman in an apron that came down to her ankles, convinced that she had created the main dish alone—a dish she particularly enjoyed because it allowed her to use a word that was otherwise taboo. When she crowed, "Come get the sonofabitch," Sandy decided this had gone too far. But Ted Quantrill could not stop laughing, and Childe wallowed in her small victory.

Sawing away at a loaf of sourdough bread, Quantrill broached the subject of Wardrop's training. "If you can keep Ba'al down home here for a couple of weeks," he said, mostly to Childe, "our crazed Brit will probably give it up. He can't afford to hire scout choppers forever, and the first blue norther that blows down here will teach him who the real enemy is."

"He won't stay hid," Childe said with authority. "I'll have to stay with him."

"You will be in school in Rocksprings next week, young lady," Sandy said, brandishing a wooden spoon like a paddle. "I can keep him busy hauling mesquite now and then, but he loses interest in it pretty fast. If anybody fires one shot at Ba'al on my spread, he can count on me shooting back.''

Around a mouthful of succulent bread-soppings, Quantrill said, ''Not Wardrop. Give the fool credit for courage; he's not even carrying a sidearm.''

Sandy, perplexed: ''This man has seen pictures of Ba'al, and is going to face him with a little bitty spear?'' Her headshake consigned Wardrop to some heavenly asylum.

Childe: ''If he's crazy, and doesn't have a gun, that's the only chance he has.''

Quantrill: ''Come again?''

Childe waved a hunk of bread airily. ''You know how rabbits go weird in season? Jumping flips, stuff like that? Ba'al likes rabbit, but he lets the crazies alone.''

''This Brit will not be turning flips or making faces,'' Quantrill warned. ''In some ways he's a helluva guy. But if he ends up with his innards spread all over Wild Country, Ba'al may get a sure-'nough posse on his trail. The best answer is for them not to meet.'' The same, he realized, was probably true for himself and Jerome Garner.

''I could get him drunk as a coot on rotten apples,'' Sandy reflected. ''But only for one day, and when he wakes up you don't want to be around here.''

Quantrill thought about that and shivered. ''Christ; Ba'al with a hangover! Boggles the mind,'' he said, chuckling as he chased a hunk of kidney around his bowl with more bread. ''By the way, it's nearly eight, Sandy. Wasn't there something you wanted to see on the holo?''

''*Umbrellas of Cherbourg*,'' she said. ''An old classic. A kind of opera, really. You'll see.'' With that promise, she began to clear the table.

Soon Quantrill had a good subdued fire of mesquite going in the fireplace, and with its flicker for a nightlight they settled down on the couch with hot mugs of coffee. Childe nestled between them, secure under her old rabbit-fur blanket, and ten minutes into the show she had begun to snore. Sandy gathered her sister up, kissed the small brow, placed Childe in the closetlike bedroom. Then she returned for some serious snuggling. She knew the power of this bittersweet old film and the tenderness it provoked even if it was in the old ''flatvision'' style.

A big down comforter can cover a multitude of sins. They massaged each other while watching the holo; eventually—despite her earlier decisions on the matter—made slow, careful love made more delicious by Sandy's fear of waking Childe. When Quantrill began to moan, Sandy muffled his mouth with her own. Then they lay silent, inert, and watched the ancient film to the end.

Quantrill was gently licking away a tear from Sandy's cheek when the late *Deadline* news began. The opening item stole their attention completely.

". . . announced a breakthrough at Bell Laboratories in development of a matter synthesizer," said the announcer. "Doctor Marengo Chabrier, Bell project scientist, refused comment, but a spokesman for the Federal Recovery Administration did respond to CBS reporters. More from Denise Young."

Cut to a stunning blonde in smart tweeds who may even have understood her pitch: "Ever since the last days of the war, rumors have persisted that China developed a machine that could create many substances starting with any simple chemical."

Quantrill sat bolt upright. "Rumor, hell. Sandy, you remember that lab I trashed in Utah?" He saw her nod. "The guy I brought out with me was Marengo Chabrier. I see he landed on all four feet." But Sandy had a finger across her lips, staring at the holo.

The lady in tweeds continued her upbeat tempo: ". . . and only small fragments of the devices survived the blast, which leveled a secret laboratory funded by Boren Mills, the former head of IEE. Mr. Mills pulled a vesco; his whereabouts are still unknown.

"But Dr. Chabrier did survive. As supervisor of the IEE lab, he provided the one living link to reconstruction of the matter synthesizer. Under hush-hush contracts with Bell Labs, he has spent the past four years, in a phrase he has since disavowed, 'reinventing the torus.' Chabrier would not comment tonight, but Mr. Kelvin Broadie of the Federal Recovery Administration spoke with me here in Missouri, D.C."

Flick to a taped sequence where a graying, conservatively dressed man faced several microphones with a look of triumph. "We always felt it was just a matter of time. Bell's people deserve a lot of credit; they never lost hope. Only in a dying culture can any important technical breakthrough be truly lost." A faint wry grin, suggesting years of doubt: "Or not for long, anyway. And Reconstruction America grows healthier by the day."

At this point Broadie paused to hear a question off mike and fielded it cleanly: "Not at any price, for a while. You have to realize that a synthesizer is about the size of a breadbox; in theory we can make them smaller, but not larger; and the yield is rated in kilograms a day. We have a few of them now at Sandia National Labs, producing exotic metals."

Another unheard question, and a cautious gnawing at his lower lip before Broadie replied. "I doubt it. We might synthesize living tissue one day, but that's a tall order. Right now we can use air as input and select cobalt or a passable bourbon as output, and"—a grin creased his face—"what more could you ask for a few cents' worth of electricity?"

Cut back to the tweedy Miss Young, whose doubtful smile faded as she showed, to millions of investors, the other side of this coin. "Trading on the Columbia market was heavy and mixed as the news broke this afternoon. Bell stock showed a sharp upturn, but firms engaged in the production of rare metals and pharmaceuticals did not fare so well. Trading in stocks of both Teledyne and McDonnell Douglas was suspended by closing time.

"The FRA's news release hinted that this amazing device will not be used to compete against private enterprise. But as of tonight, the matter synthesizer is no longer legend or rumor. Now back to you, Matt."

In the soddy, Quantrill sipped cold coffee and stared at the mesquite embers. "Jesus freeze us," he muttered, ignoring the rest of the news. "I thought that thing was dead and gone."

Sandy snapped off the holo, leaned back, worried at a cuticle with her teeth while she watched her lover. "Dead, maybe, but not gone. It's been haunting me for years." She saw his puzzlement and tried to smile, but it was a rickety construction that collapsed into silent pleading. She had to tell him now; not "someday," and not tomorrow, but tonight.

She rose from the couch and rummaged on a high shelf near the kitchen, among her few keepsakes, for the only existing miniature of a matter synthesizer.

CHAPTER TWENTY-EIGHT • • •

She held the amulet by its chain. With its great oval jewel missing from the bezel, it pendulumed slowly in the firelight, the silvery stainless steel and black diamonds gleaming. She let him grasp it before she released the chain. "I sold the big opal in the center," she said, and set about warming their coffee.

Quantrill had never seen the thing but recognized it from sketches. "They said Chabrier gave this to Eve Simpson," he murmured, turning it over to see the display on its back. The amulet had been a calculator as well! He saw that the thimble-sized yield chamber unscrewed, sniffed at it, glanced up as Sandy handed him a hot mug. "How did you get hold of this?"

"Believe it or not, Ba'al brought it here. The chain was caught over one of his tusks, but if it had bothered him, it wouldn't have been there long."

"When?" She could read nothing from his face.

A slow sip; then, "The day after the Simpson woman was killed at the dude ranch. I didn't make the connection until you told me about the amulet—how important it was. I let Childe play with the damned thing until she managed to synthesize a stink like last year's eggs." No response; he just kept looking at the device cupped in his hand. "When I did realize what it was . . . well, *you* were the one who said a thing like this would change the world." This time she saw him nod, sun-bleached straight hair falling over his brow. "Ted, will you *please* say something? Or hit me, if that's what you feel like. My love, I was afraid! I don't want my world changed, Ted; I like it pretty much as it is—with a few reservations."

He dropped the amulet in her lap, flicked his forelock back

with one hand absently, and leaned back cradling his mug in both hands, staring at the fireplace. "Well, it isn't important anymore, Sandy. You had four years to mull it over. Do you realize you could've been filthy rich with this thing?"

"In some ways, I am. Maybe I thought you'd understand."

"Maybe I do. Hell, I don't know, honey. Hold it: you sold the Ember of Venus from this thing? My God, no *wonder* you could buy all the stuff I see around here. You must have a king's ransom squirreled away somewhere."

She told him, to the penny. "Lufo probably cheated me," she added gloomily.

"That goes without saying. But it's too late to worry about that now, Sandy. The real question is, what do we do with that amulet?"

"Give it to a museum? You said it isn't important."

"I hadn't thought it through. You tell me: what would the Japanese give for it?"

Aghast: "You wouldn't!"

"No. And I really have to talk to Jim Street."

Sniffing it: "Huh. That old man put you in harness, and you'll die in it."

"He's the nearest thing to an incorruptible man that I know of, and this time I don't want you to get chiseled out of what's coming to you. Will you trust me on this?"

"I already have, Ted." She moved nearer, her hand caressing his arm, setting his coffee mug aside. "Are you . . . terribly angry with me?"

"Oh, I'll survive," he said, trying to keep it light, pulling her near for an embrace. Then, feeling her tremble in his arms, he realized how seriously she took the matter. "Look," he murmured, "you did what you thought was right. It was your decision."

"But not one of my better ones, hm?"

"I don't know. Maybe we'll know more when I get back from Corpus."

"And it's late, and you need to be fresh tomorrow," she said, beginning to arrange the couch so that he could stretch out. She would sleep with Childe, as always.

He helped her in the dim light of embers, then sat down while she stood above him, his chin in his hands. He was laughing softly. "To think that blowsy bitch is still running our lives, four years after she dies," he said.

"Who? Oh; Eve Simpson. Should I be jealous of her?"

"That's obscene, Sandy. Forget how she looked on holo; she was very fat and *very* kinky."

Sandy put her hands on his shoulders. Almost whispering: "For all I know, that turned you on. You once said that if Eve Simpson had been on the *Titanic*, it couldn't have sunk— but it might have gone down."

"Out-*rageous*," he chuckled. "There was a time when you wouldn't repeat such a thing."

"It was just a monkey do," she said, teasing him in a near whisper, playing the contrite schoolgirl as easily as she had played the whore for him in SanTone Ringcity. "You know; monkey see, monkey do."

"Cute," he growled, and began to chuckle through it. "If you're not careful, your monkey will get something to climb on."

Now she stepped astride his legs, flouncing her skirt to free her movements, and now she was lowering herself down facing him, hands gripping his shoulders, hips gyrating over him, whispering, "Ah, yes," and, "There, love," and, "Yes, there; easy, quickly, yes and yes," as she bent to find his mouth with her tongue.

Evidently, thought Ted Quantrill as he drifted into sleep, her monkey was about half rabbit. . . .

CHAPTER TWENTY-NINE • • •

Quantrill found Concannon true to his word. The van never coughed once, either in fan mode across open country to Hondo, or on its wheels down decent roads to Corpus Christi. He checked export prices on Friday evening, slept in the van, and wired over five thousand dollars to Sandy's account late Saturday morning after buying spare parts to accommodate Garner Ranch.

En route to Alice at noon, he wondered if some of those parts would help ferry hard drugs through Wild Country. Supposing the answer was "yes," had he unwittingly crossed his own ethical borders? Perhaps not, so long as it *was* unwitting. The more you know, he reflected, the more you're responsible for. By the time he reached Jim Street's ranch home near Alice, he was ready to envy fools.

He recognized the area by the creek that lazed between grassy banks, and the huge pecan trees nearby. Street's place was less inviting now, robbed of some of its charm by cyclone fencing that stretched out of sight and a polite giant manning the gate. On earlier visits he had thought of the rambling stone house as a gracious lady; now she was a suspicious old dame with a leashed Doberman. There would be no parking inside for any van—explosives were too easily hidden—but Quantrill's appointment and his thumbprints gained him entry for a long walk along a flower-lined path to the house. The groundskeeper patted him down but showed no concern over what was in Quantrill's pockets; it happened again with the receptionist, a plain-faced woman to whom Ted Quantrill was no more than a side of beef. They found Attorney General James Street puttering among potted shrubs before a huge solar window of his study, and then the woman left them. Quantrill suppressed an urge to stare.

"Looks like you're stayin' healthy, boy," said Street, extending his hand. It had the mottled color of great age and, noting the Gov's liverish complexion, Quantrill took the twisted hand carefully. He smiled at the old man's firm grip and his welcome: "Enjoy it while you can; one of these days they may turn you into a gawdam machine, too."

Street's motorized walker surrounded the old man's squat bulk with linkages, fiber rods, and slender hydraulic tubing. It cupped him in pads up to his beltline, its power source hidden inside a hard plastic pack at the small of his back. Ungainly as it looked, it permitted the old fellow to move around without the agony of earlier days. Arthritis had ruined his hips and feet long before. Seeing Quantrill's scrutiny, Street turned back toward his potted plants. "Don't ask how I take a leak with all this plumbing, boy. You mind if I cultivate my coffee while we talk? This and football are two things I can still enoy."

Quantrill showed interest that delighted the hobbyist in the old man. Harsh winters following nuclear war had at least brought a few small improvements: hardy, knee-high citrus and corn, even tiny coffee bushes that produced a good crop in a windowbox. It wasn't a real economy, Street admitted, now that you could get the "reg'lar stuff" again. It was just something to make an old curmudgeon want to rise in the mornings.

Presently the old man leaned back, locked his walker so that he could relax, and clicked his pruning clippers with a gnarled hand. "I don't like clippin' live branches without a good reason, son. Did you know somebody clipped Boren Mills this past week?"

The parallel took Quantrill by surprise. "First I heard of it, Gov. I thought he vesçoed out to Cuba or some such."

"Or some such," said Street vaguely, with a keen glance at the younger man. He did not reveal that he had the news from Canadian sources in Oregon Territory. "I suppose you can account for your whereabouts last weekend."

Quantrill folded his arms, leaned against a huge Mexican pot, and took his time answering. Much of that weekend he had been wearing contact lenses and dyed hair as randy Sam Coulter. For damn sure, he did not enjoy the prospect of explaining *that*. "Yessir, if I have to. But I didn't come here for confession. All the same, I don't even care who took Mills out, or why. It couldn't happen to a nicer guy," he finished, grinning.

"I'll buy it," said Street, laying down the clippers. "Why *did* you drop in? To watch the Teasippers and Horned Frogs on the holo this afternoon?" Like most native Texans, the old man would never outgrow his passion for football. Names like Cy Leland, Jack Crain, Doak Walker, and Earl Campbell were permanently etched into his memory.

"Should be a close game," said Quantrill, and followed as the old man's exoskeleton walked him to a library that smelled of leather and wood polish. "I had two reasons, Gov, both business—besides seeing you again."

Street waved away the pleasantry, took his hand comm set and used it to order a tray of munchables before folding himself into a semiupright couch and adjusting the wall holo set. "Good news or bad?" he asked, dialing the audio low.

"Both, I think. You knew I took Judge Anthony Placidas's dying statement?"

The old man seemed to be watching the pregame show but shook his head. "I didn't even know he had died."

"I thought as much. So you can't know he admitted being part of a drug-running operation and fingered a young rancher while he was bleeding out."

Street sighed and dialed the audio completely out. "Maybe you'd better take it from the top, son."

Top to bottom, the account lasted through the first quarter (Texas 14, T.C.U. 3). Quantrill kept skipping details he assumed the old man knew, and Street kept spearing after those details like a linebacker. Gradually, Quantrill began to appreciate that this tenacious old codger now watched over a dominion far greater than Wild Country, with interests far more diverse than a handful of high-tech rebels. It was astonishing, now that he thought about it, to find America's top cop willing to give personal attention to the unease of a deputy marshal. Still, Texas tradition overflowed with such experts at informal one-on-one: Houston, Allred, Johnson.

"So Stearns has been trying to dump you, but now he dangles a commendation at you to keep the heat off this young Garner fella," said Street, adding an excited, "Dump it off!" as a purple-jerseyed quarterback on the holo disappeared under behemoths in orange and white. No doubt about it, Jim Street could boss two outfits at once.

"And the judge said to tell you that your channels are not secure. I'll give you odds that's not audible on the tape you get, Gov. If you get it at all."

The old man shook his head in disgust at a broken play. "The horny toads got to settle down if they're gonna win this one," he said of the T.C.U. team. "So do you, son. Now let me tell you something that doesn't go out of this room: I've known my channels were tapped for a long time. If it's Stearns, I'll soon know."

"Look, look," Quantrill burst out happily, always elated when the underdog rolled to the top. A horned frog receiver had taken a pass on a dead run from between two defending Longhorns and was streaking for a distant goal.

"Always expect that fourth down pass when the other fella's rattled. Get him desperate enough and he'll do anything," Street said, cackling. "We don't want the other side rattled, son," he added soberly. "And we don't know if Stearns is ours or theirs. You aren't an unbiased observer."

"True. I know Marv Stearns's record, it's good," Quantrill admitted. "A week ago I would've thought he was immune to a bribe."

"Nobody's immune if the right coin comes along, son. Take me, now; I might do most anything for a new set of bones that'd let me run eighty yards for a touchdown. But there's only one thing I *can* do, outside normal channels. That's to use the one man with young bones that I can sure-'nough trust in this matter." He watched the extra point, Texas 20, T.C.U. 10, then tapped a forefinger toward Quantrill.

Ted Quantrill slid down in his overstuffed chair and groaned. "Christ, and I was about ready to pack it in. I was telling Lufo Albeniz the other day, it was time I turned in my ID."

Street: "Good. Spread that news around."

Quantrill: "I don't get it."

"Long as you're a deputy," said the old man, "Stearns can put you in whatever fix he likes. If you soured on the job, got into a ruckus with him, and told him to stick his badge sideways, you'd be free to move."

"Yeah. And broke as the Ten Commandments," Quantrill said.

"Oh . . . the Justice Department funds its informants, and pays a few informal brick agents, boy. You might find it's a raise, getting a monthly check for consulting with war historians. Or some gawdam thing. But it'll be direct from me, and when I say 'frog,' boy, I want to see you hop! Some of the contraband through Wild Country goes quicker'n scat. Goddammit, are you listenin' to me?"

Quantrill had just watched an on-side kickoff recovered in midair by a frenzied T.C.U. player. It looked like frenzy might win the day in Austin. "I'm a rich consultant," he said, palms out.

Not yet he wasn't, Street replied, and explained how it should work. Ideally, Marvin Stearns would be able to show cause to demand Quantrill's badge within a week or so. That way, nobody would wonder why Quantrill had quit. What did Quantrill have to sign? Nothing, Street replied. His handshake had always been enough. The handshake came immediately.

Quantrill stood up and stretched hard as the half ended with the Longhorns leading by a thin 20–17. "I can't leave now," he said.

"Dead right, son; in the second half you learn why it's nice to have strength three deep in the trenches."

Quantrill assembled a sandwich from cold cuts; popped the top from a Lone Star bock; sat back and studied the old man carefully as he began: "And *you* may get a hot potato in your lap, Governor. You remember that toy-sized synthesizer Eve Simpson lost? Well, what if I could put it in your hand one day soon?"

CHAPTER THIRTY • • •

The grizzled eyebrows lowered as old Jim Street regarded his new brick agent. "I don't believe I'm hearin' this, right on the heels of the F.R.A. announcement."

"That's what smoked the little gadget out, sir," Quantrill replied, taking a swig of beer. "Would it be worth a lot to whoever has it?"

"Who *does* have it?"

Pause. Then, soft but firm: "My question, then yours."

Street looked at the ceiling for help while his jaw twitched. "Ted Quantrill, you are the most insubordinate son of a bitch I *ever* met! Do you know who you're talkin' to?"

Still soft: "Yessir. I'm talking to the only man on Earth I trust with my questions—and one who understands about protecting sources."

"Then you don't have it yourself?"

"It doesn't belong to me," Quantrill replied with a shrug.

The old man nodded to himself, took his time smearing a corn chip with salsa that could have blistered paint, popped it into his mouth, and relished it. "I can think of several uses for the thing," he mused, dialing up the holo sound for the second-half kickoff. "Medicine on the spot; a fuel converter for those little bitty space probes; and of course a lot of foreign powers would love to get one so they could copy it. I reckon you could trade it even-steven for, say, the Star of India."

"The owner is afraid of its side effects. I mean, couldn't people use it to get drugs?"

"Depends. Some of those smart-ass gadgeteers could prob'ly limit the stuff a synthesizer makes, but as for ginnin' up cheap drugs, I sure hope so."

Quantrill chuckled and glanced at the old man, then did a double take. "You're kidding—whoa, you're not kidding."

The second half was just beginning. Street killed the audio again and, for the next few minutes, gave Quantrill his undivided attention. "Son, any adult who wants to kill himself with drugs, it shouldn't be gummint business. I grant you he's a peawit, but it's his life. This country's tried tight controls, and wound up with too much government. I was a sprat during Prohibition; my daddy was honest as they come, but he bought his hooch from bootleggers and so did twenty million other folks, and they paid high prices. Rumrunners got into reg'lar wars, and mulched a lot of innocent people and bribed a lot of others. It was the artificially high price of liquor that called for violence.

"So we repealed Prohibition. It took organized crime over a generation to recover from that, but drugs were still prohibited, even picayune stuff like pot. That was their hole card, son. As long as heroin is worth more than silver, we'll have a lot of violent crime over the stuff.

"Now, President McCarty and the voting public are bailin' this country out from under another age of tight controls. If I read the signs right, we might be ready to decriminalize hard drugs. Imagine what would happen if ever'body had a little synthesizer to make heavy drugs cheap as aspirin. It'd break the back of organized crime without adding one honest cop to the system."

Quantrill sat without moving, all but unbelieving. His distaste was obvious: "Christ! We'd see ten thousand deaths from overdoses in a few months. . . ."

"Probably." The old man narrowed his glance. "You still haven't got over Ethridge, have you?"

Quantrill remembered sleek, athletic Kent Ethridge; recalled his courage in the rebel cause. "Should I? Shit fire, personal synthesizers would help other guys oh-dee! How can you tell me that's not wrong?"

"Of course it's wrong, like any other kind of slow suicide. But look at crime the way I have to, where folks get graunched by it just by bein' in the way. Son, the backbone of organized crime is the *cost* of drugs. All that money gives too much power to people we didn't elect. And when an addict has to

beat in a few innocent heads ever' month to rob for his
tonnage, that's just what he does.''

"Ethridge didn't."

"Nope," said Street. " 'Cause he didn't have to. He got
his tonnage in bribes.''

Quantrill burst cut, "I don't believe that!''

"I'm sorry, Ted. It's true. We knew he'd been at it for a
year, off and on. Maybe he was tryin' to get straight. He
couldn't. I think his overdose was the only quick way he
knew to solve the problem; the other ways were slow and
took more gumption. It was his own choice.''

Quantrill, acidly: "You think an addict has that much free
choice?''

"I don't think there's any such thing as *free* choice; call it
expensive choice. *Whatever you choose has its price.* A re-
formed alky pays a price ever' day of his life, wanting that
drink he mustn't have. Or he takes the booze and pays a
heavier price when his liver rots.

"Son, I'm tryin' to show you that if drugs become dirt
cheap, we take power away from folks who abuse it. And
down on the shitty end of the stick, nobody *else* pays the
addict's price. He can go to hell in his own way.''

"Like Kent Ethridge did.''

Unrelenting, but sadly: "If he can't resist a known deadly
temptation, yes; like Ethridge did. Meanwhile the rest of us
could walk crosstown or take a camping trip without guns on
our belts. We'd trade weak characters for a safer world. It's a
trade I'd make in a second, boy. Now honest: wouldn't
you?''

Quantrill stared at nothing for long moments, coping with a
concept that wrenched at his value system. Finally, "I don't
know, Gov. I wish I were as certain as you are.''

Unwilling, as if admitting some vast guilt, Street said,
"I'm not really certain; I can't be, 'til it's tried. Hell, it isn't
up to me anyhow. But when you ask tough questions about
things like this, you have to be ready for some hard answers.
I know I sound bloody-minded. I'm just tellin' you what I
think. And I've been thinkin' on it for over sixty years.''

"So how am I supposed to feel ten years from now, when I
see a friend synthesizing heroin?''

"Mad as you like. Tell him he's an idiot; I would. If it

interferes with his work, you fire him. If it screws up your friendship, find other friends. That's *your* choice. We'll always have to protect kids against their own foolishness, of course. But if your friend's an adult, he should make his own choices.''

Quantrill sighed, swigged the last of his beer. ''And free choice is expensive,'' he said, nodding.

''One way or another. It's part of evolution; always was.'' Street reached for a cold cut, still watching the younger man closely. ''There aren't many men your age I'd say these things to, but you've earned straight answers. I can't help it if I sound hard.''

''My God, you sound like an anarchist,'' Quantrill muttered.

''Actually about half libertarian and half liberal. If you want to see a lot of fat-cat industrial honchos sweating blood and howling about communism, wait 'til America starts producing synthesizers for the open market. Whenever you broaden the power base, you piss in the pocket of the fella who already has power without bein' elected to it.'' The old man jerked his head toward the holo, where the scoreboard read TEXAS 34, TCU 17. ''The Longhorns know about a broad power base. They're three deep in the skill positions.'' He turned up the audio.

Quantrill saw unfamiliar numbers on orange jerseys. Texas University was substituting freely now, and three plays later they paid the price for that choice. T.C.U.'s tight end leaped high for a very short pass and slam-lateraled to the nearside guard, taking out the linebacker as he fell. A pulling guard with a five-yard head of steam can be an engine of mass destruction in the opposing secondary. The rules permitted the play, and instead of getting the vital seven yards, the Horned Frogs got twenty-four before a free safety derailed this runaway express.

Quantrill got himself another beer and chuckled. ''Only two deep at linebacker,'' he said.

''Sucker play,'' said the old man, beaming. ''Teasippers got a cushion with their first string, so now they can afford to let their sophomores make a few mistakes, and they sure as hell do. I pity the next opponent that tries a slam lateral over that partic'lar kid. That's how you build next year's team, son. Stick him in there soon as you can afford to, and let him lose his innocence. Next year he's a veteran.''

"Mistakes make this game fun,'' Quantrill observed.

"Unless you're on the team,'' said Jim Street with a wink. "Now then: who has that damn synthesizer necklace?''

Without a word, Quantrill stripped the velcrolok closure from a thigh pocket and produced the amulet, handing it across to the old man while watching the holo. He did not see Street grin at this elaborate display of careless ease.

After a long silence, turning the amulet over and over, Street made his accusation: "You said you didn't have it.''

"Nossir, I said I didn't *own* it. And I don't.''

"How'd you get it past my friskers?''

"They found it. It wasn't a weapon, Gov.''

"Like hell; it's an economic weapon—or at least I think it is. Your friend just may be a millionaire, son. I'll have to take it up with the F.R.A. through a lot of gawdam channels, but you did right to bring it here.''

T.C.U.'s tiring first team pushed across for a touchdown, and Quantrill said, "I guess Texas will bring in the first team again.''

"Wouldn't be s'prised,'' said the old man, making a show of placing the amulet in his breast pocket. "When the issue's in doubt you go with all the experience you can muster.''

Quantrill saw the parallel. "And trust, Gov.'' He flipped a nonchalant salute to the old man. "I don't mind telling you, I'm not convinced about letting people have drugs as cheaply as aspirin.''

"I'll tell you once more: I'm not dead sure, either. I *am* sure it'll be part of getting more individual freedom and less violent crime. For what it's worth, boy, I give you credit for brains. You had to know you coulda sold this to somebody like New Israel for ten times what you'll get from your own country.''

"Fat fucking chance,'' was the reply. "A friend once called me an 'agent of change.' The least I can do is try and see that the changes are made in the best interests of my own country.''

Now the old man laughed outright. "Good luck, boy. We can never know that ahead of time. You know what the big synthesizer means to Ora McCarty's science advisers?'' He got a headshake and continued: "Californium and plutonium from asteroid dust or plain old garbage."

Quantrill groaned. "Bombs? Again?"

"Nope. A real space drive. Fuel from synthesizers can take us clean out of the solar system. This little gizmo you handed me"—he patted his pocket—"might put a stardrive within the means of lots of folks. One day soon, maybe."

"I'd rather watch football. I'm just not ready to think about that."

"Then *get* ready. Because it's gonna happen. What ever made you think you can direct all the changes you trigger off? All we can do is try. Speakin' of which"—he turned to glance at the digital clock on the holo—"I'll have other fish to fry soon as the game's over. No, sit tight," he added, seeing Quantrill start to rise. "I'll need to know where to send, um, a sizable hunk of money. And one more thing: If you stand to get much of a commission on it, you might not want to stay on with me, nickelin' and dimin' and riskin' your ass. We could put other brick agents out there in Wild Country, instead of you."

Quantrill had little doubt that other agents were already out there; Lufo among them. "Maybe later, Gov. Right now I'm just too damn interested in seeing how this game turns out."

The contest on the holo turned, as Street had said it must, on the three-deep strength of the Longhorns: Texas 41, T.C.U. 30. But the old man knew that Quantrill had not been referring to a football game.

CHAPTER THIRTY-ONE • • •

In Oregon Territory, the October madness was soccer. Keith Ames risked hemorrhoids on cold bleacher seats with two hundred others and cheered his Ashland junior high team, a losing cause this season. Later he gave a rough hug to his twelve-year-old on the sidelines. "I'm proud of you, Chris," he said, tousling the kid's sweat-damp hair. "You scared the heck out of the district champs."

"We need three more guys like Paulie," Chris gloomed, and traded handslaps with a taller boy who had just taken consolation from his own father. Paulie Ewald would be Ashland's star wing in another season or two.

"Better hit the showers, kid. I'll wait here," Ames promised, and watched the boys trot away to the gym. Then, catching the eye of Paulie's father, Ames strolled over to talk.

They dissected the game briefly. Dom Ewald had a surgeon's keen eye for analysis, while Keith Ames, like many engineers, tended to suggest odd experiments. Paulie as a fullback, for example.

"You'd make a terrible coach"—Ewald chuckled—"but a great ambulance driver."

"Hey, I meant to call you," Ames replied. "How's that woman getting along?"

"Beats me. She walked out on us night before last," said Ewald. With his almost offensive good looks, Ewald compensated with a low-key delivery and an occasional practical joke.

Ames thought this might be one of those occasions. "Su-u-re she did. Seriously, Dom—or can't you tell me?"

Ewald cocked his head and thought about it. "Well . . . she was unknown and foreign, and you have a close mouth. You'll have to keep it closed, Keith." Ames nodded. "Seriously: she had a ruptured spleen with a lot of internal bleeding, so I repaired the splenic capsule first. And still we almost lost her because of something else. Good thing she was in such great physical condition. We pumped three liters of perfluosol into her, just getting her stabilized for surgery. Man, she's going to have some scarring, to judge from her mammoplasty."

"Dom, you're gargling Greek again."

"Silicon breast implants. They're what saved her life."

"I never know when you're bullshitting me," Ames said wryly.

"A breast implant is a little polymer bag full of liquid silicone, Keith. It goes about a centimeter under the skin and subcutaneous fat. Well, before she went over that cliff, somebody shot the lady with a tiny flechette." He saw Ames lift his eyebrow. "Swear to God. This little dart carried some kind of botanical alkaloid—a poison. I still don't know what the devil the stuff was, but it was lots more potent than, say, belladonna. Her pupils were dilated, heart rate like you wouldn't believe, hair standing on end, hallucinations worse than jimsonweed. Stuff like that might be used to immobilize you, make you so suggestible you'd answer any question—and then you'd die anyhow. Nice, huh? If she'd got the whole dose into her bloodstream, she'd have been dead before you got her to us. But the flechette lodged in the silicone implant. She just lucked out."

Ames shook his head, staring out across the valley to distant heights where he had found the woman. "Well, that explains why Chief Gannon came to my office last week. I didn't know much to tell him about it, and he wouldn't tell me a damn thing."

"I'm not surprised. He's got some, ah, other problems on his hands that are probably connected, and I can't talk about that. She said a lot of weird things while that alkaloid was in her. 'Course you couldn't understand much. Her face had gone through a glass mapfiche."

"Made me sick to look at her," Ames muttered. "I hope she wasn't a pretty girl . . . ah, hell, you know what I mean."

"I gather she was very fond of her face," was all Ewald said.

"Can't it be fixed?"

"Maybe, but not by me. I got her cheek sewn together; had to swing some little skin flaps down to cover denuded places at the jaw; put a few stitches in tension areas. But her face looked like a jigsaw puzzle, and from those old mammoplasty scars I'd say she was a keloid former."

"The only Greek word I know is *skataa*," Ames said with a mock-dangerous squint.

"That *proves* you're an engineer," Ewald riposted. "I'm saying that she develops scar tissue. I injected some proprionit—uh, I did what I could to keep the scarring to a minimum. But I guess we'll never know now. I'll say one thing: she's one determined lady, just to walk out in that condition."

Ames jerked in astonishment. "No joke? She really did disappear on you?"

"Would I kid you?"

"If you'd spread cracked corn on a ticklish, sleeping buddy and turn a chicken loose on him—yeah, maybe."

Ewald hung his head and murmured, "Mea maxima culpa," but his mouth would not stop twitching. "The woman did pull out on us, really; wearing a roller bandage that covered everything but her eyes."

"I really feel sorry for her." Ames sighed.

"Me too. But I got the idea she knows who tossed her into the blender. That's probably whom we should feel sorry for," Ewald finished. They began walking toward the gym, comparing notes on the hunting season. For them, Marianne Placidas would remain an enigma.

CHAPTER THIRTY-TWO • • •

Felix Sorel sunned at his poolside near La Mariposa and, for the umpteenth time, scanned the proposal in his hands. The letterhead from Películas Clásicas, classic pictures, seemed genuine enough, and the return address was in Argentina. It was not the first time a holodrama producer had offered a part to Sorel, who was still something of a hero in Latin America.

But that cover letter smelled wrong; had probably been intended to smell wrong; perhaps it was the passing reference to financing from New Israel. Sorel understood the real proposal on his first reading of the "treatment," a brief synopsis of the plot with one scene included as a sample.

Sorel had never said yes to a holodrama, but on reading that single scene he felt compelled to agree to this one. He would play the role of a courageous smuggler, running guns to insurgents in some (unnamed) country ripe for overthrow. An arms manufacturer had lost three men trying to contact him, but bygones *might* be bygones.

On the surface, the scene made as little sense as most holodramas. It was when Sorel mentally substituted drugs for guns, and the prospect of legalized drugs for a liberal gun law, that he saw the part they *really* wanted him to play.

Stripping away the clever camouflage from the Argentine treatment, Felix Sorel wondered if, indeed, this were an offer he could refuse and live to brag about it. Probably not. No matter what he claimed, the Israelis took it for granted that he had iced their men in Oregon Territory.

Now, reading between the lines of a holo script, he saw that they were willing to forgive that small lapse of politeness. They had something far more important to discuss, something that might powerfully affect his fortunes and those of New Israel.

No doubt of it: if Americans could cheaply and legally synthesize drugs, there would be no further point—certainly no money—in Sorel's conduit through Wild Country. Besides which, the Israelis saw clearly that any country that owned synthesizers would have a tremendous advantage over those that did not. It was almost like membership in the nuclear club of the last century, but with an edge that was economic instead of thermonuclear.

New Israel—if Sorel was interpreting the plot correctly— had reason to hope they would soon get their hands on a synthesizer. Meanwhile, having long since abandoned emotional ties to Earthbound countries, they could throw sand in the American gears in two ways.

One, they just might be able to sabotage the American production plant. That would delay the American advantage while others fought to create, or steal, the same technology.

Two, they could certainly provide a sudden and dramatic increase in hard drugs to the American heartland, at dirt-cheap prices. They would need someone to push the stuff through Wild Country for a year; perhaps longer. Very soon, old addicts could wallow in the stuff and give samples away. It would probably mean new addictions, overdoses, and a widespread national revulsion.

At exactly the time when legalization was under debate.

The scenario had loads of appeal for Felix Sorel, especially when he saw that the producer offered him something highly unusual: the right to select alternate endings. In plot one, his character made alliance with the arms suppliers and lived happily ever after. In plot two, Sorel refused that alliance.

Plot two had a tragic ending.

Sorel flopped onto his belly to toast his back a deeper golden brown and thought about living happily ever after. This new alliance could not last forever; a year, two or three at most. But in that time he would gain much, and his enemies to the north would suffer much. Whether New Israel gained or lost, in the long run, was of no importance whatever. Whether the Israelis blew him away in the short run was of the utmost importance, and those *chingaderos* were very good and uncommonly patient at doing exactly that. Did he want to spend the rest of his life in shadow, running from other shadows? Or did he prefer to make amends for his little breach with Maazel and company and haul more *mierda* through Wild Country to be spread across Reconstruction America?

Felix Sorel knew when he was co-opted. He could admire a bunch that absorbed their losses with such easy grace. "Kaiyi," he called lazily, "bring Cipriano to the study. We must tell San Antonio Rose to alert our Anglo friends. It seems," he added, smiling to himself, "that I have a contract with a producer."

CHAPTER THIRTY-THREE • • •

Quantrill wasted several hours during the next week, wondering how to get himself fired convincingly. His time was wasted because, internally, he had already quit. He had endured the buffeting of Chief Deputy Stearns this long only by applying discipline he had learned during the war. Tuck away that discipline, that cautious reserve, and you had a man who exactly fitted old Jim Street's complaint: one insubordinate son of a bitch.

It was a Wednesday afternoon, ten days after he returned the Garner hovervan to Sandy, when he and a half dozen other deputies arrived in Junction, summoned by calls from Stearns. The men lounged on wicker chairs, sipping soft drinks and talking shop as they waited for the meeting to begin.

The deputies were all young men, the kind who preferred backslaps and hard work in the open to handshakes and soft cushions at a desk. Three or four times a year they were assembled like this, and good-natured rivalry was likely to involve horseplay. Quantrill accepted his share of it but never kept it going.

Randy Matthews, a stump-legged farmer from Menard with a quick wit, was offering his plug of tobacco to Quantrill as Marvin Stearns strode into the room. "You'll need a chew to keep you awake," he muttered, selecting the chair behind Quantrill's.

Stearns stepped to a lectern, looked over the men, consulted the display screen of his flat 'corder. "Settle down, boys, there's good news."

Quantrill smiled and shook his head at Matthews as he took a seat. "Thanks anyway, Matthews." Words could not convey his distaste for plug tobacco, but he tried: "I'd rather chew a horse muffin," he whispered over his shoulder.

Matthews whispered back: "So would I, but this is the next best thing."

So Quantrill was laughing as Stearns began his spiel: ". . . a seminar in DalWorth next week, and that means you, too, Quantrill." The younger man nodded, trying to wipe the mirth from his face. Trouble was, anything that is the least bit funny becomes twice as funny when you're not supposed to laugh.

"You'll all go by air from SanTone, all expenses paid, with a little per diem you can spend at Six Flags if you don't find the cathouses first," Stearns said smugly, then in an aside: "Goddammit, Quantrill, if you're gonna choke, do it quietly."

Quantrill struggled with his expression, honestly trying to look alert, expectant. A week at government expense in the Dallas–Forth Worth area was a rare treat, and he was as pleased as his fellows for the opportunity.

But Stearns misread amusement as insolence in the green eyes. Midway up Stearns's list of punishable offenses was insolence from a deputy. At the top of that list was insolence *in the presence of other deputies*. No matter that he had his own reasons for wanting his part-timers far from Wild Country during a particular week soon. If one of those peons asked for disciplinary action, he was going to get it. Especially that deadly little bastard who seemed to be laughing at him now, in public.

"I've had enough, Quantrill." Stearns tried to stare the other man down. It wasn't a wild success. "How funny would it be if I canceled your freebie to DalWorth?"

Even the most trivial threat can be a trigger. Quantrill leaned back in his chair. "A side-splitter," he said.

In a cold fury: "Consider it done." Stearns saw a new sobriety on the faces of the other men. This was as good a time as any to demonstrate his power over them. To the group he said, "I was processing a commendation for Mister smart-ass Quantrill. I can still hold it up."

Quantrill stuck one hand behind his back. "Hey, Stearns," he said lazily, "guess what *I'm* holding up."

Behind him, Randy Matthews saw the upraised finger and covered his mouth to hide his smile.

Raising his arm, jabbing a forefinger to pace each word: "You're on a month's suspension, Quantrill. No pay, no commendation."

"Commend this," was the reply, with a suitable gesture. Quantrill got up and walked toward the door.

For one instant, the other men thought Stearns would hurl the 'corder at his deputy's back. "*Six* months. The maximum," Stearns said instead, choking on his rage.

"The maximum is forever. I like it better that way," said Quantrill. The room was very quiet, so quiet they heard the soft click of the doorlatch as Quantrill eased the door shut behind him.

CHAPTER THIRTY-FOUR · · ·

He could not say why at first, but Quantrill put off telling
Jess Marrow that he had drawn his last wages as a part-time
deputy marshal. It was not that he could still leave WCS land
for days at a time without any explanation, though that was
true enough. The fact was, Quantrill felt ashamed of the way
he had taunted Marv Stearns. The big man might be crooked
as a dog's hind leg, or he might not; but he'd had the look of
a man blindsided from ambush when Quantrill had walked
out on him. As if, by refusing to play by the rules as Stearns
understood them, Quantrill had taken unfair advantage.

There had been a time when Quantrill had taken unfairness
for granted. When the government implants a radio monitor
in your head and can detonate it for your slightest mistake,
you tend to simplify your ethics. When they gave you a cheap
shot, you took it; if they said "kill," you killed. In the few
years since that implant was removed from his mastoid—and
that government was removed from office—Quantrill had
learned again to savor ideals: fairness, affection, trust. In a
way, the government had been right. For a manhunter, ideals
are shackles.

If you stayed in the hunt, those shackles would eventually
get you killed.

On his second day back from Junction, Quantrill called
Sandy on the open VHF line during his lunch break. "I really
feel naked without my shoulder patch," he said. It was a
hint.

She missed it. "I hate that thing anyway. But you can buy
another one."

"Can't; it's illegal. My ID and belt video are gone, too; the
whole nine yards."

"You mean somebody stole your— I don't believe it, Ted Quantrill, what are you hiding from me?"

He told her and grinned as she whooped with glee. Then, confusing him, she was crying. "Predictable as Texas weather," was all he could think to say.

"You go to hell, Ted, I can cry if I feel like it," she sniffled. A moment later she was suggesting that he come to her place and pat her shoulder—among other things.

"Nothing I'd like better, honey, but I'd better stick around here. I'm waiting for a call from, uh"—he remembered it was an open channel—"a friend who owes you. Besides, I need to stay up-to-date on the Brit's progress. He still talks to me, God knows why. And now he's using a chopper to canvass the big ranches around these parts. He's offering money for information, but so far, as he puts it, no joy."

Touched at his concern for Ba'al, she promised much in the way she murmured their special phrase: "Soon, love."

He agreed, said goodbye, shrugged into a denim jacket for the afternoon's work. He'd thought Marrow was joking when the job was first mentioned. Wild Country Safari boasted a lot of spooky animals, but only one kind that could be mentioned in the same breath with Ba'al. Neither tame nor game, the WCS rhinos were treated rather like moving monuments with bad eyes and dispositions to match.

He was gathering his gear behind Marrow's office when he heard a familiar voice raised in irritation. "My *dear* Marrow, I am prepared to indemnify you for it!" Wardrop.

Jess Marrow's voice was indistinct, but his tone was obvious: no dice. Quantrill strode to the office doorway wearing thick nylon brush chaps and carrying cartridges for the Nelson rifle. Marrow was saying, "Like you said, laissez-faire. You do like you want, and so do we." His voice got lower, with fewer highs and lows, with every sentence. His final statement came all in one breath, and it was low on volume, but it was a beaut. "That contract of yours don't say nothin' about loanin' you no friggin' transporter fer no friggin' horse, an' I won't, not even if you had that friggin' hawg in a hole out there, maybe 'specially not then, and now I'm sorry I didn't talk down this whole friggin' idea, but I was too goddamn friggin' broad-minded." Quantrill knew the signs; the madder Jess Marrow got, the less he sounded like a veterinarian.

Alec Wardrop did not know those signs and barked, "Broad-minded? Marrow—rhymes with narrow." He turned as if to go.

"I know what rhymes with Brit, sonny boy," said Marrow, and Quantrill cleared his throat. Livid, Wardrop spun; saw who was behind him, and seemed unable to find words.

Quantrill found a few. "Why don't we take a walk, cool off." He made it sound like a question.

The long-legged Wardrop set such a pace that Quantrill was almost trotting as they neared the tack shed. Muttering, "Chance of a lifetime," and, "Paid a pretty penny—for what?" and, "Now that I have a fresh sighting . . ." he opened the little Spanish Barb's stall. He was in the kind of hurry that horses can sense, and the barb's ears went back a trifle.

Quantrill made it casual. "You say you've got a recent sighting of that boar?"

"His track, at least. Fellow named Cannon saw fresh signs this morning," Wardrop replied, checking his saddle. This was the traditional English leather affair that you could store in a breadbox with room to spare for a family of mice. Westerners called it a kidney pad; joked of its saddle tree and skirt that they were no more than a shrub and bloomers. But it took a fine rider to use an English saddle in rough country.

Quantrill asked where the sighting had been. Wardrop whisked a trim, folded polypaper chart from the side of his boot top and tapped a finger over an orange X, then continued saddling up while Quantrill opened the map one fold.

Quantrill saw the name of a township, whispered, "Shit," then refolded the map; handed it back. "Could his name have been Concannon? Wiry, thin hair, about forty?"

"Con? Yes, I believe so; Con Cannon." Wardrop flashed an almost friendly smile and kept cinching.

For one heartbeat, Quantrill considered a bad decision. No, a few broken ribs wouldn't deter Alec Wardrop for long, anyway. And it might land Quantrill in the slammer. "A hell of a long way from here," he said. Garner Ranch was over a half-day's ride on a horse.

"I'll manage. Those people may be more hospitable than this lot, and in any case I'm ready for bugger-all." Wardrop's kit looked like a good one, inflatable bag and all. The man was determined enough and loony enough to rough it out there, in country that had incredible flip-flops of weather, plus its own annual tarantula migration. But the tarantulas had made their march two months before, and Wardrop had a VHF handset. The barb would find forage, and just maybe Wardrop would find his quarry.

"These folks are only trying to keep you from killing yourself," Quantrill said reasonably. "Beats me why Marrow takes care of your gear."

"Because I have a signed contract," Wardrop said, "for which I'm paying a small fortune."

With undisguised hope: "You could go broke chasing this four-footed ghost."

"Oh, very likely," Wardrop drawled, amused. He added somewhat pointedly, "I certainly could, if I let a fresh spoor get cold. At least I know which point of the compass to face."

"Right; only thirty million acres to search. You could lose a herd of rhinos out there."

"Rhinoceri seem to lack strong herd instinct," Wardrop said acidly, leading the barb outside. "Take it from one who has hunted them with the Zulu."

Quantrill entertained one more slender hope: Perhaps the Brit could be diverted by another danger. "I've got to inoculate our white rhinos today, Wardrop. I can knock 'em out with syringe cartridges, but I have to do the inoculations up close. Thought you might enjoy the challenge."

"That's no challenge, it's a duffer's game; armchair sport," Wardrop said. He pulled a brilliant kerchief, which opened in a silent airburst the color of blood, from a pocket of his bush jacket; tied it around his throat.

Quantrill recalled the moment when Marianne Placidas had flung that kerchief at Wardrop in scorn. "Does the woman still want you to do this?"

"I wouldn't know. Saw that Ocelot of hers in San Antonio a few days ago, but I haven't seen her since the day . . ." He let his sentence trail off.

Quantrill met his glance; nodded. Alec Wardrop would seek the woman out when, and only when, he had answered her challenge. The Brit mounted up, the lance slung across his back, its point gleaming in autumn sunlight. He rode out toward the southwest, erect, undaunted, with no other weapons than the lance. Quantrill waited until the rider was out of sight before heading for Marrow's radiophone. With luck, Sandy might be able to keep Ba'al off the range for a day or so.

CHAPTER THIRTY-FIVE • • •

Felix Sorel checked the pace of his mare, frowning as he saw the way his companion mistreated a borrowed mount. This was supposed to be a pleasurable ride on his own turf, beyond the ears of his men. Yet it was difficult to enjoy with a companion like Jerome Garner. "*Cuidado*, careful," he called as the Anglo urged his big stallion down a talus slope.

Young Garner snapped the reins too hard, with the kind of overcontrol that could turn a good horse into a bad one. The Anglo sat a saddle well, but any fool could see that he had no respect for his mount. On shifting slopes, you didn't wheel your horse around if you gave a damn about broken legs—for horse and rider both.

But the Garner luck held, as it always seemed to hold. Somehow the big dun stallion obeyed with powerful lunges that brought Garner back to the promontory, where Sorel leaned on his saddle horn, patting the neck of his sorrel mare, enjoying his view.

Why lecture the *cabrón* on the matter? Instead, Sorel smiled across at his guest. "A shame that you have no such mountains on Garner Ranch," he said. "We could move an army through here without detection."

"And it'd take a week," Garner replied. He swung down from the dun, snapping kinks from his legs, swinging his big shoulders so that his mount shied. "Whoa, goddammit," he barked, jerking the reins. Sorel judged the tall Anglo to be a couple of years under thirty. He wore his dark hair rather long, its curls falling over a broad forehead, almost to his brows. His deep-set eyes were a startling blue that seemed to skewer whatever they spotted. The nose was strong, the chin square; all he lacked, thought Sorel, was a dimple.

One day this strapping Anglo would probably grow soft

with his excesses, but now he fairly hummed with vitality. It kept him trim, with the flat belly and tight buttocks of an athlete. Sorel, who worked hard to stay in shape, appreciated bodies like that; might have made a delicate proposal to the Anglo, but he knew better than to consider it seriously. For one thing, Jerome Garner saw other men only as opponents rather than friends—let alone potential lovers. For another, the man inside that charming body had no charm to speak of. Felix Sorel smiled again into the blue eyes: too bad, *lo siento mucho, querido*.

As if noting something sensuous in his host's glance, Garner nodded toward the small scatter of tile rooftops in the far distance. "How can you stand it here, Sorel? There can't be much action in a dump like Mariposa."

"I bring the action," Sorel said. "I will shortly bring more action through your land than you have yet seen."

"That's what SanTone Rose promised, and that's why I'm here; you tryin' to spook me, Sorel?"

Sorel maintained his calm. It was easy to ignore antagonism from a man he could outfight or outmaneuver at his whim. "Merely covering every base, Jerome. After our first few shipments, the border authorities may step up their surveillance. We cannot buy off all the *federales* in Wild Country. Do you have the manpower and the cover activities to handle five times the traffic you have had in the past?"

Garner gave a silent whistle; scratched a bristly chin. He would have to make it look jake with the old man, but Mul Garner himself had often mentioned a private north-south road across the spread. It'd be stupid to build one, of course, since aerial recon might have the border cops sniffing around it. The existing route up through the Garner spread was useful only because it was *not* an obvious conduit. But with a few picked hands, he could pretend they were studying a route. The old man never left ranch headquarters anymore, so the ruse could be maintained. "I can hire more hands to guard your flanks. They're expensive people; shit, you oughta know, some of 'em have been on your payroll."

"I expected that. Who did you have in mind?"

"Longo, Slaughter; a few others that are coolin' off at the old south homestead."

Sorel knew the place: a frame house and barn with sheep

pens and shearing shed, once served by chopper when fuel
was cheap. It had fallen half to ruin since old Mul Garner's
youth, but its well still pumped sweet water. The barn would
hide several loaded hovervans if necessary. Sorel nodded. "If
we travel at night, we must go slowly. Can we use ranch
headquarters for a second stop?"

"No way," Garner replied quickly. "My old man would
have more questions than a beef has ticks."

"A stopover toward the north border of your lands, then."

This time Garner thought about it longer. He knew a place
all right, hardly more than a line shack and over a century
old. It slumped near a small creek that Mul Garner had
dubbed "Faithful" because, no matter how ferocious the
summer, it always seeped a trickle of good water. Full of
limestone minerals, it was "water so hard it'll bust your teeth
out," but the shack was special for other reasons. Only a few
people knew of its existence in a tree-choked ravine, and
Jerome Garner did not intend to share its location with anybody else. Especially not with this slippery, smiling golden
boy of a Mex soccer jock. "Nothin' but a few old deer blinds
there. Half of those are in trees."

Sorel hated to show his ignorance of gringo habits, but he
hunted in other ways. "Deer blinds?"

"Ol' board shacks you nail up near a deer trail or waterhole.
Why freeze your ass in the rain when you can hunker down in
a lean-to and wait? Come to think of it, we could knock down
two or three of 'em and make you a shack from old gray
lumber; big enough to hide a van, anyhow."

"Do that," Sorel agreed. "And then I shall make a test run
to see that all is satisfactory."

But something in Sorel's tone had lodged in young Garner's craw. Drawled slowly: "Well, my, my, ain't you king
shit."

"*Perdóname*?"

"Ain't you just the top little turd in the bucket, though?
Your Highness will inspect your fuckin' domain; as if I didn't
know how to hide a hovervan on my own land."

Very cautiously, very gently: "Jerome, the shipment—all
the way to Wichita Falls—*is* my responsibility." The sorrel
mare was basically a polo pony and sensed disquiet in the

man on her back. She became nervous enough to be a diversion for Sorel.

Watching him gentle the mare, Jerome Garner snarled, "Yeah, and on my land. Don't you ever forget that if it wasn't for me and damn few others, there wouldn't be any hiding places for brush-poppers to hole up in, and no passage of Mex goodies for long. And Wild Country would be tame in five years.''

Now the voice of Felix Sorel was so soft and nonthreatening that he almost cooed. "Do you imagine that my . . . employers . . . would permit me to run tons of contraband at a time through any route I do not know in detail?" He had tried to defuse two hissing incendiaries at once by suggesting that, far from "king shit," he was only a hireling fart, which should gratify this great childish fool. And by implying that his inspection was an absolute requirement before Jerome Garner ever saw a single peso. He waited for results.

And got them: "Aw shit no, Sorel, you can come up if you want. I just don't like folks talkin' like they owned my land.''

"The lands have passed to you?"

"Might as well say that; I run the place. The old man'll check in his Justins any month, now, and until then he's happy because he thinks his foreman makes the decisions. But we have an understanding, me and Concannon.''

Sorel cocked his head as if to ask the next question. And Jerome Garner was pleased to answer: "He understands that next time he crosses me, I kick the shit out of him and hand him his wages.'' His grin was as happy and innocent as that of a boy; perhaps a young prince who could do no wrong.

Sorel smiled back, guiding his Anglo guest back to the trail to the ruined villa, making small talk. From long experience, Felix Sorel had found that politeness was easiest granted to those he least respected. And anyhow, he only had to keep up this respectful sham until the next morning. Jerome Garner never stayed off his own turf a minute longer than he had to.

CHAPTER THIRTY-SIX • • •

The great boar had fed well on Garner land, wandering for days as he pleased and leaping barbed wire when he pleased, without taking a single animal the owner would miss. Bullsnake, rattler, succulent herb shoots, cattail roots at a pool fed by a creeklet. Ba'al had begun to avoid taking sheep and cattle when ranging over Wild Country with Childe on his back, and by now he was accustomed to a meat selection that ran heavily to varmints. Like most big omnivores he could thrive on any diet.

But he had bedded in high grasses near the pool, and the soil was soft enough to take an impression, and those impressions included dewclaw marks that lay at a ninety-degree angle to the prints of the hornlike hooves. To Cam Concannon, checking out the water thereabouts, it said "boar." But those hoofprints spanned as large as a man's open hand and that, in big block letters, said BA'AL.

Armed with instinct and experience, Ba'al knew the signs of unseasonably warm weather ahead—perhaps a few more hot days where he could bask in the sun and snore without a womanchild near to kick him for the noise. There was much to be said for traveling alone.

He was not alone for long. Ba'al could not know that Lieutenant Alec Wardrop had used his radio to arrange for a horse van, paying Garner Ranch a premium to meet him at the boundary of WCS land. It saved the hunter a half-day's ride and, by midafternoon, Wardrop had seen the huge prints. The cautious side of Wardrop's nature put chillbumps on his neck and arms. If those prints could be believed, he was hunting a beast whose head would send glad cries down musty halls in the British Museum. Unless it killed him first.

Should he try to interest Garner's ranch foreman in the

152

hunt? Wardrop sensed that the man might cut the hunt short with gunfire, and from brief conversation he knew that Concannon was not all that familiar with Russian boar. No, this was *his* quest; his and the barb's. Ugly as a full chamber pot, still the little Spanish Barb had shown his mettle with two average boar on WCS land. Wardrop waved as Concannon steered the horse van back to an old wagon trail, and let the barb drink his fill at the creek. Then he guided his mount to the south a bit, following the lip of the ravine until it became a valley filled with scrub oak and cedar. Twice he flushed wild turkey, birds that sneaked through the underbrush like quail, then finally burst into the air like gigantic pheasant. They seemed very unlike the stupid domestic bird, with intelligence to match their size. From time to time, Wardrop idly wondered whether this heraldic boar might also be wiser than the normal-sized game of his experience.

Wardrop's excitement grew when he spotted more prints, inspected the chewed bases of uprooted shrubs near a limestone seep. One of the vast prints was slowly filling with water. Wardrop placed his splayed hand over the print and shuddered with excitement. He judged that print had been made within the hour, eyed the westering sun, and remounted quickly, expecting to raise his quarry before dark.

No joy. At dusk, Wardrop stood on a hilltop and scanned the valley with his pocket monocular. Somewhere out there below him, he felt sure, the Wardrop Trophy—he was already labeling it in his mind—was preparing to bed down. Or perhaps not; this boar was known to be a night marauder. *It might use the tactics of Bengal tiger*, he thought, feeling his hackles rise, and slowly scanned in a full circle. The Bengal was capable of laying down a spoor, then doubling back on a parallel course to ambush the hunter.

Uneasy about this possibility, Wardrop turned back. He had seen a rickety contraption with a platform nailed high in a medium-sized oak, now some distance behind. He found the deer blind again with more relief than he liked to admit. He hobbled the barb and let it graze, hanging his tack neatly in lower branches that spread like outflung arms from the oak trunk. The floor slanted, but with his bag inflated and a pouchful of steak and kidney pie in his belly, Wardrop managed nicely.

Except for the damned barb.

Several times that night, Wardrop heard the barb snort; heard hoofbeats drumming, not very effectively because of the hobbles. First one direction, then another. Because he kept that empty food pouch inside the deer blind, its own musky odor masked the stink of boar that the barb was smelling. And hearing.

Ba'al took his sweet time studying the stranger. The boar had slept earlier in the evening; would amble away to sleep again before morning, if nothing turned up to interest him more. He saw the shadowy haste of the little horse in the darkness; noted that it seemed to be lame; circled around to sample the wind from a better quarter. His nose told him that only one frightened horse and one relaxed rider were near. No stink of gun oil or powder residue, either, so he found nothing to arouse his anger. Ba'al decided against climbing into the lower branches of the oak for a look into the clapboard shed, though he had found it simple enough to do in the past. Let them go their way; he had made peace with one man and had grown wise enough, with age, to avoid wars without good reason.

So Alec Wardrop slept on and awoke refreshed. He never learned what it would have been like to feel the oak shaking, to rise from his mummybag in the dead of night far from any help and see peering in at him, in faint moonlight, the head of hell's own sergeant at arms.

Wardrop pulled the thermal tab on a tea bulb and waited for it to heat, stripping the wrap from slabs of herring and biscuit, and finished his breakfast before retrieving the barb. It was very near, still nervous as a nanny, and did not settle down until he had ridden it for several kilometers. Presently it began to misbehave again, and a few minutes later he knew why. He could smell the rank odor of pig. With years of experience in the breed, Wardrop knew the kinds of cover a Russian boar favored and knew also that he was, for the moment, on poorly chosen ground. When he saw the tracks again, they led to a higher elevation. Wardrop urged the barb up an animal trail, hearing it grunt with the effort. Ba'al was listening to it, too.

Ba'al had known for some time that the man was near, and swung up on the hillside for a look. Below, trotting across the meadow on his track, was the ugly little horse with its tall rider. He decided that the horse had lied; it was not lame at all. Something starlike gleamed in the sun above the man, something like a straight tusk of steel on a slender pole. Ba'al thought about that. If a thousand-pound boar can chuckle, perhaps that was the sound deep in his throat.

Wary as he was, Alec Wardrop did not know he was near his quarry until the barb shied, dancing, with a whinny of protest. He swung the reins, urging the barb to continue wheeling around, and then saw what was behind him; what he had passed moments before without sensing it because the wind was not in his favor. The barb saw it too, and screamed like a woman.

Ba'al had squatted low behind a stone outcrop to let them pass, then placed his forehooves on the rock and thrust up with his hindquarters. Alec Wardrop whirled and saw this apparition standing on its hind legs, its ears pricked forward, the yellow-red eyes glittering. It stood as high as his own head even while he was in the saddle, and it watched quietly as Wardrop fought the barb's panic.

The horse bolted, taking most of Wardrop's concentration, but he regained control within thirty yards. Wardrop's good sense told him to give the barb its head, let it run clear to San Antonio if it could. But then one end of the kerchief swept across Wardrop's face, a scarlet reminder, and then he shrugged the lance from his back and made the barb face its terror.

Then, too, Ba'al saw a threat he could appreciate in his own way. Wardrop held the long, light spear underhanded on his right, holding the reins with his left hand, the steel tusk aimed forward. He saw Ba'al's two yellow ivory weapons lowering, their incredible sweep fully as long as a man's forearm, and realized that if the boar charged, the barb must be allowed to move freely. The usual tactic meeting a boar's charge was for the horse to leap the boar, the rider spearing down between its withers. But this towering brute was easily as big as his horse. Traditional ways of dealing with pig, Wardrop saw with sudden wisdom, were going to be instantly suicidal here.

But it did not look as if the boar were going to charge. Wardrop had seen this often; a boar would usually run until blooded, and then it might do almost anything: run off a cliff, swim a river, or charge its tormentor. A trophy-sized boar at a hard charge had been known to injure an Indian elephant and could knock a horse sprawling. Or, as legend said of the viceroy of India, his boar might literally leap over the horse to escape. This unbelievable mountain of muscle was fully *twice* the size of any other boar Wardrop had ever seen or heard of, its head larger than the barb's, its great shoulders and face crossed by old scars. Could a beast of this size perform a leap even more prodigious than his smaller kin?

His head whirling with dangerous options, Wardrop spurred the barb forward. No matter how quickly it moved, a boar needed some distance to achieve a hard charge. If the barb would take orders and charge first, Wardrop might sink the lancehead home just behind the creature's elbow with his first pass. The barb did respond and closed on their quarry with a rush. Alec Wardrop even had time to wonder whether this nightmare brute was too muscle-bound to move quickly.

Ba'al may have felt a certain flattery for a few seconds; no man had ever faced him using one of his own weapons, and this one had clearly chosen to approach him wearing a tusk. But this was a view he discarded when that tusk was lowered menacingly in his direction. Besides, the moment he went to all fours, his eyes were below those of the man. And sure enough, once his eye level became dominant, the man urged his mount forward. Ba'al had no earthly notion what was meant by the shout, but it readied them both for action.

"Marianne! *Woh jataaa!* . . ."

The barb knew to charge past so that his rider's lance arm was nearest to the quarry, and he was uncommonly smart—for a horse. He expected abrupt movement from the boar and was ready for it. He was not prepared for a beast that stood his ground, tail erect like a flag, whuffing a basso grunt and waiting for any damned thing that came his way.

Ba'al saw the lancehead reach for his body; wheeled to parry it with his nearside tusk; flicked upward with a toss of heavy neck muscles; saw the lancehead flash up as the barb thundered by.

Wardrop felt the lance shaft twist as tusk and steel clashed, and narrowly avoided slicing the barb's head with the wickedly sharp edge of the lancehead. The weighted butt of the lance might as well have been so much cotton fluff. With pressure of knees and the reins, he turned the courageous, frightened little barb still expecting the boar to explode into movement. Unruffled, alert, it stood and waited for *him* to deliver.

Briefly, insanely, Wardrop thought of hurling the lance overhand in his next pass. But in pigsticking you never let go of your lance. Never. It was as basic as honor and courage. Wardrop spurred the barb, with subtle knee pressure this time to guide it a bit farther from the quarry. Sooner or later he was bound to connect.

He had seen small boar leap backward, but never a trophy animal. He brought the lancehead in with its point a trifle high, hoping that a lightning thrust inward and down would at least draw blood.

It brought blood, all right.

Ba'al waited as if carved from limestone until he saw the lancehead arrowing down to his flesh, and then jerked backward as he flicked his head. He intended to bind the lance between his tusks and disarm this maniac, then send him packing. After all, when boar fought boar, losing was punishment enough. The winner seldom killed, and this man seemed happy to fight in the manner of a boar. But Ba'al had not counted on the lancehead dropping so much, so abruptly.

Wardrop knew joy, and battle lust, as the lancehead entered the boar's mouth. He wrenched hard to free the point, seeing bright blood on the razor edge as he looked back; by that time the boar was behind him.

Ba'al realized the lancehead was between his jaws; clamped down; felt the steel's cruel passage through the soft flesh of his underlip. He did not release the pressure of his jaws but felt the slick, shiny steel slide from his teeth anyway. His own foamy saliva had reduced friction to almost nothing, but Wardrop was lucky to wrench the lance away without being unhorsed.

And now the boar did charge. He charged with a suddenness that put him alongside the harried little barb before it could turn, and while Wardrop was twisting from the waist to bring the lancehead around. He lowered the great head almost to the ground, flicked his head to the side, and delivered a terrible slash that could have taken Wardrop's leg off at the ankle.

Wardrop saw the move, kicked backward and up without

losing the stirrup, and felt the cinch give way, sliced like cheese. In the same instant the barb felt the ivory scimitar enter its flank and screamed again, staggering. With the cinch flopping loose, Wardrop's saddle slipped from the barb like soap on tile. He managed to free himself from the stirrups, hit the ground standing, and rolled free, still grasping his lance as the barb went down.

Wardrop had seen a Masai with a four-meter assegai lion spear, using his foot to ground the spear butt against the ground to impale a lion as it leaped. Now, using his knee to secure the weighted butt of his lance, he waited for this devil to rush him.

Ba'al saw the man drop to one knee, two lance lengths away. He saw the barb and heard it, too, an agony that was not pleasant to hear, and now that he was taller than both of them he felt that dominance had been won. His sudden murderous furies of earlier times failed to take hold. Tasting his own blood and that of the barb as it ran down his right tusk, he considered the matter and decided it had been settled. Neither member of *this* team seemed in condition to challenge him again.

Alec Wardrop watched the huge boar bounce away, pink foam jouncing from its mouth like flecks of cotton candy, and knew that he had not seriously wounded the creature. At the moment he was damned glad of it. Ba'al moved like something on springs, in a distance-eating canter that took him out of sight. He was bleeding more than he knew, but he would know it when he had lost a few quarts of blood. Of that, Wardrop was certain. He moved over to the savaged little Spanish Barb, avoiding the forehoof that pawed pathetically back and forth. At least he still had the VHF radio in the pocket of his bush jacket.

CHAPTER THIRTY-SEVEN • • •

Sandy's journal, Sun. 15 Oct. '06

Childe has finally cried herself to sleep. Wish I could do that but am all cried out, mostly in anger, some of it misdirected at Ted. On lonely reflection I agree he was right not to call, but to rush straight to us as soon as that berserk Brit was airlifted to WCS with his bloodstained spear. Nothing I could have done anyway, and Ted was here for support when he told us the bad news. Can it be true that my old protector is bleeding to death somewhere on Garner spread?

Wonder where Ted is, this moment. Told me his WCS hovercycle was borrowed, but more likely he simply rustled it. Did he also borrow that vet kit with permission? An even bet that Ba'al will not allow him near enough to use it. Dam it, why did Ted refuse to let me call old Mr. Garner? Only good manners to tell a neighbor when you must follow your stock onto his land. Part of my moral code, yet I let Ted talk me out of it.

Damn our moral codes anyway, they are the razors we wield against our own fulfillments, shaving away each pleasure one thin, transparent curl at a time. If taken too far, this process leaves us jumbled and juiceless piles of severed joys, baked crisp as dry leaves in the autumn of life. I have learned, at least, to remove my code before lovemaking. Half of amorality is amor . . . and I would not be straying into this line of thought if Ted had made love to me last night. Perhaps the mother of invention was not necessity, but simple frustration.

Childe's mind is subtle. Or perhaps just pragmatic; she had never told me Ba'al survived poison three years ago. Claims she alone can find the old shanty and creek where he recovered out on the Garner spread. Insists Ba'al is certain to return there if badly hurt. Still, I'm sure Ted is right, he must search alone. Wild Country is no place for a little girl at night unless she is riding the neck of Ba'al.

To be out of this mess I would give everything I own, or expect to own. Still no word on reward for that stupid amulet. Ted talks vaguely of large sums, but even $50,000 would not buy a spread big enough to contain my old friend. Only consolation tonight is that Ted is no longer in gov't service and can gallivant off like this whenever he likes without mortal danger.

Will brew agarita tea and try to sleep now. . . .

CHAPTER THIRTY-EIGHT • • •

Quantrill kept to the valleys when he could, mindful of the possibility of radar and other sensors. The hovercycle was not one of the government's stealth models with kapton plastic and special coatings, but simply the first one he could hot-wire at Wild Country Safari. It was a Curran, a fast courier job with good mufflers and a recliner you could sleep in. He had left Sandy's place before dawn and crossed Mul Garner's fenceline shortly after first light, trusting the map because it was a duplicate of Wardrop's. It was one of the few things about this fool's errand that he *could* trust.

He couldn't trust Garner's men not to shoot him on sight. If the boar's injury was less severe than Wardrop claimed, Quantrill couldn't trust the animal not to charge him. And though he had brought the Nelson rifle with its tranquilizers, he could not trust it to deliver the right dose to pacify Ba'al without killing him. He couldn't even trust the creeks he had tried to follow. Several times this day, he had whirred down a sluggish limestone-bedded brook watching for the signs Childe had described, suddenly to find himself following a dry creekbed or even, in one case, circling a sinkhole. In South Texas, creeks around Edwards Plateau were just as likely to flow underground as above it.

Quantrill did not see deer, peccary, or anything else larger than a rabbit on this morning. He and the cycle were the only big things moving across that part of Garner land. And that made it easier for motion sensors on a nearby hilltop to follow his progress.

Now, with the late morning sun promising to blister him later in the day, Quantrill settled the cycle near a scatter of discarded plastic bags and killed the engine. Wardrop's distress call had been satellite-relayed to Kerrville, the nearest

161

Search & Rescue outfit, and they'd actually lifted that poor little Spanish Barb back to Marrow in a sling under a chopper. Having spent several years with S & R teams, Quantrill recognized the flimsy clear wraps in which virtually all equipment was packed.

In any self-respecting place, the breeze in mid-October would be cool and the sky overcast. But this little piece of Wild Country was hot enough to boil a man's brains, and it promised to get worse. Tomorrow it might play host to snowflakes or a tornado, but today Quantrill cursed its heat, sighed, and found a bulb of Pearl Light in the cycle storage pannier.

A careful scan of the shrubby area told him much. Those discarded bags began to degrade with the help of dry-packed enzymes as soon as they were opened, especially in warm weather. They were still in fair condition, so the bags had been opened within the past twenty-four hours or so. Several long scuff marks on the hardpan revealed where the chopper had landed. Scarcely ten meters away was a rust-brown stain on the earth, already sun-blackening and worshiped by a squadron of biting flies. The barb must have lost quarts of blood on that spot; a wonder it had survived at all.

Labels on the empty bags said someone had used a medical stapler, a hammock sling, and a hell of a lot of tape. Quantrill spotted several crescent-shaped heelmarks—Wardrop's, for the S & R crews left caulked patterns—and then, swigging his beer, let his glance slide up a nearby animal trail.

He said an ugly short word and strode forward, seeing the sharp incisions in the earth where a huge boar had spun, parried, and charged. Without any question, it was Ba'al that Wardrop had met; and thanks to his training at the hands of Jess Marrow, Quantrill had become a passable tracker. He needed little time to find where Ba'al's blood trail began, but he was encouraged; Ba'al had not been bleeding all that much. He considered calling Sandy on the cycle's VHF set to tell her the good news but did not want to risk giving away his position in case Garner's people had direction finders. He had no way of knowing that someone already had located his path and was moving toward cover near a point he would soon pass.

Briefly, he lost the trail in the creek. He found where Ba'al had entered the creek earlier, judging from the way the prints were oriented—and then dropped to his knees. A moment later he stood up, dusting off his knees and grinning.

Marrow was not as good a tracker as, say, an Apache; but he had taught Quantrill about print incisions. When running, a hoofed animal digs the fore tip of his hoof into the soil, and more loose soil is found behind the rear hoofprint than behind the front. It took Quantrill a moment to realize what he was looking at: the dewclaws at the rear of each hoof had dug in, and the loose soil was ahead of the prints. Ba'al hadn't *entered* the creek there; he had *left* it! Striding backward, probably at a trot to judge from the spacing.

And if he'd taken that much trouble with his tracks, he probably was not badly injured. Silently, Quantrill lifted his bulb of Pearl aloft and toasted the unseen Ba'al.

Still, most of his findings were guesswork, and he had not come this far to let his imagination draw his conclusions. Quantrill copied Sandy's "all clear; come in" whistle as well as he could. If he could whistle the big devil up, at least he could take back the news that Ba'al still reigned in his corner of hell.

No response. Nor in the next ravine, either, a narrow cleft so choked with brush that its real contours were hard to see. But Quantrill saw a sunglint from water between cedars, where the ravine widened some distance away, and took the cycle along the ridge for at least one moment too many. He never knew how many rounds were fired toward him in that first burst, but one slug gashed his windscreen and another shattered the engine's injector pump in the same instant. That meant several snipers, or one with an assault rifle, or both. Quantrill took the only evasive action he could.

A hovercycle's fans were designed to give gyroscopic stability and a low center of gravity as well, so they were heavy enough to continue free-wheeling for several seconds after the engine stopped. This feature was a real bacon-saver when an engine seized while the cycle was waist high over deep water or broken countryside. You came down quickly, but you had time to get ready. Quantrill needed two seconds to release his harness and a third to roll out of the cockpit. By this time the cycle was bouncing not far from the lip of the ravine, rebounding from a long limestone outcrop. Quantrill scrambled into the shadow of the outcrop as his vehicle crashed onto its side and rolled over with what seemed agonizing slowness.

Then silence, broken only by faint pings as the engine began to cool. Quantrill replayed the attack in his head and knew that the slug through his windscreen had come from his right. That meant the ambush had not been set in the ravine, but from the flat prairie above it. The ravine was a possible escape route, then—but he did not enjoy giving up the high ground and would have to cross several meters of open territory. The outcrop stretched for five meters parallel to the ravine but was not high enough to let him rise to his knees. He could not reach into the inverted cockpit to toggle the VHF set for help without exposing himself as a clear target. If only he had brought a weapon!

Well, he had, after a fashion. The Nelson rifle and its tranquilizers lay in his cargo pannier with the beer. That pannier hatch lay almost within arm's reach. He inched out from the limestone, hoping he was hidden by the inverted cycle, ducking back expecting more gunfire. Nothing.

He slid on his belly again, reached the pannier hatch, and opened it. Instantly, a distant burst of fire hammered a half dozen slugs into the cycle and Quantrill rolled back to the outcrop. Success, and fresh trouble, too; the rifle fell from the open hatch onto the ground, but now diesel fuel began to gurgle into the engine compartment and to trickle from there to the dirt. Snaking one arm out to retrieve the rifle, Quantrill saw his last bulb of Pearl near the hatch lip. Like an idiot, he had brought no other drinkables, depending on the filter straw in his survival kit for water on the open range. And that kit was still strapped into the cockpit. Like the VHF set, it might as well be half a world away.

A single shot impacted somewhere on the cycle. Now the stink of diesel fuel was rank in his nostrils, ten gallons of it at least, and if the damned cycle caught fire, he would be showered with blazing liquid when the tank blew. He shrugged his jacket off, poked the barrel of the rifle against it, then eased it forward as he crawled along the base of the outcrop away from the cycle. The jacket did not draw fire until he had crawled to the end of the outcrop, but whoever it was, the sharpshooter was quick and accurate. Quantrill reviewed his options furiously.

It was almost noon, getting hotter, and if that fuel caught fire, his next move should be a fast scramble over the lip of the ravine, guns or no guns. That might involve another scramble down the steep ravine, and it might begin with a fall; he could not tell how far. And a compound leg fracture meant a slow and nasty death. If he stayed healthy until dark, his chances of escape were excellent. But that meant lying half in sunlight for hours with no water. Quantrill knew he sweated more than most, knew also that a single afternoon in a baking sun could send him through the classic stages of dehydration. By dusk, his tormentor could simply walk up and shoot him while he lay there.

Look at the bright side, he thought. If this had happened in midsummer, the heat would have been ferocious; deadly. And he'd been hydrating himself with low-alcohol beer, and with luck he might get his hands on that last bulb in the cycle pannier. But not if those fumes caught fire. He poked the jacket out again, drew one round that spanged off the hardpan, and crawled quickly back to the overturned cycle. Now he was sweating from his efforts in the heat and studied the ground carefully before reaching for that spare pannier. The cycle's roll bar elevated the vehicle enough for a sharpshooter to see him crawling under it. He wished for a long stick, then sighed, cursed, and crawled back to retrieve the Nelson rifle.

With the compressed gas cylinder and the fat tranquilizer darts removed from its hollow stock, the rifle was not too heavy to hold extended with one hand. Quantrill gripped the stock with his right hand, his chin buried in caliche dirt, and eased the barrel out to nudge that little plastic bulb of beer. The confounded thing rolled back and forth but would not drop out.

His wrist was tiring, and someone must have seen movement, for the next fire was a rapid series that sent slugs into the dirt beneath the cycle and dust into Quantrill's eyes. Then he did what he should have done first: hauled the rifle in, replaced the gas cylinder, and fired through the air space beneath the cycle. He did not have a dart in the chamber, but the sound of it was convincing enough.

He counted thirty before another round hit the cycle. That suggested his return fire, harmless though it was, had caused the sniper to duck. He recharged the rifle's plenum, poked its barrel under the cycle, and triggered it again. The next instant, he scrambled furiously to the pannier, snatched the little bulb of Pearl, and rolled away again. It gained him a pint of fluid and a conversation.

"Toss out the shotgun," said an amplified voice in Texas accents. Those little loud-hailer trumpets could send a voice a long way.

Time was when Quantrill would have done as he was told, the sooner to face his enemies at close range—perhaps the sooner to bring into play a set of reflexes and martial arts techniques that the average waddie could not comprehend until he had seen them used. But that was Quantrill's risky option, one that he tended to avoid more as he thought more of "settling down." The hell of it was, when you've spent years getting comfortable with the risky options, any conservative option can be an unfamiliar game that you play badly. He faced the "less is more" paradox, and understanding it did not help him subdue it.

Quantrill cursed himself for avoiding the high-risk route, heard the man repeat his demand, made no reply. The Nelson's gas cylinder showed enough charge for another dozen loud reports, and so far it had been the only reply he needed. If that bushwhacker made a charge, Quantrill could get a dart into the chamber in time for one close-up shot. If two of them came firing at once, Quantrill was in very thick yogurt. Still, this was not wartime; few men cared to take such risks against a trespasser with—Quantrill smiled in spite of himself—a shotgun.

The loud-hailer again: "You're pinned on Garner land and we've called for help, *pocho*." The term implied a cowpoke of the border variety. Evidently they had no idea who lay behind that limestone outcrop. But the next announcement brought a silent curse from Quantrill, for it bore a different voice.

"We got shade and you ain't. Come out now and there'll be no more shooting. Or bake awhile. Suit yourself." So there were at least two of the bastards.

Where the hell was his Aussie hat? Nowhere he could see. Quantrill buttoned the sleeves of his shirt, then used a forefinger to wipe sweat from his brow and sucked his finger for the salt sweat. Every drop lost was a nail in his coffin; every bit of exertion, every minute of sun on his noggin tallied points against him. He crawled to the other end of the outcrop slowly, listening for footsteps, and drew the waist of the jacket over his head, folding a sleeve under his chin. He counted his five tranquilizer darts, restowed three in the stock. One went into the chamber, the last he placed on a stone to keep it out of the caliche dust.

And there he lay for an hour by his watch. The midday heat was stifling now, and when the distant sound of a hovercycle coughed into action, he was almost dozing. He was alert enough to realize they might be waiting for his reaction to the noise; he tossed the jacket to the top of his low outcrop behind him as a decoy. He was slow coming to his feet, but an instant was all he needed before flopping down again. A rattle of fire passed near the jacket, which he retrieved with his rifle barrel. And *still* he could not spot his enemies, except for one man accelerating away down a slight depression, two hundred meters distant. How many were left?

Time to try finding out. "Now it's just you and me, back-shooter," Quantrill called.

"Two against one suits us fine," came the reply, then two bursts of fire. Well, it had been worth a try. Two men up on the prairie—or one smart one. Quantrill tried to deny his headache but knew it was an early sign of dehydration. He opened the bulb of beer and drank it all. From his days with S & R he knew there was no point in saving drinkables when you were suffering from lack of the stuff. You hydrated yourself as much as possible and tried not to generate sweat.

He settled down again, using the jacket for headgear and chinrest. If these were Garner men, and *if* they'd been lying about help, perhaps the one on the cycle had gone to get help. That implied they had no radio. Two hours to the ranch HQ, a bit over two hours back unless they had a chopper; Quantrill could expect a showdown by sunset.

He started to spit a mouthful of cottony fluff, then remembered and swallowed it. Now and then, a singleton round sang overhead or spatted into the cycle. That tactic bore several messages: they were alert; it would be suicide to try for the VHF toggle; and they had enough ammo to waste it.

At least the diesel fumes were not so strong now. He recited an old service ditty, "Lady Luck She Is a Fickle

Bitch,'' in his head. He might be running a fever now, complete with headache and cottonmouth, but by taking care in that semidesert sun, he was still clear-headed enough to think. So think!

He was still licking his own sweat; a good sign. When you quit sweating, your dehydration was well and truly advanced. He'd spotted a bark-hided lizard—locals called it a ''boomer'' —touring the edge of his outcrop, but it kept clear of him. It wasn't poisonous and it was full of body fluid, and if it got within reach, he fully intended to do what the Apaches did: bite in like Dracula and suck the poor critter dry. It wasn't as disgusting as the idea of becoming delirious out here in a single afternoon, as many a good man had done before.

Keep thinking! Their firepower was overwhelming, and they'd sent a lot of rounds under the cycle in a hurry; yet they hadn't hit him once. They could have tried flanking him and hadn't. If they weren't plain cowards, maybe they really didn't want him dead. If they'd been drugrunners, they would have kept out of sight to begin with; either that, or they'd have taken their chances and flanked him early. Chances were that these were Garner waddies, ordinary ranch hands. Yes, that fitted the patterns. Good thinking. Too goddamn bad he hadn't given more candlepower to thinking about weapons when he'd set out on this infernal idiotic quest that was hardly less stupid than Wardrop's, rot his soul. Jee-*zus*, but his head ached. *Come just a little closer, Mr. boomer lizard, and I'll explain all about vampires.* He laughed to himself, a little dizzily, and then he slept.

He did not wake when a slug sent a light shower of dirt onto his back. Nor when the sun slid down to peer under his improvised headgear, blistering the bridge of his nose. Nor when the lizard flickered across in front of him, within easy reach. What woke him was the sound of hovercycles.

CHAPTER THIRTY-NINE • • •

He'd known worse headaches, but couldn't recall when; could not recall anything very clearly, to admit the worst to himself. At least he knew he was impaired, so maybe using the jacket for shade had kept him from delirium. And now the breeze was almost cool on his blazing cheeks, and the sun was sinking into the near horizon.

Several cycles had just moved in; maybe three, from the sounds of them. He was in no condition to leap up for a fast visual check. He made himself crawl back toward his overturned cycle, more as a physical test than anything else. Dizziness, a headache that threatened to pop the top of his skull off like a champagne cork, physical weakness, and a desire to give up: all, for Quantrill, extraordinary signs.

The loud-hailer sought him again. "All right, *pocho*, we're sending men down under the bluffs behind you." A bluff was a low cliff—but cliffs could be climbed, and the man might be lying anyhow. "We got nightscopes for us, and flares for you, in case you're waiting for dark. Couple of flares into that cycle of yours will ruin your whole day. Or would you rather come out before that? You won't be hurt 'less you do something stupid."

Quantrill kept silent, playing for time. In another half hour, the shadows might be deep enough to cover a vertical descent. Or might not; whatthehell, whatthehell, he was too dizzy to care. . . .

"On the other hand, maybe you're played out already, and Mul Garner wouldn't like to know we done that to you, so in that case we'd just as soon burn the cycle and you with it. If you don't want the Fourth of July around you—better sing out."

Quantrill kept quiet until he heard a sound like a wet bag

popping, then saw a green fireball arc through a sunset sky the hue of beaten copper. It hit the caliche twenty meters from the fuel-soaked area and fragmented before burnout. No harm done, but if they kept that up, sooner or later they were bound to flush him from cover. He stuck the Nelson's muzzle over the outcrop and fired it. Then he called out. "You want boosted slugs from this scattergun? Just use those flares again."

They already thought he had a shotgun, and boosted buckshot from a smoothbore could take you out from two hundred meters. And anybody who triggered a flaregun gave his position away to the world at large. They could not be certain he was pinned down too low to spot them. So far, so good; but before long it would be dark, and they would be wondering why his "shotgun" blasts did not emit any muzzle flash. Especially if he were supposedly using ammo with a second-stage boost just beyond the muzzle. No, he had worked that coldgas rifle scam for just about all it was worth. He stowed all the spare darts in the rifle's hollow stock and decided he still might use it. The man it hit, with a load of tranquilizer gauged for a big horse, would never be revived.

The sun was dipping below the horizon now, even as a hovercycle thrummed away somewhere off to his right, seeking a way down into that steep narrow valley. These people seemed to have little stomach for risk, and perhaps they really did prefer not to whack him out, given their druthers. But with several men surrounding him, he would soon be flushed without a safe exit.

A long sliver of shadow swept up over Quantrill, and with sudden clarity he realized what he would've known before if not for this skull-splitting headache and sun-induced fever. His pursuers were looking more or less into the sun and might not see a stealthy low form crawling to the lip of the ravine. In another minute or so the sun would be gone, and moments later their vision would be much improved. He might have a better chance later—but this was the only one he'd had yet, with any appeal.

He took it. Slowly, sliding backward, feeling with his toes as he went. If someone did see him and take a shot, at worst he would be hit in the leg.

He did not hear the pop but saw his world lit from behind with an artificial crimson glow; remained perfectly still as the red flare, fired from somewhere down in the ravine, spent its fury overhead and died in the air. He began his slow progress again now, moving as an angler moves near a trout pool, each motion so drawn out that it seemed no motion at all. He paused, hearing a single rifle report, then realized that the round had struck his cycle. At least one sniper was looking in his direction but shooting several meters wide. He hoped it meant that no one had seen him sliding out on his belly in a sunset that was now the color of blood, feet first into the open, pulling the Nelson rifle behind him.

Now he lay completely exposed, turning the rifle so that it lay mostly under him, its muzzle safely beyond his nose. If he could haul the rifle down into the ravine with him, he just might liberate himself a hovercycle with it.

Then, horrifyingly near, another loud-hailer: "He's goin' over the lip, Longo!" Someone had moved far to Quantrill's left, almost to the ravine. He probably had a weapon as well, and he had finally seen his quarry's stealthy movements.

No time to consider it. Quantrill burst into a backward crawl, feeling his feet and legs protrude out into nothingness, and let go of the rifle as he braced his arms to take his weight. The man who'd seen him obviously saw that he couldn't shoot back after committing to the lip of the bluff. No question about it now: the bluff was a ragged drop-off.

Quantrill heard footsteps pounding toward him, looked over his right shoulder, saw that he hung over a vertical drop as high as a two-story house. Below that, stony ground angled away at a forty-five-degree angle toward thick brush in the throat of the ravine. He found a foothold; lowered himself enough to get his head below the ravine lip; located crevices for his hands and lowered himself two meters before the footsteps paused above him. The man was too cautious to poke his head over the edge.

"He's gone," called the man, not using the loud-hailer and not needing to. Someone called a reply. Another green flare hurtled up over the ravine, and Quantrill, looking down into the shadowy depths, saw a ledge of caliche which the flare had tinted a ghastly shade of bile green. The ledge was the width of his hand. Standing on that ledge, a man might drop to the slope and then into cover without breaking every bone in his employ. He found two more footholds, heard someone shout from below, and dropped onto the ledge.

Caliche is rotten stuff for compression loads. The ledge crumbled instantly, and Quantrill smashed both elbows against what was left of it on his way past. The impacts checked his fall but turned him slightly, and then he struck the steep slope at a hopeless angle, cartwheeling, hands outthrust to protect his head. He never saw the ragged hunk of caliche that powdered against his skull just above his left eye, and after that gigantic white flare burst inside his head he saw nothing at all.

CHAPTER FORTY • • •

Familiar pain . . . faint pressures of hands exploring his body . . . blankness . . . splash of lovely cool wet stuff. Vaguely, Quantrill knew he was swallowing water.

Bits of talk from several male voices.

"Nothin' broke that I can tell."

"Beats me why the sumbitch ain't in more pieces than a china doll."

A deep low voice: "He will be, if I know Jer."

"I seen this one someplace, Billy Ray. Rocksprings, maybe."

"Well, take his feet, goddammit; you expect me to tote him th'u this brush and shit all by myself?"

Rough handling then, not vicious but clumsy, and a slow passage through foliage as tough as an acre of wire brush. Then curses, grunts, and cushions under his butt. The aft cockpit of a cycle, perhaps. A wave of nausea, then blankness again.

Later, Quantrill realized he was trussed and in a safety harness as a diesel thrummed in the chassis; headlights swept across him from time to time from a following cycle, and a cool wind fanned his face as they proceeded in darkness. When they stopped for a break, he managed with a struggle to sit up. They gave him more water, and a strip of salt jerked meat to chew. Against all odds, he still had teeth to chew it with.

"I think you're gonna make it, *pocho*," said one of his captors, half in wonder. The man was roughly Quantrill's age and, checking the swelling on his captive's forehead, clucked to himself. "You hearing any of this?"

Quantrill nodded, and thought his head would roll off onto the ground.

"What do they call you?"

Quantrill croaked the first thing that came into his head: "Sam Coulter. More water. . . ."

From nearby, the strong deep voice: "Watch the fucker, L. J., he might sandbag you."

"And him hogtaped like this? Ease up, Longo, I'm just givin' him water." Quantrill took the canteen, his wrists taped together, and savored a full quart of it.

From what little he could see in the multiple glows of running lights, Quantrill estimated there were five of them; taciturn hired hands, men he had perhaps nodded to at Saturday dances or on the streets of Rocksprings. At least, none of them seemed to know his name.

"Gettin' on to eight o'clock," said the leader, the one others called Longo. "If that radio of yours is fixed, Billy Ray, call Concannon. Tell him we're an hour out." He mashed a cigarette underfoot, drew on his gloves, and swung into the forward cockpit of the lead cycle. Quantrill kept the canteen and managed during the next ten minutes to empty it without heaving any water up. He had been thoroughly bound with the modern cowpoke's standby, filament tape, his upper arms bound to his sides. He could not get his wrists anywhere near his teeth, and the effort was exhausting. He tried to stay awake but eventually slept again.

He woke in a modern, well-lit equipment barn as his captors were stowing their cycles. His driver, the wiry young man they called L. J., freed him from the harness, cut the tape at his ankles, and helped him stagger onto a cement floor. Then they prodded him forward, out the folding doors into a packed-earth yard bathed by an overhead sodium-yellow light. Standing alone, fists on his hips as he studied the latecomers, Cam Concannon shook his head as he looked into Quantrill's face.

Longo, the one with the resonant basso and a barrel chest to push it, jerked a thumb toward the captive. "Says his name's Sam Coulter. Poking around where that S & R crew picked up the limey."

Concannon's eyes flickered. "Coulter, huh? That's a good name, I reckon. Well, Mr. Coulter, you got some explaining to do." He turned to the other men, considering his words carefully. "You boys find fencecutters on him? Any brush-popper hardware?"

Quantrill stood there, weaving a bit, shaking the kinks from his legs as the men made their report. They'd found very little to suggest more than simple trespass. It seemed they had taken a careful look around his cycle. Billy Ray, it turned out, had brought the vet kit and the Nelson rifle along as evidence.

"This damn rifle of his sounded like a twelve-gauge, but it's just one of them vet guns. He coulda been tryin' to knock over a few beeves," Longo rumbled.

"Oh, sure," Concannon said, running a hand through his hair as he considered the idea. "Nothing to skin a beef, not even a balisong or fencecutters; how the hell was he gonna dress out anything more than a few steaks and get over a Garner fence with it?"

"I could've told them," Quantrill began, "but the first warning I had—"

Not loud, but fierce: "You shut the fuck up, Coulter," said Concannon. "You're a major pain in my ass. Think more and talk less 'til I get you in front of the old man." His gaze augered into Quantrill's. It said a little about fairness and a lot about caution when talking among these men. Quantrill sighed and brought up his hands to show the tape at his wrists.

"I see it," said Concannon, and laughed. "Hell, I ordered it. Damn good thing you didn't bag any Garner hands out there, or the tape coulda gone over your nose and mouth, too." Asphyxiation was a terrible way to die; as bad, perhaps, as the death of the skins. The foreman was telling him, as clearly as he could, that on Garner land a rough judgment might be followed up by summary execution.

And there were still more judgments to be made.

Quantrill had few illusions about that; he had already made a rough match between the deep-chested Longo and some records he'd studied in Junction. If he had carried his wallet with him, they'd have known his name immediately—and Longo might've whacked him on the spot. Maybe that was why Concannon was pretending to buy the "Sam Coulter" charade.

After a few more questions, and praising the men for a job well done, Concannon told them the cook was waiting with peach cobbler and waited until Longo had followed the others away into distant shadows. Then, with a shove on Quantrill's shoulder, the foreman aimed him toward the main house.

CHAPTER FORTY-ONE • • •

A big rectangular two-story pile of quarried limestone, Mul Garner's home loomed out of the dark, solid as some medieval fortress, its upper windows lit like hollow eye sockets. The place seemed all of a century old, with ornate woodwork tracing the eaves of its broad wooden porch. A tangle of rosebushes, all evidently dead of neglect, flanked the porch like barbed wire. The house might stand for centuries more, but the porch had seen better days.

"I'll just keep the tape on 'til the old man sees you this way. You need all the sympathy you can get, Quantrill." It was the first time Cam Concannon had indicated their earlier acquaintance. "I told you before, you and me never met."

"Right."

Concannon knocked, waited a moment, then opened first the screen door and then the big wooden door with a squall of hinges that had forgotten the taste of oil. Inside, the hallway floor was honest oak, innocent of covering, scarred from generations of men wearing spurs—some with Spanish rowels, to judge from the dotted scars. A broad staircase angled down to the big hallway, but Concannon steered his prisoner into a library the size of a bunkhouse. No, it was a parlor, but one built to entertain whole families. It spoke in a hollow voice musty with age of quilting bees and tired ranchers toasting their boot soles before a great fireplace that now yawned cold and blackened between bookshelves at one side of the room.

"We brung him in, Mr. Garner," the foreman called, mocked by echoes in two corners where antique floor lamps lit the recesses with rawhide lampshades. "In the sittin' room." He turned; saw Quantrill sniffing the air. "Them goddam Cuban cigars of his," he said with rough affection.

176

"They don't do his emphysema no good, but . . ." He finished with a shrug.

Quantrill, toeing the enormous hooked rug underfoot: "Nice old place."

Concannon, guiltily: "Needs fixin'. When the missus was alive she kept me fartin' around here a day a week. But I can't be ever'place at once." He looked up, as if he could see through the high ceiling, following creaks of footsteps above. As the steps began to move down the staircase he added, "Wild Country Safari don't even know who-all's on its payroll, it's that big. They could have a dozen Sam Coulters for all I know, but you got your ownself into this, and your story's your problem."

Quantrill nodded silently, knowing that spoken thanks would be rejected. This way, Concannon could deny—even to himself—that he was helping this troublemaker.

The old rancher who stepped into the room had once been a giant of a man. Even with the big shoulders stooped he stood well over six feet in the western boots that poked out from worn denims, his turned-up sleeves revealing the corded forearms of a man who had wrestled many a fencepost into its socket. But from all appearances, Mul Garner no longer spent his days in the sun. He was pale, with a mane of white hair and sideburns he probably trimmed himself. His eyes were pale too, a piercing light blue of a color sometimes seen in Siamese cats.

Concannon stepped away from Quantrill; smiled half in apology like a disappointed hunter. "This is what the boys brung in, Mr. Garner."

But the old man—not so very old in years, though he had not been kind to his body—was already staring at Quantrill. "Goda'mighty, Cam, how dangerous can he *be*?" He took Quantrill by one arm, looked at the livid bruise with blood now dried and cracking near Quantrill's left temple. Speaking now to Quantrill, pacing his words with the short breaths of a man with half the lungs he should have: "My foreman carries that hogleg forty-four, 'cause he can use it. I want your word he won't need to."

"I won't cause trouble," said Quantrill, with the faintest stress on the word "cause."

"Already did," said Mul Garner, and passed his hand

across his leather vest. A flash of brass and polished bone, a flick, and the rancher had opened his balisong, the long-bladed Philippine equivalent of a switchblade.

Quantrill started to pivot, merely from reflex action; then stopped, realizing the rancher intended only to cut his bindings. Garner stood still and sucked a tooth for a moment. "I don't cause trouble either, young fella. And I only settle it when I have to."

"Sorry, sir. It's been a long day," Quantrill said wearily, and let the man slice the tape from his arms and wrists.

Garner was laughing to himself, a soft wheeze punctuated by deep breaths, as he stepped back and flicked the balisong shut with another sleight of hand. "You have a gift for understatement, judging from that goose egg on your forehead." He watched Quantrill rub his wrists, running his eyes over the trespasser. Judging. He chose a suede-covered chair, its back as high as a throne, settled into it as the others followed. Quantrill did not sit, because Concannon did not. "Let's have it, then; your name and story and whatever lame excuse you might have."

Long ago in army intelligence, Quantrill had taken crash courses in language; had never been sorry for it. Mul Garner kept the cadence and twang of Wild Country but had developed a wider range of pitch changes. His phrases were those of a man who might have acted in college plays, or perhaps he simply read as widely as Sandy. Perhaps a man with a romantic streak who would understand peculiar quests.

By now, Quantrill had a story ready. He was Sam Coulter, part-timer with WCS, he said; ex-army, now considering a career as a veterinarian with exotic game. "There's a Brit lieutenant who claims he ran up against the biggest boar in the solar system out here a day or so ago," he went on, "and I got curious. A boar like that would be worth more alive than dead, I thought." To himself, he added that it wouldn't hurt Ba'al's chances if Garner got the same idea.

Concannon: "That tallies. He was out near Faithful Creek on a WCS cycle with a vet's kit and a rifle that shoots hypos." A sudden grin, then, "Kept Billy Ray and L. J. pinned down for hours, told 'em it was a shotgun with boosted ammo."

"It's louder when you discharge it without a load," Quantrill chipped in. That told Garner he hadn't shot to kill.

Mul Garner had heard nothing of Wardrop's folly and spent five minutes questioning Concannon, irritated to find that an S & R crew had answered an emergency on his land without his knowledge. Turning again to Quantrill: "This is the dumbest goddamn story I *ever* heard, Coulter. Might as well go after a Brahma bull with a willow switch."

"That's what everybody told the Brit."

"It applies to you, too. I know that damn hog's been on my spread for years, and I know what he's done. Live and let live, I say. Even if you knocked him out with a hypo, how on God's brown prairie did you expect to haul him back to WCS on a two-man cycle?"

Quantrill told the truth: "I only figured on fixing him up, if he was hurt like the Brit said."

Garner sat back, shaking his white mane. "And make him your pet? Was that the idea?"

"Something like that."

"He'd eat your lunch and save you for supper, Coulter. They didn't name that hog 'Ba'al' for nothing. He's a devil incarnate. I can't keep you from hunting him entirely, but I sure as hell don't want him munchin' your bones on my spread. And trespassers do tend to get shot in these parts. Do I have your word you won't cross my fencelines again?"

Somewhere inside Mul Garner, amusement was bubbling to get out. Quantrill saw that the man considered him little more than a harmless ass. In some ways, Quantrill agreed. It was hard not to agree with, and not to like, the rancher. "My word on it, Mr. Garner," said Quantrill.

Concannon said respectfully, "I reckon cookie can build him a sandwich and I can drive him far as Rocksprings tonight, if you want."

"If you would, Cam. You might steer him to disinfectant and a bandage, while you're at it." The rancher reached to a squat, hand-carved table and flicked the top from a cedar box. "But I haven't heard how you got bashed up, Coulter, and I intend to. While you humor me, you fellas might join me." With that, he withdrew three big green cigars and offered two to the others.

It was hard to tell whether Concannon's sigh was for the

cigars or for the wasted time. Quantrill accepted this symbol of hospitality and took a chair when he was told to. He was thirsty again, and full of aches. The cigar, he found, was the least offensive stogie he had ever lit.

Quantrill was in the act of admitting he did not know how he struck his forehead in his fall when he heard a screen door, somewhere in the back of the house, complete its shallow skritch and bang. He paused, hearing several sets of footsteps.

"That'll be my boy," said Garner.

"I thought it might," said Concannon. The foreman's expression was carefully noncommittal.

CHAPTER FORTY-TWO • • •

Jerome Garner moved with studied machismo, slapping a Stetson against expensive whipcord breeches as he entered the parlor. He was one of those men with the kind of presence that fills a room. Quantrill recognized the other two men as Longo and Billy Ray. Jerome made a showy, unnecessary gesture seating a holstered forty-five-caliber automatic more firmly on his thigh. Jerome tossed his hat into a chair. Without a by-your-leave, he crossed to the cigar box with a few long strides, tossed cigars to his cronies, unwrapped one for himself.

Jerome Garner had already glanced at Quantrill, who was partly in shadow, before turning to his father. "Just got in from the south end, Pop. I hear the boys nailed a—" He then did a very slow, almost casual, double take; lit the cigar and squatted so that his nose was within two feet of Quantrill's. "Well," he said, smiling, savoring it as he drawled, "as I live and breathe and kick ass, look who we have here." He straightened to his full height and chuckled at the impassive Quantrill.

Mul Garner looked up at his strapping son with fondness, perhaps seeing himself across the years. He was smiling at first, but saw something in Jerome's face that brought a crease to his forehead. To Jerome: "You know young Coulter?"

"Yeah. I know him." A luxurious smoke ring curled from Jerome Garner's mouth. "He's one of those fat-cat deputy marshals out of Junction and his name's not Coulter."

Quantrill met the old man's gaze and nodded. No point in telling them he was now an ex-deputy; in fact, with the memory of Judge Placidas's dying statement ringing in his ears, Quantrill thought it might be better to let them think he was still on the force. "They call me Coulter sometimes," he said, half in truth. "My real name's Ted Quantrill."

Silence, discounting the provocation of Jerome Garner's repeated chuckle. Then, from the old rancher: "Thought your face looked familiar. You fought with the rebs; did a holo broadcast with Jim Street. Made quite a splash with Street's paramilitary people, as I recall." His face troubled now, Mul Garner put the cigar aside. "Jerome, send your men back to their poker game," he said quietly.

Without hesitation Jerome said, "Wait on the porch, boys." As the two waddies moved to the front door, Quantrill saw something very like a silent plea in the face of the elder Garner, but only grim pleasure in the reply. "This is a slick one, Pop. Regular little weasel. See that dark circle on his sleeve? S'posed to be a Department of Justice patch there. And if that wasn't bad enough, he's the one helping out on Sandra Grange's pissy little spread."

The father: "Don't bad-mouth your neighbors, Jerome."

The son: "Don't tell me what to do, Pop."

Concannon: "Easy, Jer, he's your daddy."

Jerome: "You're not, Cam. Fuck you."

Mul Garner stood up to face his son, and Quantrill was reminded of the dominance ploy of Ba'al. Perhaps Jerome Garner gave you no respect unless your eyes were higher than his. The old man nearly qualified, though he no longer stood as straight as he once had. "Jerome, how many men have you hired on, who use names they weren't born with?"

Jerome shrugged carelessly and waved the question away. "I don't know and I don't care. I shit-sure care why he's snoopin' on my—our land."

Quantrill told him.

Another mirthless chuckle, studying the ash on his cigar. Then Jerome turned to his father. "Playin' doctor to a fuckin' killer hog? You really believe that, Pop? Well, let me tell you what I think. *I* think this little stud has a hard-on for a piece of land. *I* think he'd like to marry into it; yeah, the Grange spread. And her fenceline is smack against ours, and if he could figure a way to frame a neighbor on some trumped-up charge, he might be in position to get more land in exchange for droppin' those charges. That's what I think." He jerked a thumb toward the foreman. "I think Cam knew who he was all the time. How 'bout it, Cam: didn't you loan Sandra Grange a van for this goddamn deputy to drive?''

"Couldn't say," Concannon replied, and glanced innocently at Quantrill. "Was you the fella in Miz Grange's soddy?"

"That's right," said Quantrill, endorsing the evasion. "I'm also the guy who spent half a Saturday rounding up spare parts near Corpus for Garner Ranch."

Jerome Garner felt the reins slipping from his grasp and seized them quickly. "I don't give a good shit about that, but I been watching you suck up to Sandra Grange, weaseling in next to what's mine—"

"And cuttin' Miz Grange out from your remuda of fillies, Jer?" Cam Concannon spoke softly, but the truth had a cutting edge of its own.

"You're lookin' for a fat lip," said Jerome furiously, and took a step toward the foreman.

But also toward the seated Quantrill, who came up, poised on the balls of his feet, at the ready. He hurt all over, and was now running on reserve energy, but he had seen Jerome Garner operate before at Saturday dances. The big bastard liked to crowd you. In his present condition, Quantrill could not afford to take the big man lightly.

Mul Garner reached for his son's arm and simultaneously began with: "Cam, don't push him, you know how—" But Jerome, with his free hand, flicked his cigar hard toward Quantrill's face from a double arm span away.

Quantrill's open-handed wave batted the cigar down and, without pausing to consider it, he responded in kind. The glowing end of the stogie caught Jerome at the throat, sent sparks showering under his chin.

Jerome wrenched his arm free from his father's grip, brushing with both hands at his neck, then pointed a trembling finger at Quantrill. "I'll teach you to do that when I got one hand pinned."

"Be reasonable, Jer," said Mul Garner, kicking the live cigar toward the fireplace.

"Never start until you're ready," Quantrill said to the pointing finger as calmly as he could.

"You're courtin' trouble," said the old rancher to Quantrill.

"You and me goin' to knuckletown, little man. Outside," said Jerome, pointing toward the porch.

Mul Garner lifted one hand; let it fall against his leg. "I can't let you do this, Jerome."

"You'll play hell stopping me, Pop. He asked for this. And if he tries to run for it, I'll tell the boys to shoot to kill."

"They're Jer's men more'n his daddy's," Concannon said.

"That's a fact," added Mul Garner. "My mistake. At least give me the Colt, Jer." Jerome made that one small concession, dropping the nickel-plated sidearm onto a chair cushion.

In another time, Quantrill would have forced the issue then and there, in the room, which offered several advantages. But the parlor would have ended as a shambles. He waved the big man ahead of him. "I'd hate to get shot coming out the door," he said.

Jerome Garner marched out to the dimly lit porch, pulling thin leather gloves from a hip pocket. They gave him still another advantage. The two men outside turned expectantly. He let the main door swing open, held the frame of the exterior screen door until Quantrill was passing through, then kicked the frame hard.

Ted Quantrill would have been surprised if that door *hadn't* been used as a weapon. He moved sideways, with a sudden change of pace so that the wooden frame banged harmlessly shut, and let his shoulders slide along the stone wall.

Jerome was already hurtling forward to catch his victim staggering from the door, off-balance as he swung one pointed boot at groin height.

Quantrill was not there; the wall was. A working waddie has low broad heels for everyday wear, but Jerome was more rider than worker and fancied the tapered high boot heels that added two inches to a man's elevation. As one boot caromed off the limestone wall, he bent backward to catch his balance. In that position, wearing "show-off" boots, he could be literally spun on one narrow heel. Quantrill's caulked sole caught the big man behind his lifted thigh, began the spin Jerome himself had set in motion; kept it going with an elbow in his kidney.

Jerome Garner grunted, fell sidelong, and Quantrill elected not to follow him down. The truth is, Quantrill hoped to put Garner out of action with a kick to the solar plexus. Garner had made it clear that his only rule was "win," starting with a flung cigar, and he started out on his home turf with huge advantages in height, weight, and reach. In Quantrill's position, it was a disadvantage even knowing how to *spell* Marquis of Queensbury.

But Jerome anticipated that kick, rolled to the steps, saw that he was clear, and bounced up without a pause. Now he took a boxer's stance. Left-handed. Quantrill recalled that Garner had snaked the forty-five out of its holster with his right; as a wrong-hander himself, he knew the devastating effectiveness of an unexpected change-up. Yet Garner was not especially quick.

"You're no southpaw," Quantrill said, breaking his usual rule about silence in a fight, and made himself smile. Garner's only reply was to shift into a comfortable right-handed stance, sticking his left out, but he did it without haste. That was what the smaller man had hoped.

Quantrill was in and under that left guard instantly, its wrist gripped in his own left hand, his knees bent, right shoulder down to belt level, his right foot planted between Garner's as he turned away, straightened his legs, and lifted on the man's belt. Garner's right fist caught him hard behind the ear, but the big man's feet were high in the air by this time.

Quantrill kept his hold, forming a pivot over which Garner flew, and helped his momentum by pushing off with both feet. Garner hit the porch flat on his back with a splintering crash, the smaller man flipping over with him, Quantrill's right hand sinking into his enemy's belly with most of his weight behind it. Most men would have been paralyzed by this blow to the solar plexus.

But Quantrill, trying to continue his roll, felt his hair grabbed in a big paw; was flung into the stone wall face first. He heard and felt the septum crunch; it was not the first time Quantrill's nose had been broken—but it was not a thing you got used to.

Without looking, Quantrill pushed away from the wall with both hands, dodging to one side. That is why Garner's kick, with both feet, only propelled him farther and spasmed his thigh muscle instead of breaking his leg. Quantrill went down on one knee, stuck the other leg out to quell the horrendous cramp, then watched Garner struggle to his feet, doubled over, mouth open as he fought to breathe. The big man needed another ten seconds before his diaphragm would draw air but mustered the energy for another rush, trying to drive Quantrill off the porch into the tangle of rose thickets. One hand still across his belly, Garner flung the other gloved fist in a sweeping backhand that might have shattered a man's jaw.

To give Garner his due, he had never faced an opponent whose synapses were off the normal scale of human responses. Quantrill rolled onto his back, lashed out savagely with his good leg, and caught Garner at the upper end of his shinbone. It was a miss, for Quantrill was starting to think in terms of permanent disabling techniques and had aimed at his kneecap. It was not a miss that Garner could enjoy much. With his first gasping intake of breath in too long, the big man reeled, both arms wide to keep his balance. Quantrill came up squatting, leaped up to plant one foot for a disabling kick, and ducked as a clod of hard dirt whizzed past his face to spatter against limestone.

He would never know who threw the clod; only that Mul Garner stood in the doorway shouting, "Next man who interferes can draw his wages!"

With a growling whine of desperation, the younger Garner used this tiny lapse of Quantrill's concentration, falling on him with a bear hug. Quantrill felt his feet leave the porch, butted upward against the big man's chin, and felt himself swung in a great arc as one would swing a child. When his feet struck the limestone wall he simply pushed away with all his strength. Nor did he quit butting under Garner's jaw.

Then they were toppling into the rose brambles, Garner taking most of the punishment. The stuff rustled and snapped like brittle cables, driving a thousand hard spikes through cloth into their flesh as they struggled. Neither could complete a telling blow with fists, for the thorns made any sudden movement a tug of war. But Quantrill had the advantage in that the top of his head was in position to repeatedly ram under the fine manly jaw of Jerome Garner, and he rang the Garner chimes until Jerome's mouth was bleeding worse than Quantrill's nose. But the Garner clan seemed to have more stamina than sense. Jerome kept struggling.

Long ago, Quantrill had been taught to figure ways to make anything—absolutely *any*thing—into a weapon. Now, seeing a thick rope of rose stalk sag between his face and Garner's, he managed to grip it; thrust it against the big man's throat and jerked.

Jerome Garner howled like something trapped in a cave; drew another breath.

In that intake of breath Quantrill said, "Give it up."

Garner, in a crying rage: "Fuckyouman," but he was no longer slugging against Quantrill's skull.

Quantrill, pierced in a hundred places by thorns, felt as if attacked by hornets, though it hurt worse to grasp that inch-thick rose stalk. He knew Garner must be feeling the same agonies, but, "Call it quits," Quantrill said between clenched teeth, "or I'll saw your god-damned head off."

It was exactly the kind of wild exaggeration needed for a man of Jerome Garner's excesses. His hoarse sobs might have been two-thirds fury, but through them he said, "I quit, then get off me yougoddamsumbitch, YOU HEAR?"

Quantrill released the thick stalk with some difficulty; it had driven thorns into his hand in a dozen places. Silently, letting young Garner make enough noise for the both of them, he half crawled, half tumbled onto packed dirt that had once been covered with grass. He pulled at Jerome's shirt, saw his friends hurrying near, and stepped back saying, "Help yourself, the hell with it."

Cam Concannon had moved to the steps to monitor the fight's last moments. Old Mul Garner still stood near the doorway without expression until Jerome began his litany as his waddies moved in.

"Little fucker's a trained killer, *lookoutformyface!*"

Mumbling: "Let go my hair, Jer."

"I know when I'm suckered into a fight. Just wait. Now pull, *nodon't, shitfire anyhow!*"

Quantrill hobbled farther into the glow of the porch light, trying to extract thorns from his palms with his teeth.

From the old rancher on the porch: "Cam, take the man wherever he needs to go. Rocksprings clinic, if need be. I'll pay, but I don't want to see him again. Ever."

But by now Jerome was extracted from the rose thicket, and his tears were one hundred percent pustulating fury.

"Cocksuckin' deputy tried to plain *kill* me, gonna saw my head off! No knee-high pissant does that to me on my own land. Fill my hand, Billy Ray," he said, hobbling as badly as Quantrill and spitting blood.

The cowpoke hesitated, his hand on his sidearm.

"*Fill my hand,* damn you!"

Mul Garner, from the porch, only said, "Cam," and held out his hand. The foreman drew his old-fashioned peace-maker, held it by the barrel, tossed it to the rancher at the same moment Billy Ray handed his own handgun over to Jerome. Then, in a voice that had once ruled a million acres, the rancher called, "That's not how I raised you, boy."

A stream of ropy crimson spit whacked the ground from Jerome's mouth as he raised the pistol. Quantrill whirled, saw Longo menacing him from the side with a medium-caliber automatic, and waited. Jerome: "I'm not anybody's boy. Not for a long time now."

"No, I guess you're not. But you're dogmeat if you pull that trigger." Mul Garner kept his elbow cocked so that the old Colt pointed aloft but did it in a practiced and familiar way. "I taught you fairness. I never saw a sign of it tonight."

Jerome's anguish was turning him into something half man, half child. Turning to face his father, the weapon pointing downward, staring up wet-faced onto the light, he all but bawled, "You're protecting a goddamn enemy of mine, Daddy!"

"I had to. Maybe because I protected *you* too long."

Jerome, chest heaving, stared at Quantrill. "Daddy, you have to give him to me. You have to!"

"I promised him his walking papers, Jer. I'm backing it as far as I have to. That's final."

His last phrase took something out of Jerome. "It's the same as disowning me," he snarled.

"Not you, son. But I'll always disown plain murder." Mul Garner nodded toward the distant bunkhouse and lowered the handgun. "Take your men. Come back alone and we can talk when you've calmed down in an hour. Or tomorrow."

Jerome began to limp away, handing the weapon back to its owner, spitting again, speaking loudly without looking toward the porch. "Tomorrow's too late. Goddamn you, old man, got in my way once too often. You and your lickspit Concannon," he said, and spat again, flanked by his men.

Mulvihill Garner shaded his eyes, watching them retreat, the pistol hanging in his other hand. He seemed unaware of the tears that dampened his cheeks. "I wonder if I could've done it. Cam, take this little cougar off my land right now," he said, and handed the weapon back to his foreman.

Concannon hurried off into the dark for a vehicle, and Quantrill sat down on the porch steps, holding a thumb against one nostril to stanch the blood that still flowed from his nose. "I owe you a warning, Mr. Garner," he said.

Garner tossed him a kerchief the size of a small parachute. "As a man, or a deputy?"

Wiping his face: "Same thing. I really was hunting that boar, but the Justice Department could send men after your son or some of your men, one of these days."

"I'm not an idiot, Quantrill. But I've let Jerome pretty much take over this spread, and if he's abused my trust, this is no place for a deputy to flaunt a badge. Most of the men aren't as much my men as they are his. Now it's come to a head, no thanks to you. I came within an inch of turning you over to my son, you know."

"Yessir." Quantrill hawked and spat.

Pause. Then, "You really serious about the Grange girl?"

Quantrill nodded and tried to smile. His face was numb. "Maybe 'hopeless' would be a better word."

"She's a good neighbor. Maybe you'll be one, in time. Just give Jerome plenty of room, it's all I ask."

"I will, sir." Quantrill turned, got up slowly as he heard the clatter of an old diesel four-wheel-drive vehicle. He placed the bloody kerchief on the steps.

"He just needs to grow up," Mul Garner called as Quantrill walked toward the pickup. It was as near an apology as the old man could muster, and it was offered hopefully. He would not have harbored that hope if he had heard the muffled hovercycles moving out from his equipment barn without lights, moments before Concannon drove off with Ted Quantrill.

CHAPTER FORTY-THREE · · ·

The foreman had driven for ten minutes before either of the men spoke. "We're heading east," Quantrill said finally. "To Barksdale?"

"No clinic there now," Concannon grunted. "This old road will get us to Leakey." He pronounced it "Lakey" in the old way.

The pickup's lights swept a crest in the road, and for a moment they were airborne, then slamming down an incline. "You don't have to break an axle on my account," Quantrill said. His head was hurting, the nosebleed starting up again.

"Your account, hell. I'm tryin' to get us to the stretch of blacktop ahead so we can outrun a cycle. The Longo brothers got motion sensors, Quantrill." He powered the pickup through a sharp bend, expertly.

"Brothers?"

"Reeve and Clyde; Reeve was one of the two with Jer a while ago. He's a good hand. Clyde's not on the payroll; stays on the south end of the spread and don't show his face much where the old man can see him. Clyde ain't worth spit except where you get points for meanness. He's good with a gun. But so are some of the others. That's why I wanted better protection than a cycle," he said, patting the doorsill of the sturdy old pickup as it thundered through the night.

"These guys have nightscopes, too?"

"Damn right. By the way, I stuck that rifle and kit of yours into the lockbox behind us. Some of Jer's boys was takin' that in. I think L. J. was tryin' to give me a signal, but he ain't just awful long on guts. You got me between a rock an' a hard place now."

"Sorry."

"Whatthehell. I knew I'd have to make a choice one day.

190

Knew it the day Jer whupped me the second time in a row. Only thing that kept Jer in check was knowin' the quirt was ready, an' that he'd feel it the minute he took the bit in his teeth. None of this 'maybe' shit, either. Hold on,'' he added. The pickup forded a brook in a great rush and splatter of gravel, then was scrambling up an incline again.

Concannon continued, "If Jer thinks *maybe* he can get away with a thing, he'll do it for the fun of that maybe. Right now, he prob'ly thinks maybe his daddy won't jerk his bank credit even if he puts a hole in you. If anybody could afford to risk that, it's Jer.''

Quantrill spat blood out the window. "Mul Garner won't call him to account?''

"Don't matter a lot if he does. Jer's put a pile of hard cash aside the past few years. He's still doin' it. An' the way he gets it, he was purely fuckin'-A bound to get the law on him.''

Quantrill grabbed for handholds as the pickup failed to stay on the road, but there was no shoulder and no ditch—and damned near no road, for that matter. Concannon seemed to know every step of the way and found the road again, headlights sweeping wildly across the range. "Somebody should tell Jerome that if he does a stretch in Huntsville, the Justice Department might attach every cent he has in every bank account. They do that, these days,'' Quantrill said.

"Bank? When I said hard cash, I meant it. Gold Mex coins, Krugerrands, them Mormon fifty-buck pieces the Navajos uprated with turquoise—hard money.'' Another excursion into the brush and a near miss from a cedar. Concannon cursed, reversed, set out again. "Jer's like a ole brown squirrel with a holler tree. Got a stash out here someplace, nobody knows where.'' He laughed then and spat a gob that was half dust from his window. "Says he couldn't leave a track to it if he wanted to.'' Concannon bent forward over the wheel, squinting into the hostile dark.

Quantrill let the silence grow for a time, thinking, before he said, "Sounds like he was right when he said he's not anybody's boy.''

"Well, he sure-God ain't yours; he's a thirty-year-old badass kid. You want some good advice? From here on out, watch your back.''

Two minutes later, the driver said, "So far, so good. Blacktop starts up ahead; we can really make some time then." He slid the pickup around a bend, saw the mound of brush piled in the road just ahead. "Goddamn; that's new," he said, braking hard, starting to go around it.

An instant later, all of Cameron Concannon's worst suspicions were confirmed. Quantrill saw the muzzle flashes to their left; ducked below the doorsill expecting more from the right.

Concannon was slammed sideways against his passenger with the impact of the slug that passed under his left arm and into his lungs. Quantrill felt the pickup decelerate; heard the impacts of more slugs drum against the pickup body; thrust his foot against the accelerator and grabbed the steering wheel.

The pickup slewed sideways, wheels churning hard as the automatic kickdown engaged, and burst through the mound of heavy brush as Quantrill edged up to see where he was going. Now they were dragging a cedar branch under the chassis, sweeping up a great cloud of dust as the brittle cedar disintegrated beneath them.

A corner of Quantrill's mind was tallying facts, providing guesses, even while he tried to steer the pickup with Concannon slumped against him. Mul Garner had mentioned Rocksprings, but his foreman had several other options—for that matter, had taken an unlikely direction. This ambush meant that perhaps *all* the options were covered.

Counting those that had escorted him earlier, Quantrill had seen five cycles in the equipment barn. There might be at least five paths for a pickup truck across Garner Ranch, so these *cimarrones* might have only one cycle to cover each route. And if you wanted top speed from a hovercycle, cutting cross-country, you didn't load it down with two men.

That checked with the lack of fire from his right: there was probably only one man covering this unlikely exit from the ranch. Quantrill kept his head low anyway, steered the vehicle one-handed, and saw his headlights sweep across a smooth wide ribbon a hundred meters ahead. The grinding rush of foliage beneath the chassis suddenly ceased; too bad, for it had been laying down a fine dust screen to cover them, even against a nightscope. Quantrill was lucky, covering the dis-

tance to the blacktop road without decapitating a tree or
sliding into a dry wash.

Quantrill pressed the accelerator as hard as he dared, sliding up to check the rearview. He saw no lights behind them
and, without lights, a cycle could not be driven hard through
darkness in such country. He felt Concannon's weak struggles
to sit up. "I can't tell where you're hit," he said.

Concannon managed to sit up, his head flung back as he
twisted to get his hand inside his shirt. "Left side. Up high."

"Is it very bad?"

"It'll do," Concannon admitted.

Quantrill unsnapped his safety belt; felt for Concannon's
Colt without taking his eyes from the road. "Can you hit the
brakes?"

In reply, Concannon did so. Quantrill was out of the
pickup before it stopped, the old Colt ready for action, racing
to the driver's side. Concannon needed help to get his safety
belt loose and slide across the bench seat, cursing softly.
Then Quantrill had them in motion again, relieved that he had
seen no more distant muzzle flashes.

As much to monitor the man's alertness as for any other
reason, Quantrill asked about their route: how far, where was
the Leakey clinic, was there a VHF set somewhere under the
dash. Concannon replied each time, using few words. The
upshot of it was that they were a half hour from help. The
two-way radio had long since been removed after it had given
up under the merciless pounding of Wild Country roads.

Then Quantrill saw what could be a distant glow of lights
on the horizon. Concannon sat up straight, swallowed hard.
"Dizzy as hell," he said; then, "Call the ole man, Quantrill.
Tell him about Jer's stash."

"What about it?" They were talking louder over the thunder of the engine, hurtling down a straight incline now.

"I seen it. Tell him. Tell him, faithful, under a ledge at the
fig tree. Got it?"

Quantrill repeated it. "You can call him yourself," he
promised, and turned right onto a good two-lane road at the
edge of the little town of Leakey. It was one promise he could
not make good.

CHAPTER FORTY-FOUR • • •

Leakey's little clinic had seen many a gunshot wound. "I'm sorry," said the sad-faced little doctor, removing old-fashioned glasses and pinching the bridge of his nose. "Maybe if I'd got to him a little earlier . . ." He waved a hand and let it fall. "From the angle I'd say the bullet nicked his heart. I'll know more, ah, later. Your friend simply bled to death internally, Mr. Coulter. I'll have to have a statement, of course."

The young man with the blood-caked shirt sighed. While still in his teens, Quantrill had learned the trick of divorcing himself from the dead, no matter how dear. The more you mourned, the less you were able to avenge. "You still go by the book out here, huh?"

The little doctor elevated his chin. "This country won't be wild forever," he said stolidly. He could not have known that he was endorsing Quantrill's goals.

Quantrill stared over the man's green-smocked shoulder at the body of Cameron Concannon, naked to the waist and grayish against cold, impersonal sheets. The wound had bled so little outside that Quantrill had maintained an irrational hope. "Right. But right now I need a VHF set." He saw what he took for a negative look as the doctor opened his mouth. "It may be life or death."

The doctor shrugged and led him to the front desk, where a grandmotherly woman sat dozing. Moments later, Quantrill had Mulvihill Garner's call code from the Del Rio exchange.

The old rancher did not answer for so long that Quantrill was already imagining him dead. When he did answer, Quantrill identified himself as Sam Coulter and said, straight off, that he bore the worst kind of news.

"Seems to be your specialty." Mul Garner yawned. "Put Cam on."

"I can't," Quantrill replied, and told him why. He ended the account with, "You may need some help there, Mr. Garner. Are you speaking freely?"

"Nobody in the house but me. And don't worry about me. I'll take care of my own. Always have."

"Concannon told me to say"—he paused, glancing at the physician—"that the man I fought has a big pile of hard money stashed away. He implied it was from illegal dealings." Quantrill repeated the location as the foreman had gasped it out to him. "I don't know if that means anything to you."

"Yes, but mostly it means it's dirty money, so it's not Jerome's and it's not mine. It's nobody's." Mul Garner's voice in the earpiece was old now. "I've lost my best friend, and I guess I've lost my son. You have anything else to keep me awake with?"

Quantrill denied it. He was in the act of apologizing when Mul Garner killed the connection.

He was turning away from the radiophone when he made a mental connection and wheeled back, punching a code he knew by heart, feeling icy tentacles constrict around his chest. He relaxed when Sandy Grange answered.

He told her there had been a shooting scrape without giving details. "No, I'm fine . . . well, as good as you could expect," he amended, seeing the doctor's eyebrows rise. There was no telling what the physician might make of the conversation, and he took no chances. "I had a minor accident or two while looking for our livestock." Pause. "I'm really okay, honey, will you shut the hell up and listen? Okay, you recall that neighbor of yours who used to try shaking me up at Saturday dances. Yeah, him; and his friends, too. Somebody told me today to watch my back. I figure you two may be the only unprotected back I have, so stay healthy 'til I get there."

A longer pause, and the doctor saw the young man's face split in a grin. He would never have guessed that young man had just been told that a wandering Russian boar had come ambling home. Ba'al had a deep cut in his underlip, but blue ointment was Sandy's sovereign remedy. He was near the soddy, so if she needed any help, she could whistle it up in seconds. Childe, she said, reported that Ba'al actually looked forward to his next encounter with the English lieutenant.

Quantrill: "The hell of it is, so does Wardrop." Pause, then a lopsided smile. "What *can* I do? If they're gonna fight like this, why don't they just get married?"

Her reply was unprintable. Quantrill put down the headset still smiling guiltily, then followed the physician to give Sam Coulter's version of the night's violence. At least half of his statement was true.

CHAPTER FORTY-FIVE • • •

The man known to a few as San Antonio Rose took the call on a Wednesday night during late October in his SanTone Ringcity apartment. The caller used a voder with a preset message; such a cheap voder that it did not even place graceful inflections in common phrases.

Even so, the message was too direct to misunderstand. He might care to visit a certain dubok—a word the voder botched badly—one of several drops his leader had established for business connections. There he would retrieve a sample of goods that might be of interest to someone called Caballo, the Horse. In due course, the caller would quote a price. End of message.

He pondered the mystery of a caller who knew his telephone code, yet refused to identify himself. It could mean the Department of Justice had penetrated Sorel's channels—but if so, they would already have the apartment staked, and his own channels inside the law would have alerted him. No, the caller was almost surely one of Sorel's regular contacts, because he was obviously familiar with those ringcity duboks.

That particular dubok was in a part of the latino district so conspicuously dangerous at night that only members of a local *raza* bunch dared walk the shadowed streets. And they dared it only because it was they who made it dangerous. San Antonio Rose decided that the sample, presumably of drugs, could wait until morning. He had not achieved his status in this business by taking insane chances with teenaged muggers.

The caller had chosen that dubok for precisely that reason: San Antonio Rose would almost certainly visit the drop in daylight.

Next morning, after a sidewalk breakfast of *huevos con chorizo* and a bottle of Negro Modelo beer in the barrio, San

197

Antonio Rose paid a visit to a tiny, parklike, street-corner cemetery; knelt with hat in hand at a flat headstone boasting polyethelyne tulips in a brass vase. He casually rearranged the plastic blooms, then palmed a vial no larger than a thimble and leaned back as though satisfied with his decorating talent. His guess—that the vial contained some illegal drug to be analyzed for purity—was perfectly correct. He did not guess that the cocaine sample was merely bait, sacrificed so that he would not wonder why he had been lured into the open on a fruitless errand. The man remained there for a few moments and then, satisfied that he was not to be challenged, walked away.

The challenge, when it came, was the commonest type to be met there in daylight. The boy who materialized at his side had done so with no more noise than a mouse, on bare feet with soles tough as horn. "Watch your car, shine your shoes, find a virgin, only a dollar," he chanted in locally accented English.

The man shook his head, irked because the little *cabrón* had nearly made him jump.

The boy had not kept his belly off his backbone by being shy. "Ever'body needs something, mister." He danced ahead of the man, now skipping backward to match the long strides, and waved his hands for attention. "What you doin' here, anyway? You lost? You look like an Anglo to me."

San Antonio Rose stopped, reached out casually with one hand, then swiftly with the other, grabbing the lad by the collar of a jacket much too large for him—but perhaps the right size to hide a loaf of bread. The man rattled off, in local Spanish dialect, an ugly suspicion concerning a relationship between the boy's mother and a small hairless dog. Then in English he added, "I see a cornshuck in your pocket, so you already stole your tamales for lunch. You love Anglos so much, go find one." He turned the boy around with ease, released him, moved as if to whack his rump.

Of course he swept thin air, as he had expected. Nimble as a mountain goat, the boy darted away and was instantly swallowed between the small, close-packed houses of the barrio. San Antonio Rose smiled to himself and walked on to Fredricksburg Road, where he caught a bus, once more anonymous.

But not destined to remain anonymous for much longer.
The boy hotfooted it over fences and between chickencoops
to arrive back at a street corner a block from the tiny cemetery. The slender fellow with the soft voice and the scarred
face was there, as promised, with a crisp fifty-dollar bill, also
as promised. The boy gravely withdrew the little tape recorder
from the depths of a jacket pocket; exchanged it for the reward.

They spoke in Spanish. The boy: "It was hard work to
make him talk with me. Dangerous. Worth more money."

The adult: "I watched. You were well paid." Then the
little recorder went into a tattered shopping bag, next to the
camera with the excellent four-hundred-millimeter lens.

The boy had seen the results of knife fights before; sur-
mised that this fellow with the soft voice, badly cut hair, and
uncallused hands had met with a broken bottle, and recently.
Noting the boy's interest, the fellow turned away, hitched the
shopping bag up under one arm, and strode off. The boy
thrust the money out of sight and watched his benefactor for a
block, wondering what was odd about that stride. Probably a
homosexual, thought the boy, and dematerialized into the
alleyways. He would break that bill and give only twenty to
his mother. She would, in any case, never believe he had
earned fifty dollars from a swishing *maricón* merely by provoking a stranger to curse him.

You could get many, many things in SanTone Ringcity
with cash. With cash and close connections of long standing
in the legal system, you could get almost literally *any*thing.
With several good telephoto close-ups of a man standing on a
sidewalk in broad daylight, and a voiceprint of that man in
two languages, you had a fair chance of discovering much
about him. Especially if he had any criminal record since the
war.

The owner of the recorder had everything it took to learn
the real identity of San Antonio Rose. Including the burning
will to trace his connections, using any means whatever.
Now, if San Antonio Rose was known in any capacity by the
legal system, he would be revealed by modestly illegal record
checks. And from there, Marianne Placidas knew she was not
far from locating Felix Sorel.

CHAPTER FORTY-SIX • • •

Sandy's journal, Wed. 25 Oct. '06

Ted looked much better this trip. At least that awful scab is disappearing from his forehead. He was sore as a boil over his tongue-lashing from Mr. Marrow but said he was able to pay for the cycle he lost. Refused to borrow from me. Borrowing from Marrow, or did he really quit that deputy job? I refuse to think he would divert money from that amulet that is owed to me.

Jerome G. paid me a visit today, with 3 of his bravos for company, & I decided not to whistle for help. He pretended to take his welcome for granted, full of false cheer and chickenshit, but I noticed the contents of his armpit holster as he nursed my coffee. Asked me slyly about Ted, and, giving him my best dose of baby blues, I lied and enjoyed it. As if I knew nothing of their enmity I said we had agreed to disagree, & that T. had intended to see about a job in Austin, where they need heavy equipment operators to help clear old UT campus. Hope Jer chases my wild goose to Austin: The big buffoon is now a wanted man in some quarters. But not by me! Rather than send him to T. at WCS I would stir rat poison in his coffee. I forbore asking why he no longer grins so much, because I could see the gap where 2 teeth used to be.

After Jer left, I called Lufo. No one else to turn to, if T. is correct about Jer having protection inside the marshal's office. Of course Lufo asked why I didn't call T. I said he's not a hired gun anymore & I didn't want him fetching up against those men anyway. Should I try Marshal Teague in SanTone?

Lufo quickly shooed me away from that. Said he could leak

the news without involving me. Made me repeat entire farce with Jer. Told me Jer would be crazy to show up in Austin, but he would pass the word without involving me.

God blast me, I played the weak female for Lufo but had no other weapon. Begged him to swear he would keep me & T. out of it. Only when he called me "chica" was I satisfied. Poor Lufo, I love & despise him so. . . .

CHAPTER FORTY-SEVEN • • •

Lieutenant Alec Wardrop helped fit the armored blankets to his mount, cursing the weight of each piece, admiring the work of Jess Marrow's saddlemaker. The mare accepted her synthetic hide with the patience of a saint.

Marrow pointed to the great shoulder pads that hung across a wooden railing in the tack shed. "Ted, see if you and Wardrop can adjust the buckles to fit that to the mare's breastplate."

Quantrill hefted the kapton blanket with the hard nylon plates sewn between its layers. "My God, Jess, have you weighed all this stuff?"

"About sixty kilos. Should be no problem for a draft horse. Easy, Rose," said Marrow, patting the mare as she swung her head around. Rose was a deep roan in color, weighing nearly a metric ton and standing fully eighteen hands at the withers. She was a beautiful creature with the Roman nose of a Clydesdale and the smooth, untufted fetlocks of a Percheron. A trained eye could readily identify her bloodlines as those of the "great horse" first bred in northern Europe as a draft animal. Wardrop had bought her from a circus wintering near Galveston, depending on her calm and familiarity with exotic animals for the job he had in mind. Wardrop knew the history of the "great horse"; it had carried crusaders with massive armor into battle centuries before. This one, Rose, might do it again. She had proven herself very nimble and willing when harrying smaller boars during the past few days. Wardrop felt that, this time, he had the right mount.

He also had paid for different equipment. His hardware now included a night-vision helmet, a longer and thicker assegai spear, and a saddle-mounted socket pivot for it. His saddlebags were the size of mule packs, stocked for a week's travel in Wild Country. That polymer armor, however, was the result of a blistering argument with Jess Marrow. Old Marrow would stable the mare with pleasure, sweet-tempered rarity that she was, but remained aghast at Wardrop's use of her. She was Wardrop's property, so he couldn't forbid the man to hunt boar from her back—a broad platform that seemed the size and stability of a tennis court. He could refuse to equip her for armor, though; and he did, until Wardrop took her out to flush smaller boars.

When it became obvious that Wardrop was going to put Rose up against Ba'al in any case, Marrow agreed to supervise the crafting of her armor. As he had put it, "It'd be a shame to make this pore noble beast pay for what *you* got comin'." Now, with the unwilling help of Quantrill, they were making the final fit of Rose's armor pads. From knees to neck and even passing under her ample belly, Rose's armor would stop a hurled lance. It would not stop the ridicule of Wardrop's quest.

Wardrop, connecting the breastplate to padding over her shoulders, did not at first notice the bright stitching Marrow had ordered across the close-woven kapton at the shoulders of the big mare. When he did, he indulged in a deep-breathing exercise. The stitching did not say "Rose"; it said "Rosinante." "And I," said Wardrop with a flourish but not much mirth, "Don Quixote de la Mancha. While you Philistines are falling about in glee, think of the insult you give to Rose. She's no broken-down Spanish nag."

Marrow's own shoulders were shaking with repressed laughter as he stepped back to view the mare. "Maybe not, but you realize what this will all look like? Helmet, lance, armor, that goddamn stupid kerchief like a pennant—you're a dead ringer for a throwback out of the Middle Ages."

Wardrop, coolly: "That has not escaped my notice."

Quantrill: "Has it escaped your notice that you *are* a throwback? You admit the woman who gave you this idea hates your guts. And she's disappeared in the bargain."

And Marrow: "Besides, if you ever told your fellow pig-stickers how you got a draft horse gussied up like this, you'd be laughed out of your regiment."

"Regiment be damned. Marianne Placidas and you two,

especially you, be damned!'' Grunting, Wardrop lifted his
new saddle, no English postage stamp but a special affair
with a ''tree'' high enough to provide kidney support, and
swung it onto Rose's back. ''I've invested many a bottle of
that dogsbody's whiskey, and dissolved the lining of my
throat, in hearing the local opinions. You two have been
entirely too much help keeping me from my goal. I know
who you are now, Quantrill: a man with a certain cachet in
these parts. But I know myself as well, and I tell you before a
witness that if you are trying to give serious insult, I shall
give you satisfaction now, or later.'' He tugged at one of
three broad cinches under the mare's belly. ''The choice
of weapons would be yours. I would sign a waiver; I believe
that's how it has been done recently in this barbarous place.''
He stood up and waited, looking from one man to the other.

Quantrill sighed; shook his head as he led the docile Rose
into sunshine, Wardrop following with lance and helmet. To
give an ex-assassin his choice of weapons was to give a shark
his choice of bites. It was a long vault into the saddle, but
Alec Wardrop made it with style. Quantrill handed him the
reins with: ''I don't know how you do it, Wardrop. You earn
respect from people who are laughing their nuts off at what
you do. No, I won't throw down on you or duel you—but I
don't expect to see you alive again, if you keep this shit
up.''

''You've given me that warning before,'' Wardrop replied,
snapping the lance retainers, checking the saddlebags, ''and
here I sit. Forgive me for that lapse of mine, Quantrill. You
mean well.''

Quantrill threw up his hands. ''Okay, but one more thing:
There's a legend says the boar can actually smell a gun—the
oil, maybe, or old powder residue. If you've got one, get rid
of it now. Otherwise, Ba'al will scatter your bones from here
to Waxahachie.''

''No guns.'' Wardrop smiled. ''We Quixotes only use
spears.''

''Your hand, then, while it's still attached.'' Quantrill
reached up, shook with Wardrop, then turned to see that
Marrow stood near, thumbs in belt loops, listening and rocking on his heels. Wardrop gave an abbreviated form of Brit

salute, eased Rose into a ponderous trot, and headed off for his hired horse van.

"If the Lord takes care of drunks and fools," said Marrow, "I wonder if He's put aside all His other concerns for the rest of that man's life."

"Does that mean you're for Wardrop, or against him?"

"He's a pigheaded, spoiled rich, wasteful selfish snooty cantankerous foreign-born sonofabitch of world class, but he *does* have class." Marrow clucked to himself. "But whatever he has loose up here"—he tapped himself over the ear—"he makes up for it in here." So saying, Marrow put his hand over his breast. "The Brit just hasn't had his good strong sign yet. How could I be against as great an ass as Wardrop? He's one of us, Teddy!"

Quantrill's smile was distant; sad. "Maybe somebody should root for the boar."

Marrow eyed his assistant thoughtfully. "Oh, I think somebody does. God knows how it came about, but I think somebody has, for a long, long time. . . ."

CHAPTER FORTY-EIGHT • • •

If the dead can watch the living, then perhaps Judge Anthony Placidas was venting hollow laughter in hell. His dying statement made Ted Quantrill suspect that a close connection existed between Jerome Garner and the Justice Department. The important connections, however, were between the department and Sorel. Garner, for all his dreams of power, was important only because he controlled the land that was a conduit for Sorel—and because that land was vast enough to hide Sorel's Anglo confederates. Garner knew he would be conspicuous as tits on a boar hog to any deputy strolling the streets of Del Rio, Rocksprings, or Kerrville. But just as you can best hide a lump of coal among a hundred thousand other lumps of coal, a wanted man in a city can hide in plain sight. SanTone Ringcity, for example; or Austin, only a hundred klicks to the north.

And Jerome Garner knew no one who needed killing in SanTone. While checking more loose teeth and recovering from the encounter on his porch, he'd listened to his hired hands dredging up stories about the redoubtable Ted Quantrill. Sounded to Jer like the little sumbitch was on his way to being a Texas legend—and him not even a native, originally. The fact that Sam Houston and Davy Crockett had also been imports from the southeast never crossed Jer's mind. The fact that the man who shot John Wesley Hardin in the back was known by name only to historians also did not register. Jer believed what he wanted to believe: that he could gain status and discharge mortal vengeance by bagging that rattler-quick little fucker, Ted Quantrill. Sandra Grange had said Quantrill was in Austin. And when had any little bimbo ever withstood the Garner charm enough to lie to Jer? A truthful answer to *that* one might hurt him worse than bullets.

Garner needed two days for his roundabout trip to Austin, with only Billy Ray for company. The old Texas U campus in Austin had suffered so much damage during the firestorms of '96 that the great university had made do with temporary quarters in North Austin for nearly a decade. But a school with more oil money than Harvard, more fierce traditions than a regimental combat team, would not abandon its ancient campus forever. Austin's Guadalupe Boulevard resounded, now, with the clangor of construction as determined Texans proceeded to rebuild every last structure as it had been before the SinoInd War. The Littlefield Memorial, the museum, even the ad building everyone called "the Tower"—all of it would soon look as it had looked in 1995. Some said it was all being done so that those orange lights could once again bathe the Tower every time the Longhorns won a football game. Jerome Garner did not care why it was being done, so long as everyone was too busy to match his face with a "wanted" poster.

But not quite everyone was that busy. San Antonio Rose had excellent descriptions of Sorel's people, including Jer Garner. He knew enough about Jer to approach him with care, and to watch his accomplice carefully. He spent one fruitless day scanning the heavy equipment yards, especially at quitting time when the hulking Kelley Ramscoops with their telescoping wheelbases and midchassis scoops were wheeled into their compound for the night. He was not studying the equipment operators or the bag people who picked over piles of debris for anything salable, but any big, strapping specimen who stood outside the cyclone fence to watch.

His second day of surveillance was very like the first, until a half hour before the Kelley earthmovers were due to come rolling into their compound near the stadium. Then he noticed, strolling along Red River Street, the two men wearing bulky jackets over plaid shirts.

He crossed the boulevard, walking slowly enough to hide his slight limp, whistling an old familiar tune. Of the pair that walked ahead, the tall blond with the big shoulders seemed to be doing most of the talking. San Antonio Rose proceeded with caution; no telling how many men in Austin would fit Jerome Garner's description.

The men took seats at a bus stop. San Antonio Rose spent

ten minutes with a cigarette, idly observing construction work
on the stadium. He felt more sure of his job when the two
men passed up a Congress Avenue bus. He felt almost certain
when, as the big earthmovers began to whirr toward their
compound, the smaller of the men crossed alone to the opposite side of the broad thoroughfare and took up a vigil, a
broad-brim Stetson pulled low over his brow.

Jer Garner was watching for a ramscoop driver who looked
like Ted Quantrill and scarcely glanced at the lean fellow in
coveralls who sat down, whistling softly, on the other end of
his bench. Until the man quit repeating his tune and asked for
a light. Jer pulled a lighter from his jacket pocket without a
word. Flicking the lighter, he shared the gaze of a man whose
coloring and face suggested a tough latino. A day laborer,
from the look of him.

The laborer drew on his cigarette, said, "Thanks," and
whistled a tenth repetition of the tune. It irritated Jer, who
looked away. "Bet you can't name that tune," said the
laborer casually.

"I've heard enough of it," Jer replied.

"But can you name it?" the laborer persisted.

" 'Rose of San Antone,' " said Jer, not making the
connection.

"Guilty as charged," said the laborer.

Jer swiveled his head around, made a connection, then
dismissed it too soon. "I'm busy, greaseball. Get my drift?"

"I do if your initials are J. G.," said the laborer.

Now Jer turned his full attention to the man. "And what if
they aren't?"

"I'll be disappointed, and J. G. won't live to ride his sorrel
much longer." The laborer still spoke casually, but his hand
rested in his jacket. "If I were the law, which I'm not, J. G.
would be candy. You agree?"

Jer swallowed hard, imagining a snub-nosed weapon in that
pocket. "I guess so."

"So I'll give you one name and you give me the other; fair
enough?" A nod. "Jerome."

"Garner," said Jer. "You're San Antonio Rose?"

"I said I was guilty," said the man, enjoying it. "You
jus' keep watching and don' bring your backup overhere,
I'm takin' a chance for you Anglos as it is."

Jer brought out a pack of cigarettes, lit up, and kept his eyes peeled on the street, feeling sweat form in his armpits as his informant continued to talk. The story was short, its moral bitter: Jerome Garner was unlikely to find his quarry in Austin. He was more likely to find some very rough dudes authorized to carry sawed-off scatterguns, the kind of welcome you could expect if you were a known killer.

San Antonio Rose saw beads of perspiration on Jer's forehead as he finished: "Too many bounty hunters here for your health. You think this man you're after isn' bait to get you now, wherever he is? Think again. An' if I found you, who'll find you next?"

Jer spat at the gutter. "Seems like everybody knows my business before I do. It was that little cunt set me up, sure as hell!"

San Antonio Rose donated a look of puzzlement. "You're way off, Garner. Go home an' think about it."

The word "home" had more implications than he had intended. "If it wasn't that girl, I know goddamn well who it has to be," Jer raged.

"Thought you might," said San Antonio Rose, without any clear idea who the rancher had in mind. "My channels say you're settin' yourself up for a spell in the slammer. Don' expect any more help from me. You're trouble stuck up on a long pole, man. Now do us all a favor; go get your backup an' fuck off while I catch this bus."

Jer Garner got up as if the bench were a hot stove lid and hurried across the boulevard without a backward look. San Antonio Rose caught the bus, wondering whether young Garner would continue his search for the ex-deputy. He did not wonder about the slender fellow with the scarred face who sat in a rented Chevy near a street corner two blocks down Red River from that bus stop.

San Antonio Rose checked himself often for passive dipoles and radio-frequency bugs, with a good Mantis bugfinder. Because he never found evidence of tracer bugs, he assumed that he was free to pursue his business without himself being followed. He had never heard of a pheromone tracker, a hand-held device that was almost as sensitive as moth antennae in locating stray molecules of an exact type.

Marianne Placidas knew men's habits. They might wash

their clothes daily but seldom washed the outsides of wallets and belts, nor the insides of footgear and holsters. Her phero-mone spray was undetectable to human nostrils and it worked extremely well on leather, sinking into the pores and releasing a few molecules every second or so for a period of several weeks. Even in an air-conditioned metropolitan bus, enough trackable stuff found exit to make tracking possible. Upon learning where San Antonio Rose roomed, Marianne had wasted no time making purchases from her family contact, a retired detective who kept up with the latest investigative techniques. Within twenty-four hours, taking risks only a brilliant amateur would consider, she had gained illegal entry to San Antonio Rose's rooms and, wearing surgeon's gloves, sprayed all the belts, coats, and footgear he was not wearing at the time. His hair restorer, too, now had a little something extra that was noticeable only to that pheromone tracker.

Now, Marianne put the Chevy in gear and cruised slowly past the two men who were hurrying toward their own rented car. At first she had felt a sick warmth, a tremor of intent, upon seeing the man who shared that bench with San Antonio Rose. He was tall enough to be Harley Slaughter. But her view from two blocks distant, even through a good telephoto lens, was not very persuasive. Only when she passed Jer Garner at a distance of five meters did she decide that neither of the men was of immediate interest to her. Marianne turned at the next corner and followed the bus downtown, holding the little chemical tracker at the windowsill. She had nothing better to do, might never have anything better to do, than follow San Antonio Rose. And to wait. Sooner or later, he would lead her to Felix Sorel. Perhaps even now he was hurrying toward that rendezvous. And if this tactic did not bear fruit soon, perhaps she would invest in the laser audio unit Sorel had mentioned in Oregon Territory.

CHAPTER FORTY-NINE • • •

That Sorel would have one "Rose" and Wardrop another might have been odd coincidence anywhere but the American Southwest. In Texas, it was not so much coincidence as tradition. A thing of wonder or of beauty tended to be symbolically borrowed for names, and Texas was full of people named Delight, Sunshine, and Christmas. In part because the Tyler rose festival in the piney woods of East Texas was perhaps the most gorgeous display of color north of the Big Bend, the name "Rose" was one of the commonest in the state.

Mounted on his gentle Rose, Wardrop began his hunt outside the northeast corner of Garner land and, in three patient days of search, worked his way north and west to the edge of the Grange spread. Here he found more sign of the boar, some of it very recent. Until the past few weeks, Sandy had never seriously imagined she would ever have the money to fence her land. So Alec Wardrop had no idea that he was trespassing when, on his fourth day out, he urged Rose over a ridge and onto Sandy's land. This was the only piece of real estate in Texas on which Ba'al had legal rights.

And Ba'al was sticking close to home this week. He was not especially territorial, as half-ton boars go; but if Wardrop imagined that the boar gave a damn whether Rose weighed one ton or twenty, Wardrop was mistaken. The great horse sent delicate seismic tremors through the hardpan that Ba'al felt as he lay sunning himself and digesting a bellyful of rattlers, almost within whistling distance of the soddy. From that moment on, it was hard to say who was the hunter, and who the hunted.

Wardrop and the mare were traversing a shallow, flat depression when she laid her ears back and, of her own accord, wheeled around. She had smelled something exotic and musky on the fitful breeze, and now she was hearing faint swishings through the brush that Wardrop could not hear. Yet when she wheeled to face the disturbance, her rider was not long in doubt.

Wardrop saw his quarry immediately; no wonder, with his eyes a full three meters from the ground as he sat on his own mobile Texas tower. He spoke calmly, soothingly, to the mare as she seemed for the first time to be near panic. Then he snugged the helmet down and unsnapped the lance from its lashings. This time he did not speak the name of Marianne; this quest was no longer for her, but for himself. With a cry that began low in his throat and expanded to echo across the little valley, he shouted, "*Wohhhh jataaaa!* . . ."

Ba'al had heard this challenge before and saw the slender steel tusk lowered in his direction as the mare accelerated toward him. Something in her eyes said that she obeyed Wardrop against her best judgment. Ba'al did not much care; he cared very much that the rider with the huge gleaming head could look down on him from an arrogant height advantage. This was not to be borne with good grace. The mare was not his opponent, but merely a thing to be felled, just as a man might cut down a tree that gave safety to an opponent.

Wardrop heard the tremendous trumpeting squeal; saw the boar leap forward like a quarterhorse, covering ground faster than Rose within a second. Its huge head was down, and it stared forward like a furious Brahma as it charged with its vast twin scythes aimed at the breast of the mare. As Wardrop lodged the lance butt in its socket and leaned forward in the saddle, the boar made a near perfect target. Until the last split second.

Then the boar leaped across in front of Rose, one tusk ripping across her kapton breastplate as he passed to Wardrop's left. A shiny rectangle of nylon flew spinning from the breastplate, but the tusk had wedged between the tough nylon plates long enough to make that tusk a lever. For the first time in his adult life, Ba'al was spun end for end by that leverage as the mare thundered past him. He found the experience—interesting. And a bit insulting; deserving of an insult in return.

Wardrop felt his big platform wrench to the left, stumble, regain her stride. A rider of less ability would have gone flying into the brush, but Wardrop recovered his balance, wheeled the mare in a slow, ponderous maneuver, and tried again. Immediately, Wardrop saw that the beast kept moving to Wardrop's left, deliberately avoiding the lance. He grasped the lance shaft farther ahead, pulled its butt from the socket, then held the shaft under his right arm and swung the lancehead, a honed steel sliver as long as a man's arm, over Rose's head to menace the boar afresh.

Ba'al had tried parrying a steel tusk once before and, while nicking his own ivory scimitars slightly, the maneuver had worked. He had also felt the razor-sharp thing in his mouth, and that had not worked well at all. He had plenty of time for the decision because, with her great mass, the mare simply could not manage the speed of an Arabian. He watched the long steel sliver, gauging it carefully, his own head up and watchful, and they closed with a clash. The lancehead slid up, diverted by his tusks, and then he was inside the danger zone. He slammed directly into the horse's left flank with a resounding head butt, caromed off with a slashing pass against the armoring blanket, actually between Wardrop's shin and the mare's flank.

Rose grunted, nearly fell, and neighed in fear though the armor had prevented those honed tusks from touching her hide. Wardrop felt his left stirrup go, sliced cleanly away just inside his leg, and now only the foremost of the three special cinches held his saddle. Those two loose cinches now flailed about beneath the mare, frightening her. Rose kicked forward with a hind leg and then answered Wardrop's rein and knee pressure.

Wardrop had never known perspiration to burst from him so suddenly. It streamed into his eyes and he raised the visor, blinking, once more facing the boar as Rose danced sideways, dust rising as high as a man's chest beneath her. Now the huge boar moved backward with yellow-red eyes gleaming and watchful, now sidling up the dry, hard ground, provoking Wardrop to urge the mare forward. Perhaps it was the sweat in his eyes, or perhaps the thrill of battle joined; Wardrop did not realize the boar was drawing them onto a rise where occasional rains carved crevices into dirt the color of dried blood, a crumbly composite of granite and poor soil. The boar turned suddenly and half fell on its side, scrambling up from a shallow crevice, then grunted angrily, making a great show of rage as it hobbled away. Wardrop saw his chance, kicked the flanks of Rose, and resettled the lance as she gave chase.

They gained ground for two hundred meters before the boar's lame hindquarter was suddenly sound again as if by magic, Ba'al leaping a narrow crevice into a small plateau of stony rubble, Wardrop following. And now Wardrop saw that they occupied a mound invaded by deep crevices, as though Rose stood on the back of some great hand with its fingers splayed downward. The first and most elementary principle of engagement burst too late in Wardrop's mind: *The tactic depends first on terrain.* He was not mounted on a jumper that could leap clear of the problem. This demon boar had lured him into a trap.

Wardrop wheeled the mare again, shouting to spook his enemy, but as Rose turned to retrace her steps, the great boar leaped like a deer; first to one of the finger prominences, then to the slope they craved. Wardrop had no time to wonder why the boar was not champing great flecks of foam as angry boars will do. He thrust the lance down and forward, letting it slide a bit for the extra reach, and cursed as the boar dodged with ease.

Then Ba'al reared almost in the face of Rose, his head as high as her own, his sharp split hooves menacing her, and gave voice to his own challenge, a piercing squeal that unnerved the mare completely. She tossed her head, eyes rolling in terror, and backed quickly, almost rearing as she did so. Wardrop fought to keep his balance as the saddle slipped, and Rose tried valiantly to respond to his knee pressure. In an instant the great mare had slid into a crevice broad enough for her girth and easily a meter in depth. The boar chose this moment to bound to a small prominence, then leaped behind Rose before Wardrop could bring the lancehead around. The time had come to return that insult.

For one transfixing moment, Wardrop thought the brute would climb the mare from behind to get to her rider. Rose was snorting like a warhorse, struggling mightily to gain purchase so those great mounded muscles of hers could thrust her out of a crevice that was almost a ravine. Wardrop made a decision then, not from panic but with premeditation; the damned saddle was about to go anyhow.

He jammed the butt of his lance into dirt, kicked away, and hauled hard with both arms, vaulting clear of the mare; that lance shaft, after all, had been modified from a vaulting pole. He landed on both feet, squatting, whirling the lance to impale the savage brute if it charged him. And stared. The boar seemed to have no intention of charging; instead, it was poised like some great Dall ram on the edge of the ravine, well clear of Rose's frantic kicks. While Wardrop watched, it made a parody of mounting her, lurching with false thrusts, staring *at Wardrop* all the while. Alec Wardrop shouted a wordless battle cry and leaped toward the boar, the lancehead preceding him. It was probably the long moment arm of that lancehead, plus his heavy night-vision helmet, that sent him off-balance. Wardrop sprawled headlong, the lance clattering so that it spanned the crevice next to the one that held the mare entrapped.

Alec Wardrop saw then that he'd never had a chance, and neither had Rose, weighed down with all that extra garbage as they were; and if he was any judge, that goddamned boar knew exactly how to diddle with the chinks in their armor. Before he could scramble forward to grasp the lance, the boar performed a prodigious leap over the finger prominence and into the crevice bridged by the lance. Wardrop ducked and rolled away, seeing the boar come down with the lance shaft crosswise in its mouth, hearing the dry, splintering crack as the shaft failed.

Wardrop saw Rose heaving herself up as the boar almost disappeared; saw her stumble, one foreleg entering the mouth of a small burrow that might have been that of fox or armadillo. He abandoned any hope of remounting as the terror-stricken mare crashed to the ground, screaming. He began to run then and almost immediately fell hard, his helmet bouncing away. With Rose's mortal screams keening in his ears, he did not lose consciousness, but he had taken a monumental wallop in falling on the uneven ground. Wardrop thanked God as he felt for the long-bladed dirk in its boot sheath; it hadn't come loose, and now he had *something* going for him again.

The boar came up from the depression as though fired from

a trench mortar, looking back toward Wardrop but trotting toward Rose. She was trying to rise, still screaming, her right foreleg thrashing, fractured terribly just above the pastern. Wardrop shambled off, running as hard as he could, searching for a scrub oak high enough to climb as the breath whistled in his windpipe. He did not realize exactly when Rose's screaming stopped. But when he risked a look backward, he knew why Rose would never scream again.

The huge boar stood over her, staring in Wardrop's direction, making no attempt to run him down before he found something climbable. The upthrusting tusks ran crimson with blood from a huge rent torn in the mare's throat. Ba'al waited for the mare to die, now respectful of his victim, and Wardrop had the chilling sensation that the boar had acted honorably. Wardrop himself would have had to shoot Rose, had he brought a firearm. Severing the great artery in her throat was the only kindness possible under the circumstances. Without realizing that he did so, Wardrop paused fifty meters away— long enough to find that his eyes were now wet, not with perspiration, but with tears. Briefly, for perhaps five seconds, man and boar stood immobile in requiem for Rose.

When Ba'al began to trot forward, Wardrop took flight again, the dirk flashing in his hand as he ran for the tallest of the scrubby little oaks nearby. He was in error to think Ba'al could not climb after him or cut down the little oak as he had been taught to remove mesquite from around the soddy. Wardrop soon saw that the boar would reach the oaks first, instead of simply running him down in a vicious charge. Well, maybe he could squeeze into one of those little ravines far enough to present only his steel dirk to the boar. Gasping, stumbling as he ran, Wardrop turned back. For some reason, the great boar was giving him time to do it, following at a leisurely trot.

Inexorably, Wardrop found himself herded back toward the dead mare, back to his broken lance. He was nearing the limits of his reserve strength and fell again, tumbling into the crevice and slicing the calf of his leg badly against the razor edge of that lancehead. He rolled onto his back, grasping the fore end of the shattered lance, and whirled it upward. Not in time. The boar was much too close, parrying the lance just behind its steel with a sudden, almost contemptuous toss of the great head, flinging the weapon down the ravine with an empty clatter, the scarlet pennant still tied fluttering on the shaft.

Wardrop wormed his way up the narrow declivity on his back, presenting the dirk, watching the boar, which was now so near that he could count scars through the coarse secondary hair on the shoulders and flanks of Ba'al. He struck the back of his head against an outcrop, shook himself groggily. He knew the old stories of the raj; knew that Maharajah Jai Singh of Alwar had actually taken boar with a dagger, from the back of a polo pony. But he, Wardrop, was not mounted and could not even stand. He tried anyway, sitting up to try a last valiant lunge, and the effort drew too much blood from his head. Feeling the whiteout on its way, he made one desperate sweep of the dirk, which thudded harmlessly into the embankment. His eyes were still open, but the sensations of color, then outline, fled as Alec Wardrop rolled onto his stomach, semiconscious. A moment later he felt the hot breath of Ba'al on his unprotected neck. . . .

CHAPTER FIFTY • • •

Not far from where Alec Wardrop engaged his last boar, another engagement took place to the south. The rundown headquarters at the old south homestead were, as Jer Garner said, plenty roomy to hide a hovervan, along with the cycles that flanked the van like the outriders for gold shipments of a century earlier. But the street value of Sorel's cargo, gram for gram, was currently more dear than gold. Its price would drop sharply as soon as Sorel got far enough north to begin dumping it, at unheard-of low prices, to one buyer after another. And then the strategy would be tested when, and if, stupid Americans consumed a thousand kilos of cheap, top-quality skag every month.

Now, Felix Sorel had a problem. He could have bought a small European country for the heroin that rested in cartons carefully repacked and labeled "Light Crust Flour" in the cargo section behind him. But the stuff wasn't worth a peso if he couldn't get it to market, and he would never get it out of Wild Country if the van's diesel kept acting up like this. Two of the men, Reeve and Billy Ray, were passable shade-tree mechanics, but they were unable to trace the problem that made the supercharged van engine chuff and misfire. They had found the fuel filter choked with the kind of crud that often went with Mexican fuel, and after a good flushing they pronounced the problem solved.

It wasn't solved as long as tiny particles were clogging the injectors. Further, every time the engine was hard to start, the starting procedure put extra loads on the individual diesel glow plugs, which required a contortionist midget to replace. By the time Sorel decided he must make serious repairs before going farther, he was roughly halfway between the south homestead and the shanty on the north end that Garner's men had thrown together from old lumber. For the umpteenth time, the diesel staggered so severely that the van threatened to rub its skirts on caliche dirt. "This damnable thing will not take us much farther," Sorel grumbled to Jerome Garner, who sat with an assault rifle near the right-hand window and watched the head of a cycle rider bob in and out of sight some distance away on their right flank.

"It'll have to, Sorel. There's no place else on the spread."

"Are you denying the obvious? Your own ranch headquarters is the place to pull a big engine. It will be quicker and safer than—"

"You don't know the old man. Way he is now, an outfit like this would purely bring out the border guard in him."

The diesel chuffed again and nearly died, the van bouncing its tough forward skirt from the dirt. Sorel cursed and made a hard decision. "What is the shortest distance to your headquarters from here?"

"Goddammit, I told you we can't—" Jer began with some heat, then saw Sorel's face and decided maybe they could. He pointed several points to the right. "Straight over there about seven, eight miles. You got any bright ideas what to tell my old man?"

"That is your problem, which you will solve," said Sorel tightly, steering across open country from which most of the trees had been removed a generation before. "You have always, *always* given me to understand that you command this region. Well . . . command it," he finished.

It went without saying that Sorel himself was the one man in that region whom young Garner should not even attempt to command—who would, in fact, command the commander. Jer looked out the window so that he would not have to look at the driver. This was the second time in a row that Jer had been faced down by a self-assured little hardass on his own spread. Come to think of it, Sorel and Ted Quantrill seemed to have a lot in common. Both blonds, compact, graceful in movement, going about their business with minimum fuss—and augering holes through anything that tried to box them in. Jer wished he could put the two of them in a pit together like roosters so he could watch the feathers fly. Briefly, he thought of mentioning Quantrill to the Mex, then thought better of it. Jer was not about to recount his dust-up with Quantrill, and his men knew better than to talk about it if they wanted to remain on Garner land. He was still enjoying thoughts of eventual revenge when the distant rooftops of the Garner headquarters poked up over the horizon.

Sorel took the VHF handset and, using its scrambler, advised the outriders to fall in line behind his dust trail. Here in the heart of the Garner spread, they had little to worry about as long as Jer exercised the control he bragged so much about. That control would be a lot easier to maintain if they managed somehow to get into the equipment barn without Mul Garner noticing.

Jer seemed nervous as a virgin in a cantina as Sorel guided the van to the equipment barn, Jer leaping out to slide the double doors aside, his glance darting frequently to the big limestone house a hundred meters away. The four outriders—Billy Ray, Slaughter, and both of the Longo brothers—dropped the dolly wheels of their cycles and cut their engines to minimize dust in the yard, which had once been a corral. Unlike the van, most hovercycles lacked power-driven maneuvering wheels because of the weight and cost penalties, and were light enough to be pushed by hand. Billy Ray and Reeve Longo, who knew old Mulvihill Garner well, seemed especially anxious to push their cycles out of sight. Harley Slaughter, with the instincts of a back-shooter, began an immediate reconnaissance in the barn.

Felix Sorel did not fail to notice these preparations, as if for an approaching storm. To himself, he admitted that he had taken Jer too much at face value. Now that face was changing.

Payment for this trip would come from Sorel, so it was Sorel who gave the orders to remove the van engine. It weighed roughly as much as a big man, its castings chiefly of lightweight polymers and ceramics. He had hopes of getting that engine to Rocksprings for overhaul before nightfall, but those hopes were short-lived. Sorel and Slaughter were lifting a rear body panel from the hovervan when the taciturn Slaughter jerked his head to peer into the yard. "Sounds like bad news," he said.

Sorel let go of the panel and moved in shadow so that he could monitor the trouble while Slaughter eased back into the van. Sorel did not have to ask why his confederate sought cover; Slaughter's coldgas weapon was useful only at very short range. Sorel saw a pale old fellow fifteen paces away, facing Jer, carrying a vintage pump shotgun in the crook of one arm. Even with the stooped shoulders he stood almost as tall as Jerome, and his aspect was anything but friendly. Jer looked as though he wanted to kick clods, standing with hands thrust in hip pockets, turning his head this way and that as if the old man's words were slaps. Jer tried to offer a plausible lie.

"Don't know his name, Pop. His van was about to crap out, so I brung him here."

"What's this, a good neighbor policy all of a sudden?" Old Mul strode nearer to the open doors, waved sharply with his free hand, and called, "Everybody out of my barn, for a nose count." The men in the barn glanced not at Jer but at Sorel, who nodded and strolled into what was left of the late sunshine. He stopped near the safety of the doors and waved the others out into the yard with a gesture not intended to be seen by the rancher. Mul Garner saw it anyway and decided those men were not so much under Jer's control as that of the golden-haired stranger with the face of a matinee idol. Sorel still had a backup, for Slaughter was still lying hidden in the van. No one spoke for a long moment.

"Listen up," said Mul Garner, shifting the scattergun a bit for emphasis as he scanned the men. "I won't ask what this is all about. Sifting through your lies would be worse than shoveling fleas with a pitchfork. This is my spread. I won't have any part of whatever you're up to." He stared hard at his son's flushed face. "I see you have Reeve's no-account brother with you, Jer. Why not just carry a sign that you're up to no good? I want these men to clear out, same way they got here. Loli brought the pickup back, if they need it. Take it and good riddance. You've already shot the goddamn thing full of holes and killed the best foreman I ever knew."

Jer straightened. "*Me?* I was all stove up when Cam got it, Daddy."

"And Loli was in her room near the cookhouse, and she heard you give the orders. You know how it was with her and Cam. Don't expect her to take care of your dirty laundry anymore, boy; she'll barely keep house for me now. Your orders got Cam killed, and in some ways that's worse than doing it yourself."

Now Jer was breathing deeply as though fanning some inner flame, no longer avoiding his father's gaze. "Yeah? And how about you, settin' the law on my trail in Austin? Nobody else knew where I was headed, old man. You nearly got me bushwhacked."

"That's a goddamn—" Mul Garner caught himself on the defensive and changed tacks. "If that's what you think, you and I have nothing more to say."

"Speak for yourself. I say you tried to get me killed." From long habit, Jer let his hand move toward the sidearm at his hip. It was a bluff that had worked in the past, and he tried it without thinking.

The report and the *spat* against the barn wall were almost simultaneous, and Mul Garner wheeled toward its source. "Loli, no!" he bawled toward the woman who stood on the porch, steadying her scoped varmint rifle against a pillar.

Sorel drew from his armpit holster, ducked behind the nearside door, and fired as Clyde Longo sprinted into the barn for his weapon. Billy Ray and Reeve did the best they could do without weapons: they fell on their faces. Mul Garner staggered, struck in the kidney from behind, and despite the shocking pain he spun around, bringing the shotgun to his shoulder. He knew that round had come from the mouth of the barn.

Jer had drawn his automatic by reflex, saw the barrel of that scattergun rise in his general direction, and missed his father from a distance of three paces. Mul Garner squeezed off a round of double-aught buckshot toward the barn as Loli, nearly a hundred meters away, saw Jer fire that single round. Her second shot may have been intended merely to graze, but on the other hand, maybe not. It caught Jerome Garner squarely in the forehead, taking away the back of his skull in its passage. Jer folded backward from the knees and fell on his back, legs twitching, blood pooling around his head as he stared open-eyed into the heavens.

Felix Sorel felt the load of buckshot slam against the door; squeezed off two more rounds while Mul was cycling his pumpgun and saw the old man fall. Clyde Longo got his assault rifle unlimbered and, from a prone position near the other barn door, raked the porch with his first burst. The woman screamed, dropped the little varmint rifle, and doubled over, trying to reach the front door. Longo caught her in the doorway. She lurched against the door facing, her arms hanging as if broken at the shoulders, then fell on her side and did not move again.

Now, from the bunkhouse, came more fire peppering the barn, kicking dust spurts from the ground. Reeve Longo, face down as he had been from the first shot, shouted, "L. J.; cookie! It's us, dammit!"

More firing. "They know it's us, dumbfuck," called his brother. "They seen the old man go down."

Sorel did not know how many men, or how much firepower, they faced. But there was no time now for a pitched battle; for that matter, no time to shift their cargo to a pickup truck. As Clyde Longo fired toward the bunkhouse windows, Sorel ordered the others to run for the safety of the barn and covered them with several well-spaced shots.

As Clyde kept up his fire to keep their opponents inside, Sorel and the others slapped the van's body panel in place. Harley Slaughter did not have to be told to try starting the big diesel. Coughing gouts of smoke, then steadying, it surprised them all. Maybe it would get them as far as that shanty.

All the while, half of Sorel's mind was planning. He had four men left and a VHF scrambler in the van. Even if he made it to that shanty, they'd have to remove a ton of plastic-encased heroin from the van and stash it somewhere on the Garner spread. If the van coughed its last out on the open range, he would need three cycles. Reeve and Billy Ray had helped erect the shanty, and Billy Ray seemed the more dependable of the two, so he would ride in the van as guide. The others could bring the cycles after sabotaging other vehicles in the barn that might be used to give chase. Leaving no tracks, they might yet find a place to hide.

Sorel did not explain, simply barking the orders. Slaughter accepted his role frowning, but silent, and a minute later Sorel was accelerating the van out in fan mode, a great dust cloud of yellowish gray belching like cannon smoke from the mouth of the barn. It almost obscured the following cycles.

An hour later, after cursing the van's increasing ills and Billy Ray's faulty memory, Sorel saw the waddie jab a forefinger to their left. They had found it in failing light, no more than a shed with open ends, but adequate shelter from

aerial spotters. He entertained no hope that the van would
continue for even another half hour; indeed, only by lowering
the van skirts to the soil and picking his way around the
brushy undergrowth had Sorel got the damned thing this far.
Still, it was satisfactory. They could find a place to hide the
cargo, then get that hundred-kilo diesel engine loaded onto
one cycle. With three deaders lying at Garner Ranch, they'd
be courting suicide to show up at Rocksprings. Billy Ray
would have to take that engine to SanTone, where overhauls
and ranch hands were more anonymous. That would leave
Reeve Longo at the van, with the remaining canned goods
and the assault rifle. Surely those two knuckle-bangers could
reinstall the engine without help while Sorel and his hired
guns made tracks elsewhere.

Sorel refused to permit a fire, even inside the shanty, to
warm their supper that evening. Taking the worst case, those
men at the ranch might have started an aerial search, perhaps
even with Search & Rescue satellite help. A strong IR signa-
ture was the last thing he needed. The *first* thing he needed
was to contact help using the VHF scrambler. The van's
mapfiche proved they were tantalizingly near to several sizable towns: Rocksprings, Junction, Sonora. And those towns
might already be crawling with *federales* in plainclothes.
Sorel's slight accent was enough to tag him as neither Anglo
nor TexMex, and in any case some descriptions of him did
exist.

San Antonio Rose kept late hours, and Sorel's caution
worked overtime, so no message was left on the phone in
SanTone Ringcity. Around midnight Sorel finally made direct
contact. As always, Felix Sorel made as much use as possible
of the adage, "Never *com*plain; never *ex*plain." Even though
he had worked side by side in mutual trust with San Antonio
Rose before, Sorel knew he would be unwise to let the man
know just how much he was needed. Sorel's exact location
would remain a secret as well. It was enough that San Antonio Rose knew Sorel's immediate needs. These were simple
enough: a place to obtain new clothes and to alter appearances
for three men, and access to fast transport northward. While
Sorel and his gunsels conferred with his drug outlets, Billy
Ray and Reeve could get the van ready. The two mechanic
cowpokes would also make good telltales, in case some posse

did track the van somehow. They were more expendable than they knew. If you stake a bad dog in front of your door and find that dog missing or dead on your return, it's a fair bet that you should keep walking and never return. . . .

San Antonio Rose was firing on all cylinders that night, with a brilliant solution to Sorel's needs. Wild Country Safari was larger than the Garner spread and hosted the world's widest variety of guests. At least twice a week, it received passenger flights by the huge thrumming delta dirigibles that made direct connections to DalWorth and Santa Fe. It was less than two hours away by cycle. With so many people coming and going by varied kinds of private transportation, three men should have no trouble mixing with the vacationers, gamblers, dudes, and hookers in the synthetic Old West town of Faro. The place was hard to miss, served by excellent roads with two modern hotels and adjacent state-of-the-art thrill rides just over a rise from the little sin city. Sorel should find it easily and would find reservations waiting.

CHAPTER FIFTY-ONE • • •

San Antonio Rose spoke in rapid-fire Spanish, smiling as he heard Sorel's response to his solution. A scrambler module might insinuate a buzzing quality to the voice on the other end, but it couldn't filter out the relief in Sorel's voice. Oh, yes, Felix Sorel had somehow got a tin can tied to his tail all righty. A man might demand a fat bonus for help right now, and get it. And never have Sorel's trust again. Or one might see him later, man to man, and pass over it in cavalier lightness while making it clear that he knew Sorel owed him. But lightly, lightly; for Sorel possessed the subtlety and deadliness of a poison mushroom. Too bad a man had to deal with such as this handsome, lethal *maricón*, but times were bad and money still tight. Sorel paid well, and a man didn't have to ask for all the details of his business. It was easier to sleep when one did not know those details.

He would not have slept at all had he noticed the tiny spot of red light that impinged at one corner of the window nearest his telephone. His voice was the generator of faint vibrations that shook the windowpane, to be translated from fifty meters away by a laser sensor in a newly rented room with a view of his windows. His voice fidelity was poor, but no matter. The listener understood the language quite as well as he.

During the latter part of the conversation, San Antonio Rose gave advice. "The Last Chance is small, without many rooms. The Early Bird is nearest to the staging area where the deltas fly the high rollers in, and there's a lot of serious gambling there. That means quite a bit of security muscle roving around, Sorel. Some of 'em have been cops, or bounty hunters. Somehow I don't think that's what you're after.

"The Long Branch Saloon, now; if I have a choice, that's where I'll make your reservations. It covers an acre; gift shops, slots, and roulette, lots of people cruising around looking for new ways to lose their money. . . . Right; Vegas in a nutshell. Plenty of rooms upstairs. It's old style, bathrooms at the end of the hall, pitchers and basins in the rooms. . . .

"No, just for local color. You won't care, and you can't be that picky if you want to get lost among tourists. Right. Sure, why not? See you then," he said, and killed the connection with a tingle of pleasure. Then he disconnected the scrambler and called the main exchange of Wild Country Safari.

In a room not far away, Marianne Placidas furiously scribbled notes to herself. She too was tingling, with something that was as close as she could get, these days, to pleasure: it was anticipation.

CHAPTER FIFTY-TWO • • •

Sandy's journal, Mon. 30 Oct. '06

Rumors confusing. I cannot believe that Mr. Garner and Jerome would take each other's lives. And how did Loli Carrera get involved? I recall the poor old creature shopping for her patrón in Rocksprings, savaged by overwork and perhaps also by genes. They say she was lovely once, before the war, an early bloom who shed her petals too soon. She was all of forty. I suppose we will never know exactly what happened on Garner Ranch. Mystery!

Wonder who is to inherit, or to buy that great spread. God grant me good neighbors next time.

Guess who came home, bouncing like a piglet and in a mood to cavort. The strangest thing was that torn red scarf tied to his neck ruff. Childe jealously believes he has a new friend. Certainly Ba'al could not have tied that thing himself!

CHAPTER FIFTY-THREE • • •

"I don't know any more about it than you do, Ted," said Jess Marrow as they walked, trying not to seem hurried, toward the central hunt lodge. "Seems the Brit came in late last night without the van or the mare. And five minutes ago, my office terminal asks me if Wardrop has any outstanding stable fees. And you know what that means."

Quantrill nodded, mounting the steps to the lodge verandah, giving Marrow time to navigate them with his gimpy leg. They found Alec Wardrop settling his bill, scheduling a ride to the city by the earliest available means. At first, he was not disposed to talk.

Marrow found a cultural crowbar to pry an explanation from the man. "Got some stuff at my office for a toast, on the off chance that you made it back," he said, as if begrudging it. "Harvey's Bristol Cream Sherry. Awful stuff. Thought you'd like it."

Wardrop failed to keep his face straight, hung his head as he smiled. "Wonders never cease. Very well, and with pleasure. I have a few minutes to spare." Leaving his luggage untended, Wardrop accompanied his hosts back to Marrow's office.

Quantrill's only burning question was the fate of Ba'al, but all the signs pointed to a satisfactory answer; perhaps Wardrop had just taken enough of that hard-rock country, and abruptly said the hell with it. Lots of people behaved that way. Besides, Marrow's intuition made entirely too many accurate connections every time Quantrill mentioned the boar. Quantrill listened in silence as Marrow, ushering the tall Brit into the office, said, "I'm afraid to ask about Rose."

Wardrop lowered himself into an oak armchair with the care of a man who was nursing a lot of bruises. "The

229

commonest kind of tragedy, I'm afraid. She broke a leg and—had to be destroyed. I wasn't mounted at the time," he added in self-defense.

Quantrill pulled three polypaper cups from the dispenser; flicked them to Marrow, who caught them in what was obviously a ritual game. "I hear the van's still out there. Wrecked?"

Wardrop watched Marrow pour elegant sherry into lumpen proletarian cups and shook his head. "I suppose one's palate need not know the difference," he commented to Marrow, accepting a cupful, sniffing it with eyes closed. "No, the van is intact. I've marked it on a map for you. In any case, I'm all paid up; not to worry."

"I wasn't thinking about that. How'd you get back to WCS land?" Quantrill said.

"That," said Wardrop, pausing to sip the sherry, "is none of your God—damned—affair."

Quantrill made a face that was half dismay, half amusement.

Marrow: "You sure as hell didn't hoof it."

"Not by half. I got a . . . lift. I'd rather not talk about it, Marrow. Let us say, for the record, that Wild Country has too many surprises for a decent pigsticker to ply his trade. As far as I'm concerned, that boar can have the whole bloody region and welcome."

Marrow and Quantrill had swigged the sherry as though it were strawberry sodapop from the stable dispensers. Now Marrow refilled the cups, recorked the bottle. "To Wardrop and all his pigs, then," Marrow said, and hoisted the cup before drinking.

Wardrop made the proper gesture, saw the others toss off their sherry, shrugged with good humor, and followed suit. "Fitting eulogy for a dead occupation," he said, and stood up. He knew that no one would touch his things but, "I really should see to my baggage," he said. He thrust out his hand, and Marrow took it but did not stand. Unerring as usual, Jess Marrow's intuition told him the younger men had things to say in private.

With all his aches and pains, the lank Wardrop walked slowly enough for Quantrill to keep pace with ease. They had walked half the distance to the lodge before the Brit broke his silence with, "Here, take my card, Quantrill. You did your best to protect a foreigner you thought was half-mad. If you ever need help, consider yourself a fellow officer in my regiment. I'm not certain that I could explain exactly what that implies.''

"It's an honor, and that's enough.'' Quantrill shoved the card into his denims without breaking stride. "What's your next move?''

"Oh—to Cornwall, I imagine. A week or so tramping on Bodmin Moor in my knockabouts. Then back to the regiment a wiser man.'' Wardrop seemed to be laughing at himself, and then turned a frank gaze on Quantrill. "I've bagged my last boar, you know.''

Quantrill tried to hide his alarm. "Are you telling me you killed Ba'al?''

"God knows I tried.'' The Brit seemed lost in his reflections for a moment. Then, striking from an unfamiliar quarter: "Quantrill, did you ever read something called 'The Most Dangerous Game'? A classic adventure story by Richard Connell. Butchered badly in holoplays, of course.''

Quantrill's glance, flicked at his companion, was two parts suspicion. The tale had been required reading during his advanced army training in T Section, when "T'' stood for "terminate.'' Without giving that context he said, "I think so. About a Brit shipwrecked on an island. Some Russian count hunts him like an animal and the score winds up England one, islanders zero.''

"That's the one. I've always had a horror of that story. What if the game I hunted turned out to be human?''

"You have interesting nightmares,'' Quantrill conceded.

"Nightmares come true. Even if your quarry turns out to be *almost* human, it's nightmarish enough. I'm not sure this is any great surprise to you, but from the evidence I'd say that monster boar understands fair play better than most men I've known.'' Wardrop stopped at the lodge steps, hugged his elbows, stared thoughtfully toward the southwest, and straightened. "I am no Russian nobleman on an island keen on human prey. More important still, I know when I'm beaten. It's . . . not humiliating, but humbling; an experience you probably haven't yet had.'' A wry smile: "And good luck to you and your boar.'' He turned, still smiling, and reached for the door.

Quantrill cocked his head. "*My* boar?"

"Wouldn't be a bit surprised," said the Brit, pausing, and winked. "But we all have our secrets." He turned and went inside.

Quantrill walked alone back to Marrow's office, knowing that he would miss Lieutenant Alec Wardrop. He found Jess Marrow pecking away at his computer terminal and saw curiosity in the older man's gaze. He tried to satisfy it with, "I gather Wardrop has finally found his good strong sign, Jess. Claims he's through with boar hunts."

Marrow flicked off the terminal; leaned back in his chair and sighed. "He had the look, Teddy. There's another name for that sign, you know. It's called 'failure.' "

Quantrill tried the idea on for size. "I don't know, Jess. He didn't act like a broken man."

"Broken, no; but that's because he's still young and full of piss and vinegar. Lemme tell you something, Teddy: a man is lucky if he learns to accept failure when he's young. Failure for a man is like childbirth for a woman: when you have your first one late in life, it can just about destroy you."

Quantrill thought it over. "I'm not sure I follow that," he said at last.

"'Course not, fool, you haven't seen your sign. Yet."

"I've failed at a lot of things," Quantrill objected. He saw Marrow eyeing him over the old-fashioned spectacles, smiling and shaking his head. "You mean something big, then."

"Yep. Something so big it limits your self-confidence, tells you that you're just a mortal man, after all. Tells you that on a given day there's somebody, maybe nose to nose with you, who can beat you at ever'thing you do best."

"Aw, hell, Jess. Nine-tenths of the people I meet seem to know that. They don't even need a very strong sign."

"Right." Marrow grinned and shoved the specs into place with a blunt forefinger. "And they don't count, 'cause they never really had that basic self-confidence to start with. And what's more, most of 'em hate you soon as they see you *do* have it. When I said a good strong man needs a good strong sign, I didn't mean physical strength necessarily. I guess I meant confidence, Teddy. We have it. Wardrop has it." He closed one eye and aimed a finger at Quantrill. "I will bet you anything that damn near all of our close friends have it.

Because those who don't have it, don't want to be our friends. They want to see us fail.''

Quantrill threw up his hands and smiled. "Okay, you're probably right. Give me a break, Jess; great truths should be swallowed in small doses.''

"In other words, shut the fuck up, boss," Marrow growled. "By the way, there's a call came for you while you were out with Wardrop. I got the number here; the area code is Corpus Christi or thereabouts.''

Quantrill took the scrap of polypaper and studied Marrow's scrawl, then smiled. "Could be good news," he said, and hurried to his room for the Justice Department scrambler module.

CHAPTER FIFTY-FOUR • • •

Sandy's journal, Tues. 31 Oct. '06

According to Ted, I am absurdly wealthy! Must get used to saying "rich," as the rich do. Ironic that so much money could accrue from something that was, insofar as I can see, a toy for the amusement of grown children. It makes sense, I suppose, in terms of the information it contains. Dear God, now I could live in the city without ever turning a lick of work as long as I lived!

Ted laughed uproariously when I told him of "The Case of the Scarlet Pennant," gasping out that I must keep it in memory of Don Quixote?! Well, either he will explain that, or I will tickle him mercilessly in every secret place.

I suggested that he help me decide what to do about all this new wealth, as yet unreal to me. He tells me he will come in a few days, after one last piece of business in Faro. Nothing to worry about, says he. And when he says that, I always know he is risking his stupid neck. All those riches will leave me destitute if anything happens to that man.

CHAPTER FIFTY-FIVE • • •

One advantage in undercover work for the Department of Justice was that, when you needed stylish cover, you could *do* it in style while Uncle Sugar paid the tab. The chief disadvantage was that, whatever your style, you could get yourself seriously killed hunting a man like Felix Sorel. Old Jim Street had told Quantrill the good news first, about the amulet and its price, then followed it with what he called AC-DC news, which might go either way.

To counter the burgeoning black market in used machinery, engine rebuild shops in SanTone Ringcity routinely checked the serial numbers of vehicle engines brought to them for repair. Since Mexico and Canada also had the capacity to build engines, they shared their solutions to the illegal machinery trade, and that sharing was so recent that its international flavor had not yet come to Sorel's attention. Now the registered owner of any vehicle from Saskatoon to San Luis Potosí was a matter of computer record. Billy Ray did not know this. He had scarcely walked out of the ringcity shop on Bandera Road before the shop foreman, having recorded the engine number, found himself staring at a blinker on his terminal screen. Blinkers meant trouble. They sometimes meant rewards, too.

In this case there was no reward, only a husky black dude in plainclothes who visited the shop immediately with an unquenchable interest about whoever had brought in that engine. Its owner of record was one Cipriano Balsas, a Mexican national. There was no report that the engine had been stolen, but Señor Balsas was linked to a known associate that set a blinker flashing in an office of the Texas Western Federal Judicial District headquarters, SanTone Ringcity. Ironically, district HQ was so near that rebuild shop that agents could see its Solarglo sign from their high windows a kilometer away.

Computers and justice departments being what they are, every name that passed through the engine ID program was also matched for whatever interest lawmen might have in certain people. Thanks to his excellent contacts, Sorel had been assured that Mexican records did not connect him with any illegal activity—nor, in fact, with any known illegals. He was not so well connected in the hated country to the north, where Sorel's name and his known associates were on record, including one Cipriano Balsas. According to the records, Señor Balsas did not draw a breath or scratch himself unless Felix Sorel told him to do so. The Department of Justice had outstanding warrants for Sorel. They were also anxious to get his finger, retinal, and tissue prints on file, on the slight chance that some government might bring enough pressure to bear so that Sorel would one day walk around loose again. Cipriano would have died rather than lead *yanquis* to his *patrón*, but Cipriano did not have that choice. He had bought the van himself in Monterrey on Sorel's orders, and now the engine of that van was in SanTone. Neither Sorel nor any of his men knew it, but as far as the Department of Justice was concerned, that engine was so hot it glowed in the dark.

Because Billy Ray had not been on the wanted list, he gave his real name to the rebuild shop. And because he was an idiot, he signed the same name on the register of the No Tell Motel six blocks away. Finally, because ''no tell'' was a transparent lie, the register was made available to the first man flashing a federal shield on his wallet, an hour after Billy Ray signed.

So it was that Billy Ray returned from shopping with one armload of beer and the other arm full of henna redhead to find his motel room already occupied by a black agent with ball bearings for eyes and a persuasive way of displaying armament. After being read his rights Billy Ray immediately proved the fool he was by volunteering that he had been *forced* to shoot his foreman by a rancher who could neither confirm nor deny it because the back of his head had been blown away. The born-again redhead sucked on a molar, fascinated, until the federal agent decided she was guilty only of excessive availability and shooed her back onto the street again. Billy Ray, on the other hand, had earned himself an endless train of free meals and lodging at Huntsville Prison, or worse. Whisked to district headquarters, he was then advised of his wrongs, and the feds seemed to think he was important enough to string up beside his pal Felix Sorel, when they caught him—which they implied was a foregone conclusion. Briefly, Billy Ray played a delaying game.

Agents with doctorates in psychology played the man as if he were a cheap accordion, squeezing him, punching his keys as they pleased. Was Billy Ray a close confederate of Sorel? The answer was vague. Did Billy Ray know the exact whereabouts of Sorel? The answer failed to satisfy. Was Billy Ray, perchance, as queer as his buddy Sorel?

Billy Ray sang like a cageful of mockingbirds.

It soon became clear that the waddie had only the foggiest notions of Sorel's contraband, but a precise idea where that van was stashed. Golden Boy himself had run off, taking his favorites Harley Slaughter and Clyde Longo, to Little Vegas—or so Billy Ray had heard. He wasn't sure about the "little" part.

Feds conferred. The obvious answer was to turn the Nevada sin city inside out, but not so fast: there was a Las Vegas in New Mexico, too. Though not a mecca for drug dealers, the smaller Las Vegas was a place where Spanish-speaking *cimarrones* had been known to congregate. It was also within a reasonable distance of Wild Country. The town of Faro was not even real, in the sense of mayors and tax assessments. Its reality was in its gambling income and its travel connections, and one of Faro's nicknames was "Little Vegas." It was open to the public, and on a map it lay very near the spot Billy Ray had hit with a grimy fingernail, estimating the van's location. By this time, Attorney General James Street was making executive decisions on the matter.

Without knowing how many of his channels were infiltrated, but with what sounded like a monumental drug bust on tap, Jim Street picked only undercover agents under his direct control and split the ten of them up among the likely targets. Five men flew to Nevada, two to Garner Ranch, and two to northern New Mexico. Street already had his tenth man in place near Faro. He personally warned Quantrill against taking direct action unless absolutely certain of his quarry, and then only after obtaining backups. His gut feeling, Street confided, was that Sorel and his men would head for New Mexico. Once positively identified, they could be quietly surrounded by local, state, and federal authorities. Street's last advice was to remember that Felix Sorel was a sidewinder. In Wild Country that meant the man was fast, deadly, aggressive, and would give no warning before he struck. This was no epithet to Quantrill, who had once been a government-run sidewinder himself.

Quantrill rented a gleaming new hovercycle, a Curran with all the comforts of home, and using the credit code number assigned to ''Sam Coulter'' by Street, obtained a pocketful of crisp new bills from the main hunt lodge. Less than an hour after his scrambled call, wearing his best casual western outfit with the Chiller snugged into his armpit, Ted Quantrill topped a gentle rise and scanned the town of Faro.

CHAPTER FIFTY-SIX • • •

The planners of Wild Country Safari had chosen the site with great care, placing Faro deceptively in a valley separated from sight of the Thrillkiller complex, two klicks away in the next valley. On topping that rise, a visitor saw only the clapboard structures and dusty streets of a frontier township, and guests were encouraged to dress appropriately. Its emotional impact was instant 1885. No automobiles or cycles were permitted past the underground parking facility; the stables and streets of Faro were redolent of horse muffins, not auto exhaust fumes. Guests rode the stagecoach from the parking facility into town, and the cavernous gift shop offered few items more modern than cactus candy. From clerks wearing gaiters, green eyeshades, and garters on their sleeves, you could buy good western garb, Pendleton shirts, and hand-tooled boots, or you could rent them. No beer in bulbs, no candy in wrappers, no Kleenex; you used a kerchief or your sleeve. To buy such stuff as cosmetics, cigarettes, and common drugstore items, you either went elsewhere or chose from the modest assortment at the mercantile shop. You could wear a Colt peacemaker on your hip so long as it was peacebonded with six empty chambers. Only security men, wearing stars of authority in their shirts, were allowed live ammo. Quantrill's muffled Chiller, its magazine crammed with twenty-four rounds of flashless seven-millimeter ammo, was not a thing he chose to wear openly. A spare magazine rested in the pocket of each boot top.

The memory of San Antonio Rose had been flawless. Faro's last chance to take a guest's money was the small, too neat Last Chance Saloon, nearest to the parking facility. Three blocks away across the tic-tac-toe street plan, on the way to the next valley, lay the Early Bird Saloon. The Long

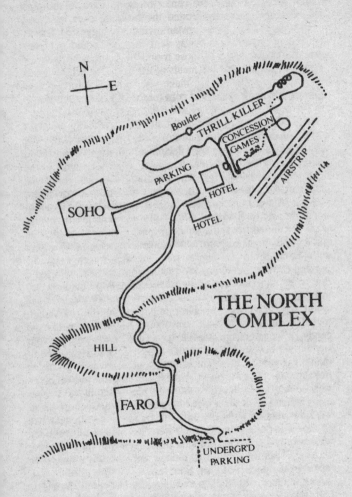

N
E

Boulder
THRILL KILLER
CONCESSION
GAMES
PARKING
AIRSTRIP
HOTEL
SOHO
HOTEL

THE NORTH
COMPLEX

HILL

FARO

UNDERGR'D
PARKING

Branch occupied the entire center-block of Faro, a shingled roof running completely around the building over its broad wooden porch. The many upstairs windows suggested dozens of sleeping rooms, and it was said that you could get your wick trimmed in some of those rooms by petticoated ladies.

It was also said that the meals at the Long Branch could, if you spent much time there, make you as fat as a forty-pound robin. The dinner fare ran to corn on the cob, succulent steaks the diameter of cantaloupe and almost as thick, sourdough biscuits with redeye gravy, and buttermilk in heavy pitchers. Some subtle manager had discovered that a meal like that could give casual gamblers a stronger sense of well-being than three shots of Old Sunny Brook.

Faro's staff spared no effort in keeping the place authentic, including the consumption of coal oil for lamps. The whole town exuded a faint odor of the stuff, reminiscent of diesel fuel and, along with wandering scorpions and rattlers, among the few real dangers in town. Faro's buried water mains were pressure-fed from a more modern installation, a valley and a century removed.

That modern complex lay sequestered in its own long valley, the two hotels and the clinic set mostly underground with huge central atriums like sinkholes walled with glass. At one end of the valley was a romantic, stuffy jumble of structures dubbed "Soho," five hundred meters square, built to resemble downtown London during the Battle of Britain in the year 1941. Its streets, hardly more than alleyways, were mostly cobbled, the buildings sprayed for the look of stone under a coal-smoke patina. Many of the upper windows were broken as if by concussion, some with proper little curtains sadly waving from them like forgotten flags of truce. Visitors entered and left Soho from only one street, Brewer, and were prevented from other exits—and from loss of the illusion—by blockades. Beyond the cordons one could see signs reading "UXB," suggesting an unexploded Nazi bomb, and rubble choking the streets with the acrid tang of cordite turning like knives in the nostrils. Now and then, from behind the barricades at a safe distance, one might see a hunk of masonry topple from a cornice into the street below.

During daylight hours, Soho's guests could see music hall hijinks or an Agatha Christie play enacted by androids who never fluffed a line and, in a distinct improvement over live actors, gauged their curtain calls to the amount of applause. Or they could buy Harris tweeds, spats, or bowler hats in Soho's shops; devour steak and kidney pie until gout set in; get laid standing up by a delicious android with Eliza Doolittle's own accent and no compunctions about copping a feel; or get viciously insulted in a small philatelist's shop. All in all, patrons of Soho thought a hundred dollars a day was very reasonable for the experience, especially since it included a night's lodging—not that anybody got to sleep much. For one thing, there were the regular percussive announcements by an unseen Big Ben, which began each brief concerto with a catastrophic clatter as if someone were using its gears to grind plate-glass windows. It wasn't precisely authentic, but it added its own brand of charm. And then, of course, there was a good, safe war.

The main show was the London blitz, three nights a week, and it was a multimedia sensation to send the craven sprinting down Brewer Street for the exit. Two WCS pilots of Confederate Air Force vintage flew the pair of half-scale, twin-engined Heinkel bombers, which were invariably picked out by searchlights to reveal the swastikas gleaming on their skins. Because a scaled-down Beaufighter was murderously hard to fly and Hurricanes lacked pizazz, other pilots chased the Heinkels in five-eighths-scale Supermarine Spitfires. Particularly on moonlit evenings, the low moan of sirens, the drone of Heinkels, the hackle-raising howl of Spits in pursuit, and the hammer of distant machine-gun fire made you suspect a time warp. The dopplering whistle of bombs and the concussions made you damn near sure of it. The choreographed march of low-level pyrotechnic flak bursts and the "crash" of a Heinkel just out of sight, complete with fireball, compelled belief.

This kind of mock-up war was expensive, and much of its timing depended on computers. The hidden kilowatt-rated loudspeakers and pyrotechnic machines were so well placed that few people suspected the aircraft were scaled down, flying rather slowly and so low that only an occasional searchlight beam could be seen from Faro. The concussions, when anyone in Faro asked, were said to be blasting operations in a distant mine. In daylight, all this carefully staged flummery would not have fooled a real Londoner for a second, but at night Soho gave added spice to drinking tepid bitter beer in basement pubs or making love in a blacked-out upstairs room. For its sky-high rates, Soho got an astonishing amount of repeat business.

Up the valley from Soho, on the other side of the hotels, lay the complex of entertainment rides. The main and most obvious attraction was a sinister assemblage of rails and individual plastic-canopied delta bullets designed by LockLever. Someone, after emerging mush-kneed from his first ride in it, had called it the Thrillkiller. After that, he'd whispered, nothing else could be a thrill if you lived through it. The name had stuck. The Thrillkiller's track stretched most of the valley's length, dipping underground soon after its early initial kinks for its spiral loop, which gave the rider the distinct impression he was spinning inside a vast, dank storm sewer to hell. Hurtling upward from this dim-lit limbo, each little capsule left its maglev rails long enough to convince a passenger that he was flying—which he was, completing an arc of fifty meters before engaging the rails again.

The viewscreen of the little capsule was not entirely for show; after the brief free-fall arc and pulling two-gee sideloads during recovery, you were asked by the screen whether you would prefer to continue on the submach track or vault to the hypersonic track—essentially, a question of the high road or the low road. If you didn't opt for the high road, you took the low one by default. Most folks, by this time, had already begun to suspect that signing the release form had been their last mortal mistake and were holding on to the grips so fiercely that they could not have punched an instruction for love nor money. This earned them the relatively mild submach track, which accelerated its spade-shaped capsules to only 150 kilometers per hour on the long stretches. It returned its sweat-soaked victims to the starting point without any more terror than they might have sustained in . . . oh, say, losing the laser boost while on a jetliner and hearing the pilot burst into tears.

If you chose the hypersonic option, you would get back to the starting point just as soon as if you'd taken the low road—but you would traverse twice the distance. Your capsule found the high road by three seconds of automatic steam boost while climbing a steep incline, and instead of a controlled descent to the low road on rails, you left those rails in a free arc that carried you to another track, perched at dizzying height near the end of the valley. You then swept the edge of a low butte, pulling three gees in the turn, before augering wildly downward toward the high-velocity run.

The bald truth was that even by firewalling your control grip, you only achieved some 350 kilometers per hour, and that for only a brief moment before the automatics kicked maglev brakes on. But you achieved it while flashing past shrubs, past the parallel outbound track, and literally through one large fiberglass boulder that seemed to have rolled onto the track just a moment before for the express purpose of making marmalade of capsule and passenger alike. The aperture that opened through the boulder was controlled by pneumatics. They had never failed. Yet. But that's what release forms were for.

The Thrillkiller's tab was twenty dollars. Survivors of the hypersonic option tended to fall into two categories: those few who would pay fifty to do it again, not today of course, but someday; and the other ninety percent who would willingly have paid a thousand *not* to. *Ever.*

Nearer to the hotels were less ambitious entertainments, some designed for children, some for adults who wanted to be children for a time. The game of Copycat involved one very flexible android and a padded room; both the Haunted Mine and the Dee & Dee layout used robotic creatures of various shapes and were chiefly underground. More of these amusements were under study by WCS planners, and the fame of the place was growing. Already, plans were under way to extend the landing strip and to expand the hangar which, at present, could swallow tiny Heinkels and Spitfires, but not a delta dirigible.

The huge deltas whispered low over the prairie on regular runs, connecting the entertainment complex with Santa Fe and DalWorth. Vacationing foreigners enjoyed the trip for its scenic value; high rollers enjoyed it because the leviathan delta provided a smooth platform for a "little game" en route, where some of those foreigners might be relieved of excess money. Felix Sorel was certain he would enjoy it because he could board a delta without showing anything more than a ticket, and could float away unseen above any posse that might be convened below in his honor.

CHAPTER FIFTY-SEVEN • • •

Quantrill's belly growled, reminding him that it was lunchtime and that Faro had many a remedy for *that*. He parked the rented cycle on the second level, noting that the place didn't seem to be overcrowded as it had been on his first visit. Guests usually elected to wait for the stagecoach—after all, it was free—but Quantrill preferred to hoof it, stretching the kinks from his legs. He wore the low-heeled western boots Sandy had bought him for Rocksprings dances, finely crafted footgear with uppers of burgundy sharkskin. Their fit and their elastomer soles were suitable for anything short of rock climbing. Sandy had refused to tell him the price of those hand-crafted beauties, lovingly put together by a man who'd learned his trade in Lubbock from the master, Willie Lusk. Perhaps they were not quite a match for the boots he'd worn with Search & Rescue, but those lugged gunboats would have given him the look of a man who expected a workout. He had dressed the part of Sam Coulter, fresh from Monahans in his best suede jacket, with a fat cash bonus and the urge to spend it. With those contact lenses and the hasty dye job on his hair, he felt anonymous enough to relax and enjoy this little junket. And that was the emergent tip of a profound mistake.

For the first time in his adult life, Ted Quantrill actively looked forward to a fruitless few days at his post. He intended to spend much of the time exercising his cover, trying his luck at the games, meeting stagecoaches and being unobtrusively on hand when the big delta came sliding to or from its moorage at the airstrip. But this was also a chance for introspection, a retreat for the inner man, where he could reexamine the facets of Ted Quantrill at leisure and consider recutting his stone, so to speak, to exclude some of its outstanding flaws. There was much to consider, now that Sandy was

245

trying to cut half a million dollars straight down the middle
with him.

Yet in entertaining these thoughts, Quantrill was letting
vital bits of his old T Section training slide. That training had
kept him alive because the army had grabbed him so young
that he'd taken their words at full face value. And virtually all
his instructors, at one time or another, had insisted that
nothing was more important, or more difficult, on a stakeout
than constant alertness. They'd phrased it in various ways,
but always it amounted to what that sublime sonofabitch
Seth Howell had drawled once, in that soft whiskey tenor of
his: "When your life rides on the game, *keep your eye on the
goddam ball.*"

Quantrill had received no refresher courses of any consequence for nearly four years. Instead of thinking in terms of
honing those skills, he was well on the way to setting them
aside—after this last mission, of course. Neither Sandy nor
Marrow had the expertise to understand, and to say, what
Quantrill most needed to hear: in the manhunting business,
the only way to quit is cold turkey. If you try to ease out,
you'll most likely get carried out.

Instead, Quantrill wandered into the Last Chance, surveyed
the tourists, then walked past a hardware store and a jewelry
store flying the false flag of an assay office before crossing to
the Long Branch. Virtually the first man he saw inside was
Felix Sorel.

CHAPTER FIFTY-EIGHT • • •

Both Longo and Slaughter had visited Faro before, but it was Sorel who thought to leave their Garner cycles in a drywash down the valley from Faro that morning. It was possible that those license plates were already on someone's shitlist. By midmorning they arrived in Faro to find that reservations had been made at the Long Branch for one Ernst Matthias, a Leo Cherry, and Clyde Longo's alias, Johnny Collier. A fourth reservation had been made as well, for the man sometimes known as San Antonio Rose. So far, the fourth man was a no-show.

Sorel had wandered around the first floor, its gaming rooms spacious as dance floors, while Slaughter signed himself in and Longo bought necessary items from Faro's shops. Then, in Slaughter's room upstairs, Sorel plied one of the many trades he had learned in Cuba.

One can create great art with razor blades, flesh-colored adhesive strips, and cotton. Sorel built lifts high as shot glasses into his own boots, and gave Longo an apparently broken left elbow by taping the naked arm with some of the tape in high tension. Longo had to rip it loose twice by flexing that arm before he was satisfied that it wouldn't impede him if he found it necessary, in his words, "to unlimber in a hurry."

A pound of cotton went into the pads at Harley Slaughter's beltline and rump, but when taped in place they gave the gaunt Slaughter the look of a well-fed rancher. By careful application of bone-tinted shoe polish to Slaughter's temples and eyebrow pencil near his eyes, Sorel added fifteen false years to the man. Sorel noted that one might profitably grow wheat under Longo's fingernails and insisted that the men attend to their manicures like gentlemen. Longo's villainous

247

beard came off next. Little more was done about his hair except send him away to have it cut at the Early Bird's tonsorial parlor.

Later, Sorel signed for his own room and made a show of striking up a conversation with Slaughter, as though they were well-met strangers, in the presence of the room clerk. The two of them then strolled around the place, checking exits. When Longo returned at midday, he walked past Sorel near the main doorway before a familiar voice made him whirl.

By the time he signed the register, Sorel's golden hair had become the blue-black of a raven's wing, and the tiny pads in his cheeks had subtly altered the hard lines of his face. He was as tall as Longo, and boasted a clear, slightly pale complexion thanks to long experience with women's cosmetics. "Matthias" and "Cherry" were standing with "Collier," enjoying the success of their deceptions, as Ted Quantrill ambled onto the porch outside.

"This calls for a drink, and a meal if we can find one worth eating," said Sorel, still smiling at Longo's surprise. After two days of heavy tension, his amusement had burst forth with unusual force.

"Best damn food in Wild Country," said Slaughter, patting his artificial belly, glancing at the dark-haired fellow with brown eyes who was pushing through the swinging doors nearby.

Longo agreed with, "They serve great grub here, and my belly thinks my throat is cut."

"Lead the way, Mr. Cherry," said Sorel.

The newcomer paused, smiling. To the man nearest—it happened to be Sorel—he said, "Best idea I've heard all day. Is the food here as good as at the Early Bird?"

"These gentlemen claim it is," said Sorel, returning the smile. "Shall we see for ourselves?"

Quantrill hesitated, with a casual scan into the nearest of the gaming rooms. Then, "Thanks," he said, "maybe in a few minutes. Don't eat it all," he joked feebly, with a nod at the other men, and moved toward the room clerk's counter.

Sorel followed Slaughter through lamplit halls. They passed a couple in western dress and a little brown man in an excellent suit of foreign cut on their way to the dining hall.

Seated at the round oak tables was only a scatter of diners, a dozen or so in all. Sorel wished the place were more crowded, wanting safety in numbers. The next delta was due on the following day and, unless business picked up later in the day, he favored staying out of sight in their rooms for the most part. In eliminating room service, Sorel felt, Faro was carrying this frontier ambience a little far. Perhaps they could add a few harmless people to their number for cover. Sorel, as usual, carried enough cash on his person to buy a condo in Austin.

Ten minutes later, Quantrill had secured a room and a quick, expensive look at the Long Branch register. He had no way of knowing that Clyde Longo or others might be with the two he sought. No men fitting his descriptions of Sorel and Slaughter had registered—certainly not together. The manager of security would be out of his office until business picked up around dark, and Quantrill's stomach was making noises like a suspicious bull terrier. He walked through the gaming rooms, with a second look at two men playing "twenty-one" near an exit, then relaxed and asked a lone croupier the way to the dining hall.

Sorel saw the sturdy fellow in the expensive sharkskin boots come through the doorway; waved a cheery greeting. "Join us," he said, and the man did so. The introductions were quickly made—all lies, by experts. Sorel found the young stranger only a bit short on easy conversation, and by the time their meals arrived he was genuinely warming to Sam Coulter from Monahans.

CHAPTER FIFTY-NINE • • •

From time to time, as the group laid waste to a heavy meal, other diners wandered into the room. Quantrill had been warned about a possible contact for Sorel, a latino in his thirties with a slight limp, broad shoulders, a little paunch above slim hips, and the look of a sullen eagle in his eye. So far, there was no sign of such a man. The faint latino accent of Sorel triggered no alarm in Quantrill's mind; one out of every four men in Wild Country claimed Spanish as their first language. At Sorel's table, no one seemed to give newcomers more than a casual glance. The four of them made their assessments without so much as a pause and polished off big helpings of apple cobbler. Sorel found himself enjoying "Coulter" and knew that part of his enjoyment was physical attraction.

He would not hear of Quantrill's paying for his meal. "In my own city of Merida, I could find no better companions," said Sorel, who knew Merida like the back of his hand. "Please be my guests at the gaming tables this afternoon, gentlemen. Or perhaps we could bring cards to my room. No risks to anyone," he added, relishing his secret play on words.

Quantrill burped gently. "Much obliged, Matthias. But I always take a solo walk after a meal like this. Later, maybe." He did not add that his stroll would take him to the desk clerk at the Early Bird.

"After siesta, then?"

Quantrill pushed his chair back and returned Sorel's smile. "Probably around dark," he hazarded, getting up. "I kinda thought I'd catch a stage to Soho and the Thrillkiller this afternoon." *And keep an eye peeled for Sorel*, he added to himself.

"An excellent idea," Sorel replied. He had his own reasons for learning the layout adjacent to the delta landing strip. Quickly he turned his smiling glance to the others. "Would you gentlemen be my guests for such a trip?"

"Whatever," said Longo lazily.

"Okay by me," Slaughter replied. "How 'bout it, Coulter?"

Quantrill made a quick decision. This was probably a wild goose chase anyhow; why not combine business with pleasure? Good sense should have told him why not; yet, "Fine," he said. "See you at the tables."

Watching Quantrill's exit, Longo muttered, "You sure we want that guy underfoot?"

"As cover, yes. We may even find that we need him. A man who uses my money can be surprisingly grateful," Sorel murmured. As he signed the tab, Sorel reflected that this was true only for simple, friendly fellows like Coulter. San Antonio Rose was a different sort: short on gratitude, long on greed. He would follow orders—making three singleton reservations for that delta at separate hotels, for instance—only because he would be paid in cash for his services.

Quantrill had found the same to be true of desk clerks. Even if he'd had a shield to flash, he would have used a crisp bill instead. It got you the information, sometimes more of it than you expected, without giving your own status away. This time he learned that the Early Bird housed a pair of tough-looking gents who might be the "friends" he sought to surprise. For a second bill, the clerk arranged to be relieved for ten minutes and, finding the pair's room empty, made his brief reconnaissance of the gaming rooms. He returned beaming, having found both men at the roulette table.

Quantrill made a wary approach, reminded himself that the Gov had insisted he obtain backups before drawing on Felix Sorel. He found one man consulting a programmable calculator, nervously scanning the display as he muttered orders to a companion. They were only men with a system to beat the wheel, and it was clearly failing. They did fit the general descriptions he gave the desk clerk, but he'd wasted forty dollars to locate a couple of incurable optimists. Quantrill sighed and moved on. Whatthehell, he might as well find

Matthias and escort him to the Thrillkiller complex. There was something about the Mexican that he liked, beyond his willingness to spend money. Maybe, he thought, it was that aura of easy self-confidence. . . .

CHAPTER SIXTY • • •

The stage to the Thrillkiller complex was loaded to its running boards, and two small boys were "forced" to sit up with the driver to their whoops of delight as they looked down on the rumps of the four-horse team. Their parents sat with Sorel's party and discussed the Thrillkiller; that is, until they saw it. Rounding a bend, the occupants of the stage all fell silent before the spectacle that sprawled the length of the valley.

They passed the quaint urban jungle of Soho to the left, on their way to a broad ground-level parking area a kilometer or so farther. A pair of sunken hotels flanked two sides of the parking area, and a vast hangarlike structure, housing most of the amusement rides, loomed beyond. Stretching alongside these structures, angling toward the butte at the head of the valley, was a well-surfaced airstrip with hangar space for small visiting craft as well as Heinkels and Spitfires. But no one spent much time staring at these secondary attractions. Even Sorel, who had come solely to see the delta moorage, stared in awe, speechless as the two boys who were first to spot a Thrillkiller capsule spiraling down from the lip of the butte several kilometers away.

From this distance, only the silver two-place capsule and its maglev rails glinted in the sun, the support structures painted to blend into the ochre tints of Wild Country. When Quantrill spotted it, the tiny bubble-topped dart was emerging from its downward spiral and onto the high-speed straight, heading in their general direction. It dropped from sight as the stage negotiated a gentle bend toward the parking area and did not come into view again until they were passing the natural earth berm of the nearest hotel. It was still nearly a kilometer away, but now over the clip-clopping and homely

253

squeaks of a horse-drawn stage they could hear the synthesized turbine howl of the capsule. Even at this distance, they found it easy to believe that the thing was streaking along at supersonic velocity.

The little capsule banked into a broad turn, arrowing nearer, then sweeping to parallel the parking area before braking for its last series of gut-wrenching chicanes. In seconds it had disappeared, heading for the start-finish arcade near the other rides. "That tears it," said the father of the boys in a hushed voice. "Nobody in his right mind would let his kids ride that thing by themselves."

"That's the hypersonic track," Quantrill offered. "Besides, WCS won't let children ride alone."

"Then that *really* settles it," the man replied. "I'm not crazy."

"I'm with you," Quantrill said, grinning. He could see his new friend Matthias studying the curve of the maglev rails, nodding, smiling. Chiefly for the Mexican's benefit and mindful of their heavy lunch, he added, "It can empty a full stomach in a hurry, they say."

Stepping from the stage near a berm walkway, they watched a double-decker London bus lurch away, half-filled with patrons, toward the distant Soho. The other passengers ambled away to leave Quantrill and his party alone. The place might be thronged by holiday season, but today the hubbub of foot traffic was light. Still gazing at the rails gleaming laserlike in the near distance, Sorel said, "I would not have thought you could resist a challenge like that, Mr. Coulter. You have been here before, without trying this Thrillkiller?"

On his first trip Quantrill had been on duty for WCS, and in any case he had not given expensive thrill rides much thought at the time. A manhunter, even a part-time deputy, found challenges enough without creating them. "I was with a miz," he lied, and followed it up with another. "Which reminds me, a girl I knew from Alpine used to work at one of these places. Really should look her up. If she's homesick, I could get lucky." He winked. "Where'll you three be in . . . oh, an hour, I reckon?"

Sorel laughed, accepting the fact that Sam Coulter liked to cruise for women alone. It also occurred to him that he could better study the delta moorage without Coulter. He looked around, saw the concession signs beyond an ornamental cactus garden, and pointed. "Under the 'Dee and Dee' sign, then, in an hour."

Quantrill entered the nearest hotel while Sorel and his companions strode off in the direction of the concessions. Longo, noting that the crowd was too sparse for his liking, said, "I feel like we're naked out here in the open."

"I must get a close look at the air terminal, such as it is," said Sorel. "Perhaps it would be better if you two separated and mingled with the tourists. If you pick up a little *puta* or two, so much the better." With that, he struck off on a perimeter path toward the airstrip, a ten-minute walk away.

CHAPTER SIXTY-ONE • • •

Quantrill drew a total blank in the modern hotels. The patrons sleeping in Soho, he learned to his surprise, could only make reservations a week or more in advance. It made sense; WCS was not about to run such an expensive spectacle as the Battle of Britain when only a handful of paying guests were scheduled. The casual tourist was encouraged to visit Soho, but the last bus left Brewer Street at Big Ben's last stroke of ten every night. A very few hardy souls might stay in the pubs until someone called, "Time, gents," but they faced a long walk in darkness to the glow of the distant hotels, and Texas rattlers did not go to sleep with the sparrows.

Logically, even if Sorel were somewhere near, he could not have known he needed reservations a week before. Besides, "Little Vegas" was a term reserved for Faro. Quantrill promised himself to visit Soho with Sandy someday but saw no reason to search the place now. The desk clerks of every hotel in the area now knew that they could earn easy money by leading one Sam Coulter, room 212 at the Long Branch, to men traveling together and matching certain descriptions. If he merely canvassed the hotels and showed up when passengers boarded the big delta at dusk the following day, he would be doing his job. The plain fact was that, by now, Quantrill did not expect—in fact, did not particularly hope—to meet Felix Sorel. Half-aware of this potentially fatal mindset, Quantrill walked across the grounds expecting, and hoping, to meet Ernst Matthias.

He saw the tall man from behind, waiting near the sign of the popular "Dee and Dee" concession, and checked his stride while tallying details with his last photo of Sorel's sidekick, Harley Slaughter. But this man had a sizable rump on him, whereas Slaughter was one lean machine. He saw as

256

he moved for a better view that this one also had the beginnings of a comfortable paunch, was gray at the sideburns, and—hell, it was only his companion, Leo Cherry! Laughing silently at himself, Quantrill greeted the man with the palm-up "how" gesture of holovision Indians and real-life Texans.

"See anything that looks like fun?"

"Little brunette, but she ain't sellin' *or* buyin'." Slaughter shrugged. "You?"

"My Alpine chick has flown," Quantrill said, aping a line from a current western ditty, complete with the catch in his voice.

If Cherry was amused, he kept it to himself. "Where the hell are—those other two?"

The others straggled up within moments, and Sorel proposed that they see what the inside concessions had to offer. A chattering jostle of parents and kids had lined up to tour the Haunted Mine, which packed four people in each artificially tacky orecart for a five-minute ride. Sorel thought it might be a trifle too tame.

The Copycat sounded tame but looked more like a challenge. Perhaps a score of tourists stood watching through large windows as a young woman, inside what seemed to be a large padded cell, vied with a programmed android. The legend "ATHLETE" glowed near the top of the windows. It seemed that patrons could choose their level of challenge, from "beginner" through "athlete" and "gymnast," to "expert." Quantrill suspected that the jeans-clad girl was a WCS shill, drumming up business by demonstrating the game. Lithe and pretty, the girl was good.

The android was better. Dressed in a floppy sweat suit, crafted to look like a burly drill instructor, it was one of the recent models with a small range of facial expressions, a belly full of energy cells, and no extension cord. It had already done push-ups, a one-legged deep-knee bend, and a cartwheel—an astonishing improvement on androids of previous years—but each time the girl copied the maneuver. As the men watched, the android performed a deep split. The girl matched it. From the scatter of objects on the padded floor it picked up a tennis ball in each hand; tossed the balls one by one up behind its back so that the arc continued over its shoulder; and caught the ball with the same hand. The girl did the same. Then, without changing its grim expression, it tossed both balls in over-the-shoulder arcs simultaneously.

"No fair," the girl laughed, and, after one or two false starts, tossed her tennis balls. She caught one, missed the other, and snapped her fingers in good-natured chagrin. The android placed its tennis balls precisely where they had been before, faced the girl again, gave an awful mechanical grin, and bowed before folding its arms and closing its eyes, inert as a concrete pillar. The girl wiped a wisp of hair from her face as she exited, smiling.

Sorel turned to his companions. "We could do that, I think. Mr. Cherry? Mr. Collier?"

The tall one made a wry face, shook his head. That coldgas weapon down his arm prevented such flexibility, and Sorel damned well knew it. The barrel-chested man lifted an eyebrow and moved his arm as if to display it. "With this gimpy elbow? Shit, no. You try it, wetback."

Sorel put his tongue between his teeth in real amusement. Longo knew he could get away with the abusive term because it formed another layer of cover over their real relationship. The Mexican glanced at Quantrill and grinned as if to say that he was not easily offended. "Then you, Mr. Coulter, and then I. My treat."

Quantrill hesitated. Old training had taught him to avoid spectacular shows of prowess. Given those uncanny reflexes, he had the ability to recover from a poor move and correct it; not in tenths, but in hundredths of a second. But nothing required him to punch the high-level options. He agreed, letting Sorel pay as he punched the "athlete" option at the Copycat doorway.

Again, the android was better. Quantrill managed the ball-toss maneuver, leaping forward to catch a fumbled ball and turning back to wave, hearing the cheers from Sorel and others. He also copied the Russian leap but found himself unequal to the android in "hackey sack." He kept the small leather beanbag bouncing from his feet and knees for only a moment before he forgot and snatched the leather bag with one hand. The android performed that ludicrous grin, bowed, and turned to stone again.

The sturdy Mexican led the scatter of applause, handed his boots to his taller companion, and punched his option. Outside, watching through the glass, Quantrill saw the glowing word "GYMNAST" and found himself hoping that Ernst Matthias was up to the challenge. An instant's memory fled through his mind of his gymnast friend Kent Ethridge, now becoming dust in a government-furnished coffin. Quantrill had been quicker at their lethal work but had never doubted Ethridge's superiority in gymnastics. Was Matthias a gymnast, too?

Whatever else he was, the Mexican was good; no, he was great. The android began with the Russian leap, and the stocking-footed Matthias did it better, legs absolutely horizontal at chest height as he touched his toes. He caused a bit of reprogramming as the android began its hackey sack routine. He flicked a foot out to intercept the leather bag, popping it upward with his other knee, crossing his other foot behind the leg he stood on to snap the bag over the android's head. The android missed, unable to whirl the massive weight of its energy cells and thermal-response plastic muscles in time to keep the hackey sack airborne.

Amid general applause begun by Quantrill, the android stopped, began a bow, stopped again. Then it squatted and—barely—performed a back flip. The Mexican laughed, then easily leaped over in a tucked position, landing with one foot only slightly behind the other. The android's handstand was quite steady, its one-armed handstand not so steady. Neither was the Mexican's, but his cheering audience did not care. Only when the android ended a cartwheel with a forward flip did the man throw up his arms, laughing. "I would break my neck," he said, accepting defeat gracefully, and made a mocking bow to the machine before walking to the exit. He did not carry himself like a man who had lost, and Quantrill clapped him on the back as they met in the hallway.

Strapping his boot closures on as he sat with his back turned to his companions, the Mexican stood up and clapped his hands together as he turned. "Somewhere in this maze," he said happily, "there must be a machine we can defeat."

"I think you licked that one, on points," Quantrill joked.

"I seen a game called 'Solo' over yonder," said Longo, nodding into the depths of the building. "That ought to tickle your balls, if you wanta kill yourself a plastic gunsel."

The heavyset Longo led them to the game, and they watched

one patron gamely go through the act of getting himself painlessly "killed" by utter strangers. This was one game, Quantrill thought, that belonged over the next hill in Faro. You paid, strapped on a black sensor-covered vest and a gunbelt with a Colt peacemaker, and strode into a small western saloon furnished with a one-way mirror behind the bar. Kibitzers watched the action through the mirror, and while that action might last only two minutes, it seemed a lifetime to some. The Colt fired a low-power laser and would do it six times, with appropriate six-gun sound effects. Your opponents were among the score of androids, some sitting in a corner at an endless poker game, some lounging at the bar or positioned above the stairway. A blowsy female leaned its ample bazooms on the top of an upright player piano and sang off key to the other machines as the piano tinkled. One android, an apparent fat drunk, roused itself now and then to vent Bronx cheers at the chanteuse. It was funny, but it broke your concentration. It was supposed to.

Because "Solo" required all the concentration you could muster. You were supposed to watch for anyone who looked your way. Every android in the place was capable of drawing some kind of old-fashioned gun, but only six—and they varied—would do so. You were not entitled to draw when you saw a face turn toward you, but when its eyes flashed crimson you had better draw fast. If you hit any part of your target, it reacted as if the laser were a slug. The android fired only at your vest, but if it hit you first the piano played a brief dirge while the androids sneered at you. Quantrill ruled out that game the instant he saw it.

"I might go for that," said the man called Johnny, watching the patron blow one mean customer off his stool.

"I just bet you would," said the one called Leo. "Busted arm and all."

"So who draws with his left?"

"I believe Sam Coulter would," said the Mexican, squeezing Quantrill's left bicep gently.

Quantrill allowed the liberty, putting aside a vague momentary feeling that his new friend had a look of fondness that verged on the feminine. Matthias, he decided, was sharp as hell to spot a left-hander so quickly. He put up both hands in surrender. "Not me. Games like that give me a pounder of a headache. You go ahead; I'll cheer."

Sorel elected to wait until the two Anglos had taken their turns, watching the action closely. Quantrill noted that two of the androids seemed always to be among the six bad dudes, and that their movements seemed choreographed to the millisecond. By waiting and watching for hours, a player might greatly improve his chances. His friend Matthias, he decided, was probably making the same calculation.

After the two Anglos had their turns, the Mexican took his time checking the freedom of his Colt in its holster before walking into the game of Solo. He seemed to have planned his moves well, drawing carefully at a moderately slow gunsel at the bar. The tall Anglo had won three of his encounters, the chunky one only two. "One down," they called. It was impossible, to tell whether the Mexican heard them, for he wasted none of his concentration on a reply.

Number two flashed its eyes from the poker table, and Sorel fired from a prone position. He almost missed number three, a lounger at the top of the stairwell, but turned sideways as he drew and got the shot off quickly. The android fell backward in satisfyingly realistic fashion, and Quantrill realized that the Mexican was cleverly twisting so that, while the vest told the machines where to aim, those vest sensors made almost no target at the instant of truth.

Number four was the bartender, which had been "watching" the gunplay at the stair and hauled out a shotgun to drill the player with an awesome report. Sorel shook his head in a flash of irritation, reseated his Colt, then quickly moved up with his back to the bartender android. *Probably*, thought Quantrill with admiration, *he's counting on only one draw from a given source. Very quick thinking, and damned quick with his body.*

Number five was a special problem, an android that flashed its crimson blink and then stepped behind three others for cover before firing. The player that shot a noncombatant lost the rest of his turn. The Mexican turned sideways again, took a one-handed stance, and moved his body abruptly from side to side. The android missed by a hairsbreadth and then, in accord with some programmer's fancy, put its hands up. Sorel shot it squarely in the chest, chuckling as he fired.

But while taking deliberate aim at his fifth opponent, Sorel had turned his torso to face the buxom machine at the piano. Though he did not see the crimson flash from its eyes, Quantrill did. Caught up in the game, Quantrill shouted, "To your left!" and actually felt his own left hand twitch in the direction of his right armpit. That would have been lovely, explaining a few explosive rounds from a Chiller through a one-way mirror.

No one noticed, for the chanteuse had drawn a derringer from its plastic cleavage and fired as the Mexican was whirling. The men outside whooped their enthusiasm, and the victim walked out muttering to himself, plainly disgusted with his performance.

Now the barrel-chested "Johnny" showed his first signs of beginning to enjoy himself. "Like my daddy said, you got to look out for them painted hussies," he rumbled. His tall companion only clucked his tongue in false sympathy.

"To be taken by a woman," the victim said, shaking his head a minute later as he handed over his gear to an attendant.

"Depends how she does it," Quantrill said slyly. "Anyhow, that was a damn fast machine made up like a woman." He was on the point of adding, like a bloody fool, that he might have done no better under the circumstances. Instead, he suggested they continue their tour.

They studied the game of Dee & Dee, reading its displays and looking over the pointedly skimpy holo maps, for the better part of half an hour before deciding against it. No doubt the maze would be tremendous fun for someone who knew all the nuances of dragons, dungeons, wizards, and trolls, but the welter of rules soon had the men laughing at the sheer complication of it all.

"Anyway, it takes a half hour, and it's as expensive as the Thrillkiller," Quantrill said.

"But it don't take the *cojones*," observed "Collier," going to the heart of it. "Why don't you go for the biggie?"

"Very well," said the Mexican. "We will follow you." His smile was innocent as a babe's.

"Collier" and "Cherry" made quite a show of unconcern as they strolled to the Thrillkiller. There was no long line of riders waiting, but the men needed a few minutes to study the paper they signed. Quantrill learned something new: it was possible to brake the capsule for an emergency stop. But if you did, you forfeited an additional fifty-dollar deposit because all capsules under way would also stop, then proceed slowly to the finish line. In case of a real malf, a huge device called a "cherry picker" slid along the maglev track to the site of the problem. Apparently, WCS and their LockLever designers had thought of everything—including the disclaimer for cardiac arrest while in a capsule.

First to climb into a capsule for his solitary ride was the heavyset Anglo, who was still smiling now, but not very convincingly. The lone attendant helped him snug into his restraint harness, including the "submarine" strap that passed between the legs and locked at the single-point disconnect low on the rider's belly. The canopy hinged at the side and snapped down with heavy thunks of probe locks. A moment later, the attendant checked a computer display and then punched a command. Inside the capsule a hidden loudspeaker began its special effects, sounding for all the world like a turbo boost. The linear electric drive, which did the real work, gradually accelerated the capsule away to the first bend. And kept accelerating through it.

The tall graying Anglo shook his head a little and sighed as his capsule trundled up to the start line. He turned to the Mexican: "Beats the shit outa me why I'm doin' this."

"You are at liberty to let the opportunity pass."

"No I ain't, and you know it." There was a hint of dark humor in the reply; Texans, even when otherwise mature, were often notorious suckers for a dare. He stepped over the high sill into his capsule and began to arrange his harness with the resignation of the damned.

"If it's any consolation," Quantrill said, "I feel the same way." This was only a slight exaggeration. Having flown government sprint choppers, he knew what to expect. But in a sprint chopper, you could plan every twist and lurch.

By unspoken agreement, Quantrill was next. By the time he waved to the Mexican, he could see a capsule far ahead, going through the second of its free-fall arcs. It dropped to the lower "submach" track, and Quantrill decided to follow suit. No point in deliberately antagonizing the others. He had little doubt that "Matthias" would take the high road.

Quantrill soon felt glad of his decision. The damned capsule whipped him from side to side, hurled itself into a tunnel, and seemed likely to screw itself down to India before straightening, accelerating up, and giving him a brief taste of zero gee before meeting the rails again. The console display gave him his choice, and he ignored it, looking ahead. That free-fall choice up ahead interested him as a problem in vertical mass switching, neatly solved. For the submach track, you scarcely left the rails at all.

The high-speed straight on the return leg was fun because it was near enough to the valley floor to give the illusion of great speed. Quantrill found himself enjoying it, reminding himself to return one day and try the hypersonic option, and the last deceleration bends came too soon. Ahead, he could see his companions, tiny stick figures outside the capsules, leaning on balustrade rails.

He got out carefully, noting the other men who were shading their eyes, watching the near distance. Sure enough, a bright dart was hurtling down the hypersonic high road, across kilometers of track at a speed that was simply appalling so near" to the ground. The boulder rocked into place across the rails, on cue, and opened on cue. Less than a minute later, their fourth member was climbing from his capsule, elated. Quantrill greeted him with what he wanted to hear: ''I took the easy way. Gotta hand it to you, Matthias; you have more big brass balls than all the pawnshops in SanTone.''

The Mexican placed his hand on Quantrill's shoulder and looked back at the rails stretching away behind them. Slowly, reflecting as he spoke, he said, ''I think—it is a matter of faith.''

''You mean like God won't let you down?''

''Oh, no. I merely remind myself that others have done this. And what anyone else can do . . .'' He let his hand fall. It was unnecessary for him to finish the sentence: *I can do better*.

CHAPTER SIXTY-TWO • • •

Quantrill could not recall all the details of the evening that followed. His only explanation—there could be no excuse short of an insanity plea—was that in his own mind he had closed the case, assuming too much. Someone had said that riding a Thrillkiller was thirsty work, and no one had denied it. After a few Dos Equis drafts in an excellent hotel lounge, they had returned by stage to Faro and downed a couple of tequila sours. Then Quantrill had accepted another—perhaps several. He did recall one special insult to his gut, a boilermaker made not with ordinary whiskey but with Gusano Rojo mezcal, the stuff with a caterpillar embalmed in state right there in the bottle where you could see it. After three hefty swigs, you would drink to its health. After two more, you would swear it was drinking to yours.

At some point, he had wisely decided against calling on any of the security managers that night. Hadn't he already covered the necessary bases? And besides, you didn't ask with a slurred tongue about the possibility of a backup for your own sidearm. That, and the decision to go to his room and stash the Chiller, were the last pieces of wisdom he used that night—with one exception. He avoided the temptation to let his good buddy Matthias in on his real reason for coming to Faro.

They had wandered arm in arm, after dark, to another saloon. They'd played cards; "bucked the tiger" in the game of faro; gone bust at "twenty-one," accepted still more drinks at the poker table. Had he finally lost, or won? Quantrill could not recall, but in any case the Mexican had put up the stakes, drinking less. Vigilant more. Some time after midnight, the little party separated. The best that could be said for Quantrill at the time was that his gait had been reasonably steady. He had long since ceased to talk much. Why bother, when his tongue was developing a Castilian accent?

Morning brought a wake-up knock that infuriated him. But he reached through the cobwebs to recall he had left orders for a wake-up when registering. He lay inert for a time, leafing through his memory, cursing at the blank passages. He could recall most of the previous evening until ten or so, and not much after that. Seems that Ernst Matthias had suggested they bunk together. Now, why the hell . . . ? No, that had to be wrong, as wrong as letting the joy of a new friendship trigger a drinking bout. If it *had* been a bout. If it had, Matthias had sure as hell won it by pacing his drinks. One more sure thing, in a booze bout nobody won the morning after. Jess Marrow had said it once: If you got hangovers, you lost then and there. If you didn't get hangovers, you lost your liver eventually.

Quantrill's hangover was a surly brute of medium ferocity. Padding barefooted on a cold oak floor, he found the pitcher and enameled basin; cursed the cruel authenticity of Faro's rooms; spilled some of that cold water on his feet (!!) while pouring it into the basin. The icy shock as he washed his face nearly knocked him over, but it soaked through more of those cobwebs—enough to make him wonder whether he had licked out a bird cage or a fireplace during the night's festivities. He drank some of that hard water, then let himself sink carefully down into the bed again. One good sign, the ceiling was not spinning. His voice seemed borrowed from a bullfrog: "Stupid jackass," he said aloud. "How many times do you have to poison yourself just for fun?"

By nine A.M. he had dressed, couching the Chiller under the light jacket, fumbling a bit as he practiced a few draws. Sitting on the bed, he essayed a ring-finger exercise he'd learned in T Section of army intelligence. Your synapses that are under least conscious control, they'd taught him, were earliest affected by booze, drugs, or concussion. Control of one's ring fingers was normally fair to poor. If you could bend those fingers and only those to a quick rhythm when sober, loss of that mastery meant your reflexes were impaired. A poor sort of evidence to stake your life on, but better than nothing.

The charge suggested by that evidence was "wasted in the

first degree.'' But he'd been hung over a half dozen times in his life and expected a quick recovery if only he could co-opt some coffee and stare down a pair of eggs, sunny-side. In the meantime, his companions could help him over the rough spots. By noon, he could put in a call to Jim Street with a clear head.

Quantrill eased down the stairs and, after only one wrong turn, wandered into the dining hall wearing a sorry smile. His companions were presiding over the remains of western omelets. He glanced at one plate in which ''Cherry'' had added catsup to his omelet. The plate looked as if someone had dropped a small animal into it from some great height. Quantrill swallowed hard as he looked away from it, sitting between ''Collier'' and the Mexican, where he could watch the door. No one, not even the waitress, entertained any doubts about his delicate condition.

When the waitress left with Quantrill's order, he managed to get a coffee cup to his lips with only one hand. It was a triumph of sorts, but Clyde Longo was not impressed. In a gravelly baritone, the man began to sing in a near whisper. The song had found fame in a holovision satire, ridiculing the essence of certain country songs that critics dubbed the ''lyrics of loserism.'' But like Archie Bunker of the old days, the ditty had become a runaway success among those it mocked, as if its ironies were subtle rather than gross. The only proper way to sing it was badly, with tears in the voice, and Longo did it right. Its title was ''Two Beers.''

> ''Ohh, pore me,
> 'Cause I got drunk.
> And killed a feller,
> And buggered a skunk,
> And wrecked the truck,
> And burnt the house,
> And kicked ole Granny,
> And swallered a mouse.
> But I can do it agin tomorry, you see—
> As long as I got yore
> Sympathy-y-y-y-y . . .''

''I need your silence more than your sympathy,'' Quantrill

said morosely to the singer beside him. The other Anglos were in only slightly better shape than he, while Ernst Matthias seemed disgustingly hale. Nevertheless, said the Mexican, he intended to spend a good part of the day recovering in his room. He did not say, of course, that he regretted raising such a high profile the day before.

Quantrill was chasing a fragment of egg with his fork when he saw the newcomer framed in the doorway. He grabbed his checked napkin and brought it to his face, coughing. The rugged, angular latino was gazing in his direction. Not so angular and rugged as he'd been a few years back, maybe, but Quantrill had no doubts. It was too late now to intercept his old friend, Lufo Albeniz. But they had shared T Section's hand signals once, and those signals composed a language you never forgot. He saw recognition in Lufo's face. The others turned casually to see the man passing between empty chairs to their table, and Quantrill lowered the napkin. He wiped his right hand across his face, saw something like consternation in Lufo's gaze, and wiped again. The gesture said, "I am wearing cover." There was absolutely no question that Lufo recognized him, dyed hair or no, because the big TexMex seemed ready to turn back toward the entrance. But now it was too late for Lufo, too; for now the barrel-chested Anglo at the table saw him and began to hum "Rose of San Antone."

CHAPTER SIXTY-THREE • • •

Every man at the table recognized the newcomer. Quantrill instantly put aside the notion that Lufo Albeniz had arrived by accident; evidently Lufo was still on the job for Jim Street. Most likely, thought Quantrill, Lufo had been sent as backup. They could confer later in private, but for the moment Quantrill felt that burning his cover meant burning a new friendship. In a sense, then, at that moment Quantrill's life was hanging on his embarrassment. He had no way of knowing Lufo's cover name among *cimarrones*, so the only inference he drew from Longo's humming was that the man couldn't carry a tune in a Kelley Ramscoop.

Clyde Longo did not give a damn what young Coulter thought. Like Sorel and Slaughter, he knew San Antonio Rose on sight and announced the fact in the usual way. The rest was up to someone else.

Harley Slaughter realized a part of the problem: San Antonio Rose might be wary of Sam Coulter who was, as of this moment, very much underfoot. Slaughter put on an uncharacteristic show of goodwill, with an expansive wave toward the man who stood poised in uncertainty before them. "I know you from somewhere. What was your name in the States?" It was an old greeting from the days when Wild Country was turning wild again.

Felix Sorel only smiled and gestured for the newcomer to take a seat. "A friend of Mr. Cherry? *Bienvenidos*." In a detached way Sorel was amused. If he found it convenient to snub young Coulter from Monahans, drive him from the pack as it were, he could do it at any time. New friends or old, it made little difference; he used them, discarded them, found others with that graceful, lethal charm.

Lufo Albeniz took his time sitting down in the only available space, between Longo and Slaughter with his back to the entrance, composing his next moves. What in seven hells was Ted Quantrill doing here, rubbing elbows with Sorel? Hold on; with those few words, Sorel had disowned their old acquaintance. And Quantrill had given him the "cover" sign, plain as day. Lufo's conclusion was that Quantrill knew his quarry. Did he also know Lufo's connection? Lufo had expected no trouble, and his only weapon was the lockblade in his hip pocket. Oh, shit. . . .

Lufo said the only thing he could: "Lufo Albeniz," and thrust his hand across the table to Sorel. Hell, they all knew his real name anyhow.

In moments he heard all the aliases he could handle. To Slaughter's casual question he replied that he had just happened by. With the tension palpable as a sheet of ice over the table, not one of them noticed the slender figure in the bulky shortcoat who had appeared in the doorway as Lufo was sitting down.

Marianne Placidas, knowing the destination of San Antonio Rose, had actually preceded him to Faro and picked him up as he got off the tour bus. And now the man had led her, with breathtaking suddenness, to within point-blank range of Felix Sorel. She did not recognize Quantrill or Longo, but Slaughter was easy to make. Almost as easy as Sorel, next to him. It all came together so quickly after her preparations that she did not give herself time to waver, nor even to tremble. Slaughter's hideously effective weapon was always drawn, so he would bear watching as closely as Sorel. It made no difference what weapons the others might use on her; Marianne had told herself many times that she had died with her beauty in Oregon Territory.

Her mistake was common among amateurs. Professionals rarely take time to savor revenge; and *never* before the fact.

"Felix Sorel, look at me." Her voice was steady. The little automatic was steady, too. Somewhere a waitress bleated, dropped a tray, scuttled for the kitchen entrance. Somewhere else, two patrons bolted for the exit. No one at the table moved quickly, except for their heads.

"*Dios mío,*" Sorel said. He realized that his expression betrayed a horrified fascination as he looked into that ruined face. The voice he knew well enough, and her eyes removed

any lingering doubt. Keeping his hands in view, he fashioned
a bright smile for her. It had always worked before. "Marianne Placidas, is it you?" If Slaughter would only make his
move, he might have time to draw on this dreadful apparition.

Standing only meters away, positioned behind Lufo so
that Slaughter would have to swing his arm, the woman faced
Sorel, her chin proud, displaying the terrible scars this man
had ordained for her. Without glancing toward Slaughter she
said, "Not anymore. I wanted you to see what you have
done."

Lufo made his decision then, twisting slowly to look at the
woman, perhaps because he was the only man at the table
who was not well armed. "Chica, you don't want to shoot a
federal agent," he said.

"*Embustero*, liar; you are San Antonio Rose," she said
without taking her eyes from Sorel's.

Mierda! So she knew. With his peripheral vision, Lufo saw
Quantrill's face harden in shock. "But this man is Ted Quantrill
of the Justice Department," he went on, pointing carefully
and slowly. "Let him do his job."

"You sonofabitch," grated Longo, his face growing cho-
leric as he stared at the man beside him, the man who had
iced Mike Rawson. Marianne might have ignored the curse,
but the reddening of Clyde Longo's face was a real endorsement.

Quantrill did not move. A half dozen tumblers within his
mind clicked into place. So all these men were old confederates, and he'd been sucked in like a fucking amateur! It
wasn't bad enough that he'd placed himself in the hands of
Sorel, but his old compadre Lufo was playing both sides of
the game. And any second now, that game would be over.

"Slaughter told me you were dead, *novita*," Sorel pleaded,
hands open in supplication, nodding toward the cold-eyed
Slaughter.

"That's a goddamn lie, Sorel," Slaughter hissed, and shifted
his arm a bit.

"If Slaughter said that, he was right. And now my spirit is
content," said Marianne, her face blazing in a ravaged, deadly
smile.

They all heard distant footfalls racing in the hall, coming
nearer. Marianne Placidas licked her lips, tossed what could
have been a look of pleading toward Quantrill, and saw

Harley Slaughter's arm slowly straighten toward the man who might, or might not, be a federal agent. If Slaughter thought so, that agent was now one second from an agonizing death. The muzzle of her little weapon flicked to a new target, and she fired without hesitation. The single slug entered Slaughter's head just above the right cheekbone, blossoming into the base of his brain. The pistol's report triggered instant pandemonium.

Even as Slaughter folded forward, his face shattering the plate before him, three of the men were reacting in almost identical ways, using other bodies for shields. Clyde Longo, without years of military training in close-quarters combat, had the horrendously bad luck to be sitting between two men who had learned from the same instructors. He found himself gripped from both sides as Quantrill and Lufo Albeniz propelled him over backward toward the woman. Sorel hurled himself sideways to the floor, taking refuge behind the inert Slaughter, reaching inside his jacket as he dropped.

Marianne stumbled back to avoid the stocky Longo as he tumbled backward from his chair, holding her little weapon with both hands. She fired again, and Slaughter's body jerked.

As he released his two-handed grip on Longo's right arm and shoulder, Quantrill continued moving in a side roll. He ended it on one knee, Chiller in hand, and saw Longo on his back near the woman's feet. Longo's teeth were bared as he looked up at her, flexing his legs, reaching into his boot top. She seemed completely unaware of the man as she fired that second round across the table.

The Chiller coughed twice, the muffled thumps of its tiny detonating slugs lost in Longo's bulk. Quantrill saw the man quiver, then relax. Kneeling between adjacent tables, his eyes above the level of the tabletops, Quantrill fired several rounds between table legs where he hoped Sorel would be; in the killing trade, the expression was "for effect." One of the slugs had its effect all right. It shattered the right rear leg of the chair supporting the corpse of Harley Slaughter, and the slug's detonation sent oak splinters flying. Quantrill selected then from between two options. He could drop prone, the aggressive option, and face Felix Sorel in a forest of spindly table legs. Or he could opt for the prudent move and vault atop a table for a commanding view and a better field of fire.

Prudence won; Quantrill's leap carried him atop the nearest unoccupied table. But the hangover won, too; he missed his footing and rolled onto his side, cups and plates scattering, the table teetering but remaining upright. At that point, a burst of firing from Sorel's vicinity said that he was still doing business. The woman gave a choking cry and staggered to the side, flinging her gun hand out as she fell toward Quantrill. At the moment, Quantrill was her only hope, and the savagery of her luck was that, in falling, she caught him across the bridge of the nose with the barrel of her pistol.

Lying on his back, Felix Sorel could see the trousered legs of Marianne Placidas from under the table. Something was happening to his left with the little brick agent, but "Coulter" had shown no deadly potential on the previous day, and the Placidas bitch was already firing in his direction. First things first: he tucked his legs, spreading them enough to fire twice from between them, and had the satisfaction of seeing the woman's right leg buckle as he thrust upward with both feet beneath the near side of the tabletop.

But before he could bring the table crashing over, Sorel was distracted by several thin, sharp reports, one near his head. He felt the peppering of wood and tiny metal fragments from the Chiller against the side of his face, then realized that the body of Harley Slaughter was collapsing on him. He flailed his left arm hard to deflect the corpse, using the impetus to continue in a back shoulder roll.

Lufo's blade was locked and in flight as the table flipped over, its blade sinking into the oak, pinning the tablecloth in place. His only other weapon was the heavy oak chair he grabbed as he ducked. It might do as a shield until he could tip another table over. He saw Ted Quantrill cut loose against Longo, saw the effects of Sorel's shots as the woman screamed and staggered to her right. Lufo began to swing the chair—it was a heavy devil, and he was out of shape—and then saw Quantrill's head snap hard against the tabletop, pistol-whipped by sheer accident.

Lufo had not been recruited into T Section for nothing all those years ago. He could reassess a problem as quickly as anyone, and his reflexes had once been almost as fast as Quantrill's. He continued the swing of that heavy chair and, instead of hurling it directly at Sorel, tossed it in a high spinning arc before he dived for the revolver poking out of Clyde Longo's boot top. A large object tumbling in a high arc tends to draw attention for a crucial second or so.

Sorel saw the chair coming as he bounced to his feet near the wall; sidestepped; saw Quantrill stunned on the tabletop and partly hidden by the woman. He fired at the only person who was in furious motion. The parabellum slug tore into Lufo's left pectoral muscle, was deflected by the high second rib, and exited after cutting a shallow trench to the sternum. Sorel skipped to one side, turned his attention to Quantrill, who had struggled to one elbow, blinking his eyes, and then realized that Marianne Placidas was again staring at him down the barrel of her little automatic. Who would have thought the bitch had so much vitality? He made a feint, then jerked back, and her next round buried itself in the wall.

Sorel fired while diving away, a throwaway shot intended to upset her aim more than anything else. Marianne Placidas spun and sat down hard on the floor, shot through the right bicep, her little weapon clattering onto the table near Quantrill's head. Ted Quantrill saw through watering eyes that his target was scrambling on all fours through the kitchen service entrance. While blinking furiously, he took a groggy sort of aim and fired a full-auto burst. One round carved a grazing welt across Sorel's back before detonating against the swinging door. For the next few seconds, Quantrill could estimate Sorel's success from the wild uproar of shouts, footsteps, and crashing of metal pans that receded through the kitchen.

Rolling from the table, Quantrill sprinted for the kitchen, went through the swinging door in a fast duck walk, bobbed up, and then stayed up, leaning against the doorframe. The shouts of alarm were now coming from the dusty street outside. Cursing himself, he reseated the Chiller and pushed back into the dining hall. Then he raised his hands. He was facing a very nervous fellow with a security star and an enormous Buntline Special.

CHAPTER SIXTY-FOUR • • •

Because most security cops knew a Chiller when they saw one, Quantrill had little difficulty making his needs understood. A federal "brick," or undercover field agent, often carried no ID beyond a Chiller, and a few even operated without that. Shaking his head to clear it now and then, mopping away runnels of blood from his nose with a borrowed bandanna, Quantrill sought to patch up the mess he had made. It didn't help that he had to ignore the troubles of Lufo and the woman.

"We've got casualties here, so I hope there's a chopper on the way."

"On the bounce," said the Buntline man, who had the look of a retired beat cop.

"I need two things *right now,* or there may be some innocent people killed. Get me a good high-gain VHF set, and throw up a cordon around Faro. Nobody, but NObody, gets out unless I see them first. Felix Sorel is armed and extremely dangerous, and I'm calling for as much expert backup as I can get."

Mr. Buntline hurried out of the room. A waitress was sitting cross-legged with Marianne Placidas's head in her lap, comforting her and thumbing a pressure point in her armpit. "Be sure you release the pressure now and then," he cautioned, and knelt beside Lufo Albeniz.

The TexMex sat with his back against the overturned table. He had torn his shirt open and was trying to make a pressure bandage of a napkin with his right hand. Now he looked up at his old friend. "Jus' like old times," he said.

"Not quite. Is it the big one? Let me see."

Lufo showed him. "The best kind, compadre. One slug,

275

two holes. Listen, you don' believe that stuff about San Antonio Rose. Right?''

''I know you match a detailed description, you dumb shit. I just never thought about you fitting it. But I'm betting Street didn't send you, so . . .'' Quantrill sighed; placed a hand on the big man's good shoulder. ''Thank God you never could stay on one side for long. You helped. Thanks.''

''I was dead slow, Ted. I think I let that crazy woman follow me here. Whatever I had in this business, it's gone.''

''That's not all you've lost. Lufo—*why*?''

Lufo shifted for more comfort and managed a crooked smile. ''To get ahead. It's not easy when you have wives and kids on both sides of the border, *hijo*.''

''You'll have years to think on that when you're inside, looking out.''

''An' my kids callin' other guys 'papa'? You know I can't think about that. Drive me loco.''

''You were loco to fuck around with the likes of Sorel,'' Quantrill said.

''Yeah. Compadre, you remember when I hauled your drowned ass outa that tunnel, about a thousan' years ago?'' He waited; got only a grunt of assent. ''You tol' me after that, if I ever wanted a favor, jus' ask. Well, I never asked. I'm askin' now.''

''For what?'' As if they didn't both know.

''For Mexico.'' He closed his eyes as he said it, drawing the word out softly, ''May-zhee-coe,'' as a child might drawl its mother's name. ''I won' come back. I'm not that stupid.''

After a long moment Quantrill said, ''Could you make it the way you are?''

''Never,'' said Lufo, rolling his eyes upward. ''I swear on the honor of Anglos.'' The crinkles above lean cheekbones said he was not to be taken seriously.

Shaking his head, trying not to grin, Quantrill stood up and spoke so the waitress could hear. ''For the record, Lufo, I can't let you go. And I'm absolutely certain you're hurt too bad to light a shuck on your own. There'll be a chopper for you any minute, and I have a job to do.'' Pause: ''Any idea where Sorel will go to ground?''

''He was waitin' for the delta. Could go anywhere now.'' As Quantrill started for the doorway, Lufo added, ''Listen, compadre, you wait for backups. You know how good you were in ninety-six? That's how good he is, I shit you not.''

''I know,'' said Quantrill, and turned away. From the tail of his eye he saw the big TexMex already struggling to his feet.

CHAPTER SIXTY-FIVE · · ·

Quantrill was patched in to Jim Street's personal circuit within two minutes, holding the VHF earpiece in place. He stood on the outside porch with a man named Bonner, the head of Long Branch security, at his side, in rapid conversation with Bonner until the Gov came on-line. The old man was not pleased with what he heard, and said so. Quantrill knew that the best excuse was none at all.

"Yessir, I blew it. His two *cimarrones* are ready for bodybags, but Sorel's running loose out here." A pause. "They were wearing good cosmetic cover, that's how. I should have made them anyway. I didn't. One of 'em was Harley Slaughter; the other one . . . I dunno; from his phenotype, could be Clyde Longo without the beard. Prints will tell you; they're not going anywhere." He said nothing about the woman and especially not about Lufo, who might indeed be going somewhere. Just how he might do it, in a town looking for a Mexican fugitive, was beyond guessing.

After another pause: "Two civilian casualties, maybe more if you don't get some people here with flak jackets. WCS security's tossing a net around Faro, but you never know, he could get to the airstrip over the hill. You might send mass and motion sensors with the teams. Divert any flights here, especially that delta. He was waiting for it."

After another pause: "I wouldn't, Gov. Bringing a SWAT team in on a delta would be like building a barricade with sticks of dynamite. . . . Beg pardon? . . . Oh; because they fill delta dirigibles with hydrogen these days. One round into a gas cell and it's a *Hindenburg* barbecue. Just send lots of backup, with intruder sensors, and hope I can whack Sorel before they get here." Another pause. Whatever Street was saying now, the little brick agent wasn't enjoying it.

278

Now a vein throbbed at his temple. He started to speak twice before, "Jesus Christ, you *know* I can't do that," he exploded, and paused again. "All right. Yessir, hands off until then. But if he starts offing more civilians in the meantime, Gov, I'm back to Job One, right? Isn't that what I'm for?" He nodded in glum satisfaction. "Yessir. I could use one. I take a size forty-two. . . . Goddammit, I *said* I would! Can't you take 'yes' for an answer—sir?"

He flicked off the toggle, handed the VHF set to the security man, hooked thumbs into belt loops, and gazed down the deserted streets. "Direct from the attorney general, you can verify if you like," he said. "There'll be three sprint chopper loads of tough meat here in a couple of hours, wearing flak jackets. Until then, nobody leaves here at all. And we don't challenge Felix Sorel; we box him up if we can. No facedowns until the place is crawling with feds carrying intruder sensors. Unless he starts taking out civilians first."

The security chief had spent twenty years in a Houston homicide detail, and men in that business tended to recall the name of Ted Quantrill. "And you hope he does?"

"No, I don't," in a flash of irritation. "I don't want some tourist on a slab just so I can slip my leash." Quantrill realized it was true only after he said it, and felt a sense of loss. "You've alerted the people over the hill?"

"Sure, for all the good it did. Bunch of pussies at the Hilton and the New Driskill, all the good men are here in Faro. I've called for recon flights from the airstrip. They only fire little tracer blanks, but at least they're eyes in the sky. Here," he added, thrusting an old-fashioned tin star in Quantrill's direction, smiling grimly. "Might keep one of our guys from nailing you by mistake."

Quantrill pinned on the star. It was just one more thing he should have thought of himself. Just as well that Jim Street had put him in a holding pattern; he was definitely not up to *mano a mano* against Sorel in this condition. Maybe not ever, in any condition. He should have known the previous day, watching Sorel operate in that saloonful of androids.

An echo stuttered from storefronts with the popping of a far-distant firecracker somewhere on the prairie. Then more of the same. Bonner ran into the street, shouted toward the roof: "Where's that coming from?"

Of course it was impossible to tell. A minute later the VHF set pinged, and they learned the answer. A man from the Last Chance, riding bareback on the perimeter with an ancient lever-action Winchester and a VHF unit, had spotted someone running hard down a drywash two minutes before. He'd seen hovercycles gleaming behind a pile of tumbleweed and fired one warning shot from over a hundred meters away. Thanks to the return fire, the Last Chance man was now transmitting from behind a gutshot gelding and could not see which way Sorel had gone after that. If Sorel had only that handgun, either he'd had incredible luck, or he was one spectacular marksman. The only good thing was that the guard still had a clear field of fire to the cycles. Sorel would be crazy to risk it, and crazier to spend his time stalking a man in the open.

Bonner replied curtly, then toggled an open transmission. The suspect, he said, was somewhere in the south end of the valley, probably doubling back toward the parking area. He must be allowed to come near enough to be boxed in. Any civilians not in their rooms must be sent inside, in custody if need be. He turned to Quantrill, standing in the rutted dirt street with him, and said, "I'm not proud. Anything else you can think of?"

"I could use a B-one shot," Quantrill said, trying to smile.

"Hell, why didn't you say so? I keep some in my desk. What brand: SubCute?"

"Whatever," Quantrill replied. The little pressure injectors delivered enough subcutaneous vitamin to send most hangovers packing, but the pop was far from painless. It was one of a thousand little improvements prodded by the technology of the recent war.

One thing Quantrill didn't need was a sore arm, so he shucked down his pants in the office and triggered the SubCute cartridge into the side of his right buttock. The security chief grabbed his VHF set as it pinged, toggled it so that Quantrill could hear both ends of the conversation. A second perimeter guard, this one afoot, had just spotted fresh prints across the sandy bottom of a drywash. They were heading east. "Probably toward the parking area," said Bonner into the mouthpiece, "and he'll have to cross a lot of open ground. Let him go, we've blocked the underground parking exits. That's where we'll have him, boys.''

In his bones, Quantrill knew better. ''Well, Sorel has caught me with my pants down for the last time,'' he said, snapping his belt buckle. ''Just for kicks, tell me where he'd be heading if he made those prints walking backward.''

''Into open country,'' said Bonner, passing his hand across an area on his wall map. ''And our perimeter men would've seen him by now. If he runs that way, our little Spitfires will spot him. If he hides, your teams will flush him out. Either way, we've got him.'' The gleam in Bonner's eye said that he wanted Sorel to try for a vehicle in the underground parking area. Wanted it so much he was taking it as a foregone conclusion. ''He can't hide out here,'' he finished, tapping the southern prairie of the map.

That open prairie area was south of Soho. Quantrill: ''Is it absolutely flat and open terrain?''

''Like a pool table,'' said the security man, smiling. Plainly, he discounted the idea that Felix Sorel had the cunning to lay a false trail while on a dead run.

''I think I'll take a look anyway,'' said Quantrill. ''You have a spare VHF set?''

''They're all in use.''

''I'll get back to you,'' said Quantrill, and hurried away.

Once into the street, he walked more casually. Turning his torso now and then, he made it easy for anyone to see that tin star on his jacket. He waved to a perimeter guard who stood on the brow of the hill, pointed to his breast, then trotted up the embankment. He was puffing at the top and exchanged handshakes with the guard who was scanning with a pair of old binoculars. From this vantage point they could see both Faro and the sprawl of the Thrillkiller, with Soho rising in a rectangular pile to the south. As he watched, a double-decker bus teetered away from Soho en route to the Hilton parking lot. Even in track shoes, Sorel could not have sprinted that far in so short a time. But he might be out there somewhere to the south.

Quantrill borrowed the binoculars, studying the bus, then sweeping the prairie. No, by God, it was *not* an absolutely flat expanse to the south. A caliche-poor prairie was rarely without its little contours and shallow runoff depressions, and this one was no exception. Damn. "Is Soho crowded this time of day?"

The guard consulted his wristwatch. "Nope. That's the second busload and she ain't full, so all the tourists are out now. They'll be pulling maintenance and cleanup from now 'til after lunch." The young man was looking at him in frank curiosity. "Your guy's headin' for the underground parking, ain't he?"

"I hope so. Don't bag me by mistake," said Quantrill, and strode back down the trail until his head was below the brow of the hill. At that point, no one watching from the open prairie could see his progress. Then he began to trot southward, wishing he had a VHF set, wishing Sorel were dead and in hell, wishing he could give Felix Sorel the throb in his head that paced his rapid footfalls.

CHAPTER SIXTY-SIX • • •

He met one more perimeter guard, who jumped and then grinned sheepishly, before striking out onto the prairie. Though only a mediocre tracker, Quantrill knew enough to think like a fugitive and to estimate the path a smart, desperate man might take. The subtle contours of the prairie would not let a man cross it unseen while walking upright. But if he could run while squatting, and crawl like a boomer lizard, yes; a man like Sorel might just possibly get away to the southwest. A man who was essentially a transplanted big-city cop—Bonner, for example—might not realize it was possible. Yet it might have been possible for Quantrill—and therefore possible for Felix Sorel.

The scuffmarks behind one long, low prominence might have been made by anybody a week before. Squatting near, Quantrill studied a faint indentation and, less than a meter away, a fainter broad groove. He got down beside it on hands and knees and found that if his toe matched the first indentation, his knee might have scuffed the second. He muttered, "Hurt like hell when you banged your knee, Sorel? Good."

He walked another fifty meters. From there he could see the rooftops of Soho, three kilometers or so to the northwest. Sorel would've seen them, too. With more than a ten-minute head start, plus another ten to the present moment, a man might make his way below Soho into Wild Country. The mating-tyrannosaur howl of a little Spitfire pierced the aching stillness, a warning to anyone who might be hiding below. *Know what I'd do, Sorel? With those little Spits boring holes in the sky overhead, I'd try to come around from the southwest and hole up in Soho 'til dark. Maybe find me a hostage and strike a bargain for a fast vehicle. Can you fly light aircraft, good buddy? I'm betting you can.*

It was a long walk to Soho's front entrance. Twice, Quantrill waved as Spitfires caterwauled overhead, removing his tin star, waving it aloft. A brief wing-waggle and the lovely little brutes were gone. He knew better than to continue the path he would have taken, had he been in Sorel's position. Best way in the world to get himself drygulched. *You don't really think Sorel is working his way back to the airstrip, sneaking into Soho to lie low until dark, do you? Yes, you damned well do. Sorel wants a fast ticket to the border, just like Lufo does. Well, good luck to you, Lufo—I wish you were my backup right now.*

Quantrill found no one manning the black iron gates that stretched across the mouth of what, a few meters inside the compound, became Brewer Street. He monkeyed over, dropping easily to the street. Nobody shouted, nobody complained. *Don't these people know there's a war on? Well, not until after lunch.* He hailed the first person he saw at the corner of Brewer and Lexington: a short, well-padded young woman wearing a frilled apron who was spearing bits of trash from the edge of the sidewalk. She took his star at face value. Where was the nearest security man?

"You're new, aren't you?" She had the flat twang of a midwesterner, the sparkle of an actress as she sized him up. "I'm Kitty—Kitty here," she went on, suddenly switching to a passable Cockney accent, "and in the pub. Off duty, I'm Kathy Diehl. You can call me Good," she added, once more Americanized. "Hey, you know you've got blood on your chin?"

"Yeah, I know. Kitty-Kathy, I need somebody in security. We can talk later."

A winsome pout: "Our ha, ha, constables took off on the bus. I think they were going to Faro for something or other. They'll have to come back after lunch. Meanwhile"—she clicked back into the Brit argot with bewildering ease—"soon as I've policed this area, ducks, I'll draw you a pint of bitter while you wait. 'Ow's that for an offer?"

Grinning in spite of everything, Quantrill shook his head. "You're a pistol, lady, but those cops of yours are probably going on guard duty in Faro when I might need 'em here. I'll take a raincheck on the beer. Look, where is everybody?

There's an armed fugitive, WML—white male, latino—who may be hiding out here. My size, black hair—''

"Your hair is black," she said.

"It's dyed. So is his, come to think of it." Kitty-Kathy was now beginning to look as though she would like to disappear from this bloody-faced man into the nearest crevice. He drew the Chiller. "Don't jump like that, for God's sake. They don't let fugitives have stars and weapons like this, okay? If you have some way to contact others here, tell 'em how I'm dressed and to avoid anybody they don't know by sight. Except me. I'm wearing the white hat."

"No, you're not," low and quivering. Now she seemed ready to burst into tears.

Reseating the Chiller, he put his hands before him as if shaking an invisible melon. "Don't go bonkers on me, lady," he said passionately. "Where the hell *is* everybody?"

"Prob'ly cleaning up at Soho Square, and some guys on Wardour Street resetting the falling building," she said, still staring at his right armpit. "Is that one of those government guns?"

Shouting: "Yes! Where the eternal fuck is Soho Square?"

"About four blocks, turn left at Frith. Can't miss it. You always talk dirty when you're mad?" Now she looked hopeful. It appeared that Kitty-Kathy could snap from one emotion to another as easily as she could adjust her accent.

He began walking backward. "If you're smart, you'll take off on foot for the New Driskill. If you're dumb, you could be a hostage." He pointed a finger at her. "You, I will *never* forget. But I'm going to try," he muttered to himself, and began to run down Brewer. *Hostages are just our speed, aren't they, ol' buddy? Guys our size need little ones. Small enough to intimidate, but not too small to hide behind. . . .*

Soho Square, evidently, was a sort of tourist promenade. It sure had its share of trash, which a grounds crew was fast removing. Five men and three women, all dressed in Brit shopkeeper garb, went about their duties, paying little attention to Quantrill until he asked for it. None of them had seen any strangers in the past half hour. They, too, accepted the star as his authority.

One tall, wiry fellow seemed to know everything about Soho. Since most of the "shops" were false, the daytime crew involved an even dozen people clearing the streets and then straightening their shops; this crew of eight who converged on Soho Square before doing room service chores at various locations; and a pair of special effects men. Quantrill asked about that pair.

"They haul the cornice and bricks and stuff back to the roof and set it up for the falling building. Realistic as hell; it's over on Wardour," he said, pointing. "You must be new. Got a map?" He pulled a fold-out brochure from the pocket of a vest shiny with use.

Quantrill sighed, took the map, and said it very slowly: "I am a federal agent, God help us all. My name is Quantrill. I want you to find everyone who works here, and carry any weapons you happen to have in plain sight, and all of you walk together out of Soho to the hotels. Tell the security people what I'm telling you: *nobody comes in here except federal agents.* I'd rather be safe than sorry; a man who looks a lot like me could be hiding here. He is very, very dangerous, and if he gets half a chance, he will take hostages. Go in groups, go now, and if you see anyone you don't know, you'd better hope he doesn't see you. And if you see a short stack named Kitty on the way, boot her butt over the gate with you. I want Soho absolutely deserted in two minutes. Understood?"

The wiry one brought his little trash sticker up like a lance. "Where're you going?"

"To the falling building on Wardour. Not your worry; I'll find it. Go on, git." They got.

The map was a godsend. Wardour led him to the southwest, the narrow street dead-ending in a three-story pile of debris. A block nearer, someone had stretched a modern cable across to bar the way. A hand-lettered sign hung from the cable, warning of deadly hazard. And mounted on a tripod near the sidewalk, farther on, was another sign: UXB. All very realistic; no sensible tourists would venture into this last block, particularly when they came to see the top of a building tumble into the street. Quantrill stood listening to a prairie wind keen across the rooftops of Soho and let the place sink into his pores. *You're here, Sorel. I can feel you. And you can probably feel me. Is your ass snipping holes in*

*your shorts? Probably not. Mine is, and it doesn't make me
like you just a whole lot.*

Somewhere above and to the left, he could hear voices
calling. The echoes garbled their content, but they carried
rebellious overtones. Great; he would have to interrupt an
argument among men at work.

Quantrill hopped over the cable. The Chiller was in his left
hand as he moved from doorway to shopfront, maximizing
his cover, eyes roving to the high ground of rooftops across
the street. Up there it was sniper country. Voices again,
almost directly above him now. Then a hammer of several
shots, thin reports like a small-caliber automatic, punctuated
by a single report, shockingly loud. Instantly, someone
screamed amid a scurry of activity.

Somewhere in the building above him, footsteps pounded
nearer. Quantrill moved into shadow, set the Chiller on full
auto, and waited.

A door at street level burst open not five meters from
where he stood and two men stumbled out, both darting
fearful glances up the steep stairs behind the door. One held
his side just below his rib cage, grimacing, blood already
beginning to stain his one-piece coverall. They turned toward
Quantrill and stopped as they saw him, the barrel of his
Chiller vertical, his right index finger across his lips. He half
expected to hear more feet coming down that stairwell. No
joy. He motioned the men nearer, into the safety of a false
stone storefront, and they came willingly once they spotted
that tin star.

Quietly: "You're the special effects men?"

The uninjured one, a heavyset black, nodded and then
jerked a thumb upward. "There's one bad sonofabitch up
there on level two. Threw down on us while—"

"I can guess. Wanted you for hostages."

"You got it," muttered the injured man, an Anglo of slight
build. He peeled his bloody hand away, looked down, grimaced. "Told me to come down alone to second level."

"Sounds like he has more than one weapon."

"Guess he does now," said the black. "You did right,
Kenny," he added, patting the little man's shoulder.

The injured man explained, "I had my nailgun when he
snuck up on us from below." He saw Quantrill's frown.

"Like a big staple gun. It'll carry fifty feet. Guess he didn't know what it was."

"Sure found out when you squeezed it off," said his companion with fond pride in his gaze.

"And the fucker made me sorry. Shot me, damn true. I dropped the nailgun over the catwalk, so I guess he's got it."

Quantrill: "Hit him?"

"Shit, I wasn't really tryin' to."

"How many rounds are left in that nailgun?"

"Eight or ten. Jeez, this hurts."

Quantrill looked at the big man. "Take him out of Soho the front way and keep going. Check in with security and give 'em the word. Do any of these other doors open?"

"They do with this," said the big man, and handed Quantrill a master key. Supporting his friend, he started down Wardour and then stopped. "Aren't you comin'?"

Quantrill shook his head and glanced upward. "You're civilians, and your buddy's hit. Felix Sorel has just rewritten my contract," he said.

CHAPTER SIXTY-SEVEN • • •

Alone on the street, Quantrill felt his skin prickle. He knew nothing of the structures behind those fake storefronts. Sorel could be strolling around, gazing through those windows at his leisure in his search for a victim. *But you wouldn't want me as a hostage, would you, pal? I might be too troublesome. You'd take me off the second you saw me, and go looking for somebody more tractable. Only there isn't gonna be anybody like that here. But you don't know that, so you'll be casting around to catch some other poor fish, moving along as quietly as you can, testing every footstep. You can't be far away. It took you a hell of a long time to flush those two special effects men. Drives a man nuts to proceed so slowly. I know, I know. . . .* Given one possible advantage in his freedom of movement, Quantrill took it.

Abruptly he began to sprint down the street, leaping the cable, turning the corner, then kneeling with that master key at the first door he came to. If he could get behind the façades of these buildings—really one single building a block wide, built to look like several crammed tightly together—he would at least know the terrain. The main thing was to get familiar with the territory; to take that advantage away from his opponent.

Even the false fronts of Soho, he found, were built with full walls and internal partitions. Perhaps WCS intended to bring the whole place to life one day. Meanwhile, West Texas dust storms had laid down a fine gray film in every empty room. You could move along the sturdy flooring without much noise, but you left tracks as obvious as if striding over fresh paint. Quantrill moved silently to the shadowed back wall; tried the old-fashioned doorknob very,

very gently, remembering to do it right. That meant standing to one side of the door, reaching over with your free hand to grasp the knob, lining your vulnerable parts up with the two-by-fours in the doorframe, just in case. If you stood forthrightly in front of the door, you could get yourself forthrightly ventilated by a slug through that door face. Or several slugs. *Hey, almost forgot; you only fired one round at that poor little guy. Low on ammo, Sorel? It should make you more cautious.*

The door was not locked and opened a hand's width without a squeak. Quantrill squinted through the opening, shifting to improve his view. The door opened onto a broad hallway floored with linolamat, showing treadmarks of many small tires as well as a welter of footprints. *A service hall, used often, with a nice quiet surface. Just the thing to gladden your heart, hm?* He eased the door open more, cursed a complaining hinge, lifted up on the knob to silence the squeak as he persisted. Now he could slip through the doorway, but now, too, he saw that the hall had no true ceiling. Instead, a catwalk of expanded metal gratings let him see two more levels above, illuminated faintly from skylights. It was a nightmare of gridwork and shadow, with tubular steel ladders spaced at intervals down the hallway, leading to higher levels through openings in the floor grate.

He was three rungs up the nearest ladder when he heard it, a single thin concussive report with a familiar ring. It seemed to have come from somewhere above. *Testing our new nailgun, are we? Good careful move. But you wouldn't do it if you knew I was here.* Quantrill gripped the receiver of the Chiller in his teeth, paused to gaze down the empty second-level corridor with its perforated metal floor, continued climbing to the third level. And saw a shadow obscure a skylight in someone's slow passage across the roof.

Quantrill moved as quickly as he dared, tempting faint creaks of the metal flooring as he hurried down the corridor. Three more skylights were spaced just above Quantrill, and that shadow had been moving in the same direction as he, but ahead of him. He paused, now realizing that some of those creaks were made by the man above him. *You're not inside this big echo chamber, Sorel, so you can't be sure whether all these damned noises are your own.*

Quantrill paused short of the next skylight, willing the heavy plastic to give him a clear view of Sorel. But dust and oxidation took their toll, and the shadow that passed above could have belonged to anybody. *I'm sure it's you up there, Sorel; who else could it be?* But bone deep in his training was that requirement to make utterly certain identification before he squeezed off a single round. It was faintly possible that some innocent dude was hiding out on the roof. Quantrill estimated his quarry's rate of advance and scurried forward again. He reached the turn of the upper-level corridor quickly, saw the ceiling trapdoor ahead in the dimness, and moved toward its interior ladder. If Sorel wanted to cross the street, he'd have to come down.

And Quantrill would be waiting. Unfortunately, not where he *should* be waiting.

He heard stealthy rustlings in the near distance, waiting for that trapdoor to open, and then felt something more than he heard it, as if a faint earth tremor had whispered through the building. He backtracked down the corridor, turned the corner, and saw Felix Sorel ten meters away, already descending a ladder to the level below. The sonofabitch had removed the skylight and dropped to the corridor floor. He'd stuffed a bulky tool, the nailgun no doubt, into his jacket front and carried his H&K sidearm in his teeth for the climb. *Just like I do*.

Quantrill made a lightning decision—the spaces of the perforations in that metal flooring might let a seven-millimeter slug pass, with luck—and fired a burst toward the head and shoulders of the man below. Though the Chiller's coughs were faint, the detonations of those tiny warheads were not. The series of blue-white flashes, spattering from the steel grate over Sorel's head, said that Quantrill's luck was poor. Sorel hit the second level, spun, and had the little sidearm aimed upward in less time than seemed possible. The muzzle of the H&K flashed and roared once; the heavy slug struck the grating near Quantrill's feet and shrilled away harmlessly, and then Sorel was sprinting away as Quantrill pounded after him on the level just above. It was maddening to pace a target in full view, from a commanding height, and not be able to fire. Correction: You could fire, but those slug fragments didn't care which target they found.

They had raced twenty meters when Quantrill realized that the next turn would lead them back to the vicinity of the "falling building," a big three-dimensional region that Sorel already knew. Holding his right hand splayed near his face for the pitifully small protection it afforded, Quantrill squeezed off another burst as he ran; saw several more flashes in the grate. But this time, one of those flashes erupted at the turn of the corridor just ahead of Sorel's pumping legs. Sorel grunted, slammed against the corridor wall as he rounded the corner to the left, and kept going. *One of my messages get through to you, buddy?*

Quantrill's next maneuver was part training, part improvisation. Instead of wheeling around the corner, he turned to face the new corridor before he reached it, bounced one-legged into the open, placed his right hand and foot against the wall, and used them to rebound backward. It gave him a fraction of a second to see ahead, and to spray a burst from the Chiller. Then he was safe behind the inside corner of the hall again.

That maneuver had saved his living bacon, for during that instant of exposure he had seen that the flooring on his level terminated with an open tubular railing, a narrow stairway leading below. Felix Sorel had been poised, his handgun extended, aiming point-blank up the stair waiting for Quantrill to appear. But that appearance had come so briefly, and with such a shower of azide-tipped lead, that Sorel had not fired once.

Did I nail you? If I did, it was sheer luck. Quantrill checked the see-through in the grip of his Chiller and saw that his magazine was nearly empty. He reached into the pocket of his right boot, the one holding a fresh magazine of explosive rounds, and made the changeover as silent and swift as possible. To cover the mechanical snicker as he slid the fresh magazine home, he spoke. "Nice try, ol' buddy."

Silence. *Naturally. Maybe I'll think you're hit, or gone, and let you shoot my eye out as I peek around to see. Yeah? Well, I can hear you if you move now, and you haven't moved.* "I can loosen your tongue, Sorel," he said, his voice echoing in the stillness.

For proof, he shifted the Chiller to his right hand, squatted, and poked its nose around the corner at knee height just long enough to fire several rounds in Sorel's general direction. He couldn't afford to waste a whole lot of ammo this way, but Sorel couldn't know that.

Now Felix Sorel spoke for the first time, softly, but with its sibilant echoes down the shadowed hall: "I am hit."

"That so? Toss that little whacker of yours out to the corner. I'll be able to see it through the grating." *And after you do, we'll talk about that nailgun. I'll bet it's your hole card for close quarters.*

"I think not," said Sorel. "You made me underestimate your talent for this work. Perhaps you enjoy killing. I must think."

"Take your time. Bleed all you like."

A low chuckle from the shadows below. "That was an interesting move, at the stair. Now I believe my friend Coulter is truly our enemy Quantrill. You refused to play Solo yesterday. Did you know me then?"

"If I had, you'd be cold cuts now."

"One of us would," Sorel replied. "How much money do you expect to see this year?"

While you talk, my backups are on the way; surely you know that. But maybe you really do think I can be bought, or rented. Hold that thought, pal—and waste more time. Aloud he said, "More than you think. And I've got you, Sorel. That's worth a lot to me."

"Would you trade me for, say, twenty thousand dollars?"

"Toss the money out here where I can see it, and we can discuss it," Quantrill taunted. He heard a rustling, but no footfalls. *I can't believe you have that much on you, and I don't really give a shit, old buddy. But take your time. . . .*

The meaning of that rustle did not become clear until a fraction of a second after Quantrill, staring down through the grating at his feet, saw the wad of currency flop scattering into view below. Of course, it drew Quantrill's attention for a wink of time.

Sorel counted on that diversion; counted on the cash to purchase time to spring five meters to the corner and empty that nailgun upward. Felix Sorel, still unhurt except for a welt across his back, knew Bonaparte's prescription for victory: audacity, always audacity. He choreographed his change of pace with wonderful precision, appearing almost beneath

Quantrill, nailgun held high, cycling its entire load of slender steel darts in the spray that lasted between one and two seconds. Quantrill reacted quickly enough to throw his forearms up before him and was leaping back as Sorel emptied the nailgun.

Those eight-penny nails were slender enough to pass easily through the grating, and five of them did. One drove itself deep into a boot heel, penetrating the tough flesh of Quantrill's right heel without doing much real damage. The second passed through Quantrill's left palm and blunted against the grip of the Chiller. The third pierced the flesh of his scalp at his hairline above the right eye, deflected by his skull, its tip emerging slightly. The fourth and fifth were clean misses.

Quantrill spun away, his Chiller clattering into the open as Sorel dived in the opposite direction. There was no reasonable possibility that he might retrieve the Chiller, because Sorel could nail him while vaulting those stairs. With one brilliant sally, Sorel had reversed the roles of hunter and quarry.

As it had done so many times before, Quantrill's body responded with that surge of noradrenaline that sent his universe into slow motion. To face Sorel at the landing was certain suicide, but the man had dived away and might need two seconds or so to reach the bottom of the stair. Quantrill was already sprinting down the hall toward the skylight Sorel had removed, ignoring the slivers of steel in his hand and forehead. He heard feet pounding up the stair and leaped for the wooden frame of the opening, catching it with both hands, unheeding of the pain in his left, hauling himself frantically upward. It was sheer luck that he kicked his legs when he did, for the nine-millimeter round, fired as Sorel paused to make an unhurried shot at twenty-five-meter range, passed between them.

Quantrill heard racing footsteps again as he levered his body over the rim of the opening and pulled his legs into a tuck, rolling to one side. He kept rolling across the graveled roof, came up in a crouch. *Thank God you're getting stingy with your ammo. I wonder if you took the Chiller, pal. And I wonder if you know what'll happen if somebody whose thumbprint doesn't match mine tries to fire it. See the pretty Chiller, Sorel. Try it out. Surprise!*

Having lost the initiative and his weapon, Quantrill saw the futility of further attacks. He grimaced, tugging at the nail through his palm. The damned thing was now blunt at both ends. He'd known a Chiller round might pass through that steel grating, so why hadn't he realized an eight-penny finishing nail could do it better? He scanned the roof as he pulled on that nail, swiping once at the blood trickling into his right eye, using the trick of turning his attention away from the site of his agony. He heard footsteps, quick but not loud, below. A moment later another in the line of skylight bubbles popped upward, falling back askew. It seemed unlikely that a man of Sorel's size could spring high enough to unseat a skylight with his hands, but it was happening. *Wonderful, you fucking soccer jock, but why?*

When a third widely spaced bubble flipped clear of its rim, Quantrill saw the point. Sorel was giving himself several well-spaced options for emerging onto the roof, and without a weapon Quantrill could not attend to them all at once. The nail in his palm was slippery now, and, running in a crouch, Quantrill chipped a tooth wrestling the thing from his flesh. It didn't hurt all that much—and then it did as he shoved the skewed skylight back into position without making himself a target. No sound came from below. *That's okay, good buddy, I see about twenty people hotfooting it down the road north of here. No more hostages but me.* It came to him then that if he were injured just enough, he might be a very useful hostage after all. His bloody handprint on that skylight rim must've been a great encouragement to Sorel. He called out, "Sorel! You want to discuss terms?"

No response. *What would I be doing in your place? Misdirecting you.* The trapdoor to the roof at the far end of the hall was fifty meters distant. Quantrill guessed right and was running across the roof expanse away from it before Sorel popped it upward.

Ventilators and vent pipes, standing proud of the roofline, made a scattered forest of metal trunks providing some cover. Quantrill passed up an external ladder that led down the backside of the building; a man who could nail a horse at a hundred long paces could certainly pick a man off a nearby ladder, even if he tried a fireman's descent. Up ahead, the roofline dropped one story, revealing external girders and catwalks behind a false front of numbered blocks that looked like stone. It was obviously the assembled falling building, and those special effects men had left it by an internal stairwell. Sorel had to know the terrain; he'd probably watched those poor devils for ten minutes getting near enough to surprise them. The upcurled rails of a roof ladder stood just ahead, and Quantrill went over the roof by grasping one rail in his right hand, swinging around and downward to keep his profile low, catching the other rail in his bloody left hand as his feet found the side rails. Sorel's slug cut a groove through the gravel and sang away between the curled rails just over his head. *Expected me to go up and over the usual way, did you? Give me some credit, pal. No, don't. Keep underestimating me. . . .*

His insteps sliding down the side rails, hands flashing down two rungs at a time, Quantrill dropped the last two meters and saw a fire door yawning open a few steps away. He fled through it, ruining a fingernail in the effort to fling it shut behind him. The damned thing was heavy, swinging shut with a lovely solid *thunkk,* but taking so much time in its swing that Quantrill heard the impact of Sorel's feet on the second-floor roof. *You wondrous bastard, you simply went over the edge without the ladder. Keep it up and you'll break your fucking neck.* But by that time Quantrill was hurtling down the dim stairwell. The way he'd been taught, only four steps at a time, gripping the banister briefly with his good hand at each bound. He dodged onto the familiar sidewalk with a flash of déjà vu, glancing up as he ran, knowing Sorel was still on the roof because no sound came from the stairwell. He saw directly above, outlined against the late morning sky and at first in eldritch silence, the upper part of the building lean out and begin to topple.

CHAPTER SIXTY-EIGHT • • •

It takes time to change direction when running full tilt in normal footgear. It also takes time for interlocked masses of fibrous plastic disguised as brick and stone to fall three stories into a street. Quantrill covered the necessary fifteen meters across a curiously yielding rubbery sidewalk in less than two seconds and was missed by the complete windowframe that cartwheeled past. But he was knocked sprawling amid the thunder of hollow masonry, sideswiped lightly by a hunk of fiberglass cornice that rebounded from that sidewalk composition. Had it been solid stone, it would have mashed him like a beetle. A cloud of grayish dust roiled up from the slithering roar of debris, and Quantrill smelled rye flour in the air as he regained his feet.

And now the sound of heavy footfalls issued from that stairwell as Sorel raced down to see the result of his handiwork. Quantrill continued almost to the face of the rubble that blocked the street but knew he could never clamber over it without giving Sorel an absurdly soft target.

He ducked into the last doorway, fumbling stupidly for that master key, and went through the door sideways cursing the squall its hinges yielded. He found himself in a room with no rear door, but with an open stairwell leading below. The room stank faintly, pungent with a once common odor, and the dust on the floor showed the passage of many feet to and from that stairwell. This corner of Soho might be off-limits to tourists, but it saw a lot of use. Felix Sorel stood in the street with his sidearm drawn, looking the other direction down Wardour, wheeling in a crouch as he heard that telltale squeal of hinges. Now he was studying storefronts across the street, moving silently, his motions fluid as an otter's as he addressed every prominence that might hide anything of Quantrill's size. *Pleasure to watch you, damn your eyes. If I close this door, it'll screech like a tomcat, and if I don't, you'll see it ajar. I'd best leave it as is, and make every second count.*

Quantrill tested each footfall for creaks, squatting below the front windows as he retreated to the stairs. He thanked a capricious providence for providing a welded steel stair that did not protest, and descended in search of something he could use as a weapon.

The basement floor was concrete, its gloom dispelled by narrow clerestory windows set at sidewalk level. Quantrill could see Felix Sorel twenty meters away, searching storefronts, listening. Moving in a crouch, Quantrill made his way around what looked like a remotely run furnace, with pipes running through the wall and a huge connected blower. A barrel-sized tank nearby sat high on metal legs, with a copper feed line to the furnace. Set into the rear wall was a door that seemed to offer hope of an exit.

It lied. The door opened silently on well-oiled hinges, and Quantrill found himself staring into a volume hardly larger than a bathroom. A row of ancient five-gallon containers stood against one wall. He opened one, damning the noise, and felt a certain satisfaction. He did not know that this basement housed the mechanism that provided Soho with its spectacular fireball during the Heinkel's "crash" just outside the compound, but he knew what he had in that metal container.

He was pulling his boots off, standing beneath the stairs, when he heard Sorel's footfalls above. He tugged at a sock, then hurriedly thrust his second spare magazine of Chiller ammo into it. If Sorel did not come down on his own, he must be enticed down. But getting Sorel down those stairs was no problem; the Mexican came down cautiously, spotted the door to the storage room, and stood assessing the place.

It had to be said just exactly right, if either of them was to live. "Don't shoot, Sorel. I'm your only hostage." His words were calm, and from his crouch behind the steel stair he was still invisible.

Just as calmly, from three meters away: "Show me empty hands."

Quantrill thrust the loaded sock into a hip pocket and stuck out his hands, very slowly, where they could be seen. "Coming out.'' He was coughing, tears gathering in his eyes, as he stood up with hands elevated to the height of his head.

Something like relief, and sadness as well, crossed Sorel's face as he trained the muzzle of his sidearm at Quantrill's belly. ''Up the stairs,'' he said, pointing with his free hand, stepping back with care, coughing softly. Quantrill stepped to the stair, blinking and coughing. Yes, he might still get out of this hole without more bloodshed, but only as a hostage, bested by Felix Sorel. In any case, he had already begun to play his own hand, and Sorel seemed unaware of it.

Quantrill stood on the first step and turned. ''Put the shooter away, Sorel, you can't use it here. And you won't get past me, but you're welcome to try.''

Sorel, too, was now blinking watery eyes as he frowned. ''Go upstairs before you suffocate, fool.''

''That's gasoline fumes you smell, ol' buddy.'' He coughed. ''Lots of it, spilled across the floor, and a hundred gallons more in storage. One muzzle flash and this whole building will be scattered from here to Faro.''

Sorel looked around him, saw the puddles and the metal jerry can standing in full view near the storage room. His face clouded. ''*Idiota*, this is not the way men fight.''

''There's a better way. I'm betting you'll take it.'' Quantrill lowered his hands to his hips, gambling, trying to make his grin a taunt even though he was now a bit light-headed from the fumes. ''If you throw that H and K and it strikes a spark, they'll hear it in Austin. Got nails in your boots? Take 'em off. Believe me, I'll wait.''

Slipping the little automatic into its holster, Sorel managed a glacial smile. His confidence seemed unshaken, though for the first time, Quantrill saw in his face the squint of a duped man. ''I love to beat a clever Anglo,'' he said. He stood on one foot, then the other, wrenching his boots off as he coughed. ''And you would bar my way, *mano a mano*?'' He might have risked hurling one of those boots if he'd had the chance.

Quantrill knew he presented a sad spectacle with blood covering one side of his face. But he was through talking, already whipping out that loaded sock, springing forward, hoping his bare feet offered purchase for maneuver as he swung at Sorel's head.

Sorel was too quick, lashing out in a footsweep that caught Quantrill's thigh and knocked him off-balance. Darting toward the stairs, Sorel felt his left hand caught by both of Quantrill's and whirled to avoid a shoulder dislocation, bringing the heel of his free hand up toward Quantrill's nose, hoping his fingers could reach those hard eyes while he shattered the septum.

Quantrill avoided the blow, his right hand forcing Sorel's arm to continue its upward sweep as he lunged forward and butted the Mexican under the jaw in a favorite move. That eight-penny nail, still embedded at his hairline, tore a gouge under Sorel's chin. Unlike Jer Garner, Sorel knew that it would be followed by a dozen more; the burst of light behind his eyes said that he could not afford them. Arching backward on the stairs, he pulled his legs up, aiming at Quantrill's groin.

Quantrill harbored no illusions about the power of those trained legs; sidestepped the ferocious kick but had to release Sorel's wrist to do it. His own heel caught Sorel's left knee at full extension, not quite at the edge of the patella, but tearing at the adjacent ligaments, and Sorel twisted away in agony instead of facing his antagonist. Instantly Quantrill fell on him, scissoring those legs between his own, grasping Sorel's left wrist with his own blood-slicked left hand while reaching for his hair with the right. Both men were panting dizzily now, locked together in a gut-churning embrace.

It is easier to snap a man's head forward than to push it to one side. Quantrill bounced Sorel's forehead against a steel riser twice before the Mexican managed to thrust up and back, lifting Quantrill's weight as he came to his knees and crashed over. Quantrill lost his slippery handgrip as they rolled, and then Sorel's left elbow caught him in the rib cage with the man's weight behind it.

As Quantrill's torso rebounded from the stair, Sorel gathered his feet under him and leaped away. He glanced behind him as Quantrill, face now streaming with gore from that scalp wound, vaulted up to follow. The distance was right, and Sorel was certain this Anglo hellion did not expect his next maneuver. It had killed more than one man.

An upward left-footed sweep, then the follow-through with his right as Felix Sorel began a bicycle kick, a backward flip with a whiplash foot that could fire a soccer ball seventy yards, or crush the skull of the man following. Sorel's glory, and much of his confidence, lay in his ability to use these skills as killing techniques.

Yet Sorel had failed to account for the synaptic edge honed into the tissues of Ted Quantrill. That murderous flashing kick missed Quantrill's head, and before he struck concrete Sorel felt a hand grip his left ankle to wrench him sideways in midair. He completed three-quarters of his flip, striking the floor on his belly, and this time Quantrill's backward heel kick against Sorel's knee found its target. The snap was audible, and the follow-up against the back of his head knocked him all but unconscious against the concrete floor.

There might be time, Quantrill thought groggily, to hammer Sorel to mush. Or time to weave up those stairs for lungfuls of fresh air. There would not be time for both. Nearly blind, lungs aflame, nauseated from the fumes, Quantrill reeled up the stairs gasping. He did not look back. If Felix Sorel chose to fire that H&K, it would make no difference where his slugs went.

Quantrill stumbled from the upper room to the sidewalk, missed his footing, and fell to his knees, retching. His fit of explosive coughs made it worse, robbing him of air, his throat muscles at last beginning to convulse from the deadly fumes. He lowered his bloody forehead to the street cobbles, shuddering, his breath whistling through a larynx that seemed to be on fire. Dimly, he imagined Felix Sorel navigating those stairs, hobbling to the street, raising that handgun. And there was not one—goddam—thing—Quantrill could do about it. He'd been breathing those fumes a half minute longer than Sorel. Coughing, fighting down his gut spasms, he waited for the sound of footsteps.

No pursuit. Too shaky to stand, Quantrill moved on hands and knees within arm's length of a clerestory basement window. He snapped his palm against the thin pane and heard shards of glass strike the concrete inside. Near fainting, he put his forehead against the sidewalk and closed his eyes, breathing deeply now. He kept down, aware that the sight of him might tempt Sorel to fire regardless of the consequences. God, how that man could move! That bicycle kick had come within a finger's width of taking his head off. "Sorel? You there?"

A disembodied voice issued from the basement. "Do you need to ask?" Then a fit of coughing.

Even from that broken window the fumes were overpowering. *You were the worst, and the best. Can't let you suffocate.* "I can see the stairs, Sorel. Toss your jacket in that patch of sunlight, and the pistol on the jacket."

More coughing. "No. This weapon is my freedom."

"Goddammit, I won't come down there for you unless you do."

"If I fired now, the result would be the same." The sounds of a tortured stomach stifled the voice.

"Why haven't you?"

"Cannot walk; the game is yours. My rules. My decision."

"Game, shit! You're goddam *dying* down there."

"Correct, in good time. Leave me. I will not say this again." Still more coughing.

"I can't, you crazy bastard. I liked you."

"Odd," said the voice from below. "We are much the same, but could never understand each other."

"We're not that complicated, Sorel. I'll visit you in Huntsville Prison and prove it, if you like. Don't ask me why."

"Prison." It was a snort. "Have you ever known the loss of all hope?"

Quantrill recalled the tiny mastoid implant that had once compelled his obedience on pain of instant death; felt again the helpless rage at learning that his lover lay dead at the hands of his own agency. But years ago. Worlds ago. "Yes. But we always get it back, somehow."

"Not the loss of youth and freedom."

"Everybody loses those. One gets taken away, the other we give away," Quantrill answered.

"Not I."

"Sure. We give away some freedom to friends, wives, kids—everybody who knows they can depend on us."

A terrible mirthless laugh, then spasmodic coughs. Then, growling it: "Not I."

"Have it your way," Quantrill said. "But when you pass out, I'll have you. You'll feel different after a spell in the slammer."

So faintly that Quantrill almost failed to hear it: "Not I. If you love me so much, then go with me."

Because the H&K's safety would make no audible click, Quantrill rolled and staggered to his feet, trying to put some distance between himself and that fume-filled hell. There was something hideously final about Sorel's final comment.

The shot was muffled, and Quantrill blinked in astonishment as he realized that it had not caused a vast explosion. The reason was not hard to find; a man's mouth will sometimes contain a muzzle flash.

CHAPTER SIXTY-NINE • • •

"I wouldn't worry about it, Teddy," said Jess Marrow, reaching for the bottle of sherry that sat between their cane-bottomed rockers. He poured a dollop into his cup, shifted his feet before the bulbous little woodstove at the corner of his office. "You coulda let a hundred Lufo Albenizes go and they wouldn't indict you now. You're a goddam *he*-ro, according to the holo. You'll be so uppity now, I got half a notion to fire you," he added with a grin, swirling the dark liquid in the bottle. "Let me top off your cup."

"One's plenty," Quantrill said. A week had passed since he'd begun a manhunt with a hangover. That was one thing he'd avoid now for the rest of his life. One of several things. He was in stocking feet at the moment, saddle-soaping one of those sharkskin boots for the third time. They hadn't felt right since he'd retrieved them from a puddle of gasoline in that basement, along with the ruin that had been Felix Sorel. It was a hard thing to admit, but on learning the full extent of Sorel's activities he knew that he would not have visited the man, even on death row. A man is not what he *has*, but what he *does*, and Felix Sorel had done all the damage he possibly could.

Now Quantrill rubbed gently at the scab near his hairline, feeling a faint twinge through the bandage covering his left palm. "I saw that holocast at Sandy's place night before last, Jess. You know as well as I do, enhanced video's a bunch of horseshit. Half of those scenes never happened."

"Try and tell that to your adorin' public."

"*That's* what really worries me. I remember what you said the other day."

Marrow sipped and nodded. "Well, it's true; there'll be a few fools lookin' for you, tryin' to make their reputations."

He sighed, fell silent for a moment. "You could take a new name. Wild Country's full of people who did."

"Like Lufo? I'd be found out just like he was." Smiling, Quantrill elevated his cup in a toast to the memory of the big TexMex. "I'd still like to know how he disappeared right under everybody's nose. He didn't get help from Marv Stearns; from what the Gov says, Stearns was already in custody. Lufo just vanished—with a nine-millimeter hole in him. Christ, he *deserved* to get away!"

"Prob'ly hid 'til the next day when the roadblocks were down and all those network people were clutterin' up the place. Made WCS management happy as a pig in shit to get all that publicity, Teddy. They'd like you to do an encore every week."

"Su-u-re they would. Like I told the Gov, Jess: I'm retired. I damn near *got* retired."

Marrow, with a sidelong leer: "Finally got your good strong sign, I reckon. Don't take this wrong, Teddy, but . . . you think you've slowed down? Or are you packin' it in at your peak?"

A long, thoughtful pause, flexing the fingers of that bandaged hand. "I was rusty. You have to keep your edge, and you can't do that and settle down, too. No, I don't think I've slowed down. Next year or the year after? Maybe."

Marrow nodded, listening to the moan of a cold prairie wind around the porch outside. He got up, chose a hunk of mesquite from the nearby pile, and thrust it into the belly of the cast-iron stove before sighing back into his rocker. Somehow the woodstove, across the office from a computer terminal, said all that needed saying about Jess Marrow. He kept what he enjoyed of the old while learning the best of the new. And he knew how to broach an idea. "There's a way to duck all that celebrity, of course." Pause. "Naw, I guess not."

"What?"

"Forget it, you wouldn't go for it. You'd say some fool thing like, it ain't your style."

"Try me," Quantrill insisted.

Marrow took his time, slipping into the slow cadences of the tale-spinner. This was the kind of day for it, a sunless day before a potbelly stove, waiting for this "blue norther" weather front to pass. "Well, I was at a WCS staff meeting yesterday at the New Driskill. Seems they expect big holiday crowds, weather or no weather, after all that holo coverage. And this robotics bigbrain named Hyson showed us a tape of some new androids they've got in California.'' The older man pursed his lips, shook his head. ''Teddy, you would not believe it. You know that Copycat 'droid near the Thrillkiller?'' He saw Quantrill nod. ''It ain't a patch on the ass of what we saw on tape. They'll cost ten thousand each, but you could enter one in a decathlon and nobody would be the wiser. 'Cept for urine tests.'' He chuckled. ''I bet they could rig that, too.''

''That tape could be enhanced video,'' Quantrill replied.

''Nope. Hyson's got a rep to uphold; he says what we saw is what WCS can get.'' Pause. ''Now, the problem is how to make one of those things pay without breakin' any laws. After the staff meeting I jawed awhile with Schreiner, Stewart, a few others. Somebody came up with a real dipshit idea. A minute ago you said, 'Try me.' You're a household word now. What if anybody at all could try you—not you, of course, but a 'droid built to your specs?''

Recalling the swiftness with which that busty mechanical bimbo had drawn a tiny derringer on the doomed Sorel, Quantrill shrugged. ''No fun in that, Jess. A 'droid could beat anybody, me included.''

''You still don't see it, do you? I mean, *exactly* to your specs. It would have your speed, but no more. In other words, your limitations. Your size and weight and, as near as possible, programmed to make the kind of decisions you'd make. Your face and voice, too.'' A dramatic pause: ''Teddy, it would fool your mother.''

Quantrill's expression suggested that he had just inhaled a fat green fly. ''What the hell for?''

''For the money it could rake in; Stewart thinks it'd pay for itself in a year. And for the royalties you'd get, if you let 'em run you through a battery of tests and answer a bushel of dumb questions by programmers.'' He saw a look of negation in Quantrill's face, then added his clincher. ''And it'd do the one thing you say you want most, Ted. It would give those piss-and-vinegar types a way to try you out on the streets of Faro, without havin' to hunt you up personally. Ultrasonics instead of lasers in the pistols; hell, it oughta double the crowd. But it was just a dipshit idea. I *said* you wouldn't go for it.''

Quantrill sniffed his sherry and thought it over, taking Marrow's reverse psychology for granted, also accepting the fact that it worked. Finally, ''Just whose dipshit idea was this?''

Marrow looked away. ''I forget.''

''Uh-huh. You realize that a copy of me might kidney-punch some poor bastard's lights out?''

''They swear it can be programmed not to. And just between me and you, they intend to do it anyway, Ted. As long as they're gonna copy somebody, why not you?''

After a moment's reflection, Quantrill began to laugh. In explanation he said, ''Jim Street may try to get that 'droid drafted.''

''More likely, they'd be interested in anybody that beats it.''

''Never happen,'' said Quantrill.

Both men were laughing now and ignored the buzz of the telephone until its eighth repetition. ''Awshit,'' Marrow grumped, and stumped over to his desk. The call was for his assistant.

Jess Marrow tried to ignore the conversation, cussing his stove and shaking its lower grate even though it was working perfectly, on the theory that if he made a hell of a racket, he couldn't be listening to a private confab three meters away. He looked around as he heard his name called and saw Quantrill press the ''hold'' button.

''Jess, just how much money could I pry out of WCS for that scheme you mentioned?''

Marrow showed a pair of callused hands. ''Five thousand. Maybe ten—if somebody on the staff thought you were worth a shit,'' he said. The higher offer was implicit, of course, because Marrow was a well-regarded staff member of WCS.

Quantrill punched another button and said to the phone, ''How would those payments look if I could put ten thousand down?'' He waited, then his face became impassive. ''Well, thanks anyway. Oh, sure, it's fair, but I couldn't make the spread pay enough to make payments that size for a long time.'' Then he was listening again.

Marrow seemed to be rumbling it to himself, but that

rumble carried: "'Course, the royalties off a concession can go a thousand a month.'' He saw Quantrill looking his way and returned to fiddling with the stove. Jess Marrow was not about to open himself to a charge, ever, that he wanted to make a man's decisions for him. But a young stud needed a prod into the right chute now and then. It sounded as if someone was turning Ted Quantrill out to new pasturage—literally. *And why not?* Marrow smiled to himself. *My daddy always told me real estate was for youth. "Get lots while you're young,'' he said. And I only thought it was the oldest joke in the world, but it's a good way to settle a man down, too.*

Quantrill rang off but did not return to his rocker as Marrow did. Instead he padded bootless to the window, staring out at the swirl of bruise-tinted cloud that rolled across the horizon. "Now I've done it,'' he muttered.

"Spit it out.''

"I want to marry Sandy Grange, Jess. She wouldn't have me until I quit the dangerous stuff. We both want to ranch that spread of hers, add to it, maybe, and she's recently . . . uh . . . come into a pile of cash. Turns out that Mulvihill Garner's property goes to a married sister in Beaumont. Sandy made some calls, says the woman likes the Bayou country and hates it out here. She'd sell the Garner spread whole or in parcels. Sandy was tickled to death at that. She called me last night, said she'd made an offer on about twenty sections of Garner land that adjoins hers.''

"Good sheep land. So where's the problem?''

Quantrill toed one of the feet of the squat iron stove and said, almost mumbling it, "I just made the woman a slightly higher offer.''

Marrow quit rocking and sat up straight. "For the same parcel?''

"Yep.''

"Well, for pity's sake,'' said Marrow, sipping and rocking, rocking and sipping. Presently he added, "I always heard there was a reason for everything, but I do believe you just blew that one out the window.''

"Jess, I'm years older than she is, but what did I have to bring to the marriage? Not a thing. I didn't want to marry property, I wanted to *combine* it.''

Marrow emptied the last of the sherry into his cup, commenced rocking again. He knew that Quantrill was watching him ruminate, tipping his cup in a game of try-not-to-spill-it as he rocked. It wasn't hard to figure; this young buck simply refused to accept himself as worthy of the union without dragging a dowry of twenty square miles along to improve his value. A ridiculous view, from a man who had the self-confidence of a manhunter. Still, it was a measure of his regard for the Grange girl that Quantrill would think himself unworthy of her without some land to sweeten the deal. Doubtless she would see that instantly; women understood these things.

"Jess?" Quantrill was still looking out that window.

"Hm?"

"I can still back out. I mean, if there's any doubt about WCS going for that up-front money or the royalties."

"Stewart's word is solid granite. If I tell him I've made you a half-assed offer, he'll chew on me for not letting *him* make it, and then he'll back it up just like he intended to all along. Truth is, I figured that call would be him calling from Kerrville, and he'd be more anxious if I let it ring awhile. He knows a good idea when he hears one, and I know him. Hell, he thought I was a genuis for . . . anyway," he trailed off, sipping. Rocking.

For perhaps ten minutes they followed their respective thoughts in silence. Then from Quantrill: "Boy, Sandy will be mad as a hornet. But I had to do this, Jess." He wheeled about, troubled, and went on. "I don't expect anybody to understand."

"Oh, I think I have it pretty well figured out."

"Then explain it to me."

Marrow was shaking silently with laughter as he met Quantrill's gaze. "The way I figure it . . . you're just a damn fool, Teddy."

Quantrill, fondly: "Screw you, Jess."

Marrow, cackling: "I'll drink to that."

CHAPTER SEVENTY   •   •   •

Sandy's journal, Wed. 14 Feb. '07

A shiny new surname for a valentine! Sweet, gruff old Jess Marrow nearly ruined my—our ceremony in the WCS chapel as he gave me away this afternoon. Ted heard his thunderous whisper to me, "Do you really take this damn fool?" and each kept the other snorting with mirth, made worse by poor nervous Mr. Hutcherson, who had jammed the ring on his pinkie and panicked when he could not get it loose. I conclude that not all men are children. But the best ones sometimes are, and at the most inopportune times!

I was simply flabbergasted to learn, over twice-spiked punch in the central lodge, that the mysterious buyer of the northern Garner parcel was MY HUSBAND! My cup erupteth over! I swear Ted seemed more apprehensive than proud, and I'm sure my tears did not reassure him. I hope the kiss did. I know it provoked applause from Childe (winsome but ill at ease in her first white frock), who did not yet know what I had just learned. When she did, she flew to Ted and tried to imitate my embrace. I know very well what the little stinker was thinking: another twenty square miles for her and Ba'al to safely roam.

Must ask Ted the identity of the woman who pressed that tiny package into my hand without a word before leaving the lodge. I know Ted saw her, though they never spoke. Wonderful proud bearing despite those thin facial scars I could see through her makeup. And a lovely body of which I should, I suppose, be envious. She must be a conduit to Lufo, for only he would know where in Mexico to locate the Ember of Venus. Nearly swallowed my teeth when I unwrapped it, now

*that I know its value. I hid it in my cleavage; chilly little
critter. If I know L., he stole it! I could never wear it in
public but, with some simple setting, may wear it at my throat
some night for MY HUSBAND when I am wearing nothing
else.*

*Childe is much too sophisticated since she started school,
for she positively demanded to spend these next few nights
with a schoolmate in Rocksprings. Not because Ted and I
would be gone from here at the soddy, but because we won't
be! Where do they learn these things?!*

*I have taken too long with you, journal, delaying until the
effects of that punch wore off while poor Ted waits, fero-
ciously patient, pretending to be interested in his holo program. I know what he is really waiting for, and I intend to be
thoroughly alert when I wife him through this night!*

*Today's entry may be déclassé with its fulsome sprinkle of
exclamation marks, but this Valentine's Day has earned them.
I feel valentiney all over, and it is my pleasure to sign myself. . .*

  Mrs. Sandra Quantrill

CHAPTER SEVENTY-ONE • • •

February and then March slipped by before the Quantrills made a decision on their new homesite. The soddy would be their retreat, but they could not run cattle or sheep from such lodgings. Sandy had a horror of credit and said it was her right to pay cash for a house.

Their choice of the site was half by accident, really, on a bright April day as they whirred Sandy's hovercycle at half speed over their new spread. Sorel's van and its contents had long since been airlifted away, and both Reeve Longo and the hapless Billy Ray would remain guests of the government for years to come. But Ted Quantrill had only a sketchy idea where, on his new property, that shed had been erected.

It was Sandy who saw its remains, like a huge box now flattened among the oaks. "Some people don't care how they litter," she complained, splendid in her sun-yellow blouse and deerskin trousers as she walked to the edge of a shallow valley nearby. She shaded her eyes and peered down the broad depression. "Where do you suppose Ba'al went to?"

"He was right behind us," Quantrill replied. "Maybe we went too fast for him." There were ways to deal with a pet dog that followed your car, he reflected; but when your half-ton boar took a notion to accompany your cycle, you might think twice before you spanked him.

"I see him. He's getting a drink at the creek. Ooh, Ted," she breathed, and stretched out her free hand. "Come look."

Hand in hand, they gazed across a depressed meadow blue with the blooms of that brief annual glory, the Texas Sunbonnet. Millions of the little lupines waved in unison, a soft breeze-borne undulation of softest sky blue across the meadow. A hawk patrolled the blue above, nearly motionless. Somewhere a mockingbird was defying nightingales. "That little

312

creek must run all year," she said, speaking low to maintain the stillness.

In the near distance, Ba'al waded into a shallow pool, flicking an ear, whisking his ridiculous tail. Above the pool the stream turned abruptly, flowing in a broad sheet over a lip of stone. "Our own waterfall," Quantrill said. It might be only knee deep, but it must be dependable. It hadn't rained in weeks. "You suppose the water's drinkable?"

"I don't care. We can treat it if we have to, honey. Are you thinking what I'm thinking?"

"If you're horny—probably," he said.

"Naughty man. Maybe after lunch. See that level area up there above the falls? We'd only have to cut down a couple of trees."

He studied the curves of the land; nodded. "Just above that old fig tree. We won't want to build too close to that waterfall, the noise could drive you nuts."

"There's one way we can find out, love. Did you ever see a better spot for a picnic?"

They spread an old blanket near the waterfall and shared the beer and barbecue sandwiches. Ba'al came ambling over, grunting lazily. "Mighty casual for a moocher," Sandy observed, and reached into the wicker hamper. "Here, I brought this just for you. Watch this," she added to her husband, offering a thick peanut butter sandwich to the boar.

Quantrill could not drink beer and laugh at the same time, but he tried. If there was one thing more crammed with solemn imbecility than a cat with a caramel, it had to be Ba'al coping with peanut butter. He snuffled, turned his head this way and that, flirting his tongue at the stuff clinging to the roof of his mouth, then sat down and tried to scrape it out with a forehoof. When he had finally got rid of the stuff, naturally he applied for more.

The Quantrills lay on their backs gasping. "He's hooked, by God," Ted insisted. "Woman, you have no pity for a poor dumb beast."

"Him, yes. You, no." She tried to finish off a bulb of Pearl but saw the reproachful look of the boar and was taken by laughter again. "Oh, fiddle," she said as beer streamed down her wrist.

Ted watched Sandy heading for the stream, sat up, and

made a scratching motion to the boar. Ba'al remained carefully clear of the blanket and Ted walked to him, scratching him around the ears, leaning against the animal, venting an occasional chuckle. It had not escaped him that Ba'al no longer cared which of them stood taller. He had suggested a leather collar, a clear sign that the great boar was domestic and not wild game, but Childe had found that her friend would have none of it. A pennant tied to his ruff, perhaps. He thought of Alec Wardrop and smiled.

The heads of man and boar jerked around in perfect unison at the urgency in Sandy's call: "Come here!" They did, Ba'al charging up first, tail erect. She was squatting on the stream bank, just above the falls, and patted the fearsome muzzle of the boar to calm him. She pointed into the water several paces from the base of the falls as Ted hurried to her side. "Is that a robin's egg? A button?"

He saw the image wavering in the water, a smooth oval object of a deeper hue than bluebonnets. "We'll soon—know," he grunted, hauling his boots and socks off, then rolling up his trousers. The bottom was limestone and it was too early in the season for algae that made it slick. He waded over, pleased that the water was not all that chill. This creeklet, like so many others in Wild Country, probably ran aboveground for only a brief distance becore plunging back to where it belonged: the measureless caverns of Edwards Plateau. Its temperature would remain fairly constant throughout the year.

He scrabbled for the thing, stood up, displayed it between thumb and forefinger, and then flipped it to Sandy. She was turning it over as he waded back. "It's one of those Mormon fifties," he said.

Briefly, after the war, the Young administration had done the best it could to make up for the loss of U. S. mints in Denver, San Francisco, and Philadelphia. The so-called "Mormon fifty" was a coin the size of an old silver dollar, minted in Ogden. Like the Susan B. Anthony dollar before it, the coin had not been a success. For one thing, its alloy was of little value—but Amerinds in the west found a partial solution. Navajo silversmiths embedded softly rounded turquoise ovals in the centers of the coins. Some were irregular, and none would have fitted a coin slot. They had been accepted at face value and were now worth twice that as rarities.

Sandy held it up. "How do you suppose . . ." she began, pushing aside a broad fig leaf that was teasing at her hair.

A gritted phrase by a dying man caromed through his mind: ". . . *faithful, under a ledge at the fig tree.*" He hurried back into the water, waded up to the base of the sluggish little waterfall, then plunged his hand through the sheet of water. Sandy was gaping at him as though he had gone mad, but her mouth fell open as he pulled his hand back. Several coins plunked into the water at his feet. He held a score more in his hand: Krugerrands, gold Mexican thousand-peso pieces, more of the reworked Mormon fifties. "I can feel hundreds of 'em in here," he said.

Sitting on their blanket, he told her of the message Cam Concannon bade him give to the old rancher. And of Mul Garner's insistence that the money belonged to no one. In any case, one Ted Quantrill now held mineral rights to that property. "And if gold isn't a mineral, what is?" he crowed. "The name of this creek is 'Faithful,' then. Must run the year 'round, honey."

They kept that solitary coin and returned the rest to the deep slot beneath the ledge, inside the falls. They didn't need the money now, Sandy pointed out, but one day they might. If Ted continued to refuse money for advertising endorsements, his name might soon be forgotten.

"God, I hope so," he said. "But even if nobody pays a dime to go up against that android this summer"—he would never call the game by its name because it was *his* name— "now we have something to fall back on."

"Maybe there is such a thing as security," she said.

"Nope. Just varying degrees of insecurity," he quoted.

"All the same, I like the idea of hearing that water from my kitchen window, and knowing what it means."

"You're pretty set on this location, I take it," he said.

"Well, not unless you are."

"I'm set, sold, and incidentally your slave, Sandy." He kissed her beneath her ear, the kind of gentle caress that implied a belly too full for stronger stuff, and then moved over to the edge of the blanket where Ba'al lay basking in the April sun. "Call me only if you find more treasure."

What if she told him, here and now, about Lufo's return of the Ember of Venus? No, she'd already decided how she was going to present that to him as soon as she found a set for it. A phrase from an old song popped into focus: "I can't cook, but you won't care," and she decided that her options were rape or active diversion.

She wiggled her fingers at him, stood up, then began to pace around the level region above the fig tree. She found stones to place at likely corners, laid a few dead oak branches down to further sketch out her imaginary foundation lines. It took her a half hour to decide where the kitchen would go. The individual rooms, modern reinforced plastic modules, could be brought in by chopper. But could they pour foundations without bringing in complete strangers? She wanted that very much.

She turned to ask him and saw that he lay with his head against the belly of Ba'al. They were both snoring. "And the lion shall lie down with the other lion," she told herself.

Which naturally directed her to think of herself lying down with her lion, with all his parts still intact after a world war and his fight to survive its aftermath. She said to her distant man, knowing he could not have heard thunder over the rumble of those snores, "You're only a man for all that, with a little edge in your reflexes. You weren't my first, and there are smarter men around, and you may not be any whiz as a sheep rancher. But you suit me right down to the ground. I don't care what they do with that silly android; turn it out to stud for the ladies, for all of me. I've got the original Ted Quantrill. And I want it now."

She tiptoed to him, shook his toe until he was blinking at her, and beckoned with a slowly curling forefinger. He rose without waking Ba'al and followed. She traced the foundations of the house with gestures, then moved to speak in his ear. "You may not know it, but I am now taking you down the hall to the master bedroom. Take off your jacket," she added, insinuating her hip against him, moving it suggestively. "Come with me."

He came with her. More than once. If the boar waked, he was too wise to show it.

AFTER GAMES • • •

Lufo's alliance with Marianne Placidas. The New Israeli hit man who finds her smudged prints in Oregon Territory.

Quantrill pitted against his android copy; the nature of the android's terrible malfunction, which programmers might have foreseen.

Billy Ray's escape from prison. His search and eventual romance of Mul Garner's dim-witted sister. Garner's south spread.

The worldwide economic panic after synthesizer theft by Brazil, and devaluation of gold as a common metal.

Childe's teenaged jealousy and ruse; separation and reconciliations.

Mating of Ba'al.

Death of Ba'al.

Assassination of Jim Street, and Quantrill's choice.

THE BEST IN SUSPENSE
FROM TOR

☐ ☐	50451-8	THE BEETHOVEN CONSPIRACY *Thomas Hauser*	$3.50 Canada $4.50
☐ ☐	54106-5	BLOOD OF EAGLES *Dean Ing*	$3.95 Canada $4.95
☐ ☐	58794-4	BLUE HERON *Philip Ross*	$3.50 Canada $4.50
☐ ☐	50549-2	THE CHOICE OF EDDIE FRANKS *Brian Freemantle*	$4.95 Canada $5.95
☐ ☐	50105-5	CITADEL RUN *Paul Bishop*	$4.95 Canada $5.95
☐ ☐	50581-6	DAY SEVEN *Jack M. Bickham*	$3.95 Canada $4.95
☐ ☐	50720-7	A FINE LINE *Ken Gross*	$4.50 Canada $5.50
☐ ☐	50911-0	THE HALFLIFE *Sharon Webb*	$4.95 Canada $5.95
☐ ☐	50642-1	RIDE THE LIGHTNING *John Lutz*	$3.95 Canada $4.95
☐ ☐	50906-4	WHITE FLOWER *Philip Ross*	$4.95 Canada $5.95
☐ ☐	50413-5	WITHOUT HONOR *David Hagberg*	$4.95 Canada $5.95

Buy them at your local bookstore or use this handy coupon:
Clip and mail this page with your order.

Publishers Book and Audio Mailing Service
P.O. Box 120159, Staten Island, NY 10312-0004

Please send me the book(s) I have checked above. I am enclosing $ _____
(please add $1.25 for the first book, and $.25 for each additional book to cover postage and handling.
Send check or money order only—no CODs).

Name _____
Address _____
City _____ State/Zip _____
Please allow six weeks for delivery. Prices subject to change without notice.